HAWAIIAN HARVEST

HAWAIIAN HARVEST

By

ARMINE VON TEMPSKI

Ox Bow Press
Woodbridge, Connecticut

Cover painting by Pamela Andelin

Copyright 1933, copyright renewed 1960

1990 reprint by
Ox Bow Press
P.O. Box 4045
Woodbridge, CT 06525

Library of Congress Cataloging-in-Publication Data
Von Tempski, Armine, 1892–1943.
Hawaiian harvest / by Armine Von Tempski
p. cm.
ISBN 0–918024–73–0. —ISBN 0–918024–72–2 (pbk.)
I. Title.
PS3543.O647H38 1990
813'.52—dc20   89–78471
                                                    CIP
The paper used in this book meets the guidelines for permanence
and durability of the Committee on Production Guidelines for
Book Longevity of the Council on Library Resources.

Printed in the United States of America

To My Beloved Dad

*Who held that the real Battle
is not winning your spurs but
keeping them shining and bright*

NOTE FROM THE PUBLISHER

In an effort to bring back into print books of an earlier period, we often encounter material that is offensive to our sensibilities. The choices are not to reprint the work, to edit out the offending material, or to leave it in place to help us understand the earlier period, warts and all. The first choice condemns us to an ignorance of the past and does not allow us to learn from past mistakes. The second allows editors to rewrite history, a practice which has been much abused in the past. The third, while sometimes painful, gives us the most honest appraisal of the sins of the past.

This work contains statements that are shockingly and repellently racist. They were the views of the fictional characters who uttered them. That they shock us so is evidence of how far we have come in an effort to understand each other. It is our hope that publishers of the future will not have to face these decisions in reviewing the books written today.

HAWAIIAN HARVEST

HAWAIIAN HARVEST

CHAPTER I

ERNEST TRAVERS thrust a fine old hand into his coat pocket, drew out a radiogram and read it for the fifth time.

> Coming Mauna Kea today stop don't want anyone but you and Glenn to meet me stop I'm a bit out of plumb but I hope not too rotten to look at.
>
> Don

Travers raised thoughtful eyes from the saffron-colored paper fluttering in the brisk Trade-wind and scanned the white-capped, indigo-hued channel upon which the smoke of an approaching steamer showed. For an instant he stood motionless, his lined tanned face looking bored and indifferent as only an Englishman's can when he is consumed with emotion. Thrusting the radiogram back into his pocket he walked to a small hotel near the beach, found a chair in the scant shade of the narrow hot veranda and sat down.

Staring about he attempted to see his surroundings through the eyes of Don Garrison, crippled in a crash with his plane during the war, detained ten years in hospitals having his back patched up, and now coming home, at Travers' insistence, on the steamer which would anchor in an hour.

The afternoon was typical of Hawaii: fierce blue spaces of sea, great pale spaces of sky broken by the shadowy shapes of islands, secret, withdrawn, under white masses of cloud. A shabby wharf and tall lonely-looking lighthouse were silhouetted against restless water glittering in the sun. Coconut trees stood like weary sentinels above green *kiawes* that waved delicate branches gaily, as though beckoning at blue sampans riding at anchor in the lagoon. Sun-drugged distances seemed to wait with awful expectancy and an occasional cessation in the sound of wind passing over the curve of the earth created the illusion that the day had paused, every now and then, to catch its breath.

Travers moved restlessly; dreadful to think of Don returning, maimed, to the vigorous life he had left in the first flush of manhood which every shadow in the hills and change in the sea would recall.

Then Travers' eyes hardened as they focused upon two men conferring a short distance away: Glenn Garrison and Randolph Morse trying to come to some decision as to the wisest course of action to pursue—before Don landed. Travers noted that Glenn's neck set into his shoulders at a defiant angle, as though Glenn felt that he was compelled to wrestle with life to his own debasement, while Morse waited, indifferent and contemptuous. Glenn could hardly be happy, Travers reflected, knowing that he had not played fair with his older brother, Don. Then Glenn's voice reached him, stifled, tense:

"What in God's name am I going to do, Ran? Don's letters are always filled with questions about the horses, cattle, trees and grass. He'll raise Cain when he finds out that the stock that old Dad bred, and that he sets such store by, have to be sold, but if he ever gets wind of the rest——"

Glenn broke off and his coffee-brown eyes, filled with a sort of furtive terror, stared guiltily at the approaching steamer. A disagreeable sensation stole over Travers, as though something cold and unpleasant had brushed him. His eyes contracted as he weighed Glenn. Glenn stood, silhouetted against the brutal glare of the sea, a serious, slack shape in a loose tweed suit. His dark, fevered eyes were vaguely unhappy, his lean face marred by dissipation, but his person was invested with the intangible distinction which breeding imparts. He was just thirty-one, but looked nearer forty, gaunt, haggard and burned out. Glenn turned from contemplation of the steamer grimacing as though he drank bitter wine, then lighted a cigarette with hands that looked flurried and cautious lest they give something away. He appeared to be consumed by secret agonies which he tried to conceal and control, agonies which confused and distracted him. Drawing deeply on his cigarette and hunching his shoulders miserably he ejaculated:

"You know, Ran, I simply can't picture Don crippled! He was such an all-round fellow, by far the best rider, roper and polo player on Maui. It would be tough for him coming home under any circumstances, but I feel a complete rotter when I realize that everything he loves and has fought to come back to has to go." He broke off, caught Morse's disdainful glance and finished miserably, "Still, it's hell that he chose to come back just when things are really getting under way. He's never questioned any move of mine during the ten years I've managed the ranch, but I know Don well

3

enough to appreciate that he'll be dead against what we're doing. When I've written I've never referred to the changes we're making, because I figured he'd stay in England indefinitely, and knowing the immense affection he has for everything pertaining to the ranch, I felt that what he didn't know wouldn't hurt him. When that wireless came yesterday saying he was in Honolulu and would be up by this boat, it about knocked the wind out of me." Glenn looked about wildly, saw Travers and said, "Ran, you don't suppose old Ernesto spilt the beans?"

Morse gestured slightly and they walked out of hearing.

Travers jerked his hat over his eyes, drew out a cigar and bit off the end. He had not, actually, written Don anything definite, he was too old and wise to mix himself up in other people's affairs, but he had stated that if Don felt strong enough to travel it was time he came home.

Weighing Morse, Travers' face hardened. The man was eminently successful as head of the pineapple industry which was revolutionizing Maui, but his sole measure of a man's worth was the amount of money he succeeded in accumulating. He was typical of an age which knew the price of everything and the value of nothing. Morse's small eyes, with lids which looked hot, were unpleasantly suggestive of a cockroach's and his slightly sloped shoulders and the brown suits he wore added to the illusion. He was like a cockroach, Travers thought indignantly, nibbling at the edges of things, spoiling them secretly. Morse coveted the wide acres of the Garrison ranch. In order to get possession of them and enlarge the output of the cannery, he had worked to gain a complete ascendency over Glenn. For the past eight months

Morse, on the pretext that his wife wished to remodel their home, had been an inmate of the Garrison household, but Travers knew him no better than on the first day he and his wife had arrived.

Travers was convinced that Morse, to further his own ends, was catering to all that was worst and weakest in Glenn. Through his wife, Morse was instrumental in having the gay, drinking set up at the ranch. Cold as a stone, with a passion only for accumulating money, Morse was unaffected by an atmosphere where it seemed to be considered the height of friendship to assist a man to rot his kidneys and blur his brain with alcohol, while Glenn's character was steadily disintegrating.

Glenn, like Don, had been an aviator, but the high excitement of flying had proved too much for his overstrung nature. He had come home from the war whole, but since then had been stumbling about, lost in dark forests of his own planting, a soiled ascetic, worshiping still—on some inner altar—the ideals his father had instilled into him, while he continually betrayed them. On one or two occasions Travers had attempted to remonstrate with Glenn about drinking; but appreciating the futility of it, as long as Morse held ascendency over Glenn's mind, he had finally written to Don, always the finer and stronger of the two, hoping that he might succeed in jerking his brother to his feet.

Then Travers' hands tightened on the arms of his chair. What if Don had gone the same way? It was possible, and he, Travers, was too old to be in a position to appreciate what men who had participated in the war had been through, so could not presume to judge either Glenn or Don. It was extraordinary, he reflected, his generation had fancied that it was their war, but the brunt of it and the consequences of it had fallen on younger shoulders.

He drew up his lower left lid slowly, like a meditative fowl, and listened to little waves slapping the smooth blue sides of sampans. He had been proud because both Don and Glenn had enlisted soon after the war started. Don, being the elder, had gone first. He had been just twenty-three and mad for the adventure—poor young fool! Travers recalled how, as the boat had pulled away from the wharf, Don had kept shouting back directions about the care of his horses, lassoes and guns. Much good they would be to him now!

Travers moved as though his chair hurt him. Dreadful to think of Don's long, fine body being messed about with by doctors, undergoing operation after operation, with their attendant indignities, solely in order that he might get well enough to come home to the tragic mess which seemed surely to await him. He wondered what years of pain, inactivity and.staring at bare hospital walls had done to Don's soul.

Life was beastly, he thought, mauling and maiming the sons of the man he had loved. To what end? For Glenn vile concealments; for Don difficult adjustments, painful revelations, changes threatening the acres he loved; for Don was, or had been, as passionate a lover of green pastures and sleek herds as his father had been before him.

Travers glanced up at the shabby hotel. It had been there that he had first met John Garrison, father of Don and Glenn. He had been newly arrived, ill, when he had heard Garrison talking in the hall with the proprietor. He remembered, still, the very words he had uttered: "Where is that

blasted British artist who is ill? I've come to take him off
your hands. It's too hot here for the poor devil. He'll be
better off at the ranch." And in he had come like a refreshing gust of Trade-wind.

There had been no resisting. Garrison had paid some
Hawaiian to ride his horse home, rented a hack and driven
Travers, himself, the fifty miles to the ranch. With his wife's
assistance John Garrison had nursed Travers back to health
and when, two years later, his wife died, he had asked Travers
to remain at the ranch. Travers contemplated the wrappings
of his cigar. For twenty years he had been a member of the
Garrison household and since John's death, in 1910, he had
attempted, despite the fact that he was a bachelor, to be a
father to his friend's sons.

Glancing up, Travers saw that the steamer was much
closer. It was dreadful, not knowing particulars about Don.
He was acquainted with the fact that his back had been
broken when his plane crashed, but beyond that knew nothing. He sat with his eyes fixed on the islands of Molokai
and Lanai. Their lower slopes seemed to have assumed
harsher aspects, as though the waning afternoon had taken
from them secret hopes and dreams.

Travers rose and began pacing the veranda, glancing occasionally at Glenn and Morse, still deep in consultation.
Glenn, despite the fact that Don requested that only he and
Travers meet him, had brought Morse, or had permitted him
to come, which proved the hold Morse had upon him. Travers watched Glenn grasping the rail of the wharf, straining
against it, staring at the steamer as though he could not

credit the fact that Don was really on the boat and coming home for good.

Travers' face twitched. Don and Glenn had been splendid boys, simple, vigorous, high-minded. He had never known two brothers so devoted, and yet here was Glenn, upset, resentful, because Don was returning; apprehensive, aside from other things, lest Don, being the elder, might menace the undisputed authority which he had enjoyed for so long as sole manager of the ranch.

Then he saw Morse stalk rapidly to a rent-car, speak to the driver and get in. The car vanished down the road and Glenn started toward the hotel with long, hasty strides. Travers drew a fresh cigar out of his breast pocket and lighted it. Evidently Morse and Glenn had concluded that it was wiser not to precipitate matters until they had got Don's measure.

"I say, Ernesto," Glenn burst out when he stepped onto the veranda, "I feel completely shot thinking about old Don. We figured that it would be best for Ran to clear out, as Don may be sensitive about being smashed up." Glenn watched the steamer pouring black smoke out of its funnel, as though mad to get to its destination. "I wish he'd waited another day and taken the boat that goes to Kahului: it would be easier for him to get off at a dock."

Glenn brought out the words with wretched fierceness and in the depths of his eyes was the expression of a man impelled toward some nameless fate of which he is always thinking with fear and contempt. Travers appreciated that Glenn was reluctant to meet Don for fear that his brother might instantly divine his changed caliber, but Travers suspected,

8

also, and despite everything, that Glenn still loved his brother, or the memory of his brother, and dreaded seeing Don lest he be too obviously crippled.

The ship swung to its anchorage on the outer side of the reef. Travers started for the wharf, Glenn lounging beside him, frowning, blinking, thrusting out his chin like a horse impatient of a bit which does not fit it. They went onto the wharf, piled almost to the roof with brown bags of sugar. Portuguese, Japanese and Filipino rent-chauffeurs jammed a roped-off space near the entrance, and at the far end, near the boat landing, dignified, leisurely Hawaiian longshoremen lounged against boxes of freight, seemingly integral parts of the amber afternoon.

Travers thoughtfully contemplated the glittering blue water. After some moments he turned and looked back at the mass of the island. Behind the tree-smothered town, mountains rose abruptly, their lower slopes swathed in cane which swept up toward deep-cleft valleys, filled with a deliberate secrecy which was vaguely disturbing. Travers weighed them, distrustful of the effect vivid ranges and vast sweeps of blue sea might have upon Don. Latitudes which brewed such violent beauty might easily shake a man's hold on himself after years of absence spent in colder, more restrained lands.

He took a deep breath, surrendering the future into the keeping of the gods, and leaned his arms on the railing. Boats were being lowered, rising and falling like white feathers against the dark flanks of the ship as great smoking swells swept shoreward.

Glenn wiped his moist face several times. Once he swore

9

under his breath, then stood absolutely still looking strangely handsome for a moment. He and Travers watched the first boat leave the side of the ship. Deftly handled oars flashed in the strong afternoon light which poured through a rift in the clouds heaped above the somber mass of Lanai. Then Glenn began looking about wildly.

"Hell!" he said, in a choked voice. "Beastly, that's what I feel—beastly! As though my skin were a dirty shirt that I can't get out of. Ever felt like that, Ernesto? Filthy, not fit to be with decent people? Christ, when I think——"

"You're not pulling your weight," Travers snapped. "Have a smoke and get hold of yourself." But he felt an immense compassion for Glenn, eaten by remorse weaker than the untoward cravings which governed him.

Travers looked at him, and Glenn moved like a bound animal staring with unhappy eyes at beautiful islands lying peacefully in the sea. For an instant the old man saw again the brown-skinned boy, direct of eye, warm as earth, lovable, who had been lost in the man beside him. In the golden light of the afternoon Glenn made Travers think of a fallen archangel, disloyal to everything he worshiped, longing to return to a foresworn Heaven but too weak to rise out of his own pit of Hell.

A clear hail, in a voice somehow thinned, set Travers' heart pounding. He forced himself to look up. The boat was a scant hundred feet away. Don stood among the seated passengers, a hand on some man's shoulder for support, chin high, white face smiling.

"Hello, you old duffers!"

"Confound it!" Glenn muttered. "An insect has flown

in my eye!" Turning aside he snatched out a handkerchief. Travers appeared not to see. Signing to Don with a slight motion of his head he studied him. In a high-necked gray sweater, worn under his dark suit, Don somehow suggested a knight in a shirt of chain-mail. His face was sharper and thinner and the blue of his eyes had, in some extraordinary way, paled, but he held himself gallantly, as of old. About his eyes were innumerable fine lines, upon his features a repression hewed from pain. He was smiling but the quality of his smile had altered. His lips were thinner, more tightly closed, as though he tried to shut in and control all that he felt, but his chin still thrust out at a fighting angle. His fine brown hair, with an indefinite wave in it, went off a valiantly modeled forehead, and to Travers it seemed that he stood for all that was fine, courageous and clean. Save for a slight lifting and cramping of the right shoulder he was as good to look at as ever, but there was an expression in his eyes which gave away the battles he had waged with himself, battles in which, Travers suspected, he had not always been victorious.

The boat bumped the platform. Passengers, aided by good-natured Hawaiian sailors, leaped and scrambled ashore. Suitcases and mail-bags were heaved onto the wharf and snatched out of the way. Don waited and Travers tried not to remember that, once, Don would have been the first man out. He stood a tall, patient, lonely figure jostled by men and women, smiling, uncomplaining, a true son of his father. Travers glanced at Glenn as though contrasting them, then was ashamed.

Glenn dashed down the steps to the boat landing and

Travers watched his emotion-racked face, feeling angry with Glenn and with himself for being upset because life had elected to run over Don.

"Rough trip?" Travers called out.

"Choppy in the channels," Don answered.

"It would be, with such a stiff Trade blowing," Travers replied, studying the fierce blue of the sea, streaked with whitecaps, which, after appearing for an instant, grayed and vanished again into blue. Don nodded, a trifle absent-mindedly, his eyes fixed upon Glenn with restrained eager-ness. Glenn hunched his shoulders as though his coat pricked him, but managed a smile, and Travers adjusted his hat to a better angle.

"Now, boys, give me a hand."

Travers' muscles tensed as though he himself were about to make the effort. Glenn leaned over the water, stretching a long arm to his brother. Their hands met and clasped.

"Easy, old man, not too fast," Don cautioned. "I must time it right. Wait until the boat lifts."

Two sailors took him deftly and firmly by the elbows, a third leaped onto the platform with his canes. A wave swelled, lifting the boat level with the landing, and Don stepped out carefully.

"Thanks, boys, *mahalo,*" he said, turning to the men sup-porting him.

Glenn released Don's hand, took the canes from the sailor and gave them to his brother. Don hoisted his weight onto them expertly.

"Great to see you, Glenn," he exclaimed. "You are as brown as a Kanaka. Wish I had some of your tan."

Glenn made an inaudible answer and Travers saw him looking at his brother, a strange expression on his face, as though he both respected and resented Don's unchanged caliber. Don started up the steps, taking them one at a time, looking about eagerly, as a horse looks at a remembered pasture. Travers noted that Don's hands were as changed as his face. They were the tired, transparent hands of an invalid and, somehow, more upsetting than the canes with which he supported himself.

"Jolly to see you, Ernesto," he said, when he was safely up the last step.

Travers' hand went out involuntarily, then he jerked it back. Don grinned.

"If you wait until I get my weight onto one of these canes, I think I can manage to crack you over the head with the other."

Travers grinned. The same old Don! Glenn dived into the press of passengers, muttering that he would look up the bags. Don studied his surroundings, then asked:

"Where is the car, Ernesto?"

"Under the big *kiawe* tree."

"That one ours?" Don exclaimed, indicating with a lift of his chin the sleek, powerful limousine under the gnarled tree.

"Yes."

"Pretty swanky—the ranch must be doing well. I'm damned glad you wrote urging me to come home. I've been in a sort of mental daze for years. I dreaded returning, but, after all, hamstrung or not, I would have had to come back

13

eventually. Let's move along. I hate crowds of people shoving me about."

Placing his canes warily on the rough planking, Don started forward, Travers walking slowly beside him. Glenn dashed up.

"Two suitcases all?" he asked.

"And a small satchel with my name on it."

"Meet you at the car," Glenn said, hurrying back to the wharf.

Travers' lips tightened. Glenn was funking it! He could have tipped any one of a dozen boys to get Don's bags.

Clear of the wharf Don halted, lifting his head as though saluting the mountains rising out of seas of green cane, running and fluttering under the wind. He glanced about like a person searching for something he has lost, then Travers saw him wince as his eyes found the road following the curve of the shore, the road which led back to the ranch! Don's knuckles grew white and shiny from the grip he put on his canes, then he glanced around as though he were wondering why Glenn did not come.

Travers debated whether or not he should prepare Don a little for what awaited him, or leave him in ignorance. Perhaps it was Don's right to have the first evening of homecoming as unspoiled as possible. He had worked long and hard to get well enough to come back to the islands he loved, but the confounded part was, Don had returned to a bigger battle than any he had fought during the war or to regain health.

Glenn approached, followed by a Hawaiian carrying Don's

14

bags. Opening the front door, he directed the boy to place the suitcases on the seat.

"Don, you better sit behind with Ernesto, more room for your legs."

His brown hand gripped Don's shoulder fiercely, then jerked down. Eaten by conflicting emotions, which he tried to conceal under an offhand manner, Glenn was giving away the state of his feelings abominably. Travers saw Don studying his brother, a puzzled expression in his eyes, probably realizing, for the first time and with a faint shock, that his return might not be entirely to Glenn's liking.

"I suppose that is the most sensible arrangement," Don agreed after an instant, but his face got a trifle paler, as though a light inside him had dimmed. Laying his canes on the floor he hoisted himself into the back seat. Travers followed, closing the door with a bang.

CHAPTER II

AS the car tore along the broad white road Don sat with arms locked across his chest trying to control emotions roused from their long sleep by forgotten smells: the fairy fragrance of indigo-bushes growing by the roadsides, the rich odor of sugar-cane in tassel, the tang of salt water breaking on clean beaches, the scent of forests growing out of wild, wet earth. Air like glass and gold streamed past his face which he inhaled with passion. Mountains and valleys, the very island, seemed to be rushing to meet him with a violent embrace.

Something inside him which had been dead stirred, quickened, woke to life. He looked away, but everywhere were the great shadowy shapes of islands lying in the sea. He folded his arms more tightly, bracing himself against their spell. He was conscious of the quick throb, the stir beneath extravagant slopes plunging downward. They had actual life, they lived, these mighty islands which had been thrust from ocean bottom to heights above the clouds. The very soil forming them pulsed, for it had lava running in its veins. He closed his eyes. After the restrained landscapes of England, the little villages, the tiny fields, the gentle contours of neatly folded hills, to come back to Hawaii! A land of vehement beauty, passionately growing vegetation, high-powered smells which aroused love incomprehensible to persons who had not been born beneath its spell. Trying to

justify the feelings rending him, Don recalled how each
summer vacation when he and Glenn returned from mainland
school, tears had blurred their eyes, when they got their first
sight, from the ship, of the islands towering above the sea.
He took a deep breath as though drawing earth, sea and
sky into his being. His nature flamed to meet the challenge
of the fierce young land, his land, the land in which he had
been born! Then he saw his canes and drew himself upward, fixing his eyes on the flat white road.

Glenn was driving like a madman. Don braced against
bumps and turns, making no protest. The car swept around
a rocky bluff and new vistas were revealed, cliffs with blue
water smoking at their bases, soaring ridges, iron-bound valleys feathered in green. Ahead in the south was the long
red streak of Kahoolawe, lying between the blues of sky and
sea, and to westward the hunched mass of Lanai crouched
under spectacular clouds.

Sight of it recalled memories of autumn hunting parties
when he and Glenn, mere boys, had gone over to it with
their father and his friends for a week of shooting. He remembered the thrill of being crowded into a small sampan
with guns and saddles and dogs. How still he had sat,
making himself small, while he listened to man-talk going on
about him, wishing for the day when he would be grown
up and able to discuss the merits of different makes of car-
tridges and guns.

He glanced at his brother crouched over the wheel.
Glenn's hunched shoulders reminded him unpleasantly of a
sick bird and even the back of his head looked tormented.
Don moved uneasily. Perhaps he should have written ahead

to tell Glenn he was coming home, then Glenn could have accustomed himself to the thought. The car swayed, regained the road and sped on as though fleeing from demons. Travers sat silent, his face a gray mask. Don frowned. He must make an effort to end the silence which had them all in its grip.

"Had any rain lately?" he called to the front seat.

"A couple of inches last week. It greened things up a bit," Glenn shouted back.

"I can hardly wait to see everything. How's the feed, good? And the thoroughbreds? Won many cups since I left?"

Glenn made an inaudible reply and stepped on the accelerator. The car leaped forward like a cruelly spurred horse.

"Trying to catch a train?" Travers demanded sarcastically.

"What?" Glenn flung back.

The car took a turn on two wheels, straightened out and raced down a long stretch of road flanked by highly colored swamps. Above them the peaks of the west Maui mountains glowed like hot metal in the light of the sinking sun. Don's chin dented and thrust out. Beyond them was the mass of Haleakala, on whose slopes lay the wide green acres of the ranch. He must prepare himself for his first sight of it!

They swung around a succession of bluffs against which the enormous swells of the Pacific burst with leisurely magnificence. There was a sound in the wind that made him forget, for an instant, his sacrificed youth, with its memories cruel and sweet, in a restless, intolerable desire for great draughts of life. He looked at the strong horizon holding back the twilight and marveled at the unbelievable beauty of the islands drowsing in the sea.

The car flung the last bluff behind it; Haleakala burst into view. Ten thousand feet it towered above the twilight dimmed sea, impressively simple, wrapped in volcanic loneliness and mystery. The crater rim was sharply etched against the flushed sky; lava wastes stained the summit, below them the land fled away, its contours attesting to a once-liquid condition, and lower still rose the splendid, rolling tree-crowned hills of the Garrison ranch.

Don caught his breath, swept away by the sheer beauty of it, then felt as though he had been struck a terrible blow over the heart. A swift, ruthless twilight had descended, dimming and blurring the sweep of the island between the masses of East and West Maui, but the outline of the great mountain lingered, bulking against the sky as though defying the dark embrace of night. Don fought with the realization that tomorrow and all the other tomorrows he would not be riding over it. His face was expressionless, but a muscle in his cheek beat like a tiny, violent heart.

He looked away at the sea and islands and it seemed as though the whole evening, the world, was emptying out through a pale gap in the clouds. Moisture damped his skin, chilling it, as he fought the seas of desolation drenching him.

A car roared up behind and passed, a topless, green roadster driven by a bit of a girl. Her hair streamed in the wind, fox terriers with wise faces and flattened ears stood with paws braced against the doors. Don got a brief glimpse of the girl's face and for some reason it made him think of white wings flashing in the sky. The car lurched through a rut, regained the road and vanished, leaving a smoking trail of dust behind.

"Good God!" Don exclaimed, irritably, "are there no speed limits on Maui? We must be doing sixty miles at least and that girl not less than seventy. I'd like to have her arrested for startling me so."

"There are traffic regulations, but no one pays the least attention to them," Travers replied. "As far as I can see, this generation believes that laws are made simply to be broken."

Don smiled.

The car rushed on, made a wide sweeping curve and squared away down a long level stretch of road flanked by cane which rustled and whispered in the wind. Looking at the vast isthmus joining the two halves of the island Don thought warmly of the march of progress in Hawaii, contrasting it with the march of civilization elsewhere. Here progress had brought beauty instead of ugliness in its wake. There were no smoke-soiled cities with factory chimneys sticking into the sky, no festering seaports, no forests wiped out leaving naked mountains behind.

Before white men came, these flowing plains of sugar-cane had been barren reaches covered with a scant growth of *pili* grass and *ilima* bushes, broken by red gulches piled with gray boulders. When the great winter rains and *kona* winds shouted through the skies, these dry gulches had roared and choked with yellow water that, in a few hours, streamed into the sea. The topography of each island was more or less alike: the eastern slopes of the high mountains, against which the Trade-wind hurled moisture-laden clouds, were extravagantly tropical, the western slopes for the most part arid and bare. Even as a boy Don had been conscious of a savage melancholy which seemed to brood in certain localities, as though the landscape waited, impatiently, to be fulfilled. Then white men had come. . . . Gathering up in great ditches the surplus moisture of the mighty watershed of east Maui, they had brought it to the bare isthmus, irrigated the parched land and out of the rich volcanic loam cane had been grown, waving triumphant green banners in the wind. Above the thousand-foot level, beyond which cane would not grow, were pastures and ranches dotted with sleek herds. He felt a rich possessive pride knowing that his father had been one of the splendid builders who had brought not only prosperity, but beauty, to Maui.

He realized that for years he had been starving for beauty, for beauty which was splashed about in a wholesale way. During his years in cold and careful lands he had hungered for violent colors, warmth, wide spaces which seemed to hold eternity in their core. And here it was, space, beauty— reckless and extravagant—which went to a man's head like strong wine.

The car made a swift turn, there was a screech of brakes ruthlessly applied as Glenn came to a sudden stop. Travers cursed and Don got white to the lips from the jar. Ahead, the green roadster was parked in a shallow, weed-grown ditch, and squatting beside the back wheel the girl was working to remove a flat tire. Tools lay on the running-board and dogs sat in an anxious, panting circle looking on.

Muttering something, Glenn got out and crossed over. Seeing him, the girl straightened up, bringing her slight, fluent body to a standing position with a single movement. She was beautiful as children are beautiful, in a lighted way. There was a gallant lift to the corners of her mouth and to her resolute and dainty chin, but something about the set of her lips suggested that she was not, or had not always been, happy. Hair like fire and honey glinted in the waning light. Her lack of height usually compelled her to look up at the person with whom she might be speaking, investing her with a melting appeal, which caused observers to overlook the firmness of the chin under its covering of youthful, creamy flesh. But it was her eyes that a person remarked and remembered, wide open, shining, fringed with luxuriant lashes which transformed their blue into gray.

She and Glenn conferred for a few minutes, then he squatted down and began working with the wheel. Don watched, then got out and stood in the road, a tall, lonely figure balanced on canes.

"Going over?" Travers asked, drawing on his cigar.

Don nodded. Travers made no comment, but looked away.

"Gay, this is my brother Don," Glenn said when he saw Don standing over them. "Don, this is Gay Storm."

The girl glanced up, her mind on other matters, then, all at once, seemed to be aware of him. She looked at his canes, then smiled and Don got a vivid, curious impression that she laid a small, comradely hand on his arm.

"I'm sorry to hold you up, I know you must be anxious to get home, but that damned tire simply refused to come off."

She turned her head slightly, facing the wind, and again Don thought of white wings flashing in the sky. Her small

22

face had a desperate sort of beauty, but her slight body was charged with force and determination. She seemed vaguely familiar, and Don groped about in his mind trying to recall where he had seen her. As though divining it she looked up.

"You're trying to place me," she said.

"Yes."

"I'm Harold Storm's daughter. I was just a kid when you left."

Don was amazed. It seemed impossible that this lovely girl could be the child he dimly remembered, a shy, tanned sprite all legs and eyes.

"Your father—"

"He's dead," Gay said, quietly.

Don poked at a pebble with his cane.

"I'm sorry. He was a fine man. I knew him well."

"Dad was the most wonderful man that ever lived," the girl said, her face lighting.

"Tell me about Gay," Don said to Travers when the green roadster vanished down the road and they started on.

"Gay's had rather a tough row to hoe," the old man said. "Her father was killed five years ago roping a wild bull on the mountain. He was dead when they found him. He and his horse fell into a lava hole and from appearances Storm must have lived for thirty-six or forty-eight hours. He was badly smashed up, but had managed to get his lasso on a stump and try and pull himself out. You know what a gritty chap he was. I guess he fought to keep alive for his kid's sake. They were everything to each other. As you know,

23

he didn't own Lanakela ranch, but managed it for Hughes——"

"Hell," Don said.

"It was, rather," Travers agreed. "Hughes was, or tried to be, generous—offered to let Gay have the house which she and her father had lived in and build a new one for the next manager, but the kid refused to accept it. She and her father had built a small house on one of the Piholo homesteads, near the forest reserve, where they used to go for week-ends, and she moved over to it, taking her horses and dogs with her."

"But no one except a Japanese can make a living off a Government homestead in Hawaii," Don protested.

"I know, and the kid knew it, too, but she used her head and makes good money guiding tourists up Haleakala. At first it used to make me sick thinking of that game little brat doing a man's work. She couldn't afford to hire help, and packed, saddled, guided and cooked, herself. Now she has a Japanese man and his wife living on the place, but she continues to do the mountain work herself. She's an ambitious little thing and paints covers for mainland magazines on the side. She's got great talent. We go sketching together when tourist trade is slack. If she had the opportunity to go abroad and study she'd make her mark. She has a real feeling for life and isn't afraid of work."

"It used to burn me up," Glenn said, from the front seat, "seeing her dragging a bunch of fools up the mountain, having to associate with Portuguese and Japanese guides, but Gay has quality and though she's a friendly little thing they respect her. She's tragic, but when a man looks into her eyes he feels—dingy."

Don made no reply.

"One of these days I'll take you over to see her," Travers said. "Her household is amusing and amazing. She has taken some poor Japanese woman under her wing, though her cook Sera and his wife can manage by themselves. She has a dozen horses, four dogs, a brute of a bullfrog which is minus a hind leg, a mouse which she found half drowned in a basin of water, a gawky colt she bought from a Portuguese homesteader who was starving it. God only knows what else she'll rescue as time goes on. Anything that's hurt, unhappy or out of luck she swoops on and carries off. Perhaps because life has manhandled her she has immense compassion for anything which has not been given a square deal."

Don watched cane fields flashing past.

Glenn touched a button and two flaming headlights cut the gathering dark. The engine whispered stealthily as it ate up the dim road; insects whirled into the light beams, struck the windshield and died. Trees loomed overhead for an instant and were gone. Above the cane-covered isthmus a giant sugarmill raised its stacks; lights winked from distant slopes of Haleakala, crouching like a gigantic beast against the stars.

Don could not speak. In his mind Gay's high young face shone like a white star. He saw her again, a motherless child riding with her father, sitting on his knee, laughing with him. Looking back he could not recall that he had ever seen them apart. And to have him wrenched from her so terribly

25

seemed monstrous. Rebellion surged through him for the injustice of life. Life had tricked him out of his own father; it had brought misery and suffering on countless millions who had been entirely guiltless during the war, robbed him of everything he held most dear, and had trapped this valiant girl into labor which would call the uttermost from a man. He had packed, and saddled, pitched tents, cut firewood, and knew the effort it entailed. He had risen on bleak mornings when wind and mist swept the summit of Haleakala, had wrestled with stiff ropes and carried horse feed, saddled resentful animals shivering and humping in the dark. He knew the toll that sustained exertion at rare altitudes takes of human bodies.

"Christ!" he thought, "is there no mercy?"

Then he drew himself together. Senseless getting off on that foot!

"I wish it weren't so confoundedly dark," he said aloud in matter-of-fact tones, after they had driven for a while in silence. "I want to see everything, realize I'm back."

He felt Travers stir beside him as though impatient of something and glanced at the old man's grim profile, briefly visible as they flashed past a lighted laborers' camp. The car sped up a long gradual incline, past a second mill, where engines with blazing solitary eyes pushed cars loaded with cane along gleaming steel tracks, and roared on toward the mass of Haleakala. Cane fields were left behind. Don breathed deeply of the night, then lifted his head.

"What's that new smell, Ernesto?" he asked.

"Pineapples."

"Pineapples?"

26

"Yes; practically every one is growing them now. Beastly things—they make the island look like a porcupine."

Glenn writhed his shoulders toward his head. The car rushed up a long hill, then turned into a straight stretch of road. Don sat still, remembering the many times he and Glenn had raced their ponies along it when they were boys.

A mingled odor of guavas and eucalyptus crept into the air. Cold, clean wind rushed down from the mountain charged with the fragrance of grass and damp forests. The dark about was filled with the presence of trees growing in their hundreds of thousands. The headlights cut into an avenue of eucalyptus that brooded over the dim, dusty road. Don smelled horses, saw groups of them standing under the huge trees, heads lowered, as though conferring softly together, and folded his arms.

"I say, Don," Glenn called back, "I forgot to tell you that a couple of friends of mine are staying at the ranch—a fellow called Morse, and his wife. He's the head of the pineapple company. Keen chap. Their house is being fixed over and I asked them to stay with me until it's finished."

"Okay with me, Glenn."

Despite the dark Don was conscious of the beauty about him, briefly glimpsed as the car swept along and the headlights snatched at dim tree-trunks rising out of deep grass. Occasionally they passed groups of animals resting contentedly. Pride stirred in him. No ranch on Maui could boast better stock, finer grass, or more beautifully planted trees. A warm, immense affection rose in him for his father, and for the legacy of beauty his father had left behind.

27

The car tore at a hill as though determined to demolish it; corrals, barns, a blacksmith-shop and stables whipped past; then it dived into a tree-grown quadrangle and stopped. Lanterns showed against moving legs as men crowded forward, men who smelt of saddle leather, dust and horse sweat, men with wreaths of flowers weighing their stained hats and spurs ringing at their heels.

Don got out, white-faced, master of himself; but emptiness which was kin to nausea swept him. In a great flood his old life rose up before him. For an instant he dared not move lest his memories unman him; then, balancing on one cane he thrust out his hand. It was gripped and regripped by the workers of the ranch; but a strange, hurt embarrassment had fallen on them, realizing for the first time that Don was, and would always be, a cripple. Don appeared not to notice, hailed the Hawaiians by name, the sonorous syllables falling easily and accurately from his lips.

"Aloha, Holomalia, Analu, Mahiai, Kahalewai. Well, well, Iole! How are you, Filipo? Where's Hu?"

"Come now," some one said as a grizzled Hawaiian edged out of the shadows, his face a comical mixture of joy and consternation. Don winced. Hu was realizing that Don would never ride the horses he had so carefully tended during that armful of years while he had been gone. Don gripped the old man's hand, wringing it, saw that Hu's eyes were wet and to pass off the moment glanced casually at his increased paunch.

"*Hapai?*" ("Carrying?") he asked, raising his eyebrows in feigned surprise.

The men, including Hu, laughed uproariously at Don's obstetrical allusion and the tension relaxed.

"Don, you rascal, just like before!" Hu said reprovingly, but with obvious delight.

A Japanese hurried forward.

"Mr. Don, I torr much glad you come. Humbugger stay away too long."

"Well—Taka!"

"I got hot bath ready, Mr. Don."

"I'll be along directly."

A scrawny Chinaman in a soiled apron waited, looking on.

"Well, Ah Sam! I'll be damned! I thought you were about to sail for China when I left!"

"You think I go China till you come back?" The old fellow's indignation was immense. "Gar-damn-go-to-hell, too long you stop England. No use!"

"Well, I'm back at last."

"Velly good you come. Now I go see dinner no all burn up."

"Well, I'm glad that's over," Don said when the last man had been greeted and they started for the house.

They passed through a gate into a shadowy garden sweet with the flowers of many lands. A dim white concrete walk led through it and Don's canes made a faint tapping sound upon it. An aged eucalyptus, weary with its weight of years, creaked protestingly. Making a turn the loom of the lighted house showed against dark tree-tops bending against the stars.

Pale, calm, master of his memories, Don crossed the

threshold and walked down the hall into the living-room. His face lighted for an instant, then looked puzzled, as though he felt that the kindly room, full of warm lights and wide, pleasing shadows was guarding some secret which it did not choose to disclose. His eyes went over it carefully, trying to detect some alteration in the arrangement of its furnishings to account for the curious impression which projected itself into his consciousness. Don moved uneasily. The old house had a soul: it had known black death and crimson birth; happiness and sorrow had lodged under its roof; it guarded yesterday, today and tomorrow.

On the mantel, above a cheerily burning fire, was the old array of silver racing trophies won by Garrison horses on every island track. Chinese vases with a delicate tracery of flowers stood in their accustomed corners; costly rugs lay in their old places on the floor. Shaded lights, deep chairs, ranked books, bowls of flowers, intimate trifles of ivory and porcelain, seemed to stir slightly in the uneasy firelight, as though welcoming him or warning him.

His eyes went to a pair of wide-spreading horns above the mantel, passed onto the gilded racing plates of a filly he had ridden to victory on more than one track, then lingered on a carefully coiled lasso hung inconspicuously against one of the wide panels of the time-mellowed walls. Above it John Garrison's picture hung. For an instant the beauty and fullness of boyhood memories rushed up. His father seemed to smile tenderly down on his broken-backed son, and at the room which he had loved and in which some essence of his presence lingered in an unobtrusive, well-behaved way.

Glenn cleared his throat and commenced searching his pockets for cigarettes. Finding none, he snatched up an inlaid box placed on a slender-legged table. Taking out one, he scowled at it and at the fire throwing flickering shadows on the hearth.

"I say, Don, have a drink?"

"Later, when I've cleaned up."

"Bath ready," Taka announced from the head of the stairs.

Don grinned.

"I see my fate," he said. "Taka has appointed himself my body-servant. Might as well submit to the inevitable. See you both later."

When Travers was dressed he tapped on Don's door. "Come in."

Don looked up eagerly and the old man guessed that he had been expecting Glenn. A shadow passed over Don's face, which was instantly replaced by a look of affection which warmed Travers' heart. He felt a stifled rage because Glenn was not Garrison enough to at least try and make the gestures demanded of a well-bred man.

Don was seated on the edge of his bed, coatless but in evening clothes. Beside him the cook, Ah Sam, stood with a bottle of colorless liquid in one hand and glasses clamped between the fingers of the other.

"Mr. Don and me catchee aloha dlink," he announced. "You like leele *shamshu* too, Mr. Ernesto?"

"Hell, no! Taka," Travers turned to the Japanese, who

was busily unpacking and putting away Don's clothes, "get me a whisky and soda."

"Yes, Mr. Ernesto," the man said and departed.

Don glanced at Travers.

"I'm not supposed to drink now, but I can't hurt the old fellow's feelings. He's worked in our family thirty-seven years. All right, Sam, not too much for me."

The Chinaman poured out a scant measure in one glass and filled the other, then handed the first to Don.

"Well, Sam," Don said, raising his glass, "plenty aloha!"

"All samee, Mr. Don, plenty aloha!"

The cook drained his tumbler, stared at Don and muttered darkly to himself:

"Gar-damn!"

Then he poured himself a second drink, trying to drown his thoughts.

"You like leele more, Mr. Don? This good *shamshu*. I make."

Don grinned and shook his head, and the cook grinned back. The atmosphere of the room relaxed.

"Mr. Don, this time I all reform, no smoke opium any more, just dlink one quart *shamshu* every day."

"I think it's high time you were sent to China as a missionary, Sam," Don laughed.

"I think mebbe so yes," the cook agreed, his eyes as bright and merry as a rat's. "Opium velly bad; *shamshu* no matter, make stlong for cook. But I no like go China now, too much damn-fool-kind things making. I think all Chinaman leele clazy this time, no all same before."

Don laughed, lighted a cigarette and inhaled the smoke deeply.

"I shouldn't," he said to Travers, "but I'm going to celebrate tonight in honor of getting home. All bets are off, as Dad used to say. Sam, tell Taka to get three whiskies and sodas. Where's Glenn? Unsociable old beggar."

Travers studied an enlarged snapshot of Don in polo togs astride a nervous filly, then contrasted it with the man sitting on the bed. Life was inexorable!

"I'll fetch Glenn," Travers said.

"You stay here," Don ordered. "Sam can get him. Damn it, it's great to be back with you all."

Glenn appeared shortly. Entering the room he leaned on the door, glancing occasionally at his brother as though resisting some force binding him against his will. Taka arrived with the drinks and Ah Sam filled the two empty tumblers with *shamshu* for Taka and himself.

"Here, chuck that out and take some whisky," Don ordered.

The old cook grinned, winked, tossed off his glass and held it out for Don to fill up with whisky. Taka followed suit.

"Well, aloha Ka Kou!" Don said, lifting his glass. "Love to everybody—Dad's old toast."

Glenn gulped his drink and excused himself almost immediately, but the others lingered over their glasses, and something which seemed lost crept back thankfully into the old house. Taka busied himself hanging up Don's clothes, and Ah Sam grinned from the bathroom door. Presently,

33

mumbling to himself in Chinese, he collected the glasses and went away.

The dinner gong sounded and Travers and Don went downstairs. Entering the dining-room Travers saw Glenn grasping the chair at the head of the table, creating the impression that he was contesting with, or challenging, Don for position as master of the house. Travers noted again the puzzled expression in Don's eyes which he had first noticed in Lahaina when Glenn assigned Don to the back of the car. Travers' face hardened, but Don appeared not to see and took a seat at the side of the table.

Across the snowy damask and gleaming silver Travers appraised the two brothers. There was a casual elegance about Glenn which did not go with the strained expression of his face. Don sat very still. Thinking of what? Courses came and went, talk was fitful and forced. Then, without warning, a song came from the dark, scented garden as though the island had cried out. Don's thin fingers tightened about the stem of his goblet and the pupils of his eyes contracted to points. He moved, once, and Travers saw tiny drops of moisture on his forehead.

Drawing a cigar from his breast pocket, Travers bit the end off viciously. He had forgotten, as Don had, the old island custom of workers serenading departing or returning members of a family. These Hawaiians had sung at Christmas, New Year's and the Fourth of July. They had serenaded Don's and Glenn's mother after her children were born, and sung the last songs over her and her husband's bodies when they were laid away. Now, once more they sang for a Garrison who had come back, after years of absence, to the folk who loved him, whose fathers had worked for his father before he was born.

When the song ended Don rose and walked onto the veranda.

"Thanks, boys, *mahalo,*" he said; then after a difficult pause did what was expected of him, requested the Haleakala hula.

There was a clamorous assent from the men at the bottom of the steps. The song, in honor of the great mountain on which the Garrison ranch lay, had from long association become symbolical of the family. After some tuning of instruments the cowboys began singing. Travers watched Don staring at a point of light on a leaf just above the men's heads, as though he could not bring himself to look at the careless strong figures in dusty riding clothes hugging great brown guitars to their breasts.

The men sang with passion and gusto; of the blue, shadowy bowl of the crater, of wet forests with clouds driving across them, of uplands clothed in a growth of *kawao,* of hills dozing under a hot sun, of whips cracking and the swift rush of cattle and horses, of immaculate dawns and of tired twilights gathering sea and islands to their breasts.

Don heaved himself up in his chair, all the color drained out of his face. Travers drove his teeth into his cigar, guessing the depths of despair with which Don was wrestling, trying to forget that once he had ridden and laughed and sung with these men as their fathers had laughed, ridden and danced with his father. He sat, breathing unevenly, staring at what? At his life, once filled like a brimming cup, now emptied forever of any activity.

35

Travers' eyes filmed like a bird's. A shaft of light from indoors threw Don's pale profile into relief and Travers saw the muscle in Don's cheek twitching. The music changed abruptly to a rollicking hula and two slim-hipped cowboys stepped onto the lawn and began dancing: hats tilted at rakish angles, white teeth flashing, spurs ringing faintly and sweetly at their heels. A second couple detached themselves from the singers and joined the dancers, and a boy threw his hat onto the grass and uttered a delighted caterwaul which tore through the dominant melody, becoming part of its primitive rhythm.

Don thrust against the back of his chair, his eyes as hard as stones. Travers glanced at him, then looked away as though he hated remembering how Don as a boy, and as a young man, had always danced hulas with his men, at Christmas, at *luaus,* or when the entire ranch gathered to celebrate some great victory won by Garrison thoroughbreds at the Kahului track. In his memory he could still see him, eager, slight, graceful, going through the intricate weaving steps, head flung back, eyes and lips smiling, beautiful and vital as the island underneath him, a true child of the earth.

Adaji, the houseboy, came to the door.

"Mr. Glenn, Mr. Morse like speak you."

Glenn, who had been standing in the shadows watching Don, started guiltily, then straightened up. Don glanced around, smiled at his brother, then looked back at the dancing men. Meeting Travers' eyes, Glenn flushed, but the old man appeared not to see. He watched Glenn stalking hurriedly and uneasily through the living-room. At the far end, on the wall, Travers saw Morse's shadow, distorted by the lamplight to gigantic proportions.

So, he thought, before Don had been home three hours those two had to confer, to conspire against him! With a vicious gesture Travers hurled his cigar into the dark.

CHAPTER III

DON woke from a restless sleep and lay with arms clasped under his head, listening to the rustle of dawn through the tree-tops. Gradually the familiar sounds of early morning reached him: a scurry of dogs let out of their kennels, whips cracking, the rush of horses driven into corrals, the cheerful shouts of riders, a truck warming up its engine, a stallion whinnying imperiously for his mares.

He lay still, fearful that if he moved he might loose emotions surging through him. He realized that it would require an enormous effort to forget the joy with which he used to greet each new day; to smother mind-pictures which had tapped at his consciousness even in sleep—memories of glossy thoroughbreds moving restlessly about the fresh straw of loose-boxes, wine-red bulls lumbering arrogantly about their pastures, dogs eagerly scenting through dewy grass, cock pheasants soaring from fern-grown ridges, the stately trees and peaceful pastures along his favorite rides.

He sat up and put his legs over the edge of the bed. Across the room was a *koa* bookcase which he had made when he was twelve, under his father's supervision. He remembered with what pride he had sawed the beautifully grained wood, fitted it together and polished it until it shone. The shelves were filled with books dealing with the rules of racing and polo, the care and feeding of stock, the training of hunting dogs, and other subjects fitting the active

38

life of a ranch. Staring at a rack filled with guns and at a row of polished riding-boots, with spurs hanging above them, he stifled a pang, then thrust back his shoulders to shake off the burden of his thoughts.

He tried to realize he was home, but a great emptiness filled him, an emptiness which ached. Through the squares of open windows familiar tree-tops, gilded with sunshine, moved softly as though beckoning to him to come out. He walked to a window; tree smells, garden smells and the strong smell of earth assailed him. Shifting his weight to one cane he pounded the carpet with the other. He felt entirely and forever divorced from the active life going on about him, almost like an intruder in his own home. Deliberately and dispassionately he relived the events of the past twelve hours, his shock when he saw Glenn standing behind the master's chair, driving home the fact that his return was not the pleasure to his brother which Don had taken for granted that it would be. Stupid to note such trifles, he thought, feeling disgusted with himself.

Glenn had been completely in charge of ranch affairs while he had been rotting in hospitals. It was human nature that this younger brother who had been, to all practical purposes, elder brother, should be reluctant to share the undisputed authority he had enjoyed for so long. The first evening had been strained, senseless to attempt to deny it. For appearances' sake Glenn had tried to make appropriate gestures and had failed. The old affection between them had become dimmed. Ernesto was genuinely glad to have him back, the servants and cowboys delighted, but at the same time embarrassed, realizing that he was, and always would be, crippled, never able to be wholly one of them again.

Don filled his lungs with keen morning air, holding it down until it hurt. Action, even curtailed action, was safer than thought. Best to go out of doors for a bit, get close to the earth; perhaps contact with it would fortify him. He looked about for his clothes, then, remembering that Taka had put them away, he experienced a moment of irritation.

A discreet tap sounded on the door.

"Taka?"

"Yes, Mr. Don."

"Come in."

The man entered smiling.

"Long time I wait outside for you to wake up. Now half-past five. I come at four."

Don had to wait for an instant before he dared to speak. In the old days he had always risen at four, eager to be out before his men began saddling.

"Give me the trousers I wore yesterday and my gray sweater. I want to see the boys off. After this I will rise at six-thirty."

The Japanese looked at him quickly and compassionately, then began laying out clothes. Don seated himself on the bed, wound his watch and went through various coat pockets, extracting his passport, bill-fold and letters. He glanced casually through them; then seeing one from Ernesto, written two months previously, he reread it:

> *Old man, if you feel up to the trip it's time you came home. It's hardly cricket to expect*

*Glenn to be entirely responsible for everything.
Conditions on Maui are changing fast. If you
put off returning too long you'll never be able to
get into step. It's natural that you should dread
returning; for you, things can never be the same,
but the obstacles you've overcome during the past
years have tested and proved your caliber and
strengthened it for greater fights——*

Don stopped reading. After twelve hours of being home,
Ernesto's words seemed invested with hidden significance.
The supposition disturbed him. He rose and Taka assisted him with his dressing. He was aware that the
Japanese was watching him unhappily. It was going to be
difficult until they all got accustomed to him being like
this. He waited while Taka tied his shoes. Then, assembling his forces, grasped his canes and started down
the passage toward the stairs.

Approaching Glenn's room he heard voices and recol-
lected that his brother had guests in the house, but the sound
of Glenn talking to a stranger at this early hour made him
feel thrust aside, and left out. Dejection, which he scorned,
filled him. In all likelihood his impressions of the past
twelve hours had been exaggerated and distorted.

Ridiculous to expect, overnight, to be reabsorbed into
Glenn's life. He must face facts: he was home, hamstrung. It was going to be difficult, almost unbearable for
a while, but eventually he would adjust and some niche
would be found into which he could fit and be of use. Until then, he must grit his teeth, fight down fruitless longings

which could never be realized, call on every ounce of reserve strength and courage he possessed. As he passed Glenn's door the voices ceased, but he heard them start again when he began descending the stairs.

He paused for a minute in the living-room, studying the objects about him. From the kitchen came the fragrance of coffee, recalling mornings when he had gulped it down hastily in order to ride off with his men. From the pasture below the house came the sound of a man singing a hula as he drove in work horses, and it seemed the voice of his lost youth calling to him again. A line appeared between his brows and he walked quickly into the garden.

The beauty of the new day, filled with color and life, jumped at him, taking him off his guard. Over trees, shutting out the immediate foreground, the rare lights of early morning lay on the lilac and green of cane fields covering the isthmus between the masses of east and west Maui. Beyond was the high blue wall of the sea, broken by the shadowed shapes of islands half hidden under heaped clouds, glittering, white, seemingly as imperishable as a great ideal.

Fox terriers, hearing strange footfalls, rushed out, barking. Don spoke to them, recognizing some of them, puppies when he left, but now gray about muzzles and ears. They looked puzzled when he called them by name. A pointer came slowly down the walk and waited, wagging his tail. Don's skin grew moist. No more shooting, no more tramping windy hills! With furious disgust he thrust the thought aside. Ridiculous to begin that all over again. He tried his voice.

"Shot, old man."

The dog came closer. Don put out a cane to stroke it and the animal edged away. He wondered if it had been wise to come home. Here life, highly colored, vital, shouted at him. In England it had been a monotone. He would need all the fortitude he possessed to get through the day, all the days.

He started on, passed through a gate set between stone walls covered with a mad growth of nasturtiums, and entered a rough quadrangle formed by stables, blacksmith-shop and corrals. Kanaka dogs with pale, blinking eyes lay beside corral gates where men were catching and saddling horses. From the blacksmith-shop came the sound of a hammer meeting an anvil. Beside the building, huge oxcarts, relics of an older régime, stood with weeds growing about their wheels. Sight of the clumsy wagons recalled his boyhood when each autumn his father had sent them out loaded with boxes of tiny seedlings to be planted on distant sections of the ranch. He had loved the wise, slow-moving oxen, the shouts of teamsters and the cracking of long whips.

"Aloha."

He came back to the present with a start, realizing that Holomalia, the immense Hawaiian foreman, was standing, hat in hand, regarding him with dignified compassion.

"Aloha," Don replied.

They both waited. There seemed nothing more to say, but Don forced himself to ask questions about the stock and the feed while the foreman waited for his men to finish saddling. Don kept his eyes fixed on Haleakala, visible above the tree-tops, cold, blue, withdrawn, against the gold-washed sky of early morning. All the courage seemed to

43

be ebbing out of him, the blood in his veins turning to ice. Awful, realizing that he could never ride over the mountain again, never re-see its secret remembered beauties, warm hollows with white-faced calves dozing in them, splendid hilltop views, the moist sweetness of golden green forests. He pressed his canes fiercely into the earth.

He saw a cowboy untying a horse and his palm remembered the pleasant roughness of rope; he saw the man swing onto the horse's back and the insides of his legs recalled the thrilling coldness of first contact with leather. Abominable, living as he did, cut off from the things he most loved!

He addressed men passing and repassing, busy about minor tasks before they set out for the real work of the day. He saw, or fancied he saw, them exchange startled glances when he asked questions about the ranch, and became increasingly aware of some hidden presence crouching in the blue heart of the day. He was conscious again of the constraint they felt in his presence. He was no longer the Don who had laughed, roped, danced and ridden with them. That Don had been left on the other side of the war. He glanced at his trousers, then at their leather-clad legs, and the sensation of foreignness, welling up in him again, filled him with despair and unrest. He leaned heavily on his canes. He must be careful not to get off on the wrong foot at the start or he would lose the race! Race, races, he could never ride another one, though he would be compelled to see the sleek thoroughbreds in the stable which he knew old Hu was preparing for his inspection. Conscious of some one at his elbow, he looked around.

"All right, Hu, bring out the race horses," he said in a

flat voice, then stared at the strong trees and at clouds collecting above the tawny blue mass of Haleakala. The most
difficult moment of his homecoming was upon him. He
must meet it like a man! Bracing himself, he waited. A
rush of hoofs on wooden flooring choked him and a muscle
in the region of his heart cramped until it hurt.

Hu darted out, leading a stallion the color of bronze. It
swung around on the halter, sunlight flashing on shoulders
and quarters, ears moving alertly, glowing crimson nostrils
dilating.

"Paniolo!"

The animal threw up its head at the sound of its name.

"Paniolo! Come here!"

Don took a step forward and the stallion threw up his
head and shied away. Hu jerked him down.

"I think little forget," Hu said, apologetically, when
Don had made some further overtures and failed to win
the animal's confidence. The fragrance of a well-kept
horse's hide almost unmanned Don, but he managed to
make appropriate comments. He had ridden Paniolo as a
colt to victory three times, but it was not possible for any
animal to remember ten years.

"All right, Hu, he looks fine. You've taken good care
of him. Bring out the others."

The man led the stallion back into the stable. Don looked
at the wide doors, remembering with despair the uncounted
times he had ridden out of them, then resolutely fixed his
attention on the rest of the thoroughbreds Hu was parading,
noting their small ears, splendid quarters, flashing off light,

firm round hoofs which had flung race tracks disdainfully behind them.

A tiny pain like a thin hot wire burned for an instant inside him, then dulled out, leaving him numb. Senseless to think backwards! No miracle could make it possible for him to ride again.

Looking around, he saw a young Hawaiian watching the animals from where he leaned against a tree. Don recognized the passionate absorption of a born horselover in the boy's eyes and signaled to him to come over. Would he like to ride the pick of these youngsters the next Fourth of July, Don asked in Hawaiian. The boy caught his breath, then a peculiar expression went over his face. Yes, he would like it even better than getting drunk. But people on Maui were not as interested in racing as they had been. Don assured him that he would see to it that at the next meet a cup and purse would be put up which would be worth the winning. There weren't enough cups on the mantel of the Big House. There never would be. . . .

The boy smiled understandingly.

Don saw Glenn coming through the garden and his heart grew lighter. Dear old Glenn! Of course it must be painful for him to see his brother crocked up. He tried to imagine his own feelings if their cases had been reversed. In all likelihood Glenn had absented himself the previous evening lest he give away to an expression of feeling forbidden to men. Glenn came up blinking and scowling.

"Out pretty early, what?" he asked.

"Thought I might as well—this morning," Don replied,

46

realizing, with a sort of fright, that his brother's words angered him because they implied that he was on the shelf. He must be on his guard every instant or he would succeed in making a complete idiot of himself, and he appreciated, with annoyance, that he had almost apologized to his own brother for doing the most natural thing in the world. What had come over him? He was like a riderless horse stampeding in all directions.

"I say, do have a smoke," Glenn urged, snatching a package of cigarettes out of his pocket.

Don noticed that Glenn was not in riding clothes. Thoughtful old fellow, he didn't intend to make his brother feel too out of the running. Seating himself carefully on a wagon-tongue Don held out his hand.

"Thanks, old man," he said, accepting the package and extracting a cigarette, while he watched, with a deadly aching calm, while Hu continued to parade horses. He was conscious of Glenn watching him, ill at ease, resenting and pitying him. There was a harried, irresolute air about Glenn that bothered him. He made Don think of a man so afraid of life that he could only exist by pretending to despise it.

"I say, Glenn, let's go back to the house. The horses are a bit too much for me, still. All right, Hu, *lawa!* I'll look at the rest another time."

The Hawaiian stopped leading the mare he had on the halter, staring at Don as though he could not believe that he had heard aright, then walked dispiritedly back into the stable.

47

Glenn and Don retraced their steps to the garden. Travers was waiting at the gate, a tattered felt hat pulled over his eyes.

"Well, has the round been made, dear familiar scenes revisited, appropriate sensations experienced?"

"Yes, damn you, you old scoffer," Don answered, heartened by the sharp, wholesome ridicule.

"Then let's eat before Sue Morse comes down. I can't endure women before noon."

"You're in a vile mood as usual," Don laughed; "perhaps food will improve your disposition. Glenn——"

"Have to go to the office for a minute; see you shortly," Glenn said, starting to cut across the lawn.

Don watched him walk away, then went with Travers to the broad *lanai* where breakfast was waiting. Palms and enormous hanging baskets of fern hiding cages of canaries, made it almost a part of the garden. The table, set with blue Japanese ware and hammered silver, was fragrant with island flowers and fruit. Travers seated himself opposite Don. Glenn's place, at the head, was conspicuous by its emptiness.

"Bacon, Adaji, and two eggs, soft," Travers said, curtly.

"Coffee or tea, Mr. Ernesto?"

"I'll take tea this morning."

"I'll have coffee and bacon," Don said; "and tell Taka that I want a car about nine and some one to drive me. Is there a roadster?"

"Yes, got, Mr. Don."

"Tell Taka I want it."

For a while they ate in silence, then Travers looked up.

"Don't make such an infernal row," he said, sarcastically.

"I know I deserve to be shot," Don said, "but everything seems putrid. I imagined, like an idiot, that there would be some zest in getting back, but there isn't. Everything seems absolutely flat."

Travers' eyes narrowed.

"Thank God you're honest enough to admit it. Most people would pretend, because it's expected of them, that it was otherwise. People attach so much unnecessary sentiment to departures and returns. I've always found they are just abominable days detached from, and hanging between, the rest of life."

Don grinned bleakly.

"You've hit the nail on the head. You're an old scoffer, Ernesto, but you're sound. You don't cheat yourself about things. According to the bunk with which people love to feed themselves, my return should be an occasion for rejoicing. In stories when the prodigal son——"

"Or wounded hero," Travers suggested, sarcastically, and they grinned at each other with immense affection.

"Or wounded hero," Don agreed, "returns, his dying hound crawls up to lick his hand, his horse neighs for him, but when I went out this morning the damned dogs barked at me, Paniolo shied away; the men feel strange, and Glenn, for some reason, seems to dodge and avoid me."

Travers occupied himself with a golden crescent of *papaia*.

"Is the old duffer afraid I'm going to assert my prerogative of being the elder brother and insist upon him playing second fiddle? I haven't the faintest intention of doing such a thing. Last night when he was down ahead of us, hanging

49

onto the seat at the head of the table, I felt like laughing and punching his head. I don't give a hang where I sit."

Travers' eyes, wise, cool, calculating, came up slowly. He started to speak, then seeing Glenn approaching with Morse laid down his spoon. Glenn placed his hands on the back of his chair as though for support.

"Don, this is Ran Morse. Ran, my brother Don."

"Pardon my not getting up," Don said, laying down his napkin.

"Absolutely," Morse replied, thrusting out his hand.

Don accepted it without enthusiasm and over it appraised the man. Cold, calculating, abnormally keen, was his conclusion, but as breakfast progressed he was vaguely bothered by Morse's proprietory manner, which was more that of a member of the family than that of a guest. He noted that Glenn watched Morse as though waiting for cues to guide his actions and saw that Glenn's narrow face was slightly flushed and his eyes restless.

"Sue not coming down for breakfast?" Glenn asked, after a prolonged silence.

"Too much party last night," Morse laughed. "I left her with an ice-pack on her head."

He glanced at Don, an amused expression of intimacy in his eyes to which Don did not respond. It was of no interest to him whatever if Morse's unknown wife had drunk too much at some smart gathering.

"I'm sorry my wife and I had to be absent the night you arrived," Morse said, "but we had a dinner engagement that we couldn't break."

Don nodded.

"I've asked friends to lunch," Glenn announced. "We must have some sort of shindig in honor of your return, old man."

"For heaven's sake, don't bother," Don protested.

"If you'd given us a little warning," Morse broke in, "we could have staged a proper welcome. Sue, my wife, is a wonderful organizer. She and Moll Harding about run this island, socially."

"I can't picture Molly Harding grown up," Don said. "When I left she was just a little kid. She must be—nineteen. What sort of a girl has she grown into?"

His mind flashed, briefly, to Gay Storm. It seemed incredible, almost depressing, realizing that children he had left had grown into young women. It made him feel old and worn-out.

"Moll is a perfect product of the age," Travers said.

"Why the beastly inflection?" Don asked. "Don't you like her, Ernesto?"

Travers did not reply.

The telephone rang and after an instant Adaji appeared.

"Mr. Glenn, Miss Molly on the line."

Glenn rose and returned shortly.

"Moll sent love and asked me to tell you, Don, that she will be up with some of her friends about noon to see you. Some one in Lahaina told her that you had come home."

"Nice of her," Don said.

Morse smiled at him across the table.

"Better watch out, Garrison. Moll's the champion big game hunter of Maui."

"I don't understand you," Don said.

"New man," Morse said, looking profound. "She'll give you no peace until she adds your scalp to those that already hang from her belt."

Don looked affronted.

"I'm out of the running," he said, stiffly.

"Don't fool yourself. You'll be a new experience. I envy and pity you."

Don looked indignantly at Morse, and Glenn moved sharply.

"I say, Don," he burst out, "I have to go down to Wailuku this morning. Hope you don't mind my running off and leaving you the first day you're home. I'll be back by noon."

"Okay with me," Don said, thinking that it would have been easy enough for Glenn to have asked him to go along. "I'm going to drive around and have a look at the ranch."

Morse's and Glenn's eyes leaped together, then Glenn jerked out:

"Better drive up the Kula road; the roads around Piholo are under repair at present, a foot deep in dust and bumpy. They'd be tough on your back."

Don nodded.

"I'll order a car for you," Glenn said, watching his brother from under working eyebrows.

"Don't bother; I've already told Taka that I want the roadster and some one to drive me."

Morse glanced remindingly at Glenn.

"Let's be off," he said, pushing back his chair. "See you at lunch," he nodded to Don.

When they were gone Don's eyes met Travers'.

"Filthy bounder," Don said. "How long are he and his wife to be here?"

"Until their house is finished. Months probably."

"Charming prospect," Don remarked, reaching down and picking up his canes. "Want to drive around with me, Ernesto?"

"Sorry, I can't. I have a canvas to finish. It's an order."

Some inflection in Travers' voice made Don glance at him sharply. He reminded Don of a wise old bird waiting with immense patience for the day to give up its secrets.

"Well, I'll see you at lunch," Don said.

"Don't be late. I don't relish being a receiving committee of one. Sue'll stay in bed until the Thundering Herd arrives. I loathe Moll and the type of people she runs round with. This generation is a mess."

"I rather suspect each generation seems a mess in the estimation of the one preceding it," Don observed.

Travers chuckled.

When Don went out he saw a strange Japanese sitting at the wheel of an expensive and ponderous limousine. Seeing Don the man got out and opened the door.

"I am Mr. Morse's driver," he announced.

"I ordered the roadster," Don said. "This car is much too good to take over the Kula road."

"Mr. Glenn speak I tell you he too sorry, but he need the roadster hisself. Mr. Glenn big car got broke tire so Mr. Morse speak I drive you."

Don stood thinking. Evidently Glenn's years of undisputed authority as manager of the ranch had implanted in his nature a desire to dominate, but it was sickening of him to attempt to domineer over his own brother—through a servant! The waiting man looked ill at ease.

"Mr. Glenn speak better I take you Kula side. Piholo road all broke."

Don stifled the anger rising in him, nodded and got into the car. It did not particularly matter where he went, but it irritated him because Glenn was attempting to dictate his movements. The car started, the man driving with ostentatious care. Don thrust the canes lying on the floor impatiently aside with one foot. Evidently Glenn intended to drive home the fact that he considered his brother on the shelf.

The bright day seemed to dim.

The car crawled along the winding road and Don sat thinking deeply. For the moment life was not pretty. Here was Glenn gone with Morse, a man Don instinctively disliked and distrusted, leaving him to be driven in Morse's car, by Morse's man, thereby putting him into Morse's debt. He stared at the road. He must move warily until time worked its magic, bringing him and Glenn together again. It was not possible that two brothers who had been as close as they had been could be permanently divided. The car emerged from the avenue and the sun-soaked mass of Haleakala, beautiful with the eucalyptus of his father's planting, came into view. Smoke blue, drawn up in squads, like regiments in review, they stood in their hundreds of thousands, crowning eminences, spilling down gulch sides, affording shelter for stock, supplying firewood and fence

54

posts, and adding beauty to the land. A monument to his father's memory!

His eyes grew gentle thinking about him. Of Polish and English descent, John Garrison had been, while he lived, the most outstanding and picturesque figure on Maui, a man of all time, beloved by all. He had been father, mother and friend to his sons, had introduced polo to Hawaii, upheld racing, imported pedigreed stock, rare grasses and trees from all over the world. Don looked reverently at the mountain; it seemed to him that he could see his father's hand laid fondly on the portions which had belonged to him, which he had loved and beautified.

He longed to have his father sitting beside him, smoking his pipe, thoughtful, quiet, attentive. Now he was a man himself, Don realized that his father had been remarkable in that he realized that his sons were not entirely his sons, but the sons of life also, belonging to it and to themselves. He had given them his love and his knowledge, but had not tried to live their lives for them.

Mind pictures of his father astride of a horse directing colossal plantings of trees, of him playing the banjo, of him instructing Glenn and himself how to handle race horses, rose from their graves to torment him. Vanished Sundays— when they tramped windy hills with dogs and guns, while their father explained about different species of trees and grasses as they hunted—came back, wiping the last vestige of color from his face.

He felt like pounding his fist against the glass window and smashing it, but instead wound it down. In the light wind were secret whispers, like promises of the unknown, and the piled clouds of the Trade seemed like the mountains of dreams, forever out of reach.

The car made its way slowly between the gleaming wire fences. Don studied the mass of Haleakala deliberately, and, in the full realization of what he was doing, relived his old life which had been spent almost entirely upon it. He remembered nights on the blue brink of the crater, stars shining down on vast shadowy cones cradled in the mammoth bowl, the infinitesimal sounds of erosion, minute particles of cinder rolling down precipitous slopes, the tiny noises of rocks worked upon by atmosphere, the thin cry of goats; hot days spent on beaches set between jagged headlands of lava where steamers anchored outside the reef and cattle had to be roped, dragged into the sea and tied to the sides of whaleboats to be drawn out and hoisted into the ship; the rush down green polo fields, the creak of straining leather, the brown blur of racetracks, the dark blunt nose of a surfboard set between wings of sheer, silver spray, the smell of feathers and gunpowder, the pliant strength of rawhide ropes circling overhead. . . .

All, everything, taken from him! How could he endure it? Why had he come back? It had been the supreme piece of insanity of his whole life. . . . As the car slowly and steadily mounted the long steep slopes, the island began unrolling before Don's eyes like a vast map. Don gazed at it, trying to draw comfort and strength from familiar contours. Well, beauty was left. . . . Then he sat up and stared. . . .

Distant, once-green pastures of adjoining estates had been transformed into raw red ploughed fields, planted with me-

chanical rows of gray pineapples. Like an emerald river
the broad acres of the Garrison ranch poured between the
sacrificed pastures of other holdings. A passion of protest
surged through Don, followed by emptying fear. Suppose
that during his absence Glenn had elected to follow the
trend of the times, had chosen to grow pineapples instead
of raise cattle? Terrible, even to think of it. It would almost have been like seeing his father's body mutilated, for
a vital part of John Garrison lived on in the trees and grasses
he had planted, in the stock that grazed off it and in the
wild feathered things he had imported.

He listened to the voice of the land, a great voice com-
pounded out of lesser voices welded into one: doves cooing
in solemn trees, pheasants crowing, plovers whistling and
wheeling overhead, the thunderous whirr of coveys of quail
startled by the passing car, a cow, lowing for her calf, the
thin whinny of a mare and a colt's answering nicker, the
tiny rattle of shaken seed-pods in the grass.

"Stop!" Don ordered, and the driver brought the car to
a halt.

For a minute Don looked out of the window. The
splendor, the fecundity of the land about, teeming with
growth—this was what he had hungered for, fought for,
reached for with his mind during the years he had spent in
bed. Green hills, peaceful stock grazing, trees with the
strong glitter of sunlight burnishing their leaves.

"Drive on for an hour," Don ordered; "I want to stay
here for a while."

He must be alone with the island, with no other presence
to disturb or distract him; he must feel part of it again, be

unified with it as he had always been as a boy and a young man. The Japanese subjected him to a peculiar scrutiny which irritated him, for it created the impression that the man was under orders not to leave him alone. The supposition was absurd, but Don's instinct convinced him he was right.

"Did you hear what I said?" he asked, sharply, as the man made no move.

"Yes, Mr. Garrison."

Don got out and stood in the road watching the car lurch through a rut, ponderous, mechanical, with no rightful place in such surroundings. When it had vanished he felt freed. He wondered if he could manage to get up the low bank into the pasture. He wanted to lie down in the grass, feel the heart of the island throbbing in the soil beneath him, to stretch out upon it and draw courage and vitality out of the earth.

He succeeded in getting up the bank where it had slipped, then the fence stopped him. He could no longer vault it and doubted if he could bend his back sufficiently to crawl through the wires. He attempted it twice, gave up and stood still, trying to think of all his assets—sky overhead, warm grass underfoot, trees everywhere. Studying the grave groves he thought of them as a guard of honor. They didn't care if a man was crippled or whole, defeated or victorious. They stood around, close, friendly and strong.

His eyes swept affectionately over their rounded tops, then rested on the simple, impressive bulk of the mountain, in sight but out of reach forever. A sort of rage filled him; weak, contemptible of him to feel bereft. He had it all back—differently. But the perverse human in him wanted it back in the old way.

He waited as though listening for a voice he longed to hear. His body, his very mind, seemed one empty ache. Where had all the painfully acquired self-control, gathered from difficult years, vanished? He had prided himself that he felt nothing, no pain, no gladness, no resentment. And yet, at his first contact with the island his hold on himself had vanished. Terror swept him. What was going to become of him? Was he to be compelled to refight all the old battles?

He looked at the strong hills.

Just over the fence a dozen yearling foals watched him curiously. Imported grasses from all over the world waved about their slender legs. Fluffy foretops lifted in the breeze, coral-lined nostrils flared. He brandished a cane and they streamed away with lifted heads and tails, only to circle back and inspect him afresh. He noted the short cannons of one and the long springy pasterns of another, the short, well-coupled back of a filly and the driving-power in the quarters of a colt. On the lower side of the fence cows lay chewing their cuds as they contentedly watched their calves taking unsteady steps forward as they nibbled at a new growth of grass, result of recent rains, forcing itself through the old. . . .

He was conscious, in a terrifying way, of the land all about him, feeling in his very being the insurgent cry of the teeming earth for growth, for perpetuation. Warm sky overhead, the milky fragrance of fat cattle, the odor of horses, like a sachet of hay, feathered things darting through

59

the blue, creeping things moving in the grass and the secret whispers of little leaves waiting to be born.

How could he endure contact with it, day after day, year after year, knowing himself unable to answer the call of the virile young land which every atom of his body loved? As he looked, the sunlight seemed to grow stronger and fiercer, the hills a deeper green, the sea a more intense blue. He felt like a drop of foreign matter in the immense azure bowl of the day. He moved, trying to ease the torment of pain rending him, then hurled a cane away.

It flew across the road into the lower pasture, startling a skylark out of the grass. The bird winged its way upward, singing, triumphant, earth-freed. Don watched it until it vanished, then wave upon wave of scorching color burned his skin. He felt, for an instant, that he had been facing God and was ashamed.

With a supreme effort he regained control of his emotions and waited until a familiar numbness began to creep along the edges of his mind. He waited until his mind became completely paralyzed before he dared to breathe. For a while, at least, he was safe, for he had got to a point beyond feeling, as he had so many times during the past ten years.

He glanced down, without interest, at his empty hand. Without a second cane he could not move away.

CHAPTER IV

DON stood for a long time feeling as though his entire being had been emptied onto the soil under his feet. The light wind of the morning had died away, leaving an awful stillness, as though the day were waiting with immense patience for some event already on its way to overtake it.

He studied the country about him, then weighed the distant estates adjoining the Garrison ranch. Above the cool green cane fields of the lowlands, pineapples had entirely replaced the pastures he remembered. Incredible, the changes which could take place in ten years!

Ernesto's statement of the previous night, when they were driving home, that practically every one on Maui was growing pineapples, had not registered until he saw it with his his own eyes. Probably the same thing was taking place on the other islands of the group. He remembered having noticed pineapples outside of Honolulu the day he had been there, but at the time they had meant nothing to him. Now they menaced everything he held most dear.

The pineapple leaves, like sharp gray spikes, arranged in mechanical rows, made him think of the ranked spears of a ruthless army, invading the land, driving beauty, peace, trees, grass and grazing stock before it. A succession of trucks passed, loaded with Filipino laborers on their way to till distant red fields. The men, standing jammed to-

61

gether, each with a hoe instead of a rifle over his shoulder, reminded Don of loaded lorries he had seen from his plane being hurried up to the front. But this, he reminded himself, was the army of progress. He laughed mirthlessly, recalling how only the evening before he had thought proudly of the march of progress in Hawaii which, until recent years, had brought beauty instead of ugliness in its wake.

He had no illusion about progress or civilization, for he had seen them going to pieces under the guns of the war. Progress was another name for commercialism, and commercial jealousy had been the moving factor that started the war. He had fancied when he left England that he was escaping from the prison of civilization to peace and beauty again, beauty embodied in his mind, by memories of the islands in which he had been born. Now he was back only to discover that during his absence Mammon had invaded them and captured most of the land.

He looked at the green pastures, thinking that he and Glenn must keep their land inviolate, must never permit materialism to control their lives. He would talk to Glenn as soon as he got home, impress upon him the necessity of continuing to raise stock instead of following the footsteps of the people about them who were all growing pineapples. He could bring up sound arguments, aside from the sentiment of seeing the work of their father's lifetime undone and beauty destroyed for extra dollars: beef in Hawaii had local consumption, while pineapples were a crop whose value might reach a peak, then decline when over-production flooded a world market.

Don was not a person who believed that everything was

splendid, but he was one who insisted upon having things as splendid as possible. Alone so much, isolated from contact with humanity for so many years, the idealist in him had grown immeasurably more important, more real, than the different reality of actual existence and people. In a dim way, without ever fully realizing it, he had always tried, even as a boy, and with every atom of him, to bring splendor about. Under his quiet exterior was a streak of iron, for people such as he had to fight practically the whole world.

Studying the transformed aspect of the island, terror seized him, for he realized that there was something insolent in humanity as well as something divine; and unquestionably, at the moment, he was feeling the insolence more than the divinity.

He looked at the groves, planted by his father for posterity, his gift to generations to come. He saw seedlings clustering at the feet of stately eucalyptus like children crowding against their parents. Then at the corner of a distant grove he saw a tree falling slowly toward the earth. Don clenched his cane; the tree crashed and it seemed as though the world went down with it.

Extraordinary to see a tree fall on a still day and for no apparent reason. No wind here! He strained his eyes; no wind moving the dark tree-tops below him. He studied the clouds piled magnificently above the horizon. No wind anywhere! His heart beat uncomfortably. He listened for the sound of an ax, but the grove was too distant and he realized that it could not be reached by a car. He moved resentfully, feeling bound, but his mind raced in all directions.

He must find out from Glenn if, by some oversight, that grove was being cut down. Their father had planted for use as well as for beauty, providing for the future needs of the ranch, but the hardwoods, suitable for firewood and fence-posts, had been carefully placed in concealed positions where their cutting and subsequent re-growth would not mar the landscape. The link between the man and the land was indissoluble. As long as the trees he had planted grew, blossomed and seeded, John Garrison himself, his ideals and aspirations and the motives which had prompted him to plant them, would live on.

Don knew from remembered conversations, in which his father revealed the tragedy of his own life, that he was a man who accepted the seasons of the heart as he accepted the seasons of the year. To his father the supreme adventure of life had been life. Its workings, terrible or beautiful, built toward a definite whole. As the stone of a fruit had to break in order that the life germ within might know sun and light, so pain cracked the shell enclosing understanding. His father had always given, unasked, everything he possessed within himself to his sons, to his friends and to the land destiny had entrusted to his care. Remembering back, Don appreciated that his father's most outstanding characteristic had been loyalty to those he loved, to those who loved him. He straightened up, saluting his father's memory.

Despite the shabby reception Glenn had accorded him, Don was convinced that his brother still loved him. It was some hidden thing eating at his conscience that made Glenn avoid him. He recalled the day in England when Glenn had come to say good-by to him in the hospital before sailing for

64

the Islands. He had said little, had sat by Don's bed, his face a white misery. When he rose to go he had glanced at braces, pulleys and weights, gripped Don's hand fiercely and muttered:

"That's the old fight! You'll make the grade yet. Hell, having to go home without you, but I'll be on the dock with bells when you come back. Stick by each other, that's what old Dad always said. You're a funny old ass, but in a pinch I'd rather have you than—" Then Glenn had torn his hand away and dashed out afraid that he had said too much.

Warmth suffused Don for an instant, as though the abyss between him and Glenn had already been bridged. It was only a question of time until— The thought was arrested by the falling of a second tree. He jammed his cane into the earth. Unforgivable of Glenn to be so careless as to permit the cutting of trees which were valueless for either firewood or fence-posts.

Then cold seas drenched him. . . . He knew! Glenn, without having written to tell him, was putting the ranch into pineapples!

His body seemed to be sinking into bottomless, black depths where no light had ever been, into an underworld, airless and charged with invisible violences which seemed to be tearing him apart.

A scamper of dogs coming around a turn of the road startled him. He heard the rhythmic trot of an approaching horse and hurriedly assembled his forces. Gay Storm came in sight and, seeing him on the bank, halted.

"Stranded?" she asked, smiling.

"I am, rather." Don had difficulty managing his voice. "I sent my man on——"

"I passed him."

She regarded him without curiosity, in a friendly, impersonal way. There was a suggestion of eternal things about her as she sat on her gray horse, as though she were a part of the island spread out behind her.

"What are you doing on the bank?" she asked after a moment. "Looking at the young horses?"

"Making an ass of myself."

She laughed enchantingly.

"Are you going to stay up there?"

"To be honest, I haven't a choice. I got up here forgetting that I couldn't get through the fence, then I threw one of my canes——"

"At one of your devils?" she suggested, to his amazement and delight.

"Exactly," he laughed. "But I missed it."

"I'll find your cane and you can have another try."

"Not today. My cane is in the lower pasture."

"I'll find it and shoo the devil farther away."

"You have already," Don said.

She smiled at him, dismounted, tied her horse to a post and climbed the wire fence. Watching her, Don forgot, for the time being, the shock he had had realizing Glenn's treachery. Her face piqued his interest. There was an elusive quality to her and a fine unawareness of self. She moved easily and surely, swishing the long grass aside with her boot while her dogs leaped about her or made impudent

66

sallies at grazing stock. Her skin had an odd, luminous quality, her eyes shone faintly as though she were always looking at something beautiful.

"You know," she called, with friendly gaiety, "I have them, too."

"Have what?" Don asked.

"Devils."

"You!" Don exclaimed, as though he could not credit it.

She nodded. He tried to see in the young girl the child he had casually known. He attempted to compute her age. She had been eight, possibly nine, when he left. That made her nearly twenty. And Ernesto had said that she had earned her own living for the past five years. An immense admiration swept him for the valiant spirit housed in her slight body. He noted the browned firmness of her bare arms, the straightness of her back, the grace of her slim legs in their worn boots and breeches. She seemed a being who belonged to herself. Despite her friendliness an air of distant defiance enveloped her as though she continually kept life at bay.

"I've found it," she called.

She climbed the fence, brandishing the cane triumphantly.

"Would you like to sit down?" she asked, when she got onto the bank beside him. "I'll give you a hand."

He accepted her aid as simply as though it had been offered by a boy. He noticed her work-roughened fingers. The bones were fine and small, but the skin was almost like that of an old woman, dry and hard. It shocked him, contrasting it with her vivid young face; then he remembered

67

the work she did, saddling, cooking, grooming horses and packing.

When he was seated she sank into the grass beside him and tossed out her hair. She had a misleadingly delicate face that made people overlook her courageous jaw. Her eyes were what a person marked and remembered, wide open, shining, alive.

"You know," she said, in an impersonal voice, "I've been thinking about you ever since I met you last evening."

Don plucked at a blade of grass. He felt her looking at him and at the land and suspected that she was thinking of him in connection with it, and the felled trees leaped back into his mind. In all likelihood she, everyone on Maui, knew that the ranch was going into pineapples, while Glenn had kept him in the dark. He wrestled with his feelings for an instant, then determined afresh that he would talk to Glenn, immediately he got home. The girl was still looking at him and he moved uncomfortably, fearing pity, but when he met her glance he realized that it was not pity but understanding that Gay was giving him. A truck loaded with laborers thundered by as though determined to overtake its fellows, well on their way to distant ploughed fields. The girls glanced around to assure herself of the whereabouts of her dogs.

"I'm always terrified that one of those horrible things will run over them," she explained, and some inflection in her voice suggested to Don that since her father's death they were all she had on which to lavish her love. "This road used to be safe for riding, but it isn't any more. Soon all this," she waved at the pastures about them, "will be gone, too."

Her voice filled with regret.

"Not if I have anything to say about it," Don announced.

The girl glanced at him, started to speak, then changed her mind. Don appeared not to notice. Loyalty to Glenn prevented him from asking her if what he suspected was common knowledge, as he guessed it must be. He looked at hills and pastures vibrating slightly under the hot sun, then fixed his eyes on the bank on the opposite side of the road. Lizards ran in and out of innumerable crevices in the earth, their flanks panting slightly. A shiny, black beetle tried to crawl along a crack, resting now and then and moving its antennæ warily. When he had mustered sufficient courage he looked up and his eyes swept the fair fields about them.

"All this," Don indicated the serene, green acres of the ranch, "seems part, is part, of my father to me. When we were small he used to take us out with him on horseback every autumn to select sites for the thousands of trees he set out every year after the first rains. He worked out a system of planting whereby the trees not only cost the ranch nothing, but netted it a profit. He'd fence off so many acres, put in the seedlings, and between them plant potatoes, which were taken off and sold to pay for the expenses of fencing and plowing. Later, imported grasses were sowed, and when the trees were large enough not to be harmed by stock the fences were removed and steers turned in to fatten for market. Dad loved it all so—" He broke off to stare at the rolling meadows, his own land-love mak-

ing his face beautiful. Then he asked, huskily, "Have you
a smoke?"

The girl nodded, reached into her breeches pocket and
brought out a package of cigarettes and a box of matches
which she handed to him.

"Thanks," he said.

The girl sat embracing her knees. When he returned
the package she selected a cigarette for herself and lighted it.
They smoked for a while in a warm, friendly silence, and
Don was conscious of her sympathy though she did not put
it into words. He noted her sensitive profile and the small
but exquisitely shaped proportions of her head under its
bright, flying hair.

"You know," she said, after a silence, "life seems, mostly,
a mess, but when I look at trees I'm ashamed. Since Dad
died, things have been tough. It seemed as though life had
pounced on me before I was ready for it. You probably
know that Dad didn't own Lanakela ranch—he managed it
for Hughes. He was generous, but somehow I couldn't
accept the house Dad and I lived in when he offered
it to me. It hurt to think of leaving, and when I moved
to the little place Dad built near the forest I felt as though
part of me had been torn off and left behind. But I
loved our little bungalow. Dad and I used to spend week-
ends there and have lots of fun. We used to pretend things
and build air castles of the time when I became a famous
artist. We bought ships and went to far away countries. . . .
Then Dad died and dreaming was done." She paused.
"Sometimes when I was alone I used to feel scared of life.
It seemed to be right behind me, treading on my heels,

hurrying me. Then I'd get on my horse and ride up here
and look at these trees and think. Drought or deluge they
grow on. They don't depend only on outside things to
help them, the push upward comes from inside. I love
them when they are still and waiting, like today; or when
a great wind is blowing through them, then they look angry
and brave and strong. These eucalyptus———"

"Were every one of them planted under the supervision
of my father," Don interrupted.

"All of them, all the lots on the mountain, too?" she
asked, as though she could not credit it.

"I'm surprised you don't know, that people haven't told
you," Don said, proudly, feeling as though the trees were
growing out of his heart. Then he was suddenly sad; so
soon, he thought, is a man's work forgotten despite the fact
that the fruit of his labor lives on. Gay glanced at him as
though divining his thought.

"Then these trees will help you, too, to be brave."

Don looked at her without answering, for her words were
like a reminding hand laid on his shoulder.

"You're going to have to be," she insisted, looking at his
pale face. "It's odd, but I feel as though I'd known you for
years. I suppose because we both love the same things, and
because life, for both of us, has been hard."

"I'm sorry that it has been difficult for you," Don said
gently.

"Why?"

"Oh, I don't just know why—" He hesitated.

" 'Gay,' " she suggested.

"Thanks, Gay," Don finished, marveling at her friendliness, given not from a girl to a man but exchanged equally, as between two human beings. The thought was warming.

"You know," Gay spoke with a sort of enchanting shyness, "of course I'm not very old and have hardly a right to express opinions, but it seems to me that when life hammers and pounds you, it isn't to break you, but just to shape you."

Don stared at her thrilled and amazed; her words were like a shout of victory, spurring on his tired body and soul.

"That's a splendid thought, Gay."

She smiled at him and he felt less lonely. "When I started the business I'm engaged in now——" She paused.

"Ernesto told me about it; it's rather marvelous to think of a little thing like you doing a man's work."

"You can do anything if you want to, badly enough," Gay said. "When I started guiding and packing I used to be scared of everything, scared that people wouldn't let me take them up the mountain because I was a girl, scared that my body wouldn't be strong enough for the work, scared that the other guides would laugh at me and make fun of me. I used to feel as though blank gray walls were closing around me; but after a while I found out that walls aren't put around you to shut you in, they are put there for you to break down or climb over."

Don felt as though this girl were gazing straight into his heart though she seemed to be addressing the blue day. There was a splendid sincerity about her. She was like a white flame burning upward with a clear, bright light.

"I wish," Gay spoke softly, "that it were possible for me to help you, but things aren't done that way. I can guess a little how you are feeling today. You looked so fearfully lonely, and lost, standing up here." Don blushed like an embarrassed boy caught in an unworthy act. "Sometimes one person can give another a push in the right direction or a hand over a difficult crossing, but I know, from my own life, that in the end each one of us must be his own redeemer."

Don sat silent, but he was convinced that Gay understood his torment when he looked at the island and listened to the earth whispering to him. When he did not reply Gay hugged her knees and contemplated the highly colored reaches spread out before them. He pressed his palm fiercely against the ground and stared at his canes.

He was uncomfortably conscious that while she studied the island she was taking stock of him. After a long silence she inspected a tuft of grass.

"I have a secret prayer," she said gently. "Shall I— would you like me to lend it to you? It's helped me when there seemed absolutely nothing to go on for."

Don smiled bleakly.

"That's just the way I've been feeling since I got back," he said, apologetically.

"I guessed it from the expression of your face. That's why I stopped. My prayer," she spoke shyly, "will help you to fight. It's not one I got out of a book but one I made up myself."

"Let's have it, Gay," Don said. "When you came along I felt that life had walked out on me."

She took a deep breath, filling herself with courage to surrender a part of her very self to another human being. "It's this, Don. 'Make me brave! Make me strong!

73

Make me profit by mistakes and progress beyond them. Make me believe, no matter what, that life is beautiful and sound. Make me ready for work, friendship, love, success or failure. Make me take whatever comes like a gentleman and a soldier.' "

"Thanks, Gay," he said, in smothered tones.

"If you say that and think about what you are saying it will take you through everything," she asserted.

Don saw tears on her lashes and felt upset. He listened to the voices of the day and hers was one of them, making their song deeper.

"You know, Don," Gay said, "my prayer isn't to any God; it's sort of an appeal to the great forces you feel at work about you from which you can draw strength if you choose, for you are an atom of the whole. It seems to me that when a person cries for help to whatever God he happens to believe in, it's like trying to pass your troubles on to some one else instead of wrestling with them yourself, like asking some one else to be responsible for you instead of trying to be responsible for yourself. To my way of thinking, the success or failure of a life depends almost entirely on the trend of a person's mind in the right or wrong direction."

Don felt humbled, ashamed, and suddenly very close to her. He watched her thoughtful young face and suspected that many times, since her father's death, the fires in her must have been nearly extinguished. One of her fox terriers dashed up and hurled itself against her. She laughed and caught it in her arms and the little animal began licking her neck.

"I could laugh now when I think of how I used to lie in

bed planning for the time when I got home," Don said, after a prolonged silence. "Now I'm back, the world I used to know seems to have gone to pieces about me. I feel like a ghost left over from another life; but you, your splendid prayer, make me want to fight and keep on fighting."

Gay sat very still, embracing her dog, but her young, fine face was lighted up with the radiance that comes from inside.

"That's how I hoped it would make you feel," she whispered. Then she whistled for her dogs and they rushed up, wild with excitement. "It must be past noon." She glanced at the sun. "I must be getting on my way, for I've work to do and the day after tomorrow I have to take a party of six people up the mountain."

"Thanks, for finding my cane, for shooing away my devil —" Don hesitated, like a shy boy, "—and for lending me your prayer and talking to me the way you have. It was generous of you and has helped me a lot."

"Come over and see me any time you feel blue," she said, sliding down the bank.

"Thanks, Gay. I should like to come and see you, even if I don't feel blue."

They smiled at each other.

"You bet you can," the girl said, untying her horse and passing an affectionate little hand along its glossy neck.

"I say," Don called out as she mounted, "why not lunch at the ranch? Others are dropping in. I'd like immensely to have you. Things at home," he grinned in his attractive way, "are still rather awful."

"I'd love to come, but can't take time today. Ernesto is

75

coming around to criticize a canvas I have to send away and I want to do a little more work on it."

Don watched her ride off, then turned back to contemplate the day. The sea seemed to curve up slightly like an azure bowl until it met the paler blue of the sky; Don had a sensation of distances being impelled outward. A succession of trucks lumbered down the road for fresh relays of laborers; Don did not look at them. In some extraordinary way he felt as though he had got closer to the island and to the earth beneath him and some inner part of him relaxed and expanded. Fixing his eyes on the grove where he had seen the trees falling he repeated Gay's prayer, thoughtfully, as though to test its soundness.

"By Jove! That's jolly fine," he thought, and his white face lighted. "Old Dad would have liked the stuff in it and that girl. She's a sporting little beggar."

Picking up a cane, he poked it thoughtfully through the grass. He must see Glenn at once. . . . Luck that Gay had happened along. . . . Talking to her, or listening to her talk, had helped him to get himself in hand. His skin burned faintly. . . . He had allowed himself to get all steamed up and it had taken a gorgeous kid to make him come to his senses.

The limousine appeared and Don got in. He watched trees and pastures sliding past the windows and sat lost in a fierce worship of the land. The car rounded a turn and he saw Gay sitting on the bank clutching one of her dogs while the others wagged their tails encouragingly and the gray horse grazed off the side of the road.

76

"Stop, Hiro!" he commanded, conscious of a constriction about his heart.

He got out and crossed the road, followed by the Japanese.

"Oh, God! A truck ran over Vixen," the girl cried, looking up with eyes shining as though with fever. "She's alive, but I'm afraid that her back is broken." She spoke in a hard dry voice which ended in a gasp.

Her face was filled with anguish. Don pounded the earth with one cane. If he had been whole he would have knelt down and gathered the girl and dog into his arms.

"Get in the car, Gay, and I'll drive you to the ranch and call up old Fitz. He's the best veterinarian in the Territory."

Gay rose and Don followed. When she was established in the back seat Don got in.

"Don't leave my other dogs!" she cried sharply, as the Japanese was about to close the door.

"I take in front with me," the man said.

"Please tie my horse up on the bank, or one of those damned trucks will crash into him."

"I'll send a boy to fetch him as soon as we get home," Don said, watching the girl tenderly settling the dog upon her knees. The car started and lurched heavily through a rut, jarring its occupants. The dog in Gay's lap, crazed with pain, sunk its teeth into her arm. Don attempted to make it release its hold, but the girl moved protestingly.

"Don't touch her!" she cried. "She doesn't know what she is doing. She'll let go in a moment. Oh, Vixen! Vixen!"

A quiver passed through the little dog's body and its jaws

77

relaxed. Don looked at the dull, bluish holes in the firm brown flesh of Gay's forearm and shuddered slightly.

"Wipe my face, Don, please," Gay said in a faint voice. "It's all wet. It drives me crazy inside when things I love get hurt. Yet somehow they do, and so terribly." Seeing her eyes Don guessed she was thinking of her dead father.

He wiped her face carefully and tenderly, admiring the courage and self-control which kept her eyes dry.

"My face is all wet again," Gay said, in a choked voice.

He wiped it a second time with a slightly unsteady hand.

"If Vixen is going to suffer," Gay said, fiercely, "I want her chloroformed."

"Fitz'll know," Don said gently, "and in the meantime, until he can get to the ranch, I'll give her a shot of morphine to ease her."

Gay raised grateful eyes, then, turning suddenly, kissed him on the point of his thin shoulder. Don sat as though he had been run through with a sword, realizing that the girl beside him was a being as lonely as a solitary star in a windswept sky . . . kin to himself.

He placed his arm about her shoulders.

CHAPTER V

TRAVERS was at the gate when they drove in. Don was too occupied with Gay and her dog to notice the old man's frown of annoyance when he recognized Morse's driver at the wheel.

"Ernesto," Don said, getting out of the car, "call up Fitz. Gay's dog has been run over by one of those confounded pineapple trucks."

"He dropped in to see you. I'll fetch him."

"Tell him to come to the office. Good God!" Don looked at the automobiles jamming the quadrangle.

"Every one who is any one, in his own estimation at least, is here," Travers remarked, caustically, as he started toward the house.

Don felt stopped. The presence of so many people made it impossible for him to discuss ranch matters with Glenn until the following day. Just so many more hours of not knowing, of not being sure! He debated whether or not to ask Travers, then decided that loyalty to Glenn made that impossible. He looked down at Gay standing beside him, holding her dog tenderly.

"Come," he said. "Let's go to the office."

The office was a sprawling one-story building connected with the house by a concrete walk winding through flowering oleanders and clumps of yellow-stemmed bamboo. Gay went

79

up the steps, Don at her heels, and crossing the narrow veranda entered the main room. Its walls were entirely covered with shelves to the height of a man's head, filled with books and medicines for man and beast. Above hung pictures of prize-winning stallions and bulls.

His father's desk was in its accustomed corner, covered with the same piece of faded green felt. Don recognized it by tiny holes burned in it from sunlight filtering through a crystal paper-weight made in the shape of an egg balanced on three balls. Don recalled how puzzled he had been as a boy to discover the cause of the burns and his awe when his father had explained it. At that desk John Garrison had expounded theories of breeding and planting to his sons, had counseled, planned and advised.

Don signed to Gay to take his father's chair and she seated herself carefully. The dog breathed painfully, gave a whimper and Gay's eyes leaped to Don's.

"Fitz'll be here directly," he encouraged.

The look the girl gave him was like a faint cry and Don had an impulse to place a hand on her head, but both were occupied with canes. He moved resentfully.

Travers appeared, followed by a kind-faced man in smartly cut riding-breeches and a coat which, despite long usage, retained distinction.

"Hello, old man, jolly nice to see you back," he said, going directly to Gay and taking the dog from her. She rose and waited beside the desk, her heart in her eyes.

"Don't let her suffer, Fitzie," she commanded, in a stifled whisper, folding her arms tightly, and Don saw her long throat straining and swallowing above them.

"Don't worry, Gay," Fitzmaurice said; "I'll give her a shot of morphine before I examine her."

"The hypo and drugs are in that long wooden box on the highest shelf," Don said, walking toward it.

Gay took it down. Opening it, she went through the tiny bottles while Don looked over her shoulder.

"There's no morphine," she announced.

"There must be; we always keep some on hand," Don insisted. "What's in that bottle, the littlest one?"

"Strychnine." Gay held it up.

"Careless of Glenn to run out of it," Don said, irritably.

"Here, Gay, hold your dog," Fitzmaurice ordered. "I have some in the car."

Gay took her dog and Don limped to the window and looked at the cars packing the quadrangle. He saw Morse talking to his driver. Once they glanced in the direction of the office and Don suspected that Morse was questioning the man about him. Resentment filled him. What business of Morse's was it what he did? Morse was only a guest.

Fitzmaurice returned with a battered black bag which he placed on the desk and opened.

"Hold Vixen, Gay; she may feel the prick of the needle."

He filled the hypodermic carefully, ejected some of the fluid with the plunger and jabbed the needle into a loose fold of skin in the dog's neck. After an instant the little bitch began relaxing.

"Her back's all right," Fitzmaurice announced, when he had finished examining her. "But her hip is broken. I'll set it and in a day or so you can take her home."

Gay nodded and walked to the door while Travers assisted

Fitzmaurice to set the broken hip. Don watched the men working, grew pale about the nostrils, and turned away. He limped to the doorway in which Gay was standing.

"Sit down," he urged.

"I think I will," the girl said. "I feel funny."

She perched herself on the edge of the desk and studied the spur scratches on the floor. Don stood beside her without speaking until he saw Taka passing along the walk. He called out, directing the Japanese to bring a straw-filled box and a bowl of hot water.

"You better let Fitz dress your arm, temporarily," he advised the girl.

"I suppose I'd better. It's my right and I need it for work."

When Fitzmaurice was finished with the dog he came over and examined Gay's arm.

"Hot water, creolin and a bandage will do the trick," he announced. "Thank God, there is no rabies in Hawaii." He examined the teeth holes in Gay's arm, chatting with Don while he worked. "There, Gay, that's not very fancy, but it will do," the man said, straightening up when the bandage was secured.

"Thanks, Fitzie," the girl returned gratefully.

Glenn appeared in the doorway.

"I say, Don——" he began in an annoyed voice.

"We'll be with you directly," Fitzmaurice broke in. "A truck ran over Gay's dog and we've been busy taking care of her. Hope we didn't hold up the party."

"Find everything you needed?" Glenn asked in a business-like manner.

Fitzmaurice nodded, replacing the narrow box of drugs in its proper place.

"We're out of morphine," Don announced.

Glenn flushed slightly.

"Are we? I'll make a note of it." He scribbled on a pad. "Let's get along; every one's waiting to see you, Don."

"I'll have to wash up first; I'm filthy," Don said. "Gay, make yourself at home in one of the guest rooms."

"I think I'll go," the girl replied, touching the dog lying limply in the straw-filled box. "I can come back late this afternoon and have a look at Vixen."

"Rot!" Glenn said. "Run along like a good kid and after you've had a drink and something to eat you'll feel tip-top."

"Better stay, Gay, for a bit," Don urged.

The girl glanced at him and nodded.

"If I know this crowd there won't be much eating," Travers remarked, as they all started for the house.

Passing through the court they heard the sound of laughter, music and the scrape of dancing feet coming from the *lanai*. Through open doors Don caught a glimpse of a glass-littered table, with a crowd of young people collected about it. Don saw Morse talking to a slight girl in a vivid green sweater. They were standing a little apart and both glanced up when they saw him. Morse bent over the girl as though instructing her about something.

Muttering excuses, Glenn hurried off, Fitzmaurice following more slowly. Don and Travers halted at the foot of the stairway, for Gay had dropped behind to examine a pyramid of tiny ivory elephants. Don realized with pleasure that she did not intrude her personality upon a man. He spoke and

83

she looked up and he had a strange impression that she frequently kept invisible company.

"Go into the guest room at the right, near the end of the hall, Gay," he directed. "I think you'll find everything you want there."

"Thanks, Don."

She mounted the stairs slowly, a slight appealing figure in her riding clothes, and the thought came to Don that being with her was like walking on windy hills.

"Good kid, Gay," Travers remarked when she vanished, and Don nodded.

He went to his room and prolonged the process of cleaning up, feeling a curious reluctance at the thought of mingling with the merrymakers filling the old house with noise. To postpone the moment he went to the kitchen and instructed Taka to feed Gay's dogs and put them in one of the runs. Ah Sam grumbled and muttered over the sink, clattering pots and pans unnecessarily, as though expressing disapproval of the upset routine of the day.

"Gar-damn-go-to-hell," he said. "Son-of-a-pitch make foolish like t'is all time. Too many fellas, too much dlink. Waste money. Waste time."

Don looked out of the sunny windows at stretches of lawn and listened to music coming from the *lanai*. It should have been their own Hawaiian boys singing instead of an orthophonic. . . . His mind followed the winding roads of memory; then he squared his shoulders and left the kitchen.

When he crossed the living-room he saw Morse still talking to the girl in the green sweater. The man spoke to her and she came flying across the living-room.

"Don!"

She flung her arms about his neck and her lips met his in the easy kiss of island greeting. Then she half drew back. Her thoughts were evident enough. This pale man Don? Don of the race track and polo field, of the roping pen and surf-board whom she dimly remembered? Why, this man was a cripple! Her face went blank, then she recovered her self-possession. Don got it all, but felt no resentment. It was so youthful.

"It's sweet of you to come to see me, Molly," he said. "When I left, you were only a kid."

She stared at him, trying to appraise the hidden man.

"You were a sort of god to me when I was little," she announced in a throaty, singularly disturbing voice. "That time you took me for a ride in front of you on your best polo pony, I nearly *melted* with bliss."

Morse's eyes, amused, reminding, met Don's above the girl's head and he flushed.

"Oh, you're nice!" she said, exultingly.

She stood carelessly before him. Her close-fitting sweater and pleated flannel skirt were as sure of themselves as were the lines of her perfect young body. In the dim light of the living-room her beauty had a startling quality, the double charm of youth and cleverly blended cosmetics. Her greenish, fearless, inquiring eyes, like two spoonfuls of shoal water, studied Don from beneath the brim of an impudent little hat. Her mouth, which was a deep silken red and painted deeper, created an impression of artifice which her clear skin and glossy hair denied. She seemed to have been sketched in a few bold, beautiful strokes and left to life to finish.

After a brief intense scrutiny she opened a white jade case with her initials upon it in minute diamonds and selected a cigarette. Her lips parted for it, showing small, imperious teeth which made Don vaguely uncomfortable. They were sharp and white as those of a carnivorous animal, and behind the wide pupils of her eyes restless flecks of flame moved like tiny, licking tongues.

"Well, you might as well come out and be introduced to the Thundering Herd. This is one of its favorite stamping-grounds," she said, starting for the *lanai*.

Her brief flash of interest seemed to have subsided and Don felt relieved. Morse excused himself and vanished.

Reaching the *lanai,* Moll beckoned imperatively to the young people collected about the table: girls with lips as red as lobsters, faces browned by the sun and powdered browner, thin arms and small pointed breasts showing plainly through their sweaters, lovely, brittle, as flowers cast in wax. Young men in baggy knickers and shirts open at the neck sauntered up, looking relieved when introductions were over and they could return to their glasses. Don recalled most of them, children he had met briefly and casually at race meets and polo matches, sons and daughters of sugar planters and ranch owners grown into young men and women.

Older folk came forward, friends he had anticipated seeing, and, seeing again, found strangely strange. More cars arrived, the telephone rang, messages of greeting were delivered, but Don realized with dismay that between him and these people years' separation, changed standards, had erected grim and terrible barriers, which no effort of his or theirs could demolish.

Some recalled that notices had appeared about him in local and mainland papers and were bothered because they could not recollect what had been said about him, what he had actually done. Others plunged hastily into accounts of local happenings, magnifying trivialities into events of major importance as though afraid that, coming from the outside, he might under-estimate the importance of the rôles they played in their little world.

Don felt guilty.

"I'm not pulling my weight," he thought, and made a savage effort to be interested, to try and feel some real gladness at getting home, at being once more with people who had loomed large in earlier life.

He sat on a couch talking, laughing, giving away nothing that he felt. Some one brought him a drink and he sat with it in his hand. Some one put a fox-trot on the orthophonic and couples started dancing, the young ones absorbed in themselves, the older ones determinedly gay. Outwardly it was all as it should be, but the full noon had a curious, capacious quality which was like a huge bowl holding nothing.

Don watched old friends and new acquaintances disporting themselves. Their self-importance was superb, they vibrated satisfaction and a form of stagnation of which they were entirely oblivious.

The *lanai* seethed, new arrivals came to shake hands with him, drinks circulated, men gathered in knots to tell stories, discuss golf scores and work. Women talked of things they

did and of the people they did them with. Girls giggled
and tittered, young men boasted and swanked. They were
all completely engrossed in their immediate lives. The world,
outside Maui, was vague, shadowy and unreal.

Don was conscious of an overwhelming longing to be one
of them again, but knew himself to be apart. The realization brought terrific loneliness in its train. He was lonely,
in his old home, with his old friends, lonelier than he had
ever been in his life. He wanted the lost years back, wanted
every happy experience, every beautiful happening he had
ever known, to rank themselves about him, barring out the
terrible present.

"I say, old man," Glenn said, coming over, "are you having any sort of a time?"

Glenn looked distracted and concerned.

"Bully," Don answered, warmed for an instant by the
feeling that his brother was genuinely interested in his
welfare.

"Thought it might buck you up to see the old guard
again," Glenn muttered; then jerked out, "Met Ran's wife
yet?"

"No."

"I'll get her. Fine girl, Sue."

Glenn dashed away and Don sat thinking. Glenn's effort
to spotlight Morse and his wife convinced him that Morse
and Glenn were into something together. If he was right in
his surmise that Glenn was going into pineapple raising,
Morse, of course, had been largely responsible. As head of
the pineapple company he would covet the ranch. The soil
composing it was the finest and richest on Maui. . . . He

must move warily, until he was sure. Tomorrow he would talk to Glenn. Until then he must play-act. . . . He thrust disdainfully at his canes with one foot and stared at the garden. The dreadful farce of it all. . . .

Travers strolled over and seated himself on the cushion-piled couch.

"Hope you're not missing any of it," he remarked.

"I don't get you, Ernesto."

"Don't you see what these people are trying to do?"

"I thought they'd come to see me."

"They've come to let you see and hear about themselves."

"Beastly thing to say, Ernesto, cynical."

"But it's true," Travers insisted. "They are afraid that coming from Europe you won't be sufficiently impressed by their importance; hence all the prancing."

Travers drew his left eyelid up slightly and Don weighed him: well-groomed, well-preserved, a remote humorous observer of life, looking a trifle older than his actual sixty-two years.

"Well, here comes Sue Morse," Travers announced.

Don watched Glenn approaching with a blonde, thin to the point of emaciation. She clung to Glenn's arm, laughing nervously, as the very stupid laugh at anything seen for the first time, and Don heard her say:

"Glenn, I'm scared to meet your brother. Do you suppose he'll like me?" and she looked as though she felt that she had said something clever.

Glenn presented her.

Don appraised her: straw-colored hair, thin aquiline face, small indefinite chin, retreating too quickly, but it was evident from her manner that she was entirely satisfied with her lot and appearance. As wife of the man who was head of the pineapple industry on Maui she had local distinction and prestige. Then he heard her speaking in a voice which sounded as if it had been diluted with water.

"Oh, Mr. Garrison, I do hope you're going to like me, that we're going to be friends. Glenn and Ran and I are just like one big family. I feel so at home here," she looked around prettily, "that I hope it's simply ages before our house gets done."

Don managed necessary answers.

"That makes me feel better. You know, I was afraid to meet you. Now, Glenn, I must have a drink." She looked again at Don. "I'm so glad you like me. You do, lots, don't you?"

Don assured her that he did, struggling with a desire to smile. Glenn directed a wild, uneasy glance at his brother as he and Sue went away.

"Good God, Ernesto," Don exclaimed, when the pair were out of earshot, "am I completely mad or has Morse some hold upon Glenn? Surely, from choice, he couldn't endure such a supreme idiot as that woman or such a cad as that man."

Seeing Morse approaching, he stopped.

"Coming to check up on the impression his wife has made on me," Don said in low tones to Travers.

"Your drink's getting warm," Morse observed as he joined them. "Let me get you a fresh one, Garrison."

"Thanks, this will do," Don replied, glancing at his sweating glass.

"I hope my man drove you carefully. I instructed him about your back," Morse said, seating himself on the railing.

Don appeared not to have heard.

"Glenn told me you were with the R.F.C., then with the Lafayette Escadrille. I was in aviation myself during the war. Seems as though all we long-legged fellows had a leaning that way."

A girl, passing with a flushed boy, called out:

"Hello, Re-Morse."

Morse looked annoyed.

"I suppose you wonder, Garrison, why I'm called that."

"I was not aware you were," Don said.

"It's a nickname I've had wished on me since coming to Maui. I think Moll was the originator of it—she would be!" he laughed indulgently.

Don sat looking completely indifferent and entirely polite. Morse hunched his shoulders, thrust his hands into his pockets, turning his head a little as though trying to hear above the noises of the room.

"Some one call me?" He waited just long enough. "Thought so. Sorry, I'll have to run along."

"I take my hat off to you," Travers grinned. "The first round and the honors go to you."

"It makes my blood boil to have him under Dad's roof."

Travers' eyelid went up slowly.

"Well," he said, "things begin to look interesting; life takes on a new savor. It's always refreshing to live in a house where people are at daggers' points with each other. Morse won't forget the cold shoulder you gave him in front of me.

He's accustomed to all sorts of respect and attention on Maui."

"Why, he's not even decently bred."

"He's what is of more account, today, an entirely successful business man who is revolutionizing the antiquated industries of Maui. Mind and take your hat off when the king goes by!" Travers brandished his arm.

"I've a sneaking suspicion that you're a little drunk," Don said.

"Correct. I'm drunk with joy at having you back and completely intoxicated with your high spirits."

"You're a buzzard," Don retorted, regarding the man with immense affection. The fact that Travers was helping him to act convinced him that Travers knew everything. Tomorrow, after he had seen Glenn, he could talk freely with the artist.

Gay appeared and made her way toward the group collected about the table. In her riding clothes she seemed all eyes and spirit. Don watched her, talking to the young people about her, delicate, eager, alive. Some one thrust a glass into her hand and she stood holding it, looking as though she had strayed into this gathering by mistake. She was a being entirely apart from the girls about her. Girls who wore wonderful little sweaters with flat, babyish collars, girls whose mouths were soft, pouting and pink, with lips parted, like those of a baby that has just finished nursing. Their eyes were wide open and empty, but in some miraculous way they knew the fine arts of driving men to desperation, and knowing their power they used it like brigands, taking all, giving little. They had the faces of angels and cherubs and the souls of man-eating sharks. He had seen their duplicates in England, and during his trip across America. They broke all the rules of living, eating horrible mixtures of sweets and bitter acids, drank quantities of liquor, yet their skins were like cream and velvet and their hair shining and glossy. Bewildering, lovely and dangerous creatures who moved on their way cool, serene and untroubled.

Watching Gay, he had a curious vivid impression that she lived believing that something glorious always waited just around the corner. There was a certain condescension in the manner of the young folks talking with her. She had to work, while they lived, without effort, off fortunes made by their fathers. Worlds yawned between them. . . .

After a while Gay strolled over and Travers tossed aside a cushion to make room for her on the couch. She sat, her bandaged arm resting on her knees, her eyes luminous and thoughtful.

"I lay down for a while," she said; "that's why I was so long. Silly to feel so upset, but I love dogs fearfully; I suppose because, rich or poor, good or bad, they adore you."

Don glanced compassionately at her. He had been right in his surmise that Gay was not blind to the fact that the face of the world changes toward those who have had position and then, through no fault of their own, have to earn a living.

Don observed her watching Morse and Glenn standing together drinking, and noted a faintly hostile expression in her eyes.

"Don't you like him?" Don asked before he meant to, and

Gay turned quickly, as though she had been caught in something.

"Like who?" she asked.

"Morse. You were looking at him in a strange way."

"I despise him," she said, speaking disdainfully. "He thinks success is just—money."

Don gave her a quick look which she appeared not to notice and Travers got up and walked away.

"Funny day," Gay remarked, after a silence.

"Why funny, Gay?"

"It seems to be waiting."

"What could it be waiting for?" Don asked.

She looked at him.

"For something to happen or for something which isn't here."

Don's face went all white and funny. He moved uncomfortably and she sat apparently absorbed in watching the people about her. Glancing at her delicate profile, Don felt for some reason defeated. He must, he thought, be careful or she might easily get under his skin. Marriage, for him, was no longer on the books.

Morse left Glenn and joined Moll and they chatted together and had several drinks; then Moll sauntered over and stood before Don and Gay.

"How's his line, Gay? Deadly?" Moll asked.

"I'm too old-fashioned to have a line, Molly," Don said.

"I wonder!" Moll bit at the inside of her lip as though weighing something. "Are you having a good time?"

"Very."

She stood apparently absorbed in thoughts belonging to

herself, then took off her hat and sat down. Despite her youth there was something terribly unyoung about her. She stared at Don for several moments, then opened her jade case, instilling into the little act an amazing grace. It lay like a temptation in the rosy hollow of her hand, tipped with highly glazed nails which threw off a faint scent.

Above her sweater her neck showed a rich gardenia white. Formal curls lay mockingly against her cheeks, emphasizing the painted redness of her mouth. Her eyes blazed with excitement.

"You like this sort of thing, don't you?" Don asked as he leaned forward to light the cigarette she held between her lips. After it was lighted she removed it.

"I—adore it. When lots of people get together things start to happen."

"I suppose they do," he agreed.

"I suppose you are bored," she mocked.

"Absolutely not."

"You lie like a cheap rug," she retorted; and Don laughed.

A knickered youth came up and claimed her for a dance. She rose deliberately, then melted into the circle of his arm. While she danced she studied the ceiling with meditative eyes. She was lovely. When the music stopped she dismissed her partner airily and rejoined Don and Gay on the couch.

"You know," she announced, staring at him, "I could be mad about you. You remind me of a locked door."

Don looked uncomfortable.

"I'm afraid, Moll—" he began.

95

"I'm not handing you a line," she interrupted. "I've always cherished a secret passion for you."

"You were only nine when I went away."

"I began falling in love with you when I was eight," she informed him, her eyes green and remembering. Opening an onyx vanity-box, she appraised herself coolly. "Men thrill me, and I," she gazed into Don's eyes, "make them feel the same way."

"You're a brat," Don said, amused.

"I could make you fall for me———"

"If all the other fellows didn't raise a howl," Don interrupted. "Don't waste your sweetness on the desert air, Molly."

She subjected him to a vivid, searching look.

"Those," she touched the canes lying on the floor with a smartly clad, contemptuous foot, "don't make you safe."

"But they safeguard me," Don said a trifle stiffly.

"Oo, you look heavenly when you are indignant," Moll cooed, looking at him through the fringe of her lowered lashes. "I suspect I'm not your style, but maybe I can convert you." Moll sat waving her foot, then called out, "Glenn!"

He came over.

"What is it, Moll?"

"I've decided that this party must continue all night."

"Oh, absolutely," Glenn agreed. "I nominate you hostess, Moll."

"You couldn't appoint a better one," Moll announced. "Let's eat, Glenn. I'm famished. And when lunch is over I'll organize the orgy."

Don glanced at Glenn. His face was flushed and his manner a trifle unsteady. It was evident that he had been drinking more than was good for him. As though aware of his brother's scrutiny, Glenn blinked nervously. Moll darted a quick look at Don, like a woman groping through corridors strange to her, then rose deliberately and took hold of Glenn's arm.

"Come with me and let's round up the Herd and head it toward the table."

Don sat for an instant feeling as though he were surrounded by invisible perils, then turned to the quiet girl sitting at his side.

"Gay, will you go in with me?" he asked.

She nodded.

"Good girl, Moll; decent of you to bring on your dogs, and jolly old Don up," Glenn said, as he and Moll started for the dining-room. "Poor old chap! He wasn't having any sort of a time. Putrid, his being smashed up. He's a chap in a million, and the dead spit of old Dad. Makes me feel all sorts of a rotter having him back. Sickening!"

"Child, you talk in riddles. What's sickening?" Moll asked, looking at Glenn with eyes which were stronger than his, dragging the truth from him.

"Oh, all this infernal drinking and messing about," Glenn ejaculated, miserably. "Why do we do it? Having the old fellow home makes me want——"

"What?"

"Oh, to get back where I used to be," Glenn said, unhappily.

"I suppose you'd like to be a sort of aunt, pure and rather dull," Moll remarked scornfully.

Glenn grinned helplessly.

"At times, Moll, you are rather a sickening ass. It's rotten taste to make fun of decent things and people. Don——"

"I'm not making fun of Don. He simply fascinates me. He makes me think of all sorts of exciting things, high fences, locked doors and sealed packages. He isn't an aunt. He has a devil, but he doesn't know it." She gave a high, excited little laugh.

"I say, do sit by him at lunch," Glenn urged. "You are so full of dynamite you can distract him. Everything has been ghastly for him since he got home."

"I have every intention of sitting by him: unknown quantities fascinate me. Perhaps I shall decide, after I get to know him better, that it'll be worth my while to sit beside him for the rest of my life."

Glenn gave her a dark, startled look.

CHAPTER VI

"HAVING a good time?"

Don glanced up, experiencing a moment of irritation. Why did people keep asking him that question? Glenn stood over him, a somber uneasy figure in evening clothes, dark eyes haunted, fine mouth twisted.

"Don't worry about me, old man; I'm enjoying myself immensely."

Glenn looked at him and grimaced.

"You lie like hell!" he muttered.

For an instant they were close and Don felt happier and less apprehensive about talking to Glenn the next day.

"Don't be an ass," he said. "Trot along and attend to your guests."

Glenn lingered for an instant, then lurched off. Don watched him unhappily. He had suspected from Glenn's burnt-out appearance that he drank more than was good for him, and observing him through the afternoon and evening, saw that it was so. He did not condemn his brother, for he had seen too often the after-effect and reaction of war on highly organized, sensitive constitutions, the craving for excitement in any form, the hunger for untoward things. But it worried him, for Glenn had been home long enough to have worked out of it.

From conversations overheard, he concluded that the gay young drinking set constantly congregated at the ranch.

99

He was conscious of intangible destructive forces at work, forces which menaced his brother's well-being.

Thrusting deeper into his chair, he deliberately weighed the scene before him: dancers passing, girls in frail bright dresses, boys with flushed faces, women smiling determinedly, men assuming conquerors' airs, the inevitable crowd about glass-littered tables. Young men, gathered in groups at one door were doubtful whether they would ask some of the older women to dance or to have another drink. Two of the older men lounged near the fireplace comparing golf scores. A third joined them, told an obscene story, and they laughed noisily, attracting attention to themselves.

Moll passed in the arms of a thick red youth. Her green dress clasped her slim, perfect body and he noted the absorbed expression of her face. There was a sense of adventure in the way her silken legs moved on their high heels and a hint of drama in the way she carried her head. A stout woman lumbered by, grinning vindictively at her partner, a crimson, gray-haired man who stared over her with a remote, repudiating eye. Sue passed with Glenn and Don saw Morse, leaning on the piano, watching them while saxophones hooted and laughed sardonically about him.

Fragments of the afternoon kept passing through his mind: phone calls for food and an orchestra, hurried preparations, shrieks of merriment from the swimming-pool, where scantily clad youngsters disported themselves in the water or sat on the edge of the tank drinking highballs. Boys and girls tearing away in roadsters to fetch evening clothes, for Moll had insisted that the party was going to be "doggy"; girls and women dressing hilariously in one wing of the house, men and boys in another. A noisy dinner and a noisier dance; unbelievable quantities of alcohol consumed by every one.

And this, Don thought ragingly, was the home-coming of which he had dreamed, for which he had worked and fought —ten years!

Picking up his canes, he heaved himself to his feet and started for the *lanai*. He appreciated that some of the resentment and distaste surging through him for the scene being enacted in the house was because he had had visions of more perfect islands and people, to which distance had added its inevitable enchantment. That accounted for the bitterness and dissatisfaction which had alternately swept him during the thirty-six hours he had been home. He felt condemning because all he saw constantly fell short of the better things he had had in mind.

He had come in contact with this brand of gaiety in England, had caught glimpses of it during his hurried trip across America, but for some absurd reason he had not expected to find that it had invaded the Islands. Afterbirth pangs of an older generation and birth pangs of a new! Civilization defeated, staggering down dark corridors—toward what?

He went to the steps and contemplated the garden. Its almost unearthly detachment from the things in progress indoors calmed him for the moment. Light fell on blossoming begonias and banks of ginger, trees showed darkly against stars burning with passionless serenity in the deep arch of the heavens. He listened: insects buzzing, cattle lowing in the hills, vibrations of sugar-mills and the distant, muted boom of the surf which sounded like the muffled laughter of forgotten gods.

He tried to tear something from the great night, but the panting music from indoors got between him and it. Idiotic, this sensation of having been discarded. These people were doing their best to make him feel one of them, but he could find nothing of himself in what was going on about him, and he wondered if he had come home whole whether it would have seemed different.

"It's because I'm a cripple," he thought, ragingly, "that I have no real contacts with them any more. It is I, not they, who have changed."

He knew he was lying to himself, cheating, because he was afraid to face the truth. This was not the Maui he had left! Common sense told him that it never would be, never could be, that Maui again, and terror swept him, realizing that the cornerstone on which his life had been built had been taken away.

The music stopped, dancers poured into the *lanai* and into the paved court. Moll passed, moving daringly as though to barbaric music, young men following her looking ready to melt into her embrace of alabaster and ebony. In her eyes were veiled promises and about her the suave, intoxicating perfume of her gilded youth.

Crossing to a couch, she cast herself upon it and relaxed against piled cushions while admirers arranged themselves about her. One took a guitar some musician had laid aside and placed it in her hands. She leaned over it with lounging grace, plucking disturbing minor chords from the resounding strings. Her every posture was a poem; one foot dangled down, and light, spilling through the doors, kissed it with gold; her glossy black hair, formally curled, fitted her head like a helmet, and her mouth showed an amazing scarlet against the powdered whiteness of her face. Studying her, Don appreciated that her beauty had a quality that corroded while it soothed.

Observing that he was watching her, Moll smiled mockingly and Don got the disquieting impression that she was acting for his benefit. Why on earth should she? He was entirely out of the running, crippled, years too old to attract or interest her. What made him feel, imagine, such a ridiculous thing? He felt disgusted with himself; but her eyes held his and he moved like a man trying to free himself from an unholy spell.

He went down the steps into the garden and looked at dewdrops winking between spears of grass and at clumps of wind-blown bananas which had a sort of tragic beauty about them. Tiny movements among the leaves created an impression of uneasiness walking through the heart of the night. He looked at the lighted house and at the dark scented garden. They were like strangers with whom, once, long ago, he had been intimate, whom he had trusted and loved and by whom he had been betrayed. He had once thought them beautiful and sacred; from their recesses had come boyhood's troops of dreams, and their long inviolate sanctuaries were now invaded by revolting revelry. He sickened at the thought as at remembered intimacies with people who have proved treacherous and untrue.

There seemed nothing fantastic to him in personifying the house and garden, for those who have lived close to

Nature instinctively personify its different aspects. As a boy, clouds had always been great gods, and mountains slumbering giants which at any moment might rouse themselves to hurl their wrath of lava on the land. The trees in the forests, the sun and the earth, had talked to him in strange tongues. Whispering, promising. . . .

"Supper," some one called from the house.

He went up the steps reluctantly. Glenn was waiting for him, hands thrust deep into pockets. Don noticed that he regarded every one with the stern fixity of the very drunk.

"I was wondering where you'd got to," he said.

"I went out for air."

"This way. Sue's had a table fixed for you and a few others." He steered Don unsteadily toward the living-room. "Supper is buffet for the rest of us."

"Liquid, you should say," Moll called from the depths of a chair.

Glenn gave a short, mirthless laugh; and Don, glancing around, saw Moll entwined with the thick red youth he had noticed dancing with her earlier in the evening. She looked up at Don in a moonstruck way, then called out:

"Galahad!"

"Hey, Garrison, the young lady is talking to you," the young man said.

Don halted, flushing slightly.

"I'm perfecting my technique to use on you," Moll announced, staring up at Don, then she tilted her exquisite little head against her partner's shoulder. He seemed on the point of dissolving with bliss, but protested feebly:

"Moll! Have some mercy!"

She gazed into his eyes for an instant.

"Bunny, you're lucky to get a few free feels."

Glenn and the young man laughed noisily and Don stared at a point over his brother's head.

"Oh, look like that again!" Moll implored, sitting up. "Pure, and rather disgusted, like an aunt. Oo, you're perfect! Just what a hero should be and never is. I can hardly wait to start working on you. Don't look scared. You're divine. You're safe for tonight. I want to keep you hanging in suspenders, want to get the stage set, so I'm 'making character' tonight, for your benefit, building pictures of me into your mind, so you'll keep thinking about me. Don't miss any of it. I'm an artist, I am."

"Oh, Moll, you're swell!" Bunny moaned.

His face was flushed, his fair hair lying in moist strands on his forehead.

Moll looked from Bunny to Don and caught her breath with an excited little gulp; then, leaning over, picked up a glass and poured its contents down the young fellow's throat.

"Live up to your name, Bun," she commanded, glancing up at Don. "Know why we call him Bunny?" she demanded. Don shook his head. "Because he's always bunned!" Moll laughed.

Don smiled faintly. Glenn, impatient to be gone, started for the living-room. Don followed, but he overheard Bunny protesting to Moll that she wanted to lay him out stiff so she could begin working on Don. His skin burned.

As they entered the living-room Don saw Gay with Ernesto and he realized that he had not appreciated until then what an infernal dungeon the place had seemed, despite the fact that it was crowded with people. In a daffodil gown with a wreath of honey-colored ginger, worn island fashion about her head, she seemed to be walking against a dawn, golden, chill and sweet. The flowers cast faint shadows on her forehead, and smoke, uncurling from a cigarette held between her fingers, made restless spirals on one cheek.

Seeing him she smiled across the room at him and he felt lifted. Sue came up and took hold of his arm.

"I had this fixed for you," she indicated a table in a corner, "as you——"

She broke off, confused.

"It was thoughtful of you, Mrs. Morse."

"Who would you like to have for supper partners?" Sue asked, looking about, distractedly.

"Bun and I are going to sit at Don's table," Moll announced, coming up behind them.

She waited as though expecting him to say something and the thought came to Don that this girl, who was just done with being a child, walked impersonally in the fires of herself. She stood for an instant without speaking, her eyes flaming shallows of green and gold, then threw back her head.

"Thundering Herd—action," she ordered, looking excitedly around. "Here, Glenn, Sue, Hazel," she signaled to a blonde passing with her boy. "Stew, we're having supper with the Hero. Where's Re-Morse?"

Glenn started apprehensively.

"Who stuck you in the ribs?" Bunny demanded.

"What?" Glenn answered, blinking and scowling.

"Oh, sit down before you all fall down," Moll ordered.

Glenn took a seat, leaning his elbows on the table, and staring at the cloth.

"Here, give the poor boy a drink," Hazel ordered. "It'll make him feel better. Hair of the Great Dane that bit you, eh, Glenn?"

"Don't worry about me; I haven't a care in the world," Glenn assured them.

"Gosh, you're funny," Sue retorted; "funny as you were last night at Hazel's party."

Glenn threw up his head.

"What do you mean—last night?" he demanded.

"That's a good one! Were you so blind that you don't remember staggering in on my party hours later than you said you would be?"

"It was some other fellow," Glenn insisted, watching Don apprehensively.

"Don't you remember socking Jim Henderson on the jaw? It was terribly funny. Of course, he was huffy, but people held onto him until he cooled off. But you know how he gets when any one makes passes at Nancy," Bunny said impressively.

"Glenn, did you make passes at Nancy?" Hazel screamed.

"I never make passes at any one," Glenn muttered.

Every one laughed extravagantly.

"Sue, isn't there any supper coming?" Hazel cried. "I don't see a thing in the glasses! I shall begin crying. I tell you I'm dying for want of a drink."

"Bring *oke* and ice and ginger ale," Sue ordered a waiter who was passing. Bunny shouted at him to hurry, and the

107

Japanese returned shortly with bottles of whisky and trays of small sandwiches which nobody seemed to eat.

Glenn held his head in both hands.

"Rescue party," Sue cried, pouring a glass half full of whisky and setting it before him.

Don's face clenched.

"Put water in it," Moll ordered, "or he won't eat. He didn't last night—all he would do was sing. Here, Glenn." She took the glass from him and diluted its contents and Don felt gratitude surge through him.

"Did I sing?" Glenn asked, dully, coming back from some hazy distance.

"Did you sing! We couldn't stop you. And would you eat? Eat, eat, why on earth should any one eat, you wanted to know. My, you were funny!" Hazel said. "You took a dislike to some old tourist Nancy had in tow, a banker or something heavy, said you didn't like the way his hair grew and you poured whisky on it to make it lie straight. Was he mad? I'll tell the world he was mad. But you got out okay."

"Did he walk or was he carried?" Sue asked. "I missed the big retreat."

"He walked," Moll assured him; "and you were perfectly all right, Glenn,—any one might have slipped going down the steps."

"Oh, surely," Glenn muttered. "Saint Peter or the Pope. I must have been a howling success."

"You were precious, Glenn; you always are," Sue assured him. "Maui's funniest man! We couldn't get along without our old Glenn. Drink your drink and you'll feel better or worse. It doesn't matter. You're with friends."

Every one laughed. "Friends!" Don thought, bitterly.

Glenn groped for his glass, found it, stared at Don defiantly, and drank it down. Don reached for his own untouched highball and diminished the contents by half, and Glenn, through the mists fogging his mind, saw and looked at his brother gratefully. Watching Glenn, Don thought that in every man there is a dream and a beast. The shining dream walked up and down the soiled loneliness of desire, while the beast prowled about the soiled loneliness of regret.

"I'm aching to run my finger down your nose," Moll informed Don. "It's beautiful and fills me with a vague desire."

The table screamed its mirth. Moll gave her companions a curious look from beneath her extravagant lashes. "Careful, Moll," Hazel warned. "You'll scare Don before you get started. You look like a woman who would eat her young."

Glenn rose unsteadily.

"What are you going to do, Glenn: catch a horse?"

"Oh, Glenn, do catch a horse!" Sue cried. "The dream of my life is to own a horse, so I can put brilliantine on its tail."

"Oi, oi, the little girl is getting drunk! Help! Help!" Bunny called. "Drinks all around. Must all take our daily dozens to keep fit."

"I'll order more *oke,*" Glenn said, wandering away.

"What color shall I paint my toe-nails?" Moll asked. "I feel a swim will do me good and it's not modest to go swimming unless your toe-nails are painted."

HAWAIIAN HARVEST

"Oh, Moll, you're swell!" Bunny cried.

"Don, can you swim?" Moll asked.

He shook his head.

"Then I won't. I'll sit in the shadows and larn you a lot."

Don managed some answer. He had been vaguely indignant because Gay had not been asked to sit at his table, but now he was glad. She was too clean, real and sweet to be in company such as this, tawdry and blurred. . . .

"Enthusiastic as a corpse, your hero," Bunny said regretfully. "Come, Moll, let's go and dance."

"No music," Hazel mourned; "the orchestra is refilling its tanks."

"I'll play," Moll said, rising. "Galahad, come and stand by me—you inspire me."

Don rose and followed her to the piano, determined to see, and realize it all. Moll seated herself and stared up at his white, unsmiling face for an instant, then her long fingers tore at the keys. She played, swaying from side to side, hair trembling, her body charged with restless flames. Couples went onto the floor and began dancing. Watching, Don wished vaguely that they wouldn't work so hard at their fun. The orchestra returned. Moll leaped up, grasped Don's arm, looked into his face, then laughed on a high note.

"I know all the things you are thinking about us, Galahad," she cried loudly.

Don flushed.

"I was thinking about Glenn."

"He'll be all right. Think about me. I'm beautiful; I'm young. See, there's Glenn by the door. Glenn, your brother is worrying about you instead of thinking about me. Come and tell him what a girl I am.''

Glenn turned his head, but did not move from the doorway. His eyes had the far-away expression of a person who has been drinking hard for a long time. He looked as brittle as glass and ready to fly into a million screaming pieces.

"Pull up your socks, Glenn!" Moll ordered, sharply, noting Don's expression. Then she turned to him. "You think the lot of us are awful," she accused.

"Not at all," Don assured her. "I wish I could ask you to dance, but, as I can't, permit me to excuse myself."

"Permit you to excuse yourself," Moll crowed. "Oh, you're divine! Marvelous! Nobody in all my life has ever asked me to permit them to excuse themselves. I mark you as mine. Girls, hands off Don!" She stood on tiptoe and kissed him audaciously on the mouth.

Don smiled mechanically.

"See, he's afraid of himself," Moll cried delightedly. "Galahad, I believe at heart you're a licentious old man. That's why you don't dare dance with wimmin. Run away, angel, and leave me pure. I'd run with you, but my body is all bubbles and I must have some good wholesome exercise or I'll bust."

She went into Bunny's arms and they started onto the floor. Moll waved a slim arm at Don and kissed the air invitingly.

Don made his way along the edge of the room, avoiding dancers, beyond feeling, beyond thought. He felt as though a tractor had run over his body, leaving it flat. He headed blindly for his room, and at the foot of the stairs encountered Gay.

"Good-night, Don. I'm going to have another look at Vixen, then go home."

He did not reply for an instant. He felt terrified, lonely, bewildered. For years he had been shut away from the world in a white room. . . . He was afraid to be alone again, with the sort of thoughts which were streaming through his mind.

"I'll go with you," he announced.

"Where, home?" Gay asked, looking at him in astonishment.

"Yes, I'd like to go home with you, get out of all this," Don cried savagely, "be where it's clean. God, in Dad's house—this orgy!"

Gay laid her hand on his arm.

"I say," Don burst out fiercely, "come into the garden with me for a bit. My head's full of wheels spinning to pieces. I'm not a prude; hell, I know life, or thought I knew it during the war, but there was some excuse then."

"You're tired," Gay said gently.

"Yes, tired as hell."

They walked down the hall slowly. Passing the kitchen window he saw, as in a dream, servants grinning above soup plates piled with ice-cream. Gay crossed the paved court, Don walking heavily beside her. Glenn . . . Glenn . . . a public spectacle . . . Glenn sneaking away the night his only brother got home to attend some drunken party. People like these, taking possession of him—of his home! Rebellion tore him.

Gay walked along the path winding through the oleanders and creaking bamboos. When they got to the heart of the garden she halted. Don looked about him. A stray gust of wind passed through the tree-tops, as though the night were shaking itself free of something distasteful. Ghosts of the past lurked in the shadows, reluctant to abandon the place entirely. Seeing a bench, Don sat down.

"I know no one has the right to judge fellow humans," he said; "but, Christ!"

Gay made no reply. Don looked at a giant eucalyptus partly lighted from the upper windows as though it were springing over a chasm of darkness. He possessed an aristocracy of the heart which nothing had ever been able to kill, and he was suffering intensely, for dreams which had been shattered, for ideals which had been hurled from their pedestals. He moved once like a person trying to wake from a terrible dream; and then Gay laid a consoling, comradely little hand on his shoulder.

"Say my prayer," she said, staring at stars burning above the dark tree-tops.

"I've said it many times since this morning."

"Say it again, and think about what you are saying; it will develop the muscles of your mind."

Don poked at a fallen leaf with his cane.

"You say the finest things, Gay. That's a splendid thought, that minds have muscles which can be developed as you develop the muscles of your body—by using them."

Gay sat down beside him and he looked up.

"Sorry, Gay, but something stopped working in my head for a bit. I felt like smashing the whole world to pieces at

supper. We'll have a look at your dog, then I'll tell Taka
to drive you home. I'd go with you, but——"

"No," she said gently. "You better get some sleep.
You need it."

She was right: he would need it for the ordeal to be gone
through tomorrow. They started for the office. As they
approached it, from the inside came the spurt of a lighted
match. Gay grasped Don's arm and some warning trans-
mitted to him through her fingers made his heart miss a beat.

"Some one's in there," Gay said.

"Probably old Fitz looking at your dog," Don replied.
They went on. Voices reached them.

"Ran, I'm in hell, I'm going crazy! Don can't go you,
Sue—anything. I know because he's so deucedly polite.
What on earth are we going to do? Everything's jammed
up. Everything seems different—since he got home."

Don realized that Glenn had completely and amazingly
sobered up.

"You'll have to whip him into line," Morse said shortly.

A cane dropped from Don's cold fingers and made a
tiny rattle on the cement walk. Quick footsteps came to
the door.

"Thought I heard some one," Morse's voice said.

Glenn made an inaudible reply and Morse's footsteps
went back into the room.

"Too late to back out now, Glenn, you're in to the
neck."

"For God's sake, let's get out of this, Gay," Don said
in a smothered voice. "Find my cane, will you: I can't
bend down. It's around my feet somewhere."

The girl found it, thrust it into his hand, gasping slightly, and Don knew she was shocked at the coldness of his fingers.

"Walk on the grass," Don directed. "I don't want old Glenn to think I was eavesdropping. Beastly, good God, filthy! Everything!" He breathed with difficulty. "Gay——"

"Glenn must be the one to tell you," she burst out. "Until I talked with you this morning I thought you knew. When I realized that you didn't it made me feel ill." Don wondered if she heard the indecent beating of his heart, for she whispered sharply, "Listen!"

But it was only a clock striking three and its strokes were quickly done.

"You see," Gay said unsteadily, "I thought of course that you knew. Every one else does. I thought probably Ernesto had written and told you and that's why you came home."

"Ernesto did write and tell me to come home, but he never gives gratuitous information," Don said. "But this morning, just before you came along, I saw trees falling in one grove which is useless for either firewood or fence-posts, and guessed that Glenn without writing to tell me is putting the ranch into pineapples. It's got to be stopped! But this, this explains an extraordinary sensation which has stayed with me, that every one, even the cowboys and servants, were afraid to tell me something that they all knew, but——" He frowned. "Glenn can't sell or lease an acre without my consent, because, by the terms of Dad's will, we inherit everything jointly."

His voice sounded steadier, and he felt calmed just by the reassurance of the uttered words.

"Gay."

"Yes?"

"You are entirely right. Glenn must be the one to tell me. This explains why he's dodged and avoided me ever since I got home." Relief filled Don's voice. "I was afraid that the old fellow resented my returning because he no longer cared for me."

Gay stared up at the brilliant stars.

"Don't look like that," Don said shortly. "You shouldn't, you know. You're too young——"

She gazed at him for an instant. His face was plainly visible in the luminous starlight.

"I know," Gay spoke in a slightly unsteady voice, "what Dad must have looked like when he tried to get out of that lava hole, and couldn't." She choked, and her little fingers dug into Don's arm. "Your spirit's in a deep hole and scared it can't get out."

Don nodded.

"Here's a bench," Gay said, and they sat down and remained silent for some instants. For a while it seemed to Don that gaunt empty spaces surrounded them, but gradually he became aware of the breathing of the garden. He saw a cluster of star-like frangipani blossoms growing at the end of thick juicy branches, drenching the spot with their heavy fragrance, and the dim shapes of belladonna lilies hanging from huge shrubs, like frosted globes in which the lights had been extinguished. He leaned his elbows on his knees and stared at the earth, afraid to speak. Then he put out his hand and, finding Gay's, gripped it. Gay, like the gallant little soldier that she was, drew a deep breath and forced herself to smile.

"Pray it—hard," she whispered.

Don nodded.

"Make me brave. . . . Make me strong. . . ."

CHAPTER VII

DON awoke feeling weighted and unrefreshed. The words he and Gay had overheard and the memory of Glenn's face during the evening had haunted his sleep. His brother's mind was being devoured by mental maggots which tortured and confused him and which would eventually destroy him, but Don wondered if it were fair to force Glenn's hand when he was in such a state. If he waited a few days, perhaps Glenn would come to him.

Sitting up, he carefully swung his legs over the side of the bed. No, it would be better to have a showdown at once; better for them both. The machinery of his mind felt clogged, and going into the bathroom he took a shower. The rush of cold water cleared his head, but he felt far from calm. Talking to Glenn would be painful and difficult, perhaps disastrous. There was so much at stake, the future of the ranch, and the testing of affection between them. He glanced at his watch. Ten o'clock! Probably Glenn had breakfasted and gone.

"Taka!" he called.

The man entered.

"Good-morning, Mr. Don. I tink berry fine party last night, too much noise, drink too much *okolehao,* everybody sleep late."

When Don entered the *lanai* he saw Glenn sitting at the breakfast table. Travers' and Morse's places had been

118

cleared away and only Sue's remained. It was not likely
that she would be down before noon. This was his moment,
and he was afraid to take it!

" 'Morning, old man," he said, sitting down.

" 'Morning," Glenn replied, occupying himself with a
mango.

Don unfolded his napkin and laid it slowly across his
knees. He stared at the garden, at the strong glitter of sunlight on green leaves and at the passionate growth of trees
and shrubs springing out of rich earth. The island seemed
to flaunt vigor, mocking him. He observed the haste with
which his brother was getting through breakfast—in order
to escape! Don swallowed, trying his throat, then looked
again at the garden. It seemed to ask what right had he,
a cripple, to suppose that he could in any way interfere with
or alter events already marching on their way? He would
show it! Grasping his napkin in one cold hand, he placed
the other against the table, as if for support.

"Glenn, I want to go through our affairs with you this
morning."

Glenn blinked like a person shocked out of sleep, nodded,
then busied himself again with his food.

"Let's go through the books as a starter," Don said, "and
later we can figure out some arrangement so I'll have work
of some sort to superintend. We might make a tentative
division: you handle the upper lands which can't be reached
by car and I'll take over the lower. Later we can work out
details and dovetail things so we'll pull together."

"Really no reason for you to bother," Glenn replied, wiping his mouth nervously. "You are hardly—" Seeing his

brother's face, he stopped and finished miserably, "Damn it! I apologize, old man."

"No need to," Don said. "I've been this way too long to mind allusions to my condition, but if I don't interest myself in something I'll go clean off my nut."

Glenn winced and looked away.

"Through?" Don asked when Glenn laid his napkin aside.

"Yes."

"Then let's shove along to the office."

"There is a matter I've wanted to talk over with you," Glenn said to Don's back, as they started down the hall. "But I hated to bother you when you are just home."

"I've been home forty-eight hours."

"What's forty-eight hours?"

"It's seemed like ten years."

As they entered the office Glenn lurched past Don, pulled out their father's chair, placing it for him, then seated himself on the edge of the desk. The unexpected courtesy for an instant put Don mentally off his balance. There were cells in Glenn's body which had survived or resisted the general let-down, cells which still jealously hoarded atoms of their father, and it was upon those cells and atoms that he must stake everything.

"Thanks, old man," he said, seating himself.

Glenn did not appear to have heard. Lighting a cigarette, he exhaled a great cloud of smoke. Don weighed Glenn's angular, narrow features. Sitting with one hand thrust into his trousers pocket, Glenn stared out of the window with ruined eyes, like a man lost among rubbish-heaps, a defiant, hungry silhouette searching the heart of emptiness. It was evident enough that Glenn was unhappy, but defiant in his unhappiness, as though he sought to deny it even to himself.

Don braced himself for what was coming. Glenn jabbed at a piece of paper with a pen, then straightened up. Don waited, fixing his eyes on a squat black iron safe across the room.

Sight of it recalled vanished Saturdays of his boyhood when the cowboys came to be paid off. He recalled his father's admonitions, the men's promises and the inevitable drinking of cactus beer. His father roused from sleep to quell disturbances, to punch heads and lock the right husbands and wives up together. Sunday night, repentant Hawaiians bringing flower garlands as peace offerings; half the ranch discharged only to be re-engaged Monday for another week of hard work. How his father had understood men and their weaknesses and forgiven them!

"Fire away, old man," he urged, breaking the match that Glenn had dropped on the desk.

Glenn threw back his head. "I have plans to sacrifice all the lower pastures and put them into pineapples." Don's cold hand clenched. "Cattle raising on Maui is a thing of the past. Can't make anywhere near the amount of money from beef as you can from growing pines."

Don stared at the burnt holes in the felt of the desk. He had been correct in his surmise!

"What's the ranch netting a year?" Don asked in a smothered voice.

"About forty thousand."

"Seems as though that amount of money ought to be sufficient to keep us decently."

Glenn avoided his brother's eyes and Don sat wondering if he could manage his voice sufficiently to ask another question.

"What made you think about, decide, in the first place——"

"Of going into pines?" Glenn interrupted. "Why, my dear chap, every one's doing it. Progress, you know, and all that. Have to keep pace with the times."

"My gorge rises at the thought of it," Don said, after a silence.

"You are, and always were, a confoundedly sentimental old duffer," Glenn observed.

"That's as you choose to see it," Don replied, indignantly, then wondered if Glenn was not perhaps right. Yet there was a vast difference—which most people failed to appreciate—in having sentiment for a thing and in being sentimental about it. "If we were in a hole," he went on, "I'd have nothing to say. As we aren't, I resent like hell having Dad's work undone—it's always provided us with an ample living—just for extra money which we don't really need. Beyond being a source of revenue to us, the ranch and the work which has been done here is also a monument to Dad's memory."

Glenn stirred unhappily and Don rose and began limping about the office.

"The East Maui Pineapple Company——"

"Of which Morse is the head!" Don cut in.

"Yes."

"Go on."

"Has made us an offer to buy or lease everything we have below the two thousand foot level. They have hold of all the available pineapple land of Maui except ours, which ranks with the cream of what they already have in their possession, and in order to enlarge the field of their future activities——"

"To hell with their future activities! You reel that off like a kid drilled to make a speech."

Don looked at his brother with fiery contempt.

"Implying?"

"Exactly!"

There was a charged silence, broken only by the muffled tapping of Don's rubber-tipped canes. Glenn got to his feet and Don attempted to rally his forces. Being the elder, it was his place to try and steer their craft among the reefs threatening its destruction. He glanced at Glenn. For all the world they were like two dogs walking stiffly and suspiciously around each other. The thought affronted him.

"You should have informed me when you first contemplated taking this step," he said, trying to speak calmly.

"It didn't occur to me. You've never seen fit to question or criticize any move of mine in connection with the ranch until this moment. When you were in England——"

"When I was in England I was to all practical purposes—dead!" Don said violently. "But I'm back now, hamstrung, I'll admit, but nevertheless you can't expect me to hang around doing nothing all the rest of my life. I'd go mad!"

Glenn was silenced. Don's face got a chalky white, as though all the blood in his veins had ceased to circulate.

"Confound it, Don, I understand a bit how you must feel," Glenn burst out, wiping his heated face. "I've always thought the world of you, you funny old ass—even when I was a kid—because you never did any of the beastly things most boys do."

"Rot!" Don said, turning crimson.

"You know it's the damned truth," Glenn insisted. "You've always been as clean as the sea, and, next to Dad, there's never been any one I've admired as———"

He broke off.

"I'm far from the saint you think me to be," Don interrupted. "Though I've done my damndest to be as decent as it's possible for men to be. For God's sake, let's try and get together! Let's not make any drastic changes for a while. Let's get acquainted again, before we, so to speak, start climbing hills."

"You don't understand the situation," Glenn went on, in a changed voice, and Don knew Morse had coached him for this interview. "For one thing, taxes today on grazing land which is suitable for growing pines are terrific. Takes all the profit out of stock raising. Let me show you some figures."

Glenn wrenched open a drawer and began searching through papers.

"You said our net profits approximated forty thousand a year," Don reminded him. "Good God! How much more do you want? I tell you, Glenn, I'm dead against this. I hate to think of the grass Dad imported, the trees he planted, the stock he bred with such care, being got rid of for a temporary crop; and there's another angle to this———"

"They won't all be sold off," Glenn interrupted. "Pines won't grow above two thousand feet, and everything———"

An expression in Don's eyes stopped him as though he read Don's thought, "Much good that will ever do me." Neither of them spoke for a minute, then Glenn ejaculated, miserably:

"Your attitude puts me in the deuce of a fix!"

Don felt himself getting pale.

"You see," Glenn went on, "I agreed, before you ever thought of coming home, to lease the Pineapple Company everything we have below the Kula road." It was evident the words were being wrenched from him against his will. "The papers are made out, all they actually lack is—your signature."

"Confound it! Why didn't you write to me about it or tell me the instant I got home?"

"I suppose because I knew you'd object," Glenn replied, with disconcerting honesty. "Morse and I looked at the proposition from every angle. After all, Don, we both profit from the transaction."

"I had a hunch you and he were into something together. To be frank, I can't go him."

"Awkward, what?" Glenn said, and the pen he had been playing with broke in his fingers.

Don glanced at his brother; Glenn's mouth was compressed, his whole expression fierce, like that of a criminal bracing himself against inevitable detection. Don felt ill.

"Hell, I never dreamed you'd feel so strongly about this."

"That's a lie, Glenn!"

Glenn dug his hand into his pocket as if groping for a concealed weapon, and Don tried to remember that they were of the same blood, the same background, for he had the unpleasant sensation that he was confronting a foe. Glenn a foe! Horrible!

"That lie, Glenn," he repeated, "doesn't alter the fact that the lease, lacking only my signature, is—closed."

Alarm leaped into Glenn's unhappy brown eyes.

"I say, Don, I'll be in the devil of a jam if you refuse to sign."

"I probably shall."

"But my word is given, as a Garrison," Glenn protested hotly. "On the strength of it a new cannery is going up. I can't go back on my promise at this stage of the game."

"Jolly," Don said, bitterly.

"I can't begin to tell you what a rotter you make me feel. When Morse suggested this thing it seemed a tremendous idea."

"If it seemed such a tremendous idea, it's odd you didn't write to me about it."

Glenn did not reply. He passed his handkerchief over his face several times, then returned it to his pocket.

"It's senseless beating about the bush," Don said. "I may be a cripple, but I'm not an absolute fool. For God's sake, be honest and admit that Morse has some sort of hold on you."

"Hold? Hold?" Glenn muttered, wrenching around to face his brother. His mouth twitched and he passed a hand across it as though to steady it, and scowled.

"Well, influence. You can't make me believe that a fellow of his type is feathering our nest for his health. What does he, actually, get out of this deal?"

"We grow the pines and sell them to the cannery, and he gets a percentage of the profit off our crop."

"What per cent?"

"Ten."

"Why should he get anything?"

"Well, he sold me on the idea and I felt that it was only decent."

Don meditated.

"You see, Morse is a far-sighted chap, he looks ahead——"

"Inferring that I don't?" Don demanded, then was instantly ashamed. "Sorry, old man, my temper's gone to pot since I got smashed up, but you must admit it's hardly square for you to have, practically, taken on another partner without informing me of the fact."

Glenn hunched over and snapped one of the pieces of the pen into halves again.

"Hated to bother you."

"Well, the only thing left to do is to get hold of Morse and thrash the whole matter out. Call him up."

Glenn picked up the desk telephone.

"Might be quicker if I went and fetched him. He's usually in the fields about now." Glenn watched his brother from under working eyebrows.

Don felt himself growing cold with suspicion. It was plain that Glenn wanted to see Morse before the three of them talked together. Was it possible that this pineapple growing was a smoke-screen for some other venture? Don discarded the suspicion with disgust.

"Call him up," he commanded irritably.

Glenn made the connection.

"Here, let me talk to him," Don said, starting forward, but Glenn brushed him aside.

"That you, Ran? Don wants to see you about that lease. You'll be up in an hour? Fine."

Glenn's eyes went to Don's as though he were entirely satisfied.

"That's bully; I was afraid he might be out."

"Suppose while we wait you and I take a run out and look at the land you propose leasing?"

"Sorry, old man, this powwow has put me behind in my day's work. Hadn't figured on it. Have to attend to two or three small matters and must post these in time to catch the mail."

Glenn dived his hand into the *koa* mail-box hanging by the desk, rammed a fist full of letters into his pocket and walked away.

Don went to the door. The over-bright morning had clouded over and a few large, leisurely raindrops were beginning to mark the walk. Terrible that the two of them who had been so close should feel as they did, resentful and compassionate, in a frozen way, each of the other's short-comings and weaknesses, but divided by the diverging roads of their lives. Beastly, time was, dimming affection, loyalty, taking the bloom off life.

He returned to the house by a covered walk which connected with the pantry and kitchen. Ah Sam was not there and the room seemed robbed of its soul. Don went to the *lanai* and lay down in a long wicker chair. Once Glenn had looked at him as though he hated him; but that had been Morse looking at him through Glenn's eyes. Morse, who wanted to get hold of their splendid acres; Morse, who, while professing to be Glenn's friend, was fostering his weaknesses to further his own ends. Don's brows drew together as his mind collected itself and leaped forward.

He must move carefully, but somehow or other Morse and his wife must be forced out of the house. Glenn must be saved from them and from himself. Glenn, who had once been as proud as an archangel, a tool! Glenn, who once had been the soul of loyalty, disloyal!

He heaved himself up in the chair, forgetting his back, and winced with pain. Travers strolled in and Don looked at the old man's gray, guarded face.

"I feel as if you are the only friend I have left," Don said, staring at the garden, then looked ashamed of having discarded his brother.

"What are you going to do?"

"I can't think—yet. This has just about bowled me over."

"I wanted to tell you, but I couldn't very well."

"I appreciate that."

Travers' eyes narrowed.

"Seen Morse?"

"He's on his way back from the cannery."

Don's face was ashen.

"Sorry for yourself?"

129

"Damn you!" Don laughed.

Travers strolled to the steps and Don sat feeling like a tree with its branches lopped off.

"Blast Morse!" Travers said after a moment.

"I'd like to," Don agreed.

Travers watched smoke curling from the cigar he held in his fingers.

"Where's Glenn?" he asked, keeping his back to Don.

"Gone to see Morse—first."

"What do you mean, first?"

Across Don's quietness there flamed a bar of fire. "I mean that obviously it's imperative for Glenn and Morse to talk together before seeing me. Stinking, makes me feel that there's more in the wind than you can see."

"What could there be, what makes you think there might be more than pineapple growing?"

"Instinct."

Travers squinted at the rustling rain.

"Morse has all the earmarks of a rotter," Don said, venomously. "It gripes me to have him staying in this house, polluting it."

"You can't very well kick him out, as he's Glenn's friend." The sarcasm in Travers' voice was immense. "It would lead to a break with Glenn."

"I haven't the slightest intention of doing so—yet. It would suit Morse to have Glenn and me smash up. There's only one course, to give him enough rope."

Travers nodded.

"And in the meantime, old Glenn's sliding down the wrong road," Don burst out, then broke off and listened.

He heard a car coming up the hill. "It's sickening, Ernesto," he said, watching the silver wires of falling rain, "to see Glenn so shot. Poor old chap."

"He's been more or less that way ever since he got back, but he's been getting worse since——"

Glenn came striding through the living-room and looked apprehensive when he saw the pair in the *lanai*.

"Morse here yet?" Don asked.

"He'll be along directly. Hot, what?" Glenn said. "But this rain will be fine for the pastures."

Don froze like an animal feeling a rifle aimed at it, and Glenn looked annoyed with himself. But the words, heard and spoken so often on the ranch, had come to his lips automatically. He sat down, leaning his elbows on his knees, listening.

"That's Ran's car now," he announced. "Shall we go?"

Don rose.

"Better meet Morse and tell him I'm waiting in the office," Don said, as they went down the hall.

Glenn appeared not to notice the edge to his brother's voice, but nodded and dashed away. Don's eyes hardened. Hearing footsteps behind him, he halted. Ah Sam came up.

"This time three fellas talk?" he demanded.

"Yes, Sam."

"Mr. Morse, number one no good man," the cook said, wiping his shaking hands on his apron. "You watch. Mr. Morse make bad kind things. I no business this kind talk, Mr. Don, but Gar-damn-go-to-hell I no can help. Mr. John my number one good flend and I all same papa for his boys."

"Thanks, Sam," Don said.

The cook hesitated as though he wanted to say more, clawed at the back of his head with a skinny hand, then retraced his steps to the kitchen.

Don went into the office and seated himself in his father's chair. Rain fell relentlessly on trees and flowers, freeing leaves and grass of their fine coating of summer dust. The old Chinaman's warning disturbed him. He grasped the arms of his chair, then hearing footsteps sat erect. Glenn appeared, followed by Morse, and Don watched them brushing raindrops off their coats.

" 'Morning, Garrison. I understand from Glenn that you don't wish to sign the lease that we have drawn up."

"Correct, I do not."

"What are your reasons? A lease on the terms proposed would be entirely to your advantage and treble the worth of this ranch."

"I'd like to see the papers. Have you them with you?"

Morse drew them from an inner pocket and handed them to Don. Don went through them slowly, glancing up once as though the rain, hammering the garden, distracted him.

"Well, what do you propose doing?" Morse asked, when Don laid the papers on the desk.

"I haven't decided," Don said calmly, but inside he was not calm. He was conscious of Glenn's unhappy eyes fixed upon him, but could not look up. They were like two enemies, himself and the brother he loved, both terrified of each other.

"Your attitude puts Glenn and me in a hell of a fix,"

Morse said, rescuing a fly from the ink-pot. "On the strength of this," he indicated the papers with a long brown hand, "I persuaded the stockholders of the Pineapple Company to consent to the building of a new plant. It's nearing completion and it's imperative that we have sufficient ground planted in pines to keep it going."

Don thrust the papers aside.

"Personally, I'm not the least interested in your end of it. The ranch needs those pastures. And there's another angle to this thing. Beef has local consumption; pineapples are a crop whose value may reach a peak, then decline when a world market is flooded by over-production."

He looked at Glenn while he spoke; Morse was apparently absorbed in watching the fly he had saved from an inky death crawling away, leaving a dark, shiny trail behind it. Glenn made a startled movement which filled Don with contemptuous pity.

"I—I—counted on your standing by me," Glenn said at length. "You ought to, you know; Dad always told us to stick together. Can't you? It isn't as if I'd sold the land outright."

Don did not reply and Glenn scrubbed at the backs of his hands with his handkerchief. It gave Don a peculiar, unpleasant sensation, as though Glenn were removing the stains of a crime.

"The thing that is completely beyond me, Glenn," Don said after a silence, "is your keeping me so completely in the dark. It looks rotten. Why didn't you write to me when you first contemplated taking this step? Why didn't you talk to me yesterday? Your silence makes the whole business stink."

Fixing Glenn with his eyes, Don waited. Morse directed a long reminding look at Glenn which acted like a spur.

"As I told you, I hesitated simply because I hated to bother you with business. There's no need for you to concern yourself—"

Don's expression stopped him.

"Look here, Garrison," Morse broke in, "don't jump your brother."

Don looked hotly at him.

"I'm responsible for this," he went on. "My company had to have more land in order to expand. All the other localities suitable to pineapples were already under cultivation, so I approached Glenn and he was perfectly agreeable. The transaction, as I told you, is entirely to your advantage."

"That's aside from the matter," Don said, fixing his eyes on the slashing, silver showers drowning the garden. He appeared not to see Glenn, but the expression on his brother's face ate at his heart. Glenn was torn between pity for his brother and loyalty to Morse.

"This man shan't smash up our affection," Don thought, beating violently about in his mind for some means by which he could retain Glenn's affection and keep the most valuable and beautiful portions of the ranch intact.

"You make me feel all sorts of a cad," Glenn said, jamming his hands into his pockets until they bulged. "Sickening to have to go back on an agreement and putrid to hurt you."

134

His fevered eyes, holding unfathomable depths of grief and guilt, went remorsefully to Don's. He looked a helpless ruin, putty pounded out of shape by his own and Morse's hands. Glenn must be rescued! What were even beloved acres, against his brother's love and well-being?

Don took out a handkerchief and wiped his face.

"I'll sign," he said, and felt shackled and freed, "on condition that you both agree to certain changes."

Glenn looked relieved and Morse suspicious.

"And those changes are—?" Morse asked, watching Don.

"That the lease shall be cut down from ten to five years and that none of the tree lots in the pastures leased shall be cut down or in any way harmed."

"But those plantations of eucalyptus cover hundreds of acres of valuable land," Morse protested, and Don saw Glenn's eyes leap to his with a sort of terror. Don thought of the trees he had seen fall. "Those trees will have to be cleared away if we are to realize the profits from the land which the terms of the lease justify," Morse said hotly.

Don sat still, but his eyes went to Glenn's asking a question. Glenn's face got crimson.

"Glenn."

"Yes?"

"Some of the groves are being cut down now." Don's words were both question and statement.

Glenn nodded.

"It must stop. Those trees took thirty years to grow." Don looked at Morse. "They were planted, primarily, to shelter stock and, incidentally, to add to the beauty and worth of the land. I will not consent to have them sacrificed for a temporary crop when they are essential to the purpose for which the land was originally intended—cattle raising."

Don spoke calmly, but the blood in his legs felt as though it were being slowly diluted with water. Then fury filled him, fury which shocked. It did not seem possible that a civilized man could feel as he did, like rising up and destroying the world and everything in it. He was hating Glenn because he permitted this man to come into his life and influence him to destroy beauty simply for extra money which they did not need, solely to possess extra cars, membership to clubs which were mostly drinking, a few more clothes, possibly a more imposing house than the one in which they had been born. Hoisting himself onto his canes he faced them.

"It's evident you have no intention to keep pace with the times," Morse said sarcastically. "You prefer to remain stationary instead of going forward."

Don's face got a livid white.

"A man is free to choose the manner in which he wishes to make a living. Were it not for the fact that Glenn has already signed the lease and pledged his word to the stockholders of the Pineapple Company, a thing you influenced him to do, I would not consider this move for an instant. We have all the money we need. Rather than compel Glenn to go back on an agreement, or take the matter to court, as I could, I'll sign, provided that the changes I stipulated are made. And the cutting of trees must be stopped or I'll not put my name to the papers."

He looked at Glenn and the ten lost years of Glenn's life streamed before him; the shock of war on a highly strung, unstable nature, return to a world which had been tipped over, altered standards, changed values. He knew Glenn could never be really happy wandering in strange pastures, never be at peace with himself until he re-embraced the gods he had betrayed. For an instant Don had a clear insight into his brother's soul.

He saw the man, slain by himself, but alive still, sorrow-stricken, quivering, scourged. Glenn needed a hand over this dangerous crossing rather than condemnation. He must be, he would be, the one to help and it could only be done by standing by him.

"When the necessary alterations and adjustments are made, bring the lease to me," Don said, after a silence.

Glenn's hand fell on Don's arm.

"Thanks, old man," he said, thickly.

Morse's eyes were as hard and hot as a spider's. Don guessed he resented and distrusted even the momentary fusing of his and Glenn's spirits. Don walked to the door and looked out. He shrank from the ghastly pretenses he must go through in order to retain even a shred of his brother's affection. He would have to endure Morse, condone, for a while longer, the sort of things he had been compelled to witness the previous evening, in order to try and snatch Glenn from destruction.

"Dad never funked anything," he thought. "I've got to go through with this business. If I fall down on my job——"

He dared not continue his thought.

137

CHAPTER VIII

GAY rolled up her sleeves and plunged her arms into a tub of horse feed. The sweet scent of barley and bran rose as she mixed and dampened the contents of the corrugated-iron container. Warm sunshine slanted into the stable and poured on her back as she worked, and a faint, pleasant moisture broke out on her skin. Occasionally she looked up and smiled fondly at the row of horses hanging eager heads over the closed gate dividing the pasture from the corral, or stopped to blow bran off the bandage about her right arm. When the feed was mixed to her satisfaction she scooped up bucketfuls and shot the contents into various boxes nailed to sturdy posts. The waiting animals tossed their noses impatiently and stamped until she unfastened the gate and let them into the enclosure. Thrusting and shoving good-naturedly at one another they went to their accustomed places and began eating.

She watched them, bucket in hand, for a few instants, then glanced at the blue mass of Haleakala. Clouds were gathering above the summit, hinting at rain before noon. That meant it would be fine tomorrow and for the sake of the tourists she was to take to the top she wanted good weather.

Closing the corral gate she set the bucket down and went into the saddle-room, to inspect the gear she would have to use the following day. She oiled and cleaned her rifle, went carefully over the bridles hanging in neat rows, examined stirrup leathers, took out an armful of saddle-blankets and spread them on the fence for the sun to sweeten, counted halters, rolled up raincoats and tied them onto each saddle while her terriers snuffed for mice among the grain bags or stretched out on the steps to bask in the sun.

When her work was well along she would telephone and find out how Vixen was progressing, and she must make time and drive over and get her before supper. She went about her work deftly and surely. She paused in the doorway to admire a glittering cloud poking its gigantic head toward the zenith, then ran across the lawn between stable and house and entering came out with a pad and pencil. Squatting on the steps she sketched the cloud, threw the pad inside the door, then hastened to water an enormous vegetable garden adjoining the pasture. She felt an immense pride in the neat rows of lettuce, cabbages, beans, carrots and peas. At one end rhubarb formed a background for jade-green lima beans gracefully twining around poles. A bed of strawberries afforded her an instant's keen pleasure: the dainty white blossoms and glowing berries, peeping from beneath dark leaves, sent little shivers of delight over her body. They were like jewels against the dark, rich earth.

Her finger tingled from cold water streaming against it as she held it over the nozzle of a hose to break the stream into spray. The vegetables she grew, in conjunction with her other activities, were the finest on Maui and she supplied the two biggest hotels with the produce of her garden. The back-breaking hours she put in hoeing, planting and weeding were more than compensated for when she gathered the crisp vegetables and laid them on green banana leaves in orderly piles of green, purple and gold.

Toil, until her father died, was a thing Gay had never encountered. Like most island children, born on ranches, she had driven and shipped cattle with her father and the cowboys, learned to saddle and pack horses, pitch tents, make fires, but it had been an entrancing pastime. There had been no other children on the lonely ranch which her father managed and she had grown to her teens without missing or wanting playfellows. Her father had been her god, Hawaiian cowboys her companions, and the life of the land her most absorbing interest.

Each season had its special thrill. In the spring it was new colts and calves; in the summer the round-up when red herds of cattle poured down the hills and broke like lava through the forests. When autumn came and work was slack she hunted pigs and turkeys with her father, and camped in the crater of Haleakala. In the winter when the great *kona* storms came shouting up from the south she galloped in the rain and wind, exulting in the new growth which would come to the pastures. She felt part of the thunder reverberating overhead, part of the rain slashing out of the heavens, and part of the surf growling along the coast.

She had been educated by an aunt who spent a few months each year with her and her father. There had been a disastrous attempt to send her to a boarding-school in Honolulu when she was nine. She had been entranced by the trip on the steamer, mildly interested in the town, but became a white stony image when her father kissed her good-by. After three weeks spent in storms and tears she had walked out of school and onto the steamer. The fact that she had no ticket and no money did not daunt her. The stewards knew her and when the captain sent for her she marched into his cabin without a qualm, told him why she had left school and declared that her father would pay her passage after she got home. The captain, a fat, good-natured half-caste, had been immensely amused and when the ship docked at Maui, he rented an automobile and escorted Gay to the ranch. Her father had been at breakfast when she walked in, a pale, desperate little figure. There had been a long talk, tears, then life had gone on serenely.

Gay's father made it his business to see that his daughter experienced every phase of life he lived, and shared with her the knowledge he had gathered from it. They read and talked together. Gay applied herself diligently to studies during the months her aunt visited her, and at the age of fifteen her mind was a storehouse of miscellaneous knowledge and her heart a storehouse of varied emotions.

Like most children brought up without companions of their own years, her imagination ran riot without making her impractical. A lover of color and beauty, she determined, at the age of ten, to become an artist, and her father encouraged her in her ambition, for she had a sensitive soul, a fine appreciation for life, and talent. He made arrangements with Travers to instruct her, and between teacher and pupil there sprang up one of those rare friendships between youth and age which enriches both.

The good women of Maui pitied Gay for her seemingly haphazard upbringing, but, with the exception of the three weeks which had been spent in boarding-school, her life was like a beautiful song, free, interesting and varied. While still a child, she made decisions usually devolving upon the adult mind, managed her father's household, gave all orders to the servants and frequently oversaw different phases of work on the ranch. An omnivorous reader, despite her many activities, she ordered books from the mainland several times a year and when they arrived she had orgies of reading, dipping and swooping among the various authors with a gourmand's ecstasy of indecision. In this way, at the age of fifteen, she knew the writings of Byron, Dickens, Brontë, Austin, Stevenson, Kipling and Shakespeare, but she knew as thoroughly the veterinary books and stock books lining the shelves of the office and read them as absorbedly. She talked frankly and fearlessly with Travers and her father, who, in many ways, was a very modern man.

"The more kinds of people you know, the more things you do, and the more that happens to you, the richer you are," her father always insisted. "Keep your eyes open, face facts; life's a fine show even when everything is against you."

Gay had been compelled to cling to the thought to fortify herself after her father died. People were inclined to criticize Harold Storm when they learned, aside from a small life insurance, he had made no provision for his daughter's future, but he had bequeathed Gay a finer inheritance than the largest fortune in the world: curiosity, courage, a warm heart, and a gay adventuresome spirit which was never to die.

People were kind, many offered her a home and the opportunity to grow up with their daughters, but their suggestions about the future appalled her—she could train for a nurse, be a teacher. She had always followed the gods of the out-of-doors and could not bear to forsake them; they were good gods, the only ones she knew, and following them had given her a strong body and a stout heart.

She spent ten days in the house in which she had passed such happy years, thinking, debating. When an animal was cornered it fought with teeth and claws for existence, they were the only weapons it knew. She felt it was sanest, when life cornered her and she had to earn a living, to fight in the same way, utilizing the things she had, the things she knew. She had read about dude ranches in America and did not see any reason, if people made money that way in the States, why it could not be done in Hawaii. She could begin in a small way. She had the bungalow her father had built, his life insurance to carry her over a year, twenty head of fine saddle horses, and the world's largest extinct crater almost in her back yard to attract tourists, and she knew practically everything there was to be known about horses and the out-of-doors.

Why couldn't she turn her unusual upbringing to good account and instead of ending her free, happy life direct it into new channels which would bring financial returns? She knew at the start she could not afford to hire help and must be prepared to do everything herself; but there was a distinct value in that—the work would be properly done. She deafened her ears to advice, and thrashed out the problem thoroughly with herself. She realized that she was gambling. If she followed the advice of would-be friends, in time she could be sure of a small regular income; if she followed her own program there was the chance of succeed-

ing in a big way, as well as the chance of failing and becoming the laughing-stock of the island on which she lived.

She was well known; she frequently rode in the horse
races and at fairs, and the training she had had riding races
prepared her, somewhat, to tackle life. In a race you must
be cool, fight for your place, look for openings, ride straight,
take chances, call on every ounce of courage and reserve,
and win or lose with a smile, which was just about what
was needed to handle the work she contemplated doing. It
would be hard to surrender her beautiful horses to all sorts
of riders; but that would be better than having to sell them.
If she made a success of guiding and packing she would
be able to keep her dogs, her home, her car and her freedom,
live as she had lived, close to Nature.

She had always had a feeling of kinship with the earth,
an illusion of splendor, of fulfilment, of safety, when she
was close to it. And alone, sitting in the garden looking
at the mountain, she made her decision to entrust her future
to it and to herself.

She had never regretted the step. The first two years had
been heart- and back-breaking, but there was a certain excitement to carry her along. Because of lack of finances, she
felt it would be wiser to dismiss all the servants, temporarily,
but she retained them until she was established in her new
home. With the same courage which made her leave school
when she was nine, and, unescorted, take passage on a
steamer, she embarked on this greater venture alone, brav-
ing criticism and comment as she had braved the possible
wrath of her father.

She had gone about her preparations in a singularly clear-headed fashion, considering her youth and inexperience with business. She appreciated that in order to compete with men already guiding, it would be necessary to make her trips especially attractive. She decided that her work must be conducted on de luxe lines. That meant hot food instead of the wrapped sandwiches which heretofore had been served tourists at the summit; and hot food meant more work, but that did not matter. In time, as she got ahead, she could afford to hire a man to assist her with the heavier work of cutting firewood and shoeing the horses. Until then, she would have to try to manage alone.

She had been a rather scared young thing when she took her first party up the mountain, scared lest some ridiculous or unfortunate accident might make her the laughing-stock of her competitors. Fate was kind and the trip carried through to a successful conclusion. Convinced that she could do the work better than the Japanese and Portuguese, employed by a white man long in the business, she appreciated that in order to get people to patronize her it would be necessary to advertise the advantages to be obtained by coming to her.

She wrote to the better hotels, announcing the fact that she was in the guiding business, listed her trips, the time required, the cost of each one. Everything was to be conducted on de luxe lines, hot meals served and everything supplied necessary for the comfort and safety of people taken out. No extras. Each trip personally conducted by herself!

Results had been amazing, and at the end of the first year she had been able to re-engage the Japanese man and his wife who had worked for her father during the past fifteen years. With them to relieve her of some of the heavier work she was free to be on the trail oftener. She was too clear-headed to expand too fast, and during the succeeding four years forged ahead slowly. She improved the outbuildings, bought a new car and new horses, met the steamers, lining up with the other rent-chauffeurs, who, at first resenting her presence, in time grew to be friends.

There were days when a feeling of unreality had possessed her. She, a guide, a chauffeur, a truck farmer, when she had planned to be an artist! But this work, she would remind herself, was a stepping-stone to her real ambition, and she must toil with undiminished energy until she was financially able to afford to devote her entire time to painting. The spare minutes which she found, sometimes at the end of even the busiest days, she devoted to her easel, going to Travers for criticism and instruction when the wet season came and tourist trade fell off.

The pangs and terrors of the first years lessened as time and results convinced her that the doubtful venture on which she had embarked was established and successful. The people of the island got accustomed to the sight of her packing and guiding, and often the pleasantest recollection visiting tourists had of their trip up Haleakala was the memory of Gay's face as she worked, a face often guiltless of powder, but fine, earnest and undaunted. Perhaps it was the shining softness of her eyes that caused people to overlook the strained and desperate expression behind them, as she spurred her tired body to its tasks. She was like the earth she loved, whose strong, resurgent life was unending.

Despite the fact that she now had two servants, Gay was always up at five. There were seventy acres in the homestead and numerous animals to care for and feed. Part of the land was common pasturage, but several acres were planted in elephant grass and Yuba cane, which Gay cut and fed to her animals, as well as grain, in order not to overstock her limited holding. When the cows were milked she separated the cream and made butter, and, if a mountain trip was scheduled, prepared for it. After breakfast, which consisted of coffee, drunk on the front steps if it were fine, in order to enjoy the rare lights of early morning on mountains and sea, she busied herself in the vegetable garden, sledded manure from the stable to enrich the beds, mowed the lawn, or worked among her flowers while the cook chopped wood, shod horses or repaired and cleaned the car.

The man came out to consult with her, and Gay shut off the hose while she went with him to look at a horse's hoof.

"I think better file little more short," the man insisted, picking up the animal's leg.

The man let go and Gay picked up the horse's hoof and spent several seconds inspecting it.

"No," she insisted; "it's short enough, Sera."

"You boss," the man said, grinning, "and you more smart shoe horse than me, but inside always I shame when I see you shoe horse."

"Why?" asked the girl.

"Too hard, Miss Gay. I no like Mr. Harold girl work like man."

Gay smiled.

"Change Dynamite's shoes when you've finished Pinto's.

147

The rest are okay until the fifteenth of the month." She opened a small book hanging on the wall of the little shop and consulted it to make sure she was correct, for she kept a record of each horse shod, with notes to help her remember whether their hoofs grew fast or slow, in order to care for them accordingly.

One of her dogs leaped against her and she leaned down and patted it, then, straightening up, made for the house. She missed Vixen; she must ring up and ask how she was getting on. Glancing at her watch, fastened by a sturdy leather band about her wrist, she was surprised to see it was almost noon. The bright morning had clouded over suddenly, and, as she approached the house, she gathered the puppies off the lawn, called to the Japanese woman washing the steps to take them to the kitchen, then went into the hall to telephone.

Don answered, and she wondered if she imagined his voice sounded strange and upset.

"I'm sorry, Gay," he said, "I don't know how Vixen is. I haven't seen her yet. I told Taka to take care of her when I went to bed last night. I've been talking to Glenn. . . . I'll see her and phone back."

Gay waited for a few minutes, rearranging a bowl of flowers. He had talked to Glenn. . . . Then he knew— everything. Poor Don!

The bell rang and she answered it.

"I'll come over this afternoon and get her," Gay said, when Don finished talking.

"I say," Don's voice came over the wire clear and strong,

"if it's okay with you, I'll bring Vixen to you. I want to clear out of the house for a bit."

Gay looked at the fall of the island glimpsed through the open door, watched raindrops marking the dust of the driveway, hesitated, then said:

"Come and lunch with me; I haven't eaten yet."

"You're a brick, Gay. I'll be glad to."

She hung up, stood an instant in thought, then, remembering the saddle-blankets she had put out to air, ran to take them in.

Don folded his arms and settled back in the car to watch tall trees flashing past. After the brief shower, there was elixir in the blue of the sky, the air was gay and buoyant, charged with sunlight. It rushed past his face filled with the smell of fresh puddles lining the road. There was a quality to the day which was genuine, earthy and elemental. He appreciated that his physical condition was largely responsible for the disgust and depression which had swept him alternately during the past forty-eight hours, but tearing along in the car his body seemed left behind.

At least, he thought, there were no more damnable secrets to divide him and Glenn. As the brief sharp downpour had cleared the atmosphere, so he felt cleansed by the show-down in the office. Once or twice, looking at the green fields, he winced. In order to stand by his brother, their serene beauty must be destroyed.

The car passed through the village of Makawao, with its street and a half of shabby houses. A dispirited Chinese, proprietor of the oldest store, sat watching his aged father amusing himself with innumerable grandchildren playing about the narrow veranda, while a busy Japanese filled the window of his restaurant with loaves of freshly baked bread. A newly erected gasoline station shouted from a corner where a sturdy Hawaiian filled a truck with oil. Two dejected-looking horses, tied to a pipe which served as a hitching rail, waited while the Portuguese who had ridden them bragged and boasted for the benefit of onlookers.

The car swooped down a hill and up the other side, passed a church set among tired old trees growing in a branch-strewn garden which was also a graveyard. Golden masses of coreopsis waved among crosses and head-stones, watched over by an almost life-sized Christ hanging from a huge wooden cross. The car turned into an avenue of ragged eucalyptus and through them Don caught a glimpse of Piholo hill. Sight of it recalled a boyhood memory of his father riding down the steep slopes leading a wild bull he had roped. Then he sat up with a jerk. On either side of the road, the pastures, *their* pastures, were planted with pine-apples, already heavy with fruit. Taka, at the wheel, stared ahead, making it clear by the way he held himself that he entirely and absolutely disapproved.

"Taka."

"Yes, Mr. Don?"

"How long have these pineapples been planted?"

"Little more two years."

Don folded his arms. He felt emptied, horribly cold, betrayed by everything. The fact that Glenn had not told him that this section of the ranch had already been planted in pineapples made him realize that the abyss between

Glenn and him had not been bridged. "He should have told me," Don thought, ragingly; "it was cowardly not to." He studied the well-ordered red and gray fields, wondering why they should so affront him, but the red earth was like a cry for everything lost, including his brother.

The car fought with the road, torn by heavy traffic, jerking over bumps, lurching through ruts. Through the restless old trees lining the banks, Don saw the great hill standing against a broken blue and white sky. A rush of wind came out of the canyon at its foot, bringing the gusty sweetness of shaken guava bushes, wet *kukui* trees and water rushing over clean boulders.

"Mr. Don."

"Yes, Taka."

"I think better I tell you some kind."

"What is it, Taka?"

"Already cannery little more finish. I, too, sorry, but no can help."

"I know; Mr. Glenn told me."

"All man too much like tell you every kind yesterday, but no can. All man too much sorry inside."

"I understand, Taka."

Don realized with amazement and relief that, for the moment, he felt nothing. Everything seemed entirely unreal. On all sides was a locality familiar in its contours but alien to the one he remembered, a land of waving Hilo grass, guavas and cattle.

The road made a sharp turn and an immense crude structure of unfinished lumber and corrugated iron sprang into view. Don straightened up. Glenn had not stated that the new cannery was being built on the ranch. He had led Don to believe, or had let him believe, that it was in Haiku, where the main plant was stationed. For an instant he could not think or feel; some inner part of him was dying and he wondered resentfully and wearily if it would have to be reborn.

The ground about the building was torn up, tough guava bushes which had been repeatedly run over sprawled exhaustedly against the earth; the stump of a once beautiful tree-fern, stripped of leaves, looked like the butt of a huge dead cigar. Trucks were backing up to discharge loads of machinery, roaring angrily as they fought with deep muddy ruts; men appeared and disappeared through doors like ants running in and out of a hill. From a grove behind the cannery Don heard electric saws working and heard the protesting screaming of trees being cut down. His long sensitive fingers dug into his folded arms.

To take his mind off the landscape, he bent down and gently stroked the head of the small bitch lying in its straw-filled box. The animal licked his hand and looked up wistfully.

"Like you, little Vixen," Don said, "I'm wondering why I must suffer."

He straightened up and looked at the mountain. Upon its splendidly sloping flanks, above the fields already planted in pineapples, tractors were tearing up new ground. Sharp shears turned over green sods, exposing rich earth which gave off a pungent odor. Don watched the ponderous machines, like clumsy beasts crawling up hills, lurching through hollows, but the mountain seemed unheeding of them crawling

like vermin on its sides. Aloof, detached, it remained
wrapped in serenity.

Taka stopped to open a gate and then drove down a
gulch whose sides were too steep for cultivation. The air
was fragrant with the smell of drenched ferns and trees. A
flock of plover rose from a bank whistling, light flashing
from the silver undersides of their wings. Longing for his
father swept him, for he had always used a plover whistle
when he wanted to summon his sons.

Don let his mind dwell upon him, recalling things his
father had said and done, and the beauty and fullness of
boyhood recollections rushed up and filled him.

Taka drove carefully along the winding road. Here and
there on a long strip of land adjoining the forest reserve Don
saw the shacks of homesteaders and the distance-diminished
figures of humans and horses toiling to wrest a living from
inadequate acres allotted by the Government. Sight of them
recalled his first boyhood pang when a leased section of the
ranch had reverted to the Territory, and a sort of shame
swept him. His resentment at the changing face of life
was weakness!

"Miss Gay house," Taka announced, bringing the car to
a halt.

Don got out and stood for an instant on the terrace running the front length of the bungalow. Through open
French doors he got a glimpse of a cozy casual-room with
wide window-seats, books lining the walls, a baby grand
piano and a fireplace. He entered and heard Gay call out
from some inner part of the house and went toward her voice.
A faded green curtain hung over a wide doorway, and he

thrust it aside with his shoulder. It fell softly behind him and he saw Gay perched on a high stool placed before an immense easel. There was a tray of assorted paints and brushes beside her, and a Japanese woman, in the garb of a cane-field worker, with a baby strapped to her back, was posing.

"Taka's bringing your dog, Gay," Don said.

"Thanks," she said, sliding down from the stool. "Wait here; I'll get Vixen."

Don nodded and looked at the shabby, comfortable room. In one corner was a high-backed rocker, beside it a table piled with small canvases while larger ones were stacked against the wall. Couches and chairs of uncertain age and origin were gathered comfortably together as though discussing matters of common interest. The model seated herself on the floor, unbuttoned her dress, shifted the child from her back and began nursing it. Once she smiled up at Don. Her earth-brown face was cruelly lined from years of child bearing and manual labor, but in her eyes there was no protest, but a look of patient enduring.

He moved uncomfortably.

"If you don't mind, Don, we'll eat here," Gay said, when she returned with the dog, which she placed on an old couch. She hung over the animal, tenderly, making sure that it was comfortably established among the cushions. Gay was entirely unaware of her appearance. Bare legged, in a ridiculous gingham dress, sizes too large and bulging in all the wrong places, she stood beside the couch like a gorgeous child, hair untidy, the hollow by her nostril shiny.

"I'd like to eat here; this is a jolly room."

The cook appeared and placed a tray on a low table, and Gay signed to Don to seat himself in the rocker while she curled up upon the couch beside her dog. The little creature lay with its eyes fixed upon her adoringly and Don saw the same look of worship in the eyes of the Japanese woman sitting contentedly upon the floor nursing her baby.

Don did not know what they ate; the shabby room had a restful quality which poured into his soul like balm after the strained days and nights since he had been home. When their plates were emptied Gay fished for a package of cigarettes in the pocket of the voluminous dress and they talked and smoked with pauses of appreciation for the beauty of the afternoon outside the open windows.

"Kama-san," Gay said, "more better *kaukau* now."

"You like I come back when I finish?" the woman asked, as she prepared to leave for her lunch.

Gay glanced at her watch, then at Don.

"Would you mind if I worked for a while longer?" she queried. "You can get a book and read here by Vixen."

"Of course I won't mind," Don said.

When the woman returned, Gay climbed upon her stool and Don watched her work, engrossed. There was something impressive, something magnificent, about her absorption. One of her bare feet was thrust through a rung of the high stool, the other stuck out as though pointing at the canvas. Once Gay spoke and the woman smiled a tired smile and made a negative movement with her head. Gay picked up a tiny mirror, squinted in it and put it down beside the box of paint tubes. Don, like the average man, knew little about art, but, studying the canvas, appreciated the force, truth and tragedy of rudely blocked-in figures in the picture upon which Gay was working. The baby looked indignantly and resentfully at the world, its brows gathered into a scowl, slant eyes half closed, as though trying to keep out sunlight streaming upon them, while the mother leaned upon a hoe, just suggested as yet by a line, creating an impression that she was compelling it to assist her to support the burden on her back.

Gay made a dark mark by the woman's ear, wiped it out, glanced quickly at the model and regretfully put it in again. The sound of padding footsteps crossing the living-room roused Don. A Japanese man in the soiled dungarees of a homestead worker waited between the curtains; then, as Gay seemed oblivious of his presence, he said in low respectful tones:

"Gay-san."

She turned sharply like a being startled back into the world.

"Yes, Takahashi?"

"Too much sore." He pulled up his earth-soiled breeches exposing hairy legs badly swelled and inflamed. "Sunday I chase wild pig inside forest and skin all get broke. Please you fix. Cost too much money to get doctor."

Gay slid off the stool and, squatting on her haunches, inspected the injured members.

"I'd soak them in creolin and hot water, wouldn't you, Don?"

"Nothing better, in my estimation, if there's a tendency of blood-poisoning," Don replied. A warm, happy feeling

156

went through him at being consulted. No one had asked his advice since he got home.

"Will you go and tell the cook to bring two kerosene tins of hot water and the creolin?"

Don went to the clean-scrubbed kitchen, gave the order and stood for a minute in the open doorway looking at the mountain. It seemed to send down a message to his soul. Gay did not treat him like a useless, cast-off garment! A moist wind prowled about the corners of the house and he watched white clouds drifting southward. His spirit winged its fierce way upward.

He appreciated when he returned to the studio that he must have been gone longer than he realized, for when he returned the Japanese homesteader was seated, rather ridiculously, each leg in a tin of slowly steaming water, and Gay was back upon her stool.

"I know I don't have to stop and be polite with you," the girl said, as he seated himself upon the couch. Her voice warmed him. "Interruptions of this sort," she indicated the seated man, "often come, sometimes half a dozen in a day, but I haven't the heart to disregard them. The people around here are poor and hard-working." Then she giggled. "Those kerosene tins look like misshapen pirate boots, don't they?"

Don, realizing that he had completely forgotten about Glenn, the pineapples, the cannery, everything, since he had been with Gay, felt uneasy. He made some reply and stared at the dog lying beside him. He must be careful. He must not permit himself to love her. What could his wife be except a sort of glorified nurse to an invalid?

He saw Gay lean back to consider her canvas, then she transferred her attention to the model and the woman smiled wearily.

"Isn't she grand?" Gay said in her leisurely, restful voice. "I saw her one day when I was driving home. She was piling out of the cane cars with the other laborers. They had been burning off cane and she and the baby were soot from head to foot. When I saw that splendid, battered old face under her funny bonnet, stuck on top of the cloths swathing her hair to keep it clean, I had to stop. When I told her I wanted to paint her she looked as though she knew I was insane and suspected that she was going crazy, and when I told her I'd give her whatever she got a day for burning and cutting cane and fifty cents extra, she simply stared at me. I've had her here with me three weeks. She helps Sera, the cook, and his wife about the place and by degrees I've dragged her story out of her."

"Aren't you going to tell it to me?" Don asked, watching Gay's absorbed little face when she had been painting for several moments.

She came back instantly, delightedly.

"I'd love to. I'm simply crazy about people, all sorts of people. I don't just want one sort. I don't ever want a definite place in any community; I want all of the community."

"Nice," Don said.

"If you have a definite position in a place," Gay said thoughtfully, "it means you go with the same crowd, belong to the same clubs, think the same thoughts, talk the same talk. When people run together it means they are all interested in tennis or golf, have incomes of approximately the same figure, or that their fathers and mothers came from the original stock, or something. I don't give a hoot if a man is a garbage-man or governor, it's the man and not what he stands for that interests me. Take this woman, for instance." She looked at Don in a lighted way. "She came to Hawaii from Japan, a picture bride, to marry a man she had never seen. She's worked in the fields, borne babies quickly in order to get back to work, washed, scrubbed, cooked when she got home. Her husband died a few months ago, just before this baby was born. She has ten children to provide for, all too young to work. But she doesn't complain." Gay's eyes rested with affection and compassion on the woman leaning on her hoe. "She's an unending inspiration to me; I don't mean as a model, but as a human being. She's beautiful, for she embodies the beauty of courage and carrying on."

Don could not answer. He studied the girl perched on her stool, reflecting that from one instant to another a person did not know which Gay she would be, the valiant boy in breeches who had sat and talked to him the previous morning on the bank, the tragic little figure huddled over her hurt dog, or the little beauty in evening dress. At the moment she was simply a lovely, thoughtful kid staring with awed eyes at a woman who dragged through life earthbound clay.

"You know," Gay said after a silence, "some day when I've earned enough money I'm going to Paris and study years and years. Then if I work hard enough and if my feeling for life is sound, I shall arrive. Maybe," she paused to survey her canvas, "if my luck holds good and I continue to sell pictures for magazine covers, I can stop working and go next spring." She stared out of the window, a rapt expression on her face.

Don realized with dismay that the mere thought of her leaving Maui distressed him.

"Do they pay you well for magazine covers?" he asked, after an interval of silence.

"Several hundred dollars, and I've sent four canvases east, with some of Ernesto's, and got two medals and all were sold. But I want to do portraits, oils. I feel," she paused, her head tilted on one side, "like a horse which is warming up with a preliminary canter before starting the real race."

Don looked at her. He had never known any one like her. She was unique, magnificent, appealing.

She resumed her painting and Don realized that her body was in the room, but her real self had fled to other worlds. He looked at the wooden-faced Japanese homesteader sitting with his legs immersed in creolin and hot water, then at the dry and weary woman with her child and hoe. Gay worked earnestly, absorbedly. When she rested her model, she walked about before her canvas weighing her picture from different angles. Don watched the changing expressions of her face. At times it was enchanted, at times intent, and she gave the impression that she was straining for something which kept eluding her.

"Don," she said finally, "go and tell the cook to make tea and take it into the sitting-room. I'll be finished in a few minutes."

He went out and gave the order. When he returned, Gay was collecting brushes and wiping her hands on an old piece of cloth. The sides of her dress were smeared with paint, her hair, cut just to miss her shoulders, needed brushing, and the last vestige of powder had been rubbed off her small, pale face. Don felt like walking over and taking her into his arms.

In her were all the fine selected forces of life. She seemed to be challenging the canvas above her. The figures she had been working on had gained solidity and dignity. She picked up a long brush from among those she had laid aside and standing on tiptoe placed a dab of orange on the painted child's infinitesimal nose. Its eyes seemed to close tighter against tropic sunshine pouring down on them. Gay caught her breath with a delighted little gasp and her eyes rushed to Don's.

"It's coming, it's coming," she chanted, and the Japnanese woman's face lighted, as her eyes, with Don's, drank up Gay's straight little body standing triumphant on its own exhaustion. The seated man spoke in Japanese and grinned at Kama-san.

"It's odd," Don remarked, from his seat upon the couch; "for some reason you make me think of Dad. You have some quality that he had. Dad worked for the glory of his gods, so to speak, and not for the glory of the man."

Gay flashed a warm, grateful look at him.

"Since you told me about him planting all those trees I shall never go out without mentally taking my hat off to him. It's strange, when you start out to do something you feel your work belongs to you, but after you've been working for a while you find out that it's you who belong to your work."

She seated herself upon the couch near Don and laid an affectionate hand on the little dog lying patiently among the cushions.

"I wish I didn't have to stop, but I have to get blankets and food ready so I can get away by daylight. All right, Kama-san, I'm finished. I'll give you a gold medal when this picture is done, for all the hours you've stood for me with Baby-san on your back."

The woman showed her black, rotted teeth in a smile.

"Before hoe, too," she reminded, as though it were a joke.

Gay's eyes leaped to Don's.

"Isn't she grand?" she demanded. "Isn't she beautiful and brave?"

Don's fine white face twitched.

"So are you," he said.

CHAPTER IX

DON thrust deeper into the upholstery, glancing out of the window of the car to assure himself that no one had seen him leaving. Then he looked, almost guiltily, at his long legs, clad in riding breeches and finished off with polished top-boots. It had taken his and Taka's combined ingenuity and united efforts to get them on.

Old Hu had left before breakfast, riding and leading a saddled horse, and should be waiting at the end of the automobile road which led halfway up Haleakala. Taka and Hu's younger brother, Analu, sat together in the front seat, their backs looking solemn and important. A faint smile lighted the tired whiteness of Don's face. There was a ludicrous aspect to this experiment. Then his eyes became a blaze of blinding blue.

What he had seen the previous day had disillusioned him about the possibility of any immediate readjustment of relations between him and Glenn. Glenn had been absent when he got home to dinner and Don had spent the greater part of the night pacing his room and thinking. When his brother did not appear for breakfast Don had written him a note and left it on the desk in the office.

The road leading to the halfway house was the same along which he had driven to Gay's the previous day. He watched tractors plunging, bucking, fighting with the earth, roaring triumphantly as they crawled over a pasture, tearing out its green heart. This morning an army of Filipinos was out tilling fields already planted, hoes winking and flashing busily in the sun. Far above, peaceful hills beckoned. If he could manage to ride even at a walk!

If he found that he could, he would take over the handling of the upper lands. Work, contact with the soil and with the unquestioning beasts, would help him to adjust. Don's instincts were gently bred and he chose his emotions finely, and he wanted, with his soul, to meet the situation confronting him, with intelligence.

He wanted to reason with himself as he drove along that nothing, fundamentally, was altered. The pineapples he resented grew out of the earth he loved. He went over, in his mind, the successive changes which had come to the landscape of the islands. Native forests, except in certain sections, had had to give way to cane and cattle, but there had been compensation for beauty gone in new beauty which had come with cane flowing before the wind and hills dotted with grazing herds. He appreciated that it was the stark ugliness of this new industry which affronted him, as though the island had been stripped naked and exposed to further material ends.

The warrior in him paid tribute to the men who had launched this new industry. He did not doubt that the upward curve of prosperity in Hawaii was greater since the establishment of pineapples as the leading industry, but he wondered if the Islands were better or happier than they had been before pineapples, Packards and prosperity had become synonymous.

He realized, with a sort of panic, that the car had reached

the end of the road. Conspicuously in the foreground, on a slight rise shaded by tall eucalyptus, Hu and the horses waited. In ten or fifteen minutes he would know. Then Don saw other animals saddled and tied in the corral beside the shack called by courtesy the halfway house. He had forgotten: Gay was taking a party up Haleakala. Taka and Analu got out and stood beside the car.

"Go and wait with Hu," Don ordered. "I'm going to smoke a cigarette, then I'll be along."

All at once he felt like a spectator of his own actions, and the picture of a cripple, supported by canes, incongruously dressed in boots and breeches, leaped into his mind, searing it. Rebellion for his condition, such as he had never known, even in hospital, shook him until everything inside him seemed to be crashing into ruins. Sunshine, trees, the send of the island seaward flaunted power and vigor, mocking him. His eyes grew as cold as steel and his face bitter. He who had spent his life worshiping strength and beauty to be stripped of it, forever!

Looking up he saw Gay speaking with Hu, and braced himself. After exchanging a few words with the Hawaiian, she started for the car, a strange expression on her face. Compassion and rebellion were mingled in it, but when she stood by the window Don saw only her eyes, large, tragic, luminous and brimming with tears.

He wound down the glass and she stepped on the running-board and reaching in gripped his hand.

"That's the—" she fought to control her voice, "that's the old fight, Don!" she said, bringing the words out with a rush. "Remember the prayer that I lent you, remember what I told you the day before yesterday, that when life hammers and pounds you it's not to break you but to shape you. Remember," she laughed on a high, unsteady note, "Kama-san!"

Don looked at Gay's face framed by charming wild hair and thought of the Japanese woman with her child and hoe, and the ferocity of grief and anger, which had had him in a vise, faded.

"Thanks, Gay. Inside, I was bolting. I needed the curb to get me back into my stride."

Gay wrenched the door open and sat down on the seat beside him, grasping his thin white hand fiercely between her hard brown ones.

"I wasn't riding you on the curb," she cried, tears splashing down her cheeks. "I was spurring you on. I know. Oh, Don, I know all the things you are feeling inside!"

She looked into his face and without saying a word said everything to him. Gazing into the wet depths of her gray eyes, Don saw all the grief, terror and agony of loneliness which she had hidden from the world while she fought it. With a quick compassionate movement he put his arm about her shoulders. She mustered a valiant smile, but, watching her tear-stained, sensitive face, Don knew she was suffering with him.

Then something in Gay and something in Don rushed forward, met, merged in a warm stream and Don knew, with terror, that he loved her, and suspected that he had loved her since the morning they had sat talking together on the bank. He wondered if she divined, in some deep way, his surrender to a force too strong for him, for she glanced up quickly, then as quickly looked away. Tiny pulses in his body throbbed and he changed his position, fearing that she might hear the beating of his heart.

The day was marvelously dry and warm, trees thrusting upward seemed solidly carved into the thin blue of the sky. He saw the horse saddled and waiting for him, stamping impatiently, and Hu and his companions looking toward the car. A parrakeet, like a gold and green jewel, darted out of a shadowy space among the trees whistling shrilly and was immediately followed by another. A paralysis of anguish held Don. Even birds were not happy alone. A dreadful expression of pain came into his eyes and he moved, trying to tear himself free of thoughts binding him. Then he felt the warm, encouraging pressure of Gay's fingers about his hand, reminding him to fight on. A deep line showed between his brows, then he straightened up.

"It's a long shot," he said, listening carefully to his voice, trying to make it sound natural. "There's only one chance in a thousand that I will be able to ride, but——"

The sound of an automobile coming up the hill startled them both.

"My people," Gay said, her fingers working deeper into Don's. "Stay in the car until we've gone. They'll just think you are a tourist waiting for one of the other guides." Warmth suffused Don's body at her impulse to screen him from the possibility of being an object of curiosity or compassion. Gay looked into his face, then tearing her fingers from his wound her arms savagely and tenderly about his neck. "Never say die; say damn," she whispered, then kissed him quickly and impulsively on the cheek, as she might have kissed a child. She waited for the ghost of an instant as though listening for a voice, then said: "Wait, I'm going to give you something."

Removing her arms from about his neck, she searched in her breeches pocket and brought out a tiny golden spur.

"Put that in your pocket when you try—when you get on your horse. Dad told me once, long ago, when I was a kid, that the real battle isn't winning your spurs; it's keeping them shining and bright. No one can say you haven't won your spurs, and I've won mine, too, but——"

She shook back her hair.

"I can't——" Don began.

She pressed the minute object into his hand and folded his fingers over it.

"You must take it; Dad gave me a pair of them. I have the other." She showed it to him. "They are mascots. When I used to feel licked I'd look at them and go on."

She started to get out of the car.

"Wait," Don commanded, and picking up her hand he kissed it.

She looked at him, startled, then smiled like a pleased child.

"Luck to you, Don," she said, in her rich, restful voice, then getting out went with firm quick steps to her horses. Don watched her meet her people, an eager friendly little creature, moving swiftly and deftly as she assisted them, adjusting stirrups, tightening girths. Finally she mounted, and with the lead rope of the pack-horse in her hand, headed for the mountain, followed by the motley cavalcade of nondescript humans huddled uncomfortably in their saddles. Just before they vanished she turned and waved to him.

He opened his hand and looked at the little gold spur, got out of the car and waited in the sunshine, collecting himself. He wanted to realize his love fully before pressure of immediate events made it unreal. He loved Gay, all that he had ever been, all that he ever would be, loved that which was physical in her and that which was spirit. She was warm, human, but always about her was a suggestion of eternity.

He appreciated, as never before, how terrifically lonely he had been; such solitude of soul made development difficult, but he had never realized to the full, the fierce tragedy of solitude, the terror of it, but now he knew, because, at last, he loved. The silent flood of passion and affection dormant in him had been released and was rushing forward sweeping everything before it. The knowledge of the immensity of his love for Gay, for the soul he had seen through the body, made him wonder if he had ever loved anything before. The past ten years were nothing, the pain he had suffered when his father died, the horror of war, the torment of knowing he was crippled, were nothing; there was no room in him for anything but love. For him the universe was one figure—Gay. He was unconscious of himself except as love for her.

Looking down into his love, he thought:

"Nothing matters, nothing can matter as long as I have this love in me. It safeguards me from everything."

It was permanent, eternally vital, clad in an armor of fire which nothing could penetrate or pierce, free of the terror of outside things because he had it safe and sacred in his heart.

Because he was crippled, decency compelled him to remain silent, but the immense truth of his feeling conquered everything else, made everything else seem false and small. But with the realization of the immense truth of love, came the realization of the immense sorrow which must dwell beside it. While Gay had been with him the magic of her presence made him feel safe, they were both children of the good earth; but he appreciated, with dismay, that nothing remained as it was when she was not with him, and there was something terrifying in the thought. He felt stunned and looked around as though expecting nature to take up arms for him against the fate which held him silent. Yet he did not think for an instant of taking up arms for himself. He had let Gay go without saying anything, and the idea of ever saying anything did not enter his mind, but his body, which remained passive, was full of a riot, a fury of life, for he felt within himself the insurgent cry of the abundant earth, for growth, for perpetuation.

He looked at the blue distances of sky and sea, charged with amber sunlight, and a sense of release came to him: the release of those who know they have nothing more to lose. His face was devoid of expression, his eyes blank blue stones, as though his soul had been expelled from his body. He saw, as in a dream, Hu moving about the horse saddled for him, and started forward mechanically. He glanced back, assuring himself there were no observers, considered the bank, selecting the likeliest spot from which to mount, thinking, with a grimace, that a pulley would be the most logical way of hoisting him into the saddle. Then, burying his pride, he signaled to the waiting men.

Taka and Analu assisted him onto the bank while Hu, slowly and almost apologetically, led the horse forward, coaxing it until it stood in the right position for Don to mount. Don directed Taka and Analu to hold his elbows and dropped his canes into the grass. After two attempts the men succeeded in lowering him into the saddle. The horse was uneasy and suspicious, moving about with quick little side steps, tossing its head. Pleasure which was almost like a stab of pain passed through Don when his legs clasped cold leather, but his veined hand looked unfamiliar holding the reins. The horse tried to go.

"Hang onto him until I'm settled," Don ordered, and Hu checked the animal sharply.

Taka and Analu thrust Don's feet into the stirrups—strangely heavy, for the riding muscles of his legs were weak and limp from long disuse. Taking firm hold of the pommel, he carefully straightened his back, testing it, then looked at the land laid out fearlessly before him. His heart woke to answer its reveille. Color scorched his face. The island, these three men of different nationalities, Gay, were his friends, were with him in spirit, were behind him in his attempt to discover whether or not he could ride.

"Let go, Hu," he ordered, and the man relinquished his hold of the bridle and stepped back.

The horse tossed its head and started forward with quick, eager strides. For an instant Don felt as if he had discarded his body and was free. He let the animal walk a few yards, then checked it.

"No, I can't," he said, through dry, gray lips; "it hurts too confoundedly much. Take me off."

Seeing the dismayed expression on the faces of the men trotting after him he began laughing. The whole performance was absurd: he, a cripple, attempting to ride, he, a grown man, needing three other grown men to put him in and take him out of a saddle. They hastened to him, Hu at a run, sunlight flashing off his well-worn spurs. Don thought of the tiny golden spur in his pocket.

"No," he cried violently. "Let me alone. I can! I will!"

Taking fresh hold of the pommel with his free hand he braced his back, shortened the reins and squeezed the horse with his legs and it went into an easy lope. He heard the remembered mutter of wind in his ears, and something beautiful which had been lost was given back to him completely. A rough tenderness swept over him, for the wide day, for the animal he bestrode, for the world. It hurt, it hurt hellishly, but if he managed to endure it for seconds he could school himself, later, to stand it for minutes, then hours. He had suffered more excruciating agony in the hospital. Sweat drenched his body and streamed down the backs of his legs, but his ears sang once again with the dust-muffled rhythm of a galloping horse's hoofs. His past life seemed to be falling away: boyhood, Europe, the war, the farce of his home coming, all seemed to be the life of somebody else.

He breathed out a sigh releasing his joy into the world, then slowed the horse down to a walk. He felt as if his soul, which had been in prison, was liberated. In this splendid moment he felt vigorous, carefree, rich, and longed to lavish upon humanity the happiness sweeping him. He turned the animal, experiencing an intoxicating sense of power when it yielded to leg and rein. Taka and Analu were executing absurd steps in the road to express their joy, and old Hu stood wiping tears out of his eyes with his sleeve.

"Can do, Mr. Don?" Taka asked, running up.

"No too much sore?" Analu demanded, laying his hand on Don's leg.

Don shook his head.

"*Welakahao!*" Hu shouted. "Me too much happy inside. Never mind if never can go very quick."

Don sat breathing heavily. His ravaged face, moist and blazing from exertion, had a ghostly youthfulness. He did not deceive himself, he could never really ride again, but he could manage to sit a horse and, in time, get around. The prospect of the hours of torture he must be prepared to face did not daunt him, for his body had known every conceivable variety of pain. He sat in the saddle overtaken by one of the rare moments which come to every man, moments when everything seems clear and close, and a person understands the gaps, the accidents, all that went to make the whole.

A car smoked up the road, rousing him. Glenn's! He saw his brother leaning out, an incredulous expression on his face. Glenn got out, staring at Don as though he were facing a spectre, then began pounding the side of the car with a clenched fist.

"Look here," he cried, ragingly, "you shouldn't be doing this! It's asinine! You'll—you'll—confound it, you fool, you'll finish your back completely banging it about on a horse. Do you want to spend the rest of your life in a stinking bed!"

He threw back his head with a gesture that condemned the universe, then began grinning, but his smile was like a twisted mask on his drawn, brown face.

"Here, get off; I'll give you a hand."

"That's all right, Glenn. I've found out that I can get around after a fashion, and it makes all the difference. When I'm up there," he signaled at the hills, "nothing will matter."

Glenn stared at him.

"I'm in Hell, Don; I tell you, I'm in Hell! When I found your note it made me feel rotten as all Sodom and Gomorrah."

Watching Glenn's tortured face Don felt as though he were spying, dishonorably, on his brother's soul.

"Don't be an ass," he said. "I had no intention of making you feel rotten; but I did feel that in our showdown, yesterday, all the cards should have been laid on the table. Now that they are," a terrible expression contorted Glenn's features, "let's not refer to the subject again. The tree cutting must be stopped. Outside of that, from now on, I'll only concern myself with the upper lands and you can take over the rest."

When Don got home Ah Sam was waiting in the quadrangle, muttering to himself and wiping his hands repeatedly on his apron. A scowl disfigured his lined, saffron-colored face and his scrawny throat jerked nervously.

"Can do, Mr. Don?" he asked, before Don was out of the car.

Don nodded.

"Gar-damn-go-to-hell, I too much glad. I got lunch for you inside kitchen. Other man all finish. I think may be sure you like."

"Fine, Sam," Don said, getting out of the car.

The prospect of eating in the kitchen pleased him, for it was reminiscent of life before he had gone to the war. On mornings when he had gone up the mountain before daybreak to rope wild cattle, on nights when he returned late from shipping steers to Honolulu, he had taken his meals in shirt-sleeves at the long table opposite the stove while Ah Sam piled plates with food and slammed pots and pans into the sink. The Chinaman started on, Don followed, Taka at his heels.

"I think better pull off boots, Mr. Don," Taka suggested; "s'pose wait too long, back too much sore."

"That's a good idea," Don said, limping along the walk.

His muscles were strained and aching, but a sense of well-being filled him, for he felt that, once more, he had a part in the vast, vital mechanism of a living world. Entering the kitchen, he seated himself and Taka commenced working to remove his boots.

"Easy," Don cautioned, tensing his legs and bracing; "my confounded back is giving me merry hell." The Japanese looked up, his face sympathetic and admiring. "Pull slowly, down a bit on the toe, now again. It's coming."

After some more tentative tugging the boots slid off.

"Now, Sam," Don said, leaning his arms on the table, "bring my lunch."

He watched the cook heaping a plate with rice and Hawaiian stew, and realized that he was hungry and eager for food for the first time for years.

"*Poi*, Sam, and if you have any chili peppers——"

"Got every kind you like," the cook said, hurrying into the pantry.

When the food was placed on the table, Ah Sam poured out a steaming cup of coffee, then wiped his claw-like hands, veined from four decades of washing Garrison dishes, on his apron.

"Any kind more you like?" he demanded. "More better eat plenty. This time you too much thin."

"I have enough, for the present," Don said, smiling.

The cook grunted and going to the sink began washing lunch dishes. Don glanced at a long shelf above the old man's head, filled with empty jam jars, bits of soap and soiled rags. There was the glass with Ah Sam's toothbrush, which was also an ear scratcher at the opposite end; he smiled, remembering how he and Glenn, as boys, entranced with the doubly useful tool, had begged their father to purchase them brushes of similar make.

Taka wiped off and polished Don's boots, glancing up contentedly ever so often, and it seemed to Don that the past ten years had been blotted out. He saw the cook sign commandingly at the Japanese, who was prolonging the boot cleaning unnecessarily, and after a few minutes Taka went to put the boots away. Ah Sam snatched a saucepan off the stove and thrust it into the dishpan, sending up hissing clouds

of steam. The old man looked at outs with the world, and
instinct told Don that the cook wanted to talk to him
privately. He felt apprehensive. Knowing the futility of
attempting to hurry a Chinaman, he occupied himself with
food and waited.

Happiness and unhappiness blended inextricably in Don.
He was too tired, mentally and physically, to want to think,
and stared out of the window. In the cloudless blue of the
sky there seemed magic depths, and the day was like a dream,
intense and passionate, yet touched with some unearthly
quality. He laid his fork down on the plate. Strong sunlight walking through the gay garden bred bravery, and he
felt as though his whole nature were being renewed. Within
was an active, gnawing hunger, like acid which burns and
eats away metal. Changes were taking place inside him
and he was afraid. It was going to be difficult facing his
love for Gay, which made him feel a whole man again, when
he was not whole.

"Mr. Don."

He started.

"Yes, Sam?"

"Some kind I like talk."

"Fire away." Don picked up his fork.

The cook did not look around, but occupied himself scrub-
bing off the bottom of a saucepan.

Don wondered what was coming. Ah Sam considered
himself a member of the family. The old man had worked
for their father before he and Glenn were born. He had endured boyish raids on safe and icebox and had permitted the
space behind the big kitchen range to be turned into a menag-

erie for maimed and motherless animals. He had grumbled and cursed, made passes at the boys with pieces of firewood and buckets of hot water, but they had known it was only a gesture to keep the kitchen from being completely overrun.

On one occasion the Chinaman had gone so far as to screen Glenn and himself from punishment. Because one or the other of them had cried at a fall from a horse and been reproved for it, they had decided upon a course of tortures to develop bravery. The first torture had consisted of pressing burning punks into their arms; the second, of rubbing the skin off the tender backs of their legs with prickly lantana branches, then rubbing in the milk of figs. The resulting mass of sores and blisters could not be concealed as the minute punk burns had been, and when their father inquired into the cause of the affliction and had been informed of the reason for it, he had been amused, but insisted that the tortures be discontinued.

Disregarding the command, determined to complete the development of bravery, he and Glenn had gone through the final test, eating cactus fruit without peeling it. With throats and mouths inflamed by the infinitesimal thorns, they had rushed to the kitchen and devoured every loaf of bread, trying to ease their torment. When the reason for the raid was explained to Ah Sam he had grinned, a rather pleased expression on his face, and baked more bread in order that the boys' disobedience might not be discovered.

Don glanced at the old man.

"What do you want to say, Sam?" he asked.

The Chinaman continued to keep his back to Don.

"Mr. Morse no stlaight. Mr. Glenn clazy like this man.

I no velly smart, Mr. Don; I only Chinaman; but Humbugger Mr. Morse stop inside Mr. John house. Better you kick out."

Looking at the old man's narrow, secret back, Don felt worried.

"Go on, Sam."

"Gar-damn-go-to-hell, Maui no all same before. Me like better old style. Mr. John time, sure, when fellas come home, kill pig, Kanaka boys sing, play guitar, but never waste money like other night, rent orclestla, dlink, dlink, dlink. All mans and womans clazy. What for white fellas make like this?"

"Look at me when you talk to me, Sam," Don ordered, shortly, knowing that the man, Oriental fashion, was beating about the bush before getting to his point.

"I shame look you when I talk this kind things," the cook retorted, keeping his back stubbornly to Don. "I too much aloha you and Mr. Glenn; you all same my boys; but because Mr. Glenn too much like Mr. Morse he no make stlaight with you. Gar-damn-go-to-hell, s'pose you know what kind Mr. Glenn and Mr. Morse making—you kick two fellas outside this house."

"That'll do, Sam."

"Orli, orli, no use get angry. After by and by you see."

Ah Sam slammed a fresh pot into the sink and attacked the smoke-blackened bottom viciously.

Don sat silent, feeling sick and cold. After a little he rose and went upstairs.

179

CHAPTER X

A THOUSAND thoughts raced through Don's mind as he mounted the stairs. He must be alone, he must think! He walked toward his father's room, where he would be safe from intrusion. The old Chinaman's hints disturbed him, but what possible thing could Glenn be into? There was no disgrace in growing pineapples.

His back ached intolerably, but when he reached his father's door he straightened up, grasped the knob and entered. The room was a spacious affair, with windows in unexpected places opening onto favorite views. He walked to the largest and looked out. A flock of mynah birds streamed across a bit of sunny sky and he watched a wee spider repairing its web at the end of a branch. Above tree-tops the familiar outline of Haleakala showed, a solitary puff of white cloud standing high above it, casting an immense shadow on the ranch. It depressed Don, for it was sym-bolical of the shadow on his and Glenn's lives.

He wanted to open the window, but doubted if he could manage it, so sat down in a deep chair. His eyes wandered thoughtfully over the room. Enlarged snapshots of Glenn and himself, as children astride sturdy ponies, groups at race meets and *luaus,* hung on the wall, recalling a happy childhood; but Glenn's ghost seemed to lurk in the background, making him restless and unhappy. He must remember that Glenn, himself, uncounted others, were like spent bullets. They had been shaped hastily for war, hurled at the enemy, described short brilliant arcs and dropped back to earth. He propped his head on his hand, feeling as if he faced a curtain of darkness. A tap on the door roused him.

"Come in," he called, impatient at being disturbed.

Ah Sam stood in the doorway.

"Mr. Don, you velly angly because I talk about Mr. Glenn. Me only speak because I too much aloha for Mr. John and no like his boy make shame kind things. Mr. Glenn my boss, but sometimes I like lick him. Bimeby when you savvy what kind Mr. Glenn and Mr. Morse making you clazy inside. Better you forget what kind I speaking, but you keep sharp lookout."

He stepped back and started to close the door.

"Sam," Don said, sharply.

"Yes, Mr. Don?"

"Wait."

The cook stood in the doorway like an inscrutable image. Ah Sam did not deceive himself about the perfection of the members of the family for which he had worked for so long, but loyalty sealed him to them.

"What kind you like?" the cook asked, crossly, when Don did not speak.

"I want to thank you, Sam, for———"

"Never mind thank you." The cook glanced sharply at Don, then remarked, like an afterthought, "This time your face just all same Mr. John's. Seem like he come back."

181

Don felt warmed, then caught sight of himself in the mirror across the room.

"Good God!" he thought, "did dear old Dad ever look like that?"

The Chinaman left and Don studied his reflection thoughtfully; then his eyes went to his mother's picture standing on the bureau by the mirror. The face was three-quarters full, the eyes raised as if for inspiration. Dreadful for his father, for any man, to be robbed by death of the woman he loved, before their lives were half over. His mind leaped to Gay. Well, he thought, his father had had some years of happiness at least. Rising, he began pacing the floor.

The waste, the futility of war! It had changed the face of life for him and for countless others, distorting their bodies and minds. He raged, remembering days and nights when he had been a drugged bundle of intolerable pain, dimly conscious of gassed comrades in adjoining rooms, coughing up fragments of their lungs, and howling tortures which had once been men.

And his spirit rose in revolt, calling up shapes with which he had secretly wrestled during convalescence, impulses to which he had succumbed in fury, disgust and revolt, after he had been discharged from hospital. Tortured flesh and spirit, soiled by attempts to escape, to forget, to be revenged upon life—for the time being hideous—by making it more hideous still. The folly, the futility of flesh attempting to revenge itself on spirit, and spirit trying to revenge itself on flesh, while the world walked on in beauty! The inevitable toll, sick body, sick mind, shamed of its shame, trying to hide from pure mornings born from unspeakable nights. The devastating realization, afterwards, that there was no blessed crevice in the flesh through which the spirit might creep out, timidly to touch hands with beauty again.

But that was all left behind, he reminded himself. He looked at the still garden and went downstairs. For a while he walked among the trees, trying to find serenity. He repeated Gay's prayer, but the cry of the body for its own distracted his soul. Dreadful to think that he could never tell Gay he loved her, dreadful knowing that he could never hold her in his arms!

A flock of pigeons circled over the house, delicate lovers of the air, then fearlessly alighted on the roof, strutting hither and thither, making their perpetual, characteristic motion of the head, half nod, half bow. He made an attempt to conquer the rebellion in him for the fate which had been unfairly meted him, but the gnawing hunger of the flesh, wishing to live fully, tormented him. According to old Hawaiian beliefs, everything in creation had its mate, on land and in the sea; like the *kukui*, a tree, and the *paa-kukui*, a fish in the sea, supposed to be its complement.

He did not deceive himself that Gay loved him, but he felt that he could have made her love him if he had been whole. He knew that the kindness she showed him she would show any one in trouble. He recalled Travers' remark about her the night they had driven home: "Because life has manhandled her she has compassion for anything which has not been given a square deal." He had not been fairly dealt with. For no fault of his own, he was condemned to live half a life. He came to an abrupt stop and stared at the sea. Cloud shadows lay upon it like sunken islands, and the edge of the horizon blurred into the blue of the sky. Eternity seemed to be watching him.

He felt as though he were being devoured; never in the hospital, never since he had left it, had he been tormented like this. Two-thirds of his life still lay ahead of him and he must live it alone. Seeing a bench, he sank upon it. The warm afternoon breathed softly around him and he felt the strength of the earth under his feet, the earth whose true child he was. He knew how irrevocable was his fate. The combined science and medicine of the world could not make him strong; he would always be compelled to walk with canes. He could not, would not, ask Gay, any woman, to marry him. No woman would want to marry him, for that matter. Gay was young, exquisite, courageous, gifted; life could not beat her. She would go on and on.

He thought of her as he had first seen her, changing a tire, but even when engaged in so commonplace an act she had distinction and beauty. He thought of her working in her studio, riding up the mountain, playing with her dogs, standing by the fireplace in her daffodil evening gown the night he had supped with Moll and her friends.

For an instant he allowed his imagination to run riot, fancied her arms about his neck, her head on his heart. . . . Then rising to his feet, he cursed God.

"You like I tell Mr. Don tea time?" Adaji asked Travers, when he set down the tray in the living-room. The old man nodded. Working in his wing of the house, under John Garrison's room, he had listened to the incessant tapping of

Don's canes as he paced up and down. Once Travers had started to rise, then resumed his painting. This was Don's fight and no one had any right to interfere. Later, he had heard him go downstairs and into the garden.

The old man's pupils contracted and his gray face, still faintly marked with the dissipations of a youth long past, grew worried. He had lived widely and in many lands before coming to Hawaii, but knew himself powerless to help either Glenn or Don. He listened for Don's step, wishing that he would come. It was stupid of him to keep beating himself, mentally, to death over things which could not be helped.

Don appeared and, walking across the room, seated himself opposite Travers. Light slanting in from outdoors struck Don's face; its flesh was shadowed with blue and Travers realized for the first time, and with a faint shock, that Don must suffer constant and considerable pain. The old man was overtaken by an acute sense of depression, foreign to his nature, realizing the walls with which Don surrounded the secret places of his soul. No man, or woman, would ever be permitted to know all of his heart.

"No sugar in my tea, Adaji, only cream," Don said to the man working at his elbow. "And when you've finished serving, light a fire. I'm cold."

Travers glanced at Don. Cold, on a bright day; sign of overwrought nerves. Don's stilled face seemed to contemplate enormous, deserted distances, as though some inner part of him had fallen to pieces, destroying past, present and future. Don turned to Travers and something hot and bitter stirred in the old artist. He was afraid that Don was about to make some strange, passionate revelation which he might later regret. But Don did not speak. He watched Adaji light the fire, then stretched his long legs to the blaze. Travers took out a cigar and inspected it thoughtfully.

"Well, what have you been up to today?" he asked, after the silence had prolonged itself to breaking-point.

"You'd never guess," Don said, grinning bleakly.

"Well, what have you been doing?" Travers demanded, after another silence.

"I went to Olinda and experimented riding."

"Ass!" Travers announced, disgustedly.

"I found out that I can get about after a fashion. Luckily, I couldn't see myself. I fancy I don't cut a very inspiring figure on horseback."

"What do you plan to do?"

"For the immediate present, take charge of the upper lands and forget everything below. You know, Ernesto, at times I feel confoundedly disgusted with myself. It's asinine to feel so upset over a few damned pineapples, but it's the motive behind that gripes me: that money is the measure of success and happiness. It jolly well isn't! A certain amount is necessary in order to live, but it can't buy peace, happiness, love——"

Some intonation in Don's voice made Travers look up. When Don commenced speaking it had been tired, even hopeless, but with the last word it sounded hard, full of love, sex and passion. Studying Don's white face, Travers wondered what red pageant of thoughts was marching through the other man's mind. He looked like a lost man trying to find his way home, a man who, at the moment, was keeping a fierce companionship with spectres and savagely longing for the re-creation of himself.

The old man did not like the expression in Don's eyes, for it was that of a man who hated his Creator, and he wondered what secrets the day held which Don had not disclosed.

"I hear a car coming," Travers announced.

He was glad of any one who might call, bringing fresh atmosphere, for that in the old house was muddied with the emotions which the past three days had stirred up. He stared into the fire, leaping and straining up the chimney as if irresistibly drawn upwards by some strong influence sucking it away from the whirlpool of human life.

"Well, if you aren't a pair of spinsters, having tea by the fire!" Moll jeered. "Here I sneaked up on you hoping for excitement," she laughed as she crossed the room, "and I find a completely depressing scene. Can't you raise something stronger than tea for me, Don?"

"Of course, Molly. Like a cocktail?"

"A flock of them."

Taking a cushion from a nearby chair she tossed it onto the hearth and seated herself upon it. In the firelight her beauty was startling. She was in a smart white flannel dress with a tiny green monogram over her left breast. Her gorgeous, artful, crimson mouth stood out like a tempting flower against her face, and from behind thickened lashes, her eyes shone disturbingly. She smiled at Don, then leaning forward scratched at an infinitesimal speck of dust on a conspicuously slender and shapely ankle, directing attention toward it. Then straightening up she fished in the depths of a large green leather purse and drew out a cigarette case and lighter.

Travers noted that she was watching Don absorbedly.

Adaji came to gather up tea things and Don dispatched him to make a cocktail. The man returned shortly with a frosted shaker and a glass which he set upon the smallest of a nest of teakwood tables, placing it within Moll's reach. Travers did not listen to what Moll and Don were saying, for he was busy analyzing the girl. She appeared obvious, but he suspected that there were hidden depths in her to be plumbed.

"Pour me one, Don," Moll commanded.

She accepted the glass from him, instilling into the little act an intimacy which startled Travers. Moll, with a skill hardly in accord with her years, was deliberately setting out to break down the wall of Don's reserve.

Don was sufficiently different to arouse Moll's curiosity, fast tiring of her crowd and craving new excitements. Don leaned toward her, elbows on knees, talking. In the instant he resembled his father, almost ridiculously, and Travers knew that Don possessed the same aristocracy of spirit, but the old artist knew that even the best of men, in black moments, drink of dead waters and in his present mood Don might easily swing off at some unexpected tangent.

"Well, what have you been doing these last two days?" Moll asked. "I haven't laid eyes on you since the party."

"Oh, just mulling around."

The girl moved her cocktail glass so that firelight, shining through the liquid, cast a restless spot of color on her mouth. Her face was grave and thoughtful, but her eyes gleamed like sunlight on shallow water. Then she stared at Don mischievously from under her lashes.

"Would you like me to put a charge of T.N.T. into your life?" she asked.

Don smiled.

"Think I can't?"

"I know so, my dear."

"You'd be surprised," she announced, appraising him; then she asked airily, "Are you easily shocked? You look as though you might be."

"You are an absolute brat, Molly. Some one should spank you."

"Well, that would be a new experience," she announced, her eyes fixed speculatively on the close line of Don's mouth. After an instant she transferred her attention to Travers. "Is he?"

"Is who what?" the old man asked, sarcastically.

"Is Don easily shocked? I'd like to know, as it will make a difference in my method of approach."

Don laughed, but Travers' expression was condemning. He did not answer Moll's question and she regarded him with immense scorn, which he appeared not to see. He listened to her meaningless patter, confined to a few stock phrases which were the vogue of the moment, while he watched her bewildering eyes, one moment veiled, then as suddenly wide open, polished briefly with unbearable excitement, then calculating and cold.

"I know exactly how you would kiss, Don," Moll announced, from some depth of thought. "A peck and next morning you'd be wondering if you oughtn't to marry the girl."

Don got crimson, but was compelled to smile.

"Call off your dogs, Molly; you are entirely too much for me. I can't talk your talk."

"Then I'll learn yours," she announced.

Travers watched grimly. Moll looked outrageously lovely, glamorously youthful. Travers had no respect for girls of Moll's type, but knew they were unusually successful when they set out to get a man. Moll was no fool and he suspected that she appreciated that the easy, established intimacy between island families made it permissible for her to come to the ranch as often as she pleased. That a girl in the whirl of her first season would take time to be nice to a man so obviously out of the running, the disparity in their ages, would make gossip impossible and leave her field clear.

There was no telling what her motives might be, probably youthful vanity, hunger for new conquests, but she was utterly ruthless and could easily make mincemeat of a man's life. There was no denying that she possessed the mysterious power to arouse men, to affect them more than she affected herself; and she was aware of the fact. Then some fleeting expression in Moll's eyes brought another thought. Moll might fall in love with Don, and then there would be hell to pay. She was the sort of girl who, regardless of what people might say or think, would go with tooth and claw after the man she wanted. Don's reserve was a challenge, hinting at depths which she might imagine she could succeed in plumbing.

"Don't watch me in that perfectly poisonous way," Moll said indignantly to Travers.

The old man did not reply.

Glenn and Morse arrived, and Don became cold and withdrawn. Glenn looked wretched and unhappy, Morse insolently at ease.

"You are a fortunate fellow, Garrison," he remarked, "to have Maui's most popular débutante at your feet."

Glenn's expression was terrified, but Don seemed not to have heard Morse's remark.

"Pose effective, Re-Morse?" Moll asked.

"Ask Travers: he's an artist," Morse replied carelessly, conscious of Glenn's eyes imploring him not to go too far.

Travers glanced contemptuously at Moll.

"It couldn't be more effective if you'd rehearsed it."

"Coming on, prehistoric!" Moll cried. "Of course I rehearse scenes, stage situations in my mind, when I set out to get a new scalp. Don's new material, so I have to use a new technique. I figured that if you sit at a man's feet, like this, and look up at him," she laughed at Don, watching him from under her lashes, "you make him feel important."

"You're a scamp," Don said, amused at her impudent, confident youth.

Travers threw his cigar into the fire. It seemed a blasphemy for this girl to be so beautiful and for Don to be so oblivious of her intentions. Travers knew that Moll did not deceive herself. She realized that it was going to take all her skill to make an impression on Don, aloof, unlike the men of her acquaintance. Extraordinary, Travers reflected. Outwardly, any afternoon: twilight gathering out of doors, a fire leaping up the chimney, clink of teacups and glasses being lifted up and set aside, smoke curling from the ends of sociably glowing cigarettes; but, beneath placid surfaces, life hurrying forward to unknown goals.

The clock, with preliminary whirrings, chimed six. Glenn looked at it like a person roused from a troubled sleep.

"Going to Stew's party, Moll?" he asked.

She nodded. "Are you?" she turned to Don.

"I was not aware that there was a party tonight," he replied.

"Stew's staging a binge," Moll said.

"Stew?" Don asked, puzzled.

"Stuyvesant Webb, commonly known as Stew because he's usually stewed," Moll explained. "He was at your party and told me to dig you up and drag you along. I came on purpose to tell you, but forgot because you fascinate me so."

Morse laughed.

"Thank Webb for me, will you, Molly? I'm too tired to go out tonight," Don said.

"It'll do you good to go out. People who stay at home all the time get mildew on their minds," Moll asserted.

Don winced behind his smile.

"I must beg off this time, Molly."

She rose and stood beside him, circling his arm with magnetic fingers.

"Well, if Stew's binge gets boring, I'll be back," she announced. "I crave real excitement." She studied Don for an instant, then turned to Glenn and Morse, "Coming with me or you going to clean up?"

"I'll shove along as I am," Glenn muttered.

"I'll follow with Sue," Morse said.

Glenn rose.

Moll took possessive hold of his arm. "I'm going to ride hard on you tonight," she announced. "It's stupid to pass out at every party. You miss all the fun."

Don looked at her gratefully and Moll smiled a secret smile.

"Good kid, Molly," Don remarked, when she was gone. "I'm inclined to fancy her pose is all bluff. She's an audacious little devil, but underneath she's kind. Decent of her to try and jolly along an old crock like myself, and damned decent of her to keep an eye on Glenn. The other night at supper she did the same thing."

Travers stared into the fire. Moll was clever—damn her!

When dinner was over Travers and Don adjourned to the living-room and seated themselves before the hearth. Wind mourned about the house and the night was filled with disturbing secrecy. Travers stared into the hot heart of the fire, then his eyes began wandering thoughtfully around the room. He was impressed by the air of serenity pervading the house. It was untouched, undisturbed by the events which had streamed through it, a shrine guarding Garrison memories.

He and Don talked fitfully and the old man appeared not to see the frozen storms in Don's eyes. Travers studied his face, fine, sensitive, restrained. Life, for Don, until the war, had been an intense waking dream; now he looked world-old. Years had brought knowledge, paid for with the dreams of youth, and yet Travers was convinced that Don was not entirely disenchanted. Sound as the earth he loved, he kept his eyes resolutely fastened on the pillars of a better life, a larger world than the one a person could touch and see. He sat, legs stretched to the blaze, a slender, lonely giant, smoking cigarette after cigarette. Travers stirred unhappily. Each man's city of refuge, he reflected, must be built within himself, of shattered dreams.

He loved Don as he had loved his father. Don's hair, which was still a boy's hair, swept back from a forehead, clean, sensible and brave, but his mouth was a man's, tightly closed and at the moment bleak. The old man sighed. A person fancied at the start that love, work, success or disaster were the big things, but, looking back, saw that they were little unnoticed corners where you turned to left or right. The old man felt depressed, and when the clock struck ten rose and said goodnight.

Don sat listening to the snapping of the fire. The room itself was so still that it seemed to be shouting for attention. He looked fondly about it. It was filled with the friendly ghosts of flown years: Sunday morning shooting parties, when men gathered to talk of guns and game while dawn walked over the mountain with cold, blue feet. Evenings when hunters trooped in smelling of powder and feathers, and the day's adventures were relived while the atmosphere of hills mingled with that of the glowing, hospitable room. This house had a soul which was like a song of warm, autumn days; it had been a vineyard and was now a winepress, crushing out lives.

The wind dropped and gradually a vague, enormous rustling, which grew steadily louder, filled the night and he realized that heavy rain was falling. Clean, rich scents crept into the air from the drenched and hidden earth. He felt want aching in his being. He had slept little the night before, there was a gritty dryness behind his eyes, but he was burningly alive. He knew that there were few men who did not feel, at some period of their lives, that all was over for them, that there was nothing to hope for, that happiness was a dream which would visit them no more.

He was tired, limbs and back ached, temples felt compressed, but he was conscious of a latent excitement stirring in him, roused by the splendidly falling rain which brought fulfilment to the island. Outwardly always reserved and quiet, he was inwardly a human fire, a human storm. That day Nature, so often calm and indifferent, as one too complete to be aware of incompleteness, had imperiously summoned him to her worship. Who could remain cold and calm in latitudes of fire, where days went by like dreams in which was the stir of constant re-birth? What was the worship of a man's heart given only to a locality, or a man's soul given only to the earth?

The night smelled damp and rich, as if its arms spilled with offerings, and he drew the wealthy atmosphere into his nostrils. He contrasted the desperate dirt of London mornings, the sooty, breathed air brooding over black houses and greasy pavements, with the dawns that came to the islands of the Pacific, immaculate, sacred and clean, as if each one was the first one of creation when mountains swooped downward and sea sprang upward to meet in a vast embrace from which the fierce vitality of day was born.

A door slammed somewhere in the back of the house and after some instants cold air came down the hall and touched him. Glancing up, he saw Moll leaning against the doorjamb watching him, a curious, intent expression in her eyes. There was something avid, sultry and brooding about her. For an instant he was amazed to see her, then thought of Glenn and straightened in his chair.

"Want something, Molly?"

She did not reply, but crossed the room lashing a black velvet wrap excitedly about her.

"Stew's binge was boring, so I thought I'd come and talk to you."

"It's bit late for calling," Don said, smiling faintly, as he glanced at the clock.

Moll ignored the remark, tossed the wrap into a chair and stretched her arms toward the blaze. Don was glad of the intrusion which helped to thrust out the burden of profitless thoughts.

"Glenn okay?" he asked, after a moment.

Moll nodded indifferently. Her face was a small white mask with emeralds for eyes. Formal curls cast black shadows on her cheeks. The mask of her face was not one of concealment, but the likeness of her very self which knew not good or evil, honor or dishonor. Conscious of Don's scrutiny, she smiled and with a graceful movement sank upon the hearth.

"You haven't told me how you like my dress," she said, gazing up at him.

"You are looking particularly gorgeous, Molly. Did they melt and pour you into that?" Don ventured, looking at the slight figure clasped in satin so black that it looked wet. About her neck was a string of pearls, lustrous as the warm young flesh beneath it. She changed her position slightly, leaning against his knee.

"Do I," she stared up at him, "blind you?"

Don could not help smiling. Moll's exotic, upturned face was smooth and open. Nothing, as yet, had been written on it and he wondered what life would do to it or what Moll would do herself.

"You might very easily if I were a younger man and if——" he broke off.

"The gap in our ages is chic," Moll announced; "I'd adore being an old man's darling." She laid her arm across his knees.

"My dear child," Don began, laughing; but her eyes stopped him, for he saw, despite her youth, that she was a being old as the earth.

She stared into the fire, pressing thoughtfully on her lower lip with small, sharp teeth.

"You," she fixed him with her eyes, "make me feel all wobbly and queer inside."

The hush of her waiting breathing distracted Don. She sat, coiled in firelight, watching him with unclouded, shameless eyes.

"Moll," he began.

She waited, expectantly. Her left hand was hanging down and knocked against his, and pity swept him. The heat of her fingers, the shiver that ran over her body at the brief contact, made him afraid that life had marked her for disaster, and yet she sat in ordered loveliness, every wave of hair and fold of gown in place.

"Sit in that chair, Molly, where I can see you," Don said.

"Are you afraid to have me near you?" she asked, hopefully. "Because you can see me better where I am."

"Why should I be afraid of you?" Don inquired.

"I like you; you are so brutal," Moll said. "Why aren't you crazy about me, as I am about you? I've been thinking of you ever since I met you. You do all sorts of exciting things to me inside." She sat, eyes fastened on his face, and Don felt a sort of exquisite trouble moving through him like a wave, and fixed his eyes on a picture across the room. She waited.

"Moll."

"I'm listening." Lacing her fingers, she pressed both elbows down upon his knees, giving a breathless, pregnant little laugh which became part of the restless, rustling dark.

"I can guess how these," she touched his canes contemptuously with her foot, "make you feel since you got back to the Islands. I'm young, I'm pretty. Kiss me. I can make you forget—everything."

She waited expectantly for him to follow up her provocations, as the other men of her acquaintance undoubtedly did. Don thought disgustedly that had it not been for Gay, she could have made him forget, for a while at least. In his present savage mood of frustration. . . . He went hot and pale and reached into his breast pocket for his handkerchief. A tiny sound of some minute object falling onto the hearth made him look down. The golden spur Gay had given him that morning glinted in the dull glow of the dying fire. Moll swooped upon it, looking puzzled; then a strange expression dawned in her eyes.

"Gay gave you that," she said.

"Yes; give it to me, Molly."

She retained it. "I suppose," she said in a voice of immense scorn, "you think she loves you."

"I know she doesn't."

"But you wish she did! Can't fool me! I may be bad, but I'm smart. I get vibrations. The first day you were home I knew you were crazy about her when you were sitting together on the couch before we went to lunch." Yes, Don thought, unconsciously he had loved Gay even then. "I bet she hasn't told you that she has a boy. He doesn't live on Maui, but they've been engaged ever since she was sixteen. When he is twenty-one next spring they are going to be married. He's rich, and after they are married he's promised to take her to Paris so she can study art." The contempt in Moll's voice was enormous.

Don recalled the lighted expression on Gay's face when she had spoken of going to Paris, and felt suddenly very tired.

"Now, I'm crazy about you," Moll declared, breathing quickly. She glanced at his canes. "I think it would be fearfully exciting and different to be your wife. I'm badder than any one knows, but I never feel wicked when I am— just excited, and always hungry for more."

"That'll do, Moll," Don said, stiffly.

"Oo, you look handsome when you're shocked. Look like that again, it's marvelous. Don, you—you've got me! I know because I can't do my stuff properly when I'm with you. I feel as if I were married to you and you were lecturing me. I'd adore it. I'd like to be just a little scared of you." She breathed fast, visioning herself tyrannized over by a man. "You are wonderful. You make me think of a locked door. You give me gooseflesh. Don," she rose to her knees, "marry me. I'm crazy about you. You thrill me to the core, and I can thrill you."

"Can't you understand, Molly, that I have no wish or intention of getting married. It simply isn't on the books for me—now."

"You're lying. You'd like to; you're crazy to be loved, but, being old-fashioned, think because you are a cripple you shouldn't marry." She watched his tense figure. "But you have a devil and I knew it the first time I saw you and told Glenn so. I'll get you through your devil because I have one, too."

"Give me my spur, Molly, and my canes; I'm going to bed."

"You're scared to stay with me, scared of yourself!" She laughed into his eyes in a wild high way.

"You—your——"

"I know what you're going to say," Moll interrupted. "Me, my sort appeal to all that's worst in a man. And we get them! Our mothers preached that girls who chased men, men didn't want. That's bunk. Look at Pansy Wetherill, she ran Pete Sullivan to ground. She went after him—every way; she got him. If our mothers knew, they'd label her bad; and she isn't bad, she's smart. She keeps Pete crazy about her. She knows all the tricks. So do I. But when I'm with you my style is cramped—because I'm mad about you. You don't love me; I disgust you. You think you won't marry me, but, old thing, you will."

Don reached for his canes, realizing that Moll was trying to thrust out Gay, the secret companion of his mind, invade his thoughts, perhaps his life, in exchange for a puny pleasure which needed love to exalt it. He saw, with alarm, that Moll was no longer playing; she was swept away by a loose, adolescent passion, and he wondered if he could make her understand that romance did not steal in through the fleshy portals of the heart. He rose and Moll rose with him, breathing fast.

He looked at her, resenting what she was trying to do, but it was balm to know that he, or the wreck of what he had been, could stir such a violent and lovely creature. Trembling seized him, as if she had stabbed him with the up-trust of her bosom. Suddenly her arms were about him.

"Don."

He attempted to wrench himself free of the vise of her arms clinging about his body.

"Let go, Moll."

"I love you, Don. I want you. It's silly of you to long for Gay when she loves some one else. I'm as beautiful, more beautiful than she is, and can love much harder."

Disengaging one arm, she threw the spur into the fire. Rage swept Don, shaking his hold on himself. He cursed and she laughed delightedly, reached up, got her arms about his neck and dragged down his head until her lips found his.

"Oo, you're swell," she crooned.

Her warm breath reached him, her hands pressed palm against his back so that the shape of them burned through the material into his flesh, and his face, which he averted, reddened with a slow tide which ran upwards from his collar. Something wild and lawless, something passionate, strong and savage, kin to the great forces imprisoned in the earth, was rising in her nature to face a similar force in him, which called it and which it answered without shame.

A log broke and fell into the coals, sending up two flames which leaped into a red tongue of fire. Don felt Moll's body trembling against his as if the violence of the spirit confined within was shaking it to pieces. Outside rain continued spilling with splendid recklessness, becoming part of the great charged darkness enveloping the earth.

"Moll, let go. You can't . . . get me . . . that way! Get out!"

She released him slowly, giving him a look of scorn, but made no move to go.

"You heard me, Moll. Get out!"

Moll laughed, delighted. "Bravo, Don! Spoken like my very own man. The scene's mine, now. I adore to have you domineering."

Picking up her cloak, she wrapped it about her with a royal gesture while Don reached for a fallen cane. The spur! He must retrieve what was left of it. Moll's heels clicked, as she walked triumphantly toward the door.

"I'm going, angel," she called. "But one of these days I'll return and it will be because you want me."

The door closed.

Lowering himself to the hearth, Don poked among the coals with the tongs until he found the little lump of melted gold. Foolish, idiotic, to want to keep it. He looked at it lying on the hearth, distorted, thinking bitterly that it was like his dreams. When it was cool he wiped the ashes off the nugget and slipped it back into his breast pocket.

CHAPTER XI

MOLL lay between sleep and waking, indifferent to strong sunlight walking over the island. Mynah birds consulted noisily in the tree-tops and somewhere in the garden a boy was singing and clipping a hedge. Rolling over, Moll buried her head in her arms. The cells of her body jarred minutely and continuously against one another and her limbs were weighted from excitement, alcohol and fatigue.

The door opened carefully and an elderly Japanese woman entered. Her mild, flat face became indignant as she glanced at Moll's black dress thrown across a chaise-longue, piled with small lacy pillows. Her velvet wrap lay on the floor, shoes and stockings beside it. The woman moved about softly, collecting strewed garments, inspecting them, shaking them out. She emptied a brass tray filled with cigarette butts, straightened out the dresser, arranging the gold-stoppered bottles in a neat row. Picking up a flask she smelled it and muttered under her breath in Japanese.

"What time is it, Taki?" Moll asked.

"Eleben o'clock," the woman answered, without turning around. Her broad back in its neat blue kimono looked condemning. Moll sat up and embraced her knees.

"You like somekind eat?" Taki asked, busying herself with the articles on the dresser.

"I'm not hungry; bring me some iced ginger ale."

Unable to contain herself longer the woman wheeled.

"Ginger ale!" she exclaimed. "What for all time you making foolish, Molly-san? After by and by you sorry. No use girl stay up all night, drink *okolehao*. Look you *loli*, all on top floor." She held up lace underthings. "This kind cost too much money. See dirt on top and new dress broke." Wrathfully she displayed a rent in the hem.

Moll contemplated it indifferently.

"Molly-san."

"Yes?" the girl answered, yawning and stretching like a luxurious kitten.

"S'pose me mother, I lick you. Before baby-time when you naughty I give castor-oil——"

"And now you can only yap," Moll interrupted. "Get my ginger ale. I'm thirsty."

The woman departed and Moll looked at her room with satisfaction. It had been recently done over in a pale shade of gold which set off her dark beauty. Getting out of bed she went to the mirror and inspected herself interestedly. She felt that she had grown more beautiful overnight, invested with the glow, the roseate exhalation which envelops a woman in love. Picking up a powder-puff she passed it over her chin, then looked at her nails. Her long fingers tipped with vermilion, which emphasized their milky whiteness, pleased her.

Walking to the window, she stretched in the sunshine, enjoying the sensation of hard young muscles moving under velvety skin. She thought of Don, of his quiet face, of his well-bred, well-shaped hands, which were not ruthless and possessive as were the hands of the men she knew. Odd, how he fascinated her. Thrilling to make a cripple love you, like playing with chained forces. Something new!

She walked about the room in her transparent pajamas, picking up a magazine, putting it down, fingering an ashtray, examining a photograph, smoking a cigarette from the box on the bedside table. Restless, nervously alive. She must see Don again! Sue was giving a luncheon that day at the ranch for the Twelve Club. Of course Don would absent himself, but she would contrive to see him some time during the afternoon. She quivered in anticipation, remembering the electrical current which always went through her when she touched him.

Far from being affronted at his ordering her out, she was enchanted, for it proved that under his quiet exterior he was violent. If she had not thrown Gay's spur into the fire she might never have discovered it. Gay, she thought contemptuously, always messing about with paints and work! But Moll did not cheat herself, and she knew that Gay, as well as herself, appealed to men's imagination. Gay would bear watching. She possessed some quality hard to define that made a direct bid for sympathy. Perhaps her aloneness. Well, she had pricked that bubble!

Walking to the bureau, she looked into the mirror again. Her small face with its large eyes which slanted a little at the corners, her long slim throat, and dark little head, were exotic and dangerous. Don, no man, could be proof against her forever. Taki returned with the ginger ale, interrupting her train of thought. Moll accepted the long, frosted glass and, stretching out on the chaise-longue, sipped it while the woman ran a bath, collected perfumed bath salts and body powder.

"What dress you like?" Taki asked, walking to the cupboard and inspecting the array of clothes hanging limply in it.

"My red and white figured silk and the hat and shoes that go with it." Moll's eyes narrowed, watching bubbles stringing upward and bursting with tiny, cracking noises. She would, she knew, achieve distinction with her crowd by being in love. For the first time her life had a definite purpose. She did not honestly know why she wanted Don so overwhelmingly, but he represented an unknown world and was, therefore, worth exploring. Taki's voice roused her.

"Molly-san, what for always you go out? You tink you catch mans that way?"

Molly smiled, secretly.

"You tink this damn fool *baka-tari* kind fellas you go out with, mans?" Taki demanded, scornfully.

"I know they're not," Moll said, draining her glass and setting it aside. She sat like a breath carved in fire, all desire, then got up and pulled off her pajamas. The woman looked at her slim, naked body with sudden affection.

"Molly-san, baby-time I take care you. I love berry much. You nice baby, nice little girl, but this time I no like you any more."

"You're lying, Taki," the girl said, walking into the tiled bathroom, which was like a green and white lily cup. "You like me as much as ever, but you don't like the things I do."

She slipped into the warm, scented water and tossed a handful over one round shoulder.

"You speaking true. I like all same before, Molly-san,

207

but I sorry and shame for you. You tink I catching Yama-ichi before, girl-time, if I make like you, come home morning-time with dronk fellas? Sure, Yama-ichi sleep with me, but never he marry with me. You young, you pretty, you got nice father and mother, but always you doing cheap kind things. I too much angry when dronk mans bring you home. *Baki-tari!* I feel like slap you face and boys' faces, too. That one you call Bunny, why you go out with him? Why father and mother no kick this kind fellas out? Never you catching good mans for husband if you making like this. Waste time!"

"I'll catch a good one, Taki, you see," Moll said, soaping her long arms.

The woman watched her, then going to the edge of the tub, tucked back the long sleeves of her kimono, and began washing the girl's back. Her plump, dimpled hands moved lovingly across it. Once she halted to push up a damp strand of Moll's hair and the girl glanced up and smiled.

"From now on, Taki, I'm going to walk in purity—like an aunt," Moll announced.

Taki snorted.

"What kind things you talking, Molly-san? I no onderstand."

"Well, I'm going to be good, for a change," Moll announced.

"For what?" Taki asked suspiciously.

"Because I'm out to land a good man."

Moll fingered the bright faucet. Taki soaped her, waiting.

"Tell Taki what kind you making," the woman urged. "Who this new man you liking now? Too much I like you get marry quick, then after bime-by I take care baby-sans like before I take care you."

"There probably won't be any babies," Moll giggled.

"What for speak all same?" the woman demanded, indignantly.

Moll stepped out of the bath and stood taut while the woman dried her. Taki's hands looked expectant, and the girl laughed.

"Tell Taki," the woman urged. "You finding some good mans last night?"

"Wouldn't you like to know!" Moll said, feeling important.

Taki powdered Moll, her hands working expertly about the girl's fresh body.

"I'm going to marry Don Garrison," she announced without preliminary.

Taki jerked up.

"Mr. Glenn brother?"

Moll nodded.

"But he all broke!" the woman protested.

Moll did not seem to hear. Her face was thoughtful, absorbed, her eyes veiled. The woman looked at her aghast, then her face grew crafty.

"He nice mans," she agreed, "but——"

"But what?" Moll demanded, suspiciously.

"Never this kind mans marrying with girl who make like you. Before I know Mr. Don father. He all same kind mans. Berry good. I too sorry Mr. Don all broke."

Moll stared at her pink foot.

"Already he ask you for marrying?" Taki asked, hopefully, after a few moments.

"No, but I'm going to make him."

"What for you like marry with this kind mans, Molly-san?"

"Oh, I don't know, Taki, he makes me want—oh, things!"

"I no onderstand what kind you speaking, Molly-san," Taki said, "but I tell you true, spoke you like catch this kind mans, better you make like Miss Gay. She number one good girl. Very kind to all peoples, work hard, never make foolish."

"Gay!" Moll exclaimed venomously, and her face went hard, blank and ruthless.

"I know he's crazy about her," Moll said, as if talking to herself, "but he'll never say anything to her, because, as you express it, he's all broke. But I'll make him ask me. See if I don't."

Taki weighed her critically.

"Maybe can, maybe no can."

"I bet you, Taki, that before this year's out, I'll be Mrs. Don Garrison. I simply have to have him or I'll bust."

"Then better quick you make like I speak," the woman advised. "No show off any more, no drink too much, go nice and easy and after bime-by——"

"I'll show you, old Pie-face, I'll show you!" Moll cried, embracing her.

When she released Taki, the woman grimaced at her kimono, all white with powder. Observing Taki's expression, Moll seized the box and threw its contents over her.

Taki shrieked with simulated fury and ran into the bedroom, Moll pursuing her about it scattering powder. Finally, laughing and exhausted, Moll cast herself on the chaise-longue and Taki sat down on a chair panting. Her eyes shone, her brown face was tender.

"Inside you only baby-san, like before," she announced with relief. "All this kind you only making show off."

Moll watched her from beneath heavy lashes, then hearing footsteps, threw a silk wrapper across her. Her mother opened the door and the Japanese woman rose apologetically, dusting her kimono.

"Molly-san make foolish with powder," she explained.

Ella Harding smiled.

"Tired after your party, Molly?"

"Rarin' to go."

"What is it today?"

"Sue's having the Twelve Club to the ranch for lunch."

"If you see Don give him my love."

Moll darted a quick look at her mother and nodded indifferently. She knew that Don's father and her mother had been lifelong friends. Her mother would like . . . . that, she thought with inner glee. She'd surprise them all yet, knock them all cold. When she succeeded in landing Don she would focus attention upon herself, gain real distinction. To be married to a man like Don, so different, so distinguished, a war cripple, would ensure her spotlight for the rest of her life! She, the island's loveliest, most dashing débutante, to capture a man of Don's caliber, with slues of medals and decorations, would be a triumph. She knew just how the talk would go!

"My deeah! My deeah! Can you feature it? Moll's gone and done it, absolutely done it! She would. She's simply carried Don Garrison off his feet. He never had a chance from the moment he met her. He's completely gone on her. He's marrying her! Can you feature it! Isn't it simply precious? But then you know we all felt, despite her glitter, that the girl had depths," and they would all look profound, the girls she had run with. She shivered with excitement and anticipatory pleasure.

"Will you be home for dinner?" her mother's voice disturbed her, and she frowned and thought quickly.

"We're going to Hazel's for a swim after the lunch and will probably stay for supper, as the boys are dropping in."

"Do you want the car?"

"Hazel's coming for me."

Ella Harding waited for an instant, glancing at the garden shears in her hand, then closed the door. Moll stared out of the window, lost in thought, her eyes wise, steady as stars seen out of a cave. Then she rose and started dressing.

Her toilette was careful and complicated. On her bureau were great glass jars that contained fine meal, there were rows of pots holding cream, massage cream, vanishing cream, cleansing cream. There were little crystal and gold bowls of scarlet and yellowish pastes, a perforated container sprouting cotton, toilet waters, perfumes, atomizers, unguents. It wasn't a dressing-table but a laboratory.

When her toilette was completed, Taki withdrew a step and regarded her admiringly.

"Too much nice, Molly-san. You number one pretty girl on Maui."

Moll smiled and passed expert fingers over her hair, shining, undulated, carefully pressing already perfect waves into place.

"Give me my dress."

Taki held it and she slipped expertly into it. Through the heavy silk of the material, her uncorseted, pliant figure was bewildering, lovely, dangerous. She held out her hand for a small white hat which Taki gave her. It had three crimson gardenias painted against the crown which just matched the lipstick on her mouth. Down, down with two fingers of her right hand Moll pulled the brief brim until it hid one eyebrow and emphasized the slight upward tilt of her chin. Taki opened a drawer and brought out a large, white purse.

"Find me a hankie," Moll ordered, moistening the tip of her fourth finger and carefully passing it over the visible eyebrow. Then she sprayed herself with expensive perfume and regarded herself with immense satisfaction.

"Think I can wreck him, Taki?" she inquired.

The woman looked puzzled, but nodded emphatically.

Moll snatched her into her strong, young arms and kissed her. She had more genuine respect and affection for Taki than for either of her parents. They had never crossed her, but the Japanese woman did not hesitate to express her disgust or disapproval when it suited her.

"I love you, old Pie-face," she declared, when she released her. "I think it will be thrilling to be good. . . ." She stared at the silver, monogrammed flask lying on the dresser, picked it up and thrust it into the woman's hand.

"What for you give me this kind, Molly-san?" the woman demanded, suspiciously. "I no like drink *okolehao*."

"Well, give it to Yama-ichi."

The woman looked at the flask, then at the girl.

"I keep. *Okolehao* I put inside ginger ale bottle and Yama-ichi drink Saturday night. This silver kind, after bime-by when you catch nice broke man, better you give him for marry present." She laughed noisily, and Moll squealed with glee.

"Hot idea, Taki!" she cried.

Taki slipped the flask into the bosom of her kimono and smoothed down the folds. Moll gazed at her own reflection. It was lovely, stimulating. She felt as though Don was already her husband, and a little mounting sensation of excitement filled her. Life had at last a real zest! She knew men, how to drive them to distraction; deep underneath they were all the same. Don had trembled when she clasped him . . . . She smiled a Mona Lisa smile and left the room.

Taki listened to the important click of her heels descending the stairs, then started tidying the room. Presently the orthophonic was turned on and she heard Moll singing. Taki paused in her work to listen to the defiant hootings and squealings of saxophones above the deep, full tones of other instruments, visioning Moll executing dance steps while she waited for Hazel to come and pick her up and take her to the ranch. Taki murmured a prayer, invoking the gods of love and luck, both Japanese and Hawaiian, to surround her baby-san. Young, impudent, irresistible . . . no man could be proof against Moll forever.

CHAPTER XII

DON, having been warned by Ernesto of Sue's luncheon, absented himself for the day. He rode for a short time, then drove over all the portions of the ranch which were accessible by car. There was no turning back. For the time being he had pledged himself to stand by Glenn and must face the consequences. The race-horses, excepting one or two, would have to be sold, the herd reduced from five thousand to about eighteen hundred. The upper lands would not carry more without overstocking and ruining the pastures. Barracks would have to be erected to house the hundreds of Filipinos necessary to till a pineapple plantation, sheds built to shelter trucks, implements and machinery.

He ordered Taka to drive him again around Piholo, trying to see beauty in ploughed fields, in gray spiked leaves set about the golden globes of pineapples; but when he listened instinctively for the voice of the land, it had been replaced by the noises of civilization, the endless rumble of trucks coming and going, the roaring of tractors, the chattering of monkey-like Filipinos. The smell of gasoline, exhaust, dust, sweating humanity, fermenting pineapple tops, had replaced the fragrances of trees, cattle and grass.

Looking at the cloudless summit of Haleakala he thought of Gay riding upon it and a mirage of romance invaded the common light of day. Her just being in the world made it more beautiful, and thought of her was like a blue spirit standing between him and the storms of life. Then, remembering Moll, his proud face closed. So thin a line between the beautiful and the unbeautiful in every man. Had it not been that he loved Gay . . .

It was late when he got home and he went directly to his room. When he was bathed and dressed he determined to go and chat with Glenn. Limping slowly down the hall, he tapped on the door. There was no answer and he wondered if Glenn and Morse had gone out without his hearing them. They had come in together while he was taking his bath. He was about to go when some impulse made him turn the handle and enter.

The room was in semi-darkness and for an instant he thought it was empty, then saw an inert figure sprawled across the bed. Don hurriedly switched on the light. A whisky bottle stood on the bedside table and a coil of tinfoil, like a gold and silver twisted leaf, lay on the floor. The bottle had been full; Glenn had drunk himself insensible!

Crossing to the bed, Don seated himself upon it and placed a hand on Glenn's shoulder. Glenn shivered and buried his head deeper into the pillow, breathing terribly, then flung out one arm, and the bottle and a cup full of whisky went clattering to the floor. The bottle rolled under the bed as though trying to hide itself.

"Glenn, Glenn, old man," Don said, passing his long fingers over his brother's burning head. Glenn rolled over and his unguarded face, flushed a deep telltale red, was bloated and tortured. Don looked away for an instant, leting his eyes wander about the room, which he had not once entered, or been asked to enter, since he got home. It was much as he remembered it and he was consumed with compassion and felt closer to his brother than at any time during the past days.

He knew most of Glenn's agony was self-chosen, but, despite appearances, was convinced that Glenn still possessed a high, clean heart, else he could not be so desperately unhappy knowing he was in the wrong pasture. Remembering his own strayings after he had been discharged from hospital his body felt hollow with sympathy and his heart a coal burning in emptiness. How far he and Glenn had wandered from the things of their boyhood!

He thrust his fingers through Glenn's moist hair; somewhere inside this body the real Glenn crouched, dismayed, frightened, revolting, forever seeking escape from its prison. He wondered if a doctor should be called, and felt his brother's pulse. Glenn's brown wrist seemed too thin to contain the stream of blood jerking through it.

He should at least call a servant and get Glenn undressed. Fury ate him because he could not manage to do it himself. He hated subjecting Glenn to the eyes of even the faithful Taka, because his state was too pitifully obvious. Going to the door he called out. The Japanese appeared and Don told him to undress Glenn. When the covers were decently arranged, Don contemplated him, wondering passionately if there was no way of reaching him.

Lying on his back, his long form outlined by bedclothes, Glenn looked as though he might be dead, but his features wore the convulsed expression of one who had reached the limit of endurance, the expression they had worn the previous morning when he had come upon Don unexpectedly riding. It was evident that Glenn's spirit, even aided by alcohol, had not succeeded in escaping. In some dim region, beyond help or reach, it was still being tortured and twisted.

"Take away that cup and bottle," Don ordered, pointing under the bed with his cane.

Taka collected them. "Some more kind you like?" Taka asked, his eyes unhappy and concerned resting on Glenn. From the expression in them it was clear that Taka knew, as Don knew, that this was no ordinary passing out. Don computed; it had been less than an hour and a half since he had heard Glenn come in and the tinfoil testified that the bottle of whisky had been consumed during that time.

"Yes, Taka, get an ice-pack for Mr. Glenn's head and put another at the base of his neck. And stay with him."

"Sure, I no leave. I too much sorry. Mr. Glenn number one good man."

The words consoled Don. He was not the only one who felt that Glenn, the real Glenn, was fundamentally unchanged.

"I'll wait here until you bring the ice."

Don limped about the room inspecting it, thinking of the times he and Glenn had had together as boys, the joy they had shared in the clean beauties of Nature, the zest with which they had taken part in the lusty life of the ranch.

Taka returned and arranged the ice-packs, then seated himself respectfully on a straight chair he placed beside the bed.

"Is Mr. Morse dining at home tonight?" Don asked, without looking at the Japanese.

"One hour before, Mr. and Mrs. Morse go Honolulu. No come back for one week."

Don experienced a moment of fury. He had intended to see Morse and tell him to get out of the house. Well, he consoled himself, at least he would be rid of him temporarily.

Travers was waiting at the dinner-table when Don came down.

"Glenn's laid himself out stiff," Don said, as he took his place. "I don't know whether or not I should call a doctor."

"It might be advisable; he's been at it a damn long time."

"Think he may be in for a bout of the D.T.'s?"

"If he hadn't the constitution of an ox he'd have had them months ago."

"God blast Morse! I'm going to tell him he's got to clear out. He's largely responsible for Glenn being like this, the blackguard!"

"Morse is not a blackguard," Travers said. "He merely happens to be entirely unscrupulous. Glenn was hitting it hard before Morse appeared and he, to further his own ends, helped that which was already under way."

"Well, I won't have him here. Wish he hadn't gone to Honolulu. I'd like to get it over."

Before dinner was half done Taka appeared. Don laid down his napkin and reached for his canes.

"What is it, Taka?"

"Mr. Glenn too much crazy talk. Better you come."

Don went up, followed by Travers. Glenn was muttering and gesticulating, his face purple, veins standing out on forehead and neck like worms.

"Call a doctor," Don said, hurrying across the room to the bed. "Glenn, Glenn, old man———"

Glenn tipped his head back, straining against the pillows, then sunk back into himself. Don gripped his brother's hand fiercely.

"I'm here, Glenn," he said a trifle huskily, seating himself on the edge of the bed beside the dark, tragic thing which had once been Glenn Garrison. Just thirty-one, Don thought, watching him with awful compassion. Such a tragedy!

"You know," Travers said, after the doctor had come and a nurse had been established in Glenn's room, "it's fortunate that things happened as they did."

"What do you mean, Ernesto?" Don asked.

"I had an idea that the young ass might blow out his brains."

"Why on earth should Glenn do such a thing?"

"He and Morse are in something foul. I got the first wind of it the day you came home when I overheard them talking on the wharf. It seemed so preposterous that I tried to believe that my instincts were tricking me. Because of you, Glenn's felt bad about the ranch going into pines, but that isn't sufficient to get him into such a state."

"Ah Sam collared me yesterday when I came in from riding and hinted at the same thing, but being a confounded tight-mouthed Chink didn't commit himself to anything."

"Well, this is an excellent opportunity for you to find out what they're up to while Glenn is laid out and Morse away. Glenn was no drunker than usual when they came in; I saw him. Morse never counted on Glenn laying himself out or he would never have left. Whatever it is that's bothering Glenn got too much for him when Morse cleared out."

The telephone began ringing shrilly.

"Shall I answer it?" Travers asked.

"Will you? It's Adaji's night off."

Before the old man was halfway across the room Taka appeared.

"Some man like talk Mr. Glenn," he informed them.

"I'll take the message," Don said, rising.

When Don rejoined Travers there was a hard glitter in his eyes.

"Some fellow wanted Glenn, and when I told him Glenn was ill and I'd take the message he hung up on me."

"Which proves——" Travers began.

Taka came to the door.

"You like I stop house tonight, Mr. Don?" he asked.

"No need to, Taka. Glenn has a nurse to take care of him and we'll be going to bed shortly."

"Then s'pose all right I take my small boys to movie show?"

"Do, by all means."

Don and Travers sat for a minute in silence while wind ran around the corners of the house whimpering like a lost hound. Don was aware of the pressure of the night; it appeared to stoop nearer, blind, impassive, but intensely aware. The telephone began ringing again and Don's eyes went to Travers.

"You go this time," Don suggested.

Don sat tense. Ridiculous thinking that the bell sounded different, shrill and excited. Events crowding too fast on his heels had distorted and exaggerated happenings out of all proportion. He tried to imagine what Glenn and Morse could possibly be doing. Probably the lot of them, himself and Travers included, were all going crazy. Hearing the old man's returning step, he glanced up and was astounded by the expression on his face. He looked blanched and ill.

"What the hell——" Don began.

"Gay's been hurt and the cook wants us to come over immediately."

"Hurt, what do you mean hurt?" Don asked, feeling as if some one had struck him a numbing blow at the base of the skull.

"Coming down the mountain she opened the gate and her gun——"

Don snatched his canes off the floor. His mind blurred, then cleared. He had dismissed Taka; it was Adaji's night out; Travers had never handled a car. . . . He had ridden. Well, he would drive.

"See if Glenn's okay, tell the nurse where she can call us. I'll wait for you in the garage."

Travers made no comment when he came out and saw Don at the wheel. Don jammed in the gear, winced, then rushed the car out backwards, slued it around and headed down the avenue. Roadsides were flung behind, stars tossed about in bits of sky glimpsed between tree-tops, dark streamed past Don's and Travers' faces. They tore through the street-and-a-half of Makawao, past the church, and swung into the Piholo avenue. Tree-trunks and rows of pineapples leaped into sight and vanished as, armed in silence, wrapped in light, the great car sped along.

Don drove recklessly, but with assurance, his strained face illuminated by the tiny dashboard light. They passed the cannery and, arriving at the gate in the gulch, Don jammed on the brakes and the car slid to a stop. While Travers was opening it Don realized, with amazement, that during the past week, under pressure of terrific emotion, he had torn two bars out of his prison—ridden a horse and driven a car.

High on the swell of the ridge, at the edge of the forest reserve, lights shone from the doors and windows of Gay's house. Travers did not attempt to speak to Don. He looked entirely removed from earthly things when, in reality, he was wholly occupied with them. They rushed into the yard. A mass of sweat-stained horses waited patiently in the corral to be unsaddled. A dog was silhouetted for an instant against a lighted doorway, then trotted into the house. The cook was waiting on the terrace, holding a lantern, and in its striped light his face looked worried and angry, lines carved into it like scars.

"Torr much I like you fellas come quick," he said. "Gay-san torr much *pilikea.* Torr much blood come. Gar-damn what for Gay-san all time carry gun for shoot goat meat? Humbugger this girl no got enough money."

Don seemed not to hear him, but stalked into the house. Gay was lying on a couch in the living-room propped against hastily piled cushions. She was still in her riding clothes, and on the front of her shirt was a spreading crimson stain. Kama-san, her baby strapped to her back, was on her knees hanging onto one of Gay's hands and crying silently. Japanese homesteaders, men and women, who had been sum-

223

moned or who had come voluntarily, stood in unhappy groups looking on helplessly.

"Call a doctor, Ernesto," Don directed, seating himself on the couch, and his canes went rattling to the floor.

"One time call already, but no stop," Sera, the cook, said. "Gar-damn-son-of-a-pitch every kind no good."

Travers went to the telephone.

Gay opened glazed eyes then closed them slowly. Information was flung at Don. Nishimoto had been working late spreading Paris green about his potatoes when he heard the sound of a shot on the trail coming down the mountain. A few minutes later Takahashi, who lived higher up, came running in, his face blanched as though he had seen an *umbogi*. He had hardly been able to talk. Gay-san was lying in the road amid a tangle of dogs and horses and the rifle she always carried was beside the gate.

Looking at the girl's pinched face, Don felt as though all the gods had forsaken him. He spoke to her, but she did not answer, and with shaking hands he unfastened her shirt and saw a ragged wound above her small breast. It had bled profusely, soaking her left arm and shoulder, but now there was only a slow, thick ooze.

"Get ice and towels," Don ordered, and the cook went for them.

One of the dogs whined and leaped onto the couch, sniffed, then, drooping its tail disconsolately, jumped down. Don directed one of the men to put out the animals, but Gay made a faint protesting movement.

"Let them stay," she whispered through dry gray lips. "I

224

love them and want them all with me. And open the doors wide so I can see outside."

The muscle in Don's cheek began beating. Life had robbed this girl of love, brutally and cruelly, as it had robbed him. She had lavished the wealth and warmth of her heart on animals and given the worship of her soul to Nature, and in her hour of trial she turned to them instinctively for help and courage, rather than to her fellow humans. One of the Japanese women pushed the door wide and Gay turned her face to the great starry night. From the forests came the clean scent of running water and damp vegetation and the mystical exhalation of animate green things in the process of growth and creation. Gay's eyes rested contentedly for an instant on the great dim shape of the mountain, then a spasm convulsed her features.

"Hurt very much?" Don asked, wadding up his handkerchief and holding it against the wound.

Gay nodded.

"Lie still," Don begged in an unsteady voice.

Gay's wide-open eyes left the stars and came to his face.

"Want to tell you how it happened. Coming through the gate my rifle caught and I bent over . . . . Don, will you keep my dogs and horses?" Her hand went out, seeking his. "No one will ever know what loving them and having them love me has meant . . . . since Dad died. I couldn't bear anyone to have them who didn't love them as I do."

Her eyes wandered about the room until they found a dog, then rested upon it. She lay against the pillows, a dazed child. Life had been too hard and hasty with her. There were things she would have liked, that she should have had, but there had been no time to find out what they were, though she had felt want of them aching in her being.

"You shan't die!" Don said fiercely.

She did not answer for a moment, then said, with a deep sigh: "Tired!"

Kama-san began crying audibly, as though understanding that cry. Don grasped Gay's fingers. This girl was part of him, molded in another shape but the substance was the same. Life should not wrest her from him! She was his to care for, protect and love. At the moment they seemed to be the only two people in the world, invisible threads spun between them.

"Don't leave me," Gay said faintly. "I can be brave as long as I hold your hand. When I'm with you——"

"I won't leave you, dear. I'll never leave you again," Don said, speaking like a man in a dream.

Travers entered.

"The doctor will be here shortly," he announced, "and is bringing a nurse."

The cook arrived with ice and towels and, with Travers and the Japanese, helped Don wash and dress the wound temporarily. Gay lay with her eyes closed while they worked. Once she winced and Don's hands shook violently.

"Hurt?" he asked, mechanically.

"A little. Wipe my face, it's all wet."

The muscles in Don's throat contracted. Her words recalled the morning when Vixen had been run over. In his ears sounded again the thin, piercing cry of the hurt dog as the car lurched through the rut, a cry with centuries of pain behind it and the age-long terror of small things helpless

before the onslaugh of great. Taking out his handkerchief
he gently wiped her forehead and the hollows under her
closed eyes. When the wound was dressed, she opened them.

"Hold my hand, Don," she said in a ghost of a voice.

"I'm holding it, Gay."

"Hold it harder, so I can feel it. And don't leave me.
. . ." Her eyelids fluttered down like tired birds, hiding
agony in the dark pupils. For an instant she lay so white and
still on the pillows that Don thought she had gone, then she
shifted a little and his heart resumed its hurried beating. He
roused himself from his egotism of despair and instructed the
waiting men to unsaddle and feed the horses. Hearing, Gay
smiled without opening her eyes. Travers walked to the
window.

"Don——"

"Yes, Gay?"

"It's beginning to hurt dreadfully, all down my arm and
in my side and shoulder."

"Get some whisky, Ernesto."

The old man walked to the sideboard.

"Lift me a little."

Don slipped an arm behind her head and it slid into the
hollow of his shoulder. Rigidity paralyzed the muscles of his
body for an instant. Gay opened her eyes and looked up at
him and they sat together motionless, like two creatures
caught in the same vast intangible snare. The night seemed
unreal despite the fact that men worked about the stables and
the occasional flash of a lantern passed across the lawn. A
cock crowed from far away.

Don looked at Gay's head, resting like a bright flower

against his neck, and in his being strange forces waked and warred. He felt echoes of great voices long silenced, cries of vast strange beasts which had once dragged their weight across the earth, the silent, sullen strivings of creatures wrestling in slime, the tyranny of life stirring in the womb, the upward push of spears of grass thrilling to sun and dew, and the magnificent pageant marching yearly through the jade-green temples of opening bud and leaf.

"Don."

"Yes?"

"Don't look so unhappy," she begged, watching him with pain-glazed eyes.

"I can't let you go, Gay; I love you!" The words were wrenched from him by a force greater than his own will.

"Don, say it—again. I must hear."

A thrill like white-hot fire, of pain, of rapture and unbelief, pierced Don, and he knew that in the scheme of things there are blessings undreamed of by man that must come with a shock of surprise, showing him the faultiness of what he had thought were perhaps his most magnificent imaginings. He was conscious, in a deep way, of the girl beside him, who seemed indissolubly linked with him to the trees growing in the adjacent forest, unobtrusive, majestic, standing with roots planted deeply in the earth.

"I love you, Gay. I've loved you in every beautiful thing I've ever seen. Since yesterday I've wanted more than I've ever wanted anything in my life to ask you to be my wife, but I felt, because I'm as I am, that I shouldn't, that I hadn't the right to speak. But this," he indicated her wound, "got me off my guard."

"Nice gun," Gay whispered so low that he could hardly hear her, but he felt the vibrations of her words in his body. "If I—had died—before you told me, I could never have forgiven—God! Kiss me, Don."

She looked up and there was no mistaking what was in her eyes. The whole love of her being was his; he had miraculously filled the place of Nature and her love of helpless creatures and at the same time deepened both. All the clean instincts of love, the beauty of passion, the forgetfulness of self which creates self, the crying of the spirit from its marble chalice of flesh, the wistful ascending answer of flesh to spirit, was looking at him from the ivory oval of her face.

Don had always loved normal things. He was not one of those persons set apart by the strange aloofness of genius whose soul burns with a wild light instead of the steady glow of a hearth-fire. He was an ordinary man loving normal, ordinary things, for in those very things were all the glory and wonder of the earth. For an instant he passed into a region where self had no existence. His whole soul was intent upon Gay, to whom he had given all the stored treasures of his heart. Then he bent and kissed her, as a man kisses the woman he loves when he knows it may be for the last time, long and close, with a desperation of love that feels frustrated by the very lips it is touching, as though the flesh got between the fusion of souls.

"You've let me out of prison, Gay," Don said, when he lifted his head. "You've unlocked the door that sets me free ——" His voice broke.

A tiny smile fluttered about Gay's white, quivering lips. "Happy," she whispered, "and—scared."

"Scared of what, Gay?" Don asked, quickly grasping her hand.

"Tell the doctor to try hard. I wasn't afraid of dying before, but I am now. I don't want to; I want to stay with you."

"You shall!" Don cried. "Nothing shall take you from me." He stared intently at her small fingers locked into his.

"What are you thinking about so fiercely?"

"About you. I'm thinking, Gay, that as soon as the doctor has fixed you up we'll get married. That will give me the right to stay with you, to take care of you. I won't let you go, I won't leave you now that I know you love me. They," he looked out of the wide open door as though addressing the great forces lurking in the universe, "can have everything else, but not you!"

Tears slid down the girl's cheeks and her lips moved silently. Don bent closer, thinking that she was talking to him, then heard her murmuring:

"Thank you, God! Oh, thank you, thank you!"

CHAPTER XIII

TRAVERS pulled up the collar of his coat and sat back in the car. He was tired and cold. The false dawn was beginning to quicken the east and great planets blazed above the solemn slopes of Haleakala. It had taken the better part of the night to wake the city clerk, get a special license issued, and rouse the parson. Keoke, the clerk, being Polynesian, had evinced no surprise when Travers walked in.

"Sure, if Don Garrison like marry quick with Gay I fix up everything. He fine fella. But take little time," he had said, removing his pajamas while Travers was still talking.

Keoke sat in front with the driver, his brown ears just visible above the rolled neck of his sweater. The Reverend Doremus, seated beside Travers, looked mildewed and sleepy and kept repeating under his breath: "A most extraordinary business."

His murmurings annoyed Travers, whose nerves were on edge. Slowly, sacredly, light opened the sea. Venus shrank from a golden pool to a golden point, the mountain assumed vaster proportions, trees looked taller and a solemn presence seemed to crouch in each one, and the grass, gray and weighted with dew, appeared to have been tramped and retramped by invisible feet. The hour was gravid with the future.

He wondered what the doctor's verdict had been in regard to Gay, and how Glenn was progressing. When they drove into the garden he instructed his companions to wait and entered the house alone. The doctor, a harried little man, was just coming out of Gay's room. He looked tired and worried, and his overcoat flapped irritably about his knees.

"How is she?" Travers asked.

"So-so. If no complications develop within the next thirty-six hours she'll pull through. She's got a splendid constitution and the grit of a man. Nasty accident, though. The bullet grazed the top of her lung, tearing the tissue, and lodged under the shoulder-blade. The nerves and ligaments are torn and will affect the use of her left arm for a while. It was a ticklish business removing the bullet. It'll be ages before she can take any more trips up the mountain. I had to give her chloroform finally. She's about out of it. I'm going to run around and see Glenn; the nurse phoned for me about fifteen minutes ago. I'll come up here about noon. If I should be needed before that, phone me at the office."

His rough coat gave a vindictive flounce as he went out and yet he was a kindly man. Travers wondered how many island secrets he guarded behind his rather unprepossessing exterior, then started reluctantly toward Gay's room. He dreaded seeing her. He tapped on the door and after an instant the nurse opened it.

Don was seated at the bedside holding Gay's hand. Her eyes were closed and she looked diminished, hardly larger than a child in the clean white bed. Her wild, charming hair was brushed back tidily, but one strand of it lay like a golden flame against her cheek. Travers heard the faint regular hush of her breathing. Could there be better news than knowing she was asleep, breathing like a baby? Then

232

her eyes were wide open and staring at him. They wished to say something; queer things moved in the dilated pupils; the memory of pain and terror. Then she looked at Don and Travers understood. She was terrified that she might die, and, dying, be robbed of Don. Her face was gray and drawn, but there was a gallant quality to her bright head, flung back against the pillow. The nurse crossed the room quickly and bent over her patient, her starched white uniform crackling pleasantly.

"Get everything fixed up, Ernesto?" Don asked.

"Keoke and Doremus are waiting outside."

Bending over, Don spoke to Gay in a low voice and she made a slight, assenting movement with her head.

"Tell them to come in, Ernesto, will you?" Don said.

The old man nodded; he did not trust his voice sufficiently to reply. Don looked as though during the hours of the night he had been bled by a ruthless surgeon. Travers retraced his steps. Daylight was beginning to creep timidly through the house. He noticed a dog curled up on the couch where Gay had lain. From the kitchen came the murmur of lowered voices talking in Japanese. Going to the door, he signaled to the men waiting on the terrace. The Hawaiian tiptoed up the steps like a huge concerned boy and asked softly:

"How the little girl?"

"All right," Travers answered.

When they entered Gay's room Don was standing by the bed leaning on one cane. The nurse waited on the opposite side of the bed with a professional, detached air. Walking forward, Travers placed his hand on the back of a chair, noticing that day had come, stealing over the island with mysterious vitality, edging everything with gold.

Keoke crossed the room, license in hand, and Don felt mechanically for the fountain-pen he carried in his breast pocket. He looked like a man lost in a dream and groping to wake.

"Think you can manage to sign, Gay?" he asked.

"If you hold my hand."

Keoke picked up a book off the bedside table and placing the paper on it handed it to Don. He stared at it for an instant, collected himself and sat down. Taking Gay's fingers in his, he placed them upon the correct spot and her hand dragged slowly over the paper, like a winged bird, forming the letters of her name. When she was finished Don scratched his own signature hurriedly beneath it as though mad to get the preliminaries done.

Watching him, Travers thought that a man never knows from what corner his luck will come. An accident had made this marriage possible which, otherwise, would never have been. Don handed the paper back to the Hawaiian and Doremus came forward, Prayer Book in hand. He paused to pull down his cuffs, then drew himself erect.

"Dearly beloved, we are gathered together——"

Everything seemed entirely unreal. Travers fixed his eyes on brittle sunshine glinting on the edge of small leaves quivering outside the open windows, and on horses moving about in the pasture in the unreserved way that animals have in the early hours before the restraint of human company is put upon them.

Then he forced himself to look at Don and Gay. The

234

thought came to the old man that in youth there was a deep mystery. In Don's and Gay's eyes, fastened upon each other, was a suggestion that they were seeing things which were still to come to pass, things of the future which fate entrusted to their keeping. Don's voice shook slightly as he repeated the words after the parson, and Gay's responses were inaudible whispers. Light streamed over the island and Travers thought it was fitting that these two should be married at break of day.

"The ring?" Doremus' voice startled Travers.

"I haven't one," Don said.

Mechanically Travers removed an emerald he always wore on his little finger and held it out. Don looked at him gratefully, but Travers was shocked at the coldness of Don's hand when it touched his.

Dreams, clouds, faces, mists, phantoms, Travers thought. The only thing which seemed real was his ring. He had bought it in Delhi and remembered having bargained shamelessly for it. In those days he had not known John Garrison, and John's sons had not been born.

"For richer, for poorer, for better, for worse, to love, honor and cherish until death do ye part."

Travers moved sharply, resenting the last. When the blessing had been given Don seated himself, looking as if he had reached the limit of his endurance. Some one spoke and Travers found himself signing as the first witness; he fancied the nurse was the other. He felt tired and his mind was fogged.

"Well, everykind fix up, better you get well quick now,

little girl," Keoke said, roguishly, restoring the moment to normal.

Gay smiled weakly, and reaching out Don possessed himself of her hand. Travers escorted the men to the living-room and crossing to the sideboard took the stopper out of a cutglass decanter of whisky.

"Like a drink, any one?" he asked, turning to his companions.

"Thanks, I don't," Doremus said.

"Hell, I do," Travers retorted, looking at the new day walking bravely over the island. He heard the infinitesimal rustle of new leaves unfolding, and felt the faint stir of the earth waking to the sun.

"I take a little drink, too," Keoke said, coming forward. "Better us make a little aloha for the marry fellas. Bring good luck."

Don walked through the living-room and paused in the doorway to look at the mountain; the afternoon was fading, crouching in remote valleys and hesitating on the hills. An immense peace had descended upon him. He no longer questioned life, he accepted it, for during the hours of that day it had held him by the hand and its hand had been Gay's. He had spent hours in her room, stretched in a chaise-longue which the nurse drew near the bed. He was conscious of Gay even when he dozed, but it seemed impossible that she was his wife. When the doctor called at noon he roused himself, learned that she was progressing, then slept as he had not slept since he came home.

He breathed deep of the fragrant evening, then went to

Gay's room. She was sleeping, her head turned sidewise against the pillow, and the nurse smiled from her post.

"She's resting nicely, Mr. Garrison, and hasn't the slightest vestige of a temperature."

"I'll sit with her and you go and have your dinner."

The woman rose and the faint professional crackle of her uniform soothed Don, reminding him of dogs pushing through dry brush. Seating himself, he laid his canes on the floor, and watched the quiet passing of the evening through the open windows.

Piled clouds, like splendid gods, marched overhead, and a faint breeze, like a quick, cold kiss, came from the forests, whispering that the deeper sorrow carved into a person's being, the more joy it could contain. For years he had walked in loneliness, doubting, fighting the forces ranged against him, and life had come to a standstill; now he was going forward again.

He watched Sera feeding the horses and Kama-san watering the vegetable garden. The day melted into a blue twilight that gradually blurred the outlines of the island. Looking at Gay in her deep sleep, he tried to realize what this unexpected turn of events would mean in his subsequent life. He who had been lonely would never be lonely again; and this girl, who had fought her way since she was fifteen, would have him, henceforth, as her protector. She was his, destined to him as he had been destined to her, since the beginning of time. For an instant life was set in a glory of fire.

Don's face at all times suggested strength, but sitting in the twilight this was more noticeable than ever. It was transfigured with a manliness that had the fervor, the glowing

237

vigor of a glory that had suddenly become aware of itself.

A breeze came through the windows, loaded with the rich fragrances of the earth, like a secret messenger whispering of the future. When he took Gay back to the ranch his real life would begin. All the rest had been a preparation for it. He was glad; he thanked God that his past years had been empty of joy and robbed of ordinary pleasures. He was grateful that he had come to maturity without knowing love. It seemed to him that in ordinary cases to love early was almost pitiful, a catastrophe, an experience for which the soul was not ready and could not appreciate to the full.

Gay stirred slightly and he gathered her hand, lying palm uppermost on the coverlet, into his, but his touch did not disturb her. Looking at her quiet face he called around him the vast congregation of his past sorrows, blessed them and bade them depart. He was conscious of kinship with the angels, because he was aware that he was fulfilling his divine mission at last. Thousands of years ago men had been told to love one another. He had fancied he loved his fellow beings, but realized that he had not really known the meaning of the word until Gay had whispered: "If I had died before you told me you loved me——" Now, it seemed a blasphemy to finish her sentence even in his mind.

For him all things had fallen into order: stars and men, silent, growing green things, seas and mountains, formed a complete circle.

Dark had come and out of the window the two stars in Scorpio's tail burned like bright eyes watching him through the tree-tops. Then he saw other stars here and there in the heavens. He had often watched stars and known the longings and almost terrible aspirations they wake in watchers, but they looked different tonight, nearer the earth, brighter, more living, like strange tenderness made visible and peopling the night with vast sympathy.

The nurse returned and placed a small night light on the table, shading it carefully.

"Don't you want to go and get something to eat, Mr. Garrison?" she asked.

"I'm not hungry."

"Then I'll lie down in the next room for a while and get some sleep. Wake me about midnight."

When the woman had gone Don stretched out on the chaise-longue. Peace stole into him, part of the vast night spreading over the island, and the voice of the wind wandering over the forests, pastures and ploughed fields whispered softly outside the windows. The thin, blue notes of a samisen wandered down eerily from some Japanese house; horses moved about the pastures as they grazed; and a dog came in and curled up on a rug, sighing contentedly.

Don's mind went to Glenn; Travers was with him. Then he realized that Gay's eyes were open. She was looking at him without wonder, as though expecting him to be there, and warmth, which was life-giving, permeated him.

"Want something, Gay?"

"Get Vixen and bring her in here with us," she whispered.

He smiled and rose, went out and found the dog and got the cook to bring her in.

"Put her on the foot of my bed," Gay directed.

The Japanese obeyed, smiled and withdrew. Don bent

down and touched the little thing gently on the head, then reseated himself.

"Shoulder hurt, Gay?" he asked, passing his fingers through her hair.

She shook her head.

"I've been lying here with my eyes shut, thinking and thinking," she said, in a low, happy voice.

"So have I."

Their smiles met.

"I used to be afraid to think, but I won't be afraid any more. I was thinking about when we go over to the ranch. All my animals and people can go with us, can't they, Don?"

"Of course, Gay."

"And don't let's sell this little house—I love it. Let's keep it to come to sometimes like Dad and I used to. I feel," her eyes rested upon him, "as if I had found Dad, and more. I always forget that he isn't here and when beautiful and exciting things happen I start to tell him about them, like I've been wanting to tell him about us."

Don's eyes dimmed.

"Thank you, Gay," he said, and bending, kissed her.

Her fingers worked deeper into his, like a confident and trusting child's, and he knew that the supreme adventure for man is woman, and for woman, man. In finding each other, he and Gay touched the ultimate and became part of the earth which lived on forever. Too often the grave, majestic meeting of the sexes, holding as it does the golden pageantry of the future, is regarded simply as the satisfaction of appetite, but Don, who had lived worshiping inviolate Nature, appreciated its deeper significance. From being outcast and set aside, he now belonged to the happy and companionable company of men who work, marry, bring up children, girls like lilies and boys like blades, and then, passing the standard of race to younger hands to carry on, in the full knowledge of the glory of fulfilled days, lay down their heads on the pillow of endless sleep.

They sat, with locked hands, talking softly, marveling at the fate which had been coming to them through the years, planning as simply as children for the days which were to come.

"Nothing matters now, Don, does it?" Gay whispered . . . . "Even pineapples. . . ." Her voice rippled into weak laughter.

His eyes lighted and he raised her hand to his lips and kissed it.

"Yes, even pineapples are beautiful," he replied.

Gay lay very still, her eyes fixed on his face.

"Want something, darling?" he asked.

"Water; I'm hot."

The nurse entered and fetching a glass held it to Gay's lips. Don thought he saw the woman frown slightly as she assisted the girl to drink it, and his heart turned over with fear. He computed hastily: the doctor had declared that if there were no complications within thirty-six hours. . . . It was nearing thirty.

"Is she all right?" he asked, in smothered tones.

"She has a slight temperature."

"I'm all right," Gay announced from her pillow. "I heard the doctor talking last night. He said that my lungs might fill up with water because the bullet passed through the top of one, tearing the tissue, but they won't. We've been talking too much."

Don caught her hand tighter, pressing his palm against hers with tenderness, admiration and terror. This girl had a soul as strong and brave as a tree's, but her assertion was like a challenge flung to listening, jealous gods peopling the starry darkness. For himself, he did not fear or resent death; to die was only to become part of the earth which persisted forever, but to lose Gay . . . . after getting her so miraculously!

The nurse got the thermometer and stood with it in her hand, waiting for the effect of the water to wear off before taking Gay's temperature. She smiled at the pair while she chatted, then glanced at the clock and put the slender, crystal tube into Gay's mouth. It seemed eons to Don until she removed it.

"A little over a hundred, Mrs. Garrison; nothing to worry about."

Surprise showed in Gay's eyes, then they went to Don's.

"I am Mrs. Garrison, now." She spoke thoughtfully. "Hold my hand, Don." He took it closely into his again and the girl smiled in her lighted way. "Happy," she whispered. "Love you. I feel safe and rich."

"No more talking," the nurse said, smiling, then her eyes filled with tears and she went out of the room. The look on their faces was made in the image of God.

CHAPTER XIV

MOLL stamped viciously on the accelerator and her long, glittering roadster swayed resentfully as it smoked up the rutted road leading past the Piholo cannery. Trucks loaded with pineapple tops, destined to be planted in newly ploughed fields, lumbered up the mountain. Usually a limp, expert, fearless driver, Moll swerved, avoiding them adroitly, missing hubs and banks by an inch, but she looked venomously at each new one ahead of her hindering her way, as if she felt they were directly responsible for the seas of fury tearing her. She clutched the wheel with hot hands, spinning it unnecessarily on turns, tearing to get it back, spurting the car when the way was clear, jamming on brakes when it was blocked.

When she got to the gate in the gulch she stopped the car within an inch of it, got out, flung the gate open and shot through without pausing to close it, indifferent to the fact that cows, grazing on the roadsides, belonging to homesteaders, might stray. Sighting Gay's house on the ridge, she flung back her head, raced the car into the garden and brought it to a throbbing stop.

For an instant she sat under the polished wheel thinking. She must collect herself, play her cards skilfully, but it would be difficult when her heart was a coal burning between her ribs. Getting out a vanity, she powdered carefully and considered her reflection. She had put on a simple white silk

243

sport dress which emphasized the youth of her slim body. The red leather jacket she wore over it was flung open; the collar standing out on each side framed her heart-shaped, exquisite face. A succession of flat red buttons marched diagonally across her dress, ending over her left breast, and a small red hat perched daringly on the side of her head, disclosing carefully waved hair. She looked like a white, red-tipped lily growing carelessly in a neglected garden waiting for some one to pick it.

Getting out, she looked around. Don's car was not in sight. He had probably gone to see Glenn. She would talk to Gay first and Don afterwards. If she were clever she might succeed in breaking up this marriage which, as yet, was no marriage. Gay was sensitive and proud. It would confound her if she were told that Don had declared that he never intended to marry, make Gay feel that this deed had been compassion instead of love. And Don must be made to feel that by his impulsive marriage he had robbed Gay of the boy who wanted to marry her. The fact that Gay had not returned young Carlton's love need not be mentioned. Anything would suffice so long as it would prevent them from getting together. She looked at the house, an expression of hatred frozen on her face. Gay had successfully robbed her of the man she had marked as hers and everything belonging to her was detestable. Entering, she stared about like a person invading enemy territory. She had never been under Gay's roof: she and the set she ran with had no time to waste on grubbers. Her eyes swept the appointments scornfully. Old stuff, which must have belonged to Gay's father.

Moll was blind to the charm and peace of the room, with its books, bowls of flowers, doors and windows opening onto sunny stretches of lawn. She saw only the shabbiness of the furniture. It was silly of people to despise, or to pretend to despise money, luxury, ease, splendor, furs, jewels, silks, the enchantment that the skin loves. With half or two-thirds of the ranch going into pineapples Glenn and Don would soon be among the richest men in the Islands. Money was a sword, it permitted its possessors to do what they pleased, gave people the courage of their checks. This marriage was entirely to Gay's advantage, aside from the fact that she had got Don!

She thrust one hand into the pocket of her jacket and stared at the floor. A step sounded and she flung around. The cook stood in the doorway and gave a polite little bow.

"Somekind you like, Missie?" he asked.

"I've come to ask how Miss Storm is. I'd like to see her."

"No Missie Storm any more; Mrs. Garrison," the cook corrected her with obvious satisfaction. "Before last night Mr. Don marry with Gay-san. I torr much glad Gay-san catch number one good soldier-mans. Lucky. And Mr. Don lucky too to get number one good girl like Gay-san. Me too much happy inside. Gay-san speak bime-by when she go ranch me, *wahine,* Kama-san, boys all go too. I proud work for Mr. Don. Sometime I speak please dress in soldier clothes so my boys can see. Bime-by my boys soldier for Japan Emperor. Me soldier before I come Hawaii. Soldier mans number one good."

Moll's face went blank. Even this Japanese appreciated

245

Don's extra dimension and flaunted Gay's good fortune in her face. Her eyes scanned the room rapidly.

"Mrs. Garrison," she uttered the word with difficulty, "is my friend. I want to see her."

"Sure, sure; I ask nurse s'pose can little time speak. Gay-san more good today, so Mr. Don go ranch look sick brother."

Moll nodded; her surmise as to Don's whereabouts had been correct. She would see Gay, then wait until he came back. The cook went to Gay's bedroom door and tapped upon it. The nurse opened it.

"One fren Gay-san stop, like little talk-talk. Can do?"

The woman hesitated and Moll came forward.

"I wonder if I could just slip in," she said. "I won't stay long."

"Mrs. Garrison is sleeping; if you care to wait until she wakes it won't hurt her to see you for a few minutes. She's better—in fact, doing nicely. If things keep on like this, in a few days she can be moved to the ranch. Mr. Garrison is eager to get her over there because his brother is very ill."

"I know," Moll replied. "I spend most of my time at the ranch. We are all friends."

"What name shall I tell Mrs. Garrison?" the woman asked.

"Just say Moll wants to see her and offer congratulations," the girl said carelessly.

The woman nodded and closed the door.

Moll stared at the floor then opening her purse took out a cigarette. All of a sudden Gay had become a person of consequence, because she was Don's wife! The cook, this

246

nurse, every one, stood about for her and would continue standing about. Her hands shook.

The Japanese lingered as if feeling responsible for the hospitality of the house.

"Anything you like?" he asked.

Moll glanced at the tiny diamond watch on her wrist. Eleven o'clock! Don would probably return about one to have lunch—with his wife!

"Get me a highball," she ordered, flinging herself into a long chair.

"Sure, sure," the man said, hurrying away.

She smoked with furious absent-mindedness for a minute, then crushed out her cigarette on a small marble-topped table standing near the chair. Snapping open her case, she selected another and lighted it, then stared at the long slope of the island framed by the open door. She blew out a cloud of smoke and watched it sucked out of a nearby window.

Her nerves were getting the best of her; she felt scattered. Waiting was torture, and she must wait while Gay slept! Her dry lips ravaged her cigarette. She had fallen in love with a stab and a flash. Two days ago it had been a great adventure, now it was plain, unadulterated hell. Because of a silly gun getting caught in a gate and going off, she had been robbed of Don, who, given time, she was convinced she could have got. He had felt his hold on himself slipping the night she had gone to see him; that was why he had been angry. Men like Don got angry when they were scared, angry with themselves. Recalling the expression on his face when she had thrown Gay's spur into the fire, her eyes grew thoughtful, then her hands tightened on the arms of her chair.

The cook came in with the highball and set it on the table. Moll reached for it and drank deeply, then relaxed, fortified by alcohol.

"You like sandwich?" the man asked. "One, two minute I can make."

"No, thanks; I've just finished breakfast," Moll replied, dismissing him.

She finished her drink and waited impatiently. She thought she heard a car coming up the hill and went to the door. She must see Gay before she talked to Don. The car passed and she glanced at her watch. Eleven-thirty! Hours seemed to have dragged by since she arrived. She looked at her roadster; then a thought came and she went out and honked the horn loudly and retraced her steps to the house. She could tell the nurse that she had gone for her purse and, reaching for it, had accidentally leaned on the horn. She waited and after a few minutes the door opened. Glibly she told her story.

"Mrs. Garrison says she will be glad to see you. Come in."

Moll walked in. Her eyes swept the room, taking stock of it. Beside the bed stood a small table with a bouquet of white gardenias upon it. Moll wondered if the flowers were Don's gift. She avoided looking at Gay for as long as she could, afraid that Gay might read the thoughts in her eyes.

She stood, one hand thrust in her coat pocket, noting details. There was a watercolor on one wall of a desert sunset, a simple thing of gray wastes of sage deepening to lavender near the flushed horizon; and opposite, another of an island rising precipitously from the sea. Both were signed with Travers' name. The dresser, the bed, were unpretentious, suitable for a child; probably both had been bought for Gay by her father when she returned from school. Then her hand clenched in her pocket. On the dresser lay a tie, carelessly, intimately. One of Don's which he had left or had forgotten. It brought the reality of Gay's marriage home as nothing else could have done. She pictured him sitting on the plain little seat brushing his hair before he had gone to see Glenn. She caught her breath and went forward. Gay held out her hand.

"Nice of you to come and see me, Moll."

Moll took the small brown hand into hers for an instant, then seated herself in the low rocker which the nurse had vacated.

"Mind if I smoke?" she asked carelessly.

"Of course not."

She chose a cigarette with unnecessary care and lighted it.

"Like one?" she inquired, without looking at Gay.

"You better not, Mrs. Garrison," the nurse warned. "It might make you cough and you must be careful of your lung for a while." Turning to Moll, she explained details. When she had finished talking Gay turned toward Moll and smiled.

"Silly of me to have an accident when I've handled guns for years. But it was dark and I was tired." Then her wan little face lighted. "But I'll always bless that bullet." She stared dreamily at the wall. "Funny how one little ball of lead could change a whole life, two lives, mine and Don's."

Moll bit her lower lip, thinking angrily that the accidental shot had changed the course of three lives, instead of two. She looked at the ring hanging loosely on Gay's fourth finger.

"That's Ernesto's," she said.

"I know," Gay replied. "He lent it to Don till he can buy another. I don't remember very much about being married. Everything was hazy because the doctor had to give me chloroform when he dug out the bullet. I'm glad it wasn't my right arm, because of my painting."

The memory of pain lingered in Gay's eyes, her hair was limp, her lips colorless, but her face was lighted for marvels. Moll ground out her cigarette in the tray placed on the table.

"Painting?" she said. "Do you still intend to keep on doing it?"

"Of course," Gay answered, amazed. "How could I stop?"

"But you don't have to earn your living now you are Mrs. Don Garrison." There was a grate in Moll's voice.

"I know, so I'll have more time for work. Don is full of plans for it. We talked most of last night."

The nurse walked over and smiled at the two girls.

"I think I'll take a walk in the sunshine and leave you to chat," she said. "You can stay," she smiled at Moll, "for twenty minutes. I'll come back when time is up."

Moll managed to nod carelessly, but she pulled off her hat, which of a sudden seemed too tight. She had exactly twenty minutes in which to accomplish what she had come to do. The door closed and Gay reached out and touched one of the gardenias.

"Like one, Moll?" she asked, pulling out a blossom. "Don brought them to me last night. You know," her face grew thoughtful, "I simply can't realize that I'm married to him. I didn't even know that he loved me, but when we were talking he told me that he'd loved me from the start. You can't imagine how it feels to me, because you have a father and mother, to have some one to love, to know there is some one I belong to. Since Dad died———" She wiped happy tears from her eyes. "Silly to cry," she said, apologetically, "but I feel so happy and rich."

Moll inspected the petals of the gardenia with a slightly unsteady forefinger and Gay, eager to talk, eager to have some one with whom to share her unexpected and recently found joy, went on: "It seems like a dream to me; everything. I can't realize that I won't have to take any more parties up the mountain, that all I have to do is to make Don happy, and paint. I'm bursting with ideas already." She laughed like an excited child. "Last night I couldn't sleep and Don and I talked and talked. He's going to let me use his father's bedroom for my studio, and he's given me Paniolo. He says that I'm to ride—for him." Her voice caught. "Poor Don!"

"Yes, poor Don!" Moll echoed, studying the white flower held between her fingers. She got up and walked to the window and stared at the garden for a minute. "You know, Gay," she said, keeping her back to the girl, "I feel I should tell you something."

"What?" Gay asked from the bed.

"I wouldn't tell you this," Moll said, choosing her words carefully, "if you hadn't said what you did about not giving up your painting. That clears the way. . . . The night before you got hurt I was up at the ranch and Don and I had a long talk. You know, I love him, too." She turned around and looked at Gay.

"I can't imagine any one who couldn't love Don," the girl said, slowly and thoughtfully.

"Well, I mean I love him the same way you do," Moll said sharply.

Gay looked at her amazed.

"But——" she began, "he isn't——"

"He *is* the sort of man I want to marry," Moll broke in; "and I told him so, and he said that he never wanted to marry, that marriage wasn't on the books for him. I accused him of loving you and——"

"And what?" Gay asked, faintly.

"He said he liked you, was sorry for you——" She stopped, cleverly letting Gay's mind finish the sentence.

Gay lay very still.

"I suppose you don't believe me," Moll cried. "Well, ask him what he did with the spur you gave him! When I heard that he was married to you I was sick, sick for him. You say that you love him; if you really do you will set him free. It can be done easily—you'll just have to say that marriage and a career won't mix. He's generous; he'll give you money so you can go to Paris and study." Gay made a faint protesting gesture. "I, I was crazy with jealousy. I thought he loved you when I wanted him to love me, and then, after we talked, I knew that I loved him more than I loved myself and whatever he wanted I wanted too." Walking back, she stared at the girl in the bed. "So I left, and if you really love him you'll leave too."

"I'm tired," Gay whispered. "I can't think."

"I suppose you'll cry and the nurse will be mad with me and say I've upset you. I don't care if I have. It's Don who matters."

"Yes," Gay said faintly. Her forehead was damp and she passed her fingers over it.

"I suppose you'll tell Don," Moll said scornfully.

Gay did not answer.

"Please, Moll, go away."

"I'm going," Moll snapped, picking up her hat. Walking over to the mirror, she put it on carefully, then turned around. "Now you're crying, I suppose."

"I'm not crying," Gay answered. "I'm——" Hearing a car coming up the hill, her voice died.

Moll glanced out of the window and, seeing Don's roadster, walked out of the room. Her heart was beating unevenly and her hands shook as she opened her purse and inspected herself afresh in the small mirror. Her face looked like a small white hatchet. She must get that expression off it! Drawing herself erect, she took a deep breath, got out a cigarette and lighted it, then crossed the room with casual indifference, timing her gait to arrive at the door just as Don entered.

"Hello," she said, halting.

Don glanced at her with quick suspicion.

"What are you doing here, Moll?" he asked a trifle shortly.

"Me? Why I came to see Gay and offer her my congratulations. You may not think a hell of a lot of me, but I can be a generous loser."

Her voice mocked him. "Sorry, Moll. It was decent of you to come up so soon. How is Gay?"

"She's a bit weepy. Don't look so alarmed. It's natural. She's beginning to realize——"

"What?" Don asked quickly.

"Why, what you've done by marrying her."

Don looked puzzled for a moment, then he got pale. Moll glanced at him, satisfied.

"You've got between her and the boy I told you about. She was all muddled up with pain and chloroform when you got the big idea of marrying her right off the bat."

Don looked at his canes. Moll watched him, mercilessly, noting the changing expression of his face. His years of lack of contact with the world had left his feelings unblunted, his sensitiveness was almost abnormal, that of a youth, alive to the tiniest whisper, set on fire by a word. To such a nature life in the world would be a perpetual torture. That which manifested by another man would have moved her to impatience and contempt, in Don woke other sensations.

"I," Don seemed to be speaking to himself, "forgot everything when she was hurt, except that I loved her, wanted to have the right to stay with her." He broke off, and threw back his head. "Did she say anything to you?"

Moll nodded and looked profound.

"You've smashed up her life," she declared, quiet with triumph at being able to deliver her dart. She flicked the ash off her cigarette and watched it make a fine, gray dust on the floor. "Now I suppose you'll go and tell her I told you and——"

"I shall do nothing of the sort," Don said, sharply. "There are other ways." He spoke thoughtfully.

With a swift stride Moll was beside him and laid her hand on his shoulder.

"Don."

"Yes?"

"I'm sorry I have to be the one to tell you and make you unhappy, but it's better, because in the end you would have found out and that would have made you unhappier." Her fingers tightened on his shoulder. She was thinking harder and faster than she had ever thought in her life. "I know you love Gay; it's all over you. . . ." She spoke reluctantly, as if hating to admit it. "Gay's upset and weak. Of course, I can't help being jealous of her, but I don't hate her. Be careful what you do and say. She's tender-hearted; it will hurt her to know she's hurt you. She isn't ready yet for——"

Don shook Moll's hand off his shoulder.

"I don't believe you," he said. "I know that Gay loves me."

Moll laughed.

"Gay'd die rather than have anything hurt, even mice and frogs, and rather than hurt you she'd pretend——"

Don stood, his eyes on the floor, thinking deeply; then the expression came to his face of a person who has passed into a region where self has no existence. Moll watched him, satisfied. That had been the right tack. . . .

"Yes, Gay is like that. I was headlong." He spoke heavily. "But I'm not a complete fool. There will be time enough after we are back at the ranch for me to figure a way out for her."

Moll glanced at him sharply. There was danger in delay, but greater danger having them talk at once; she might get found out. Delay would have to be chanced. Each feeling as they did, as she had made them feel, she thought triumphantly, the restraint between them would grow, steadily parting them.

"Well," she announced, "I must get along. You probably hate me, but one of these days you will appreciate that I was a real friend when I told you the truth."

Don did not seem to hear. Moll looked at him; he was eating out his heart, jealous of what he did not know of Gay's life. Then, in a second, with an effort that he superbly hid from Moll's eyes, he was calm.

"You need not be afraid," he said stiffly, "that I will betray Gay's confidence. I shall not, out of consideration for her." He drew himself erect with a quaint formal gesture.

It maddened Moll, emphasizing again his difference, enhancing his desirability. All at once she was terrified at the thought of leaving them alone lest they might still find their way to each other. Don loved Gay with all of him, and, if she suspected it, it was not to be thought that she could refrain from loving him in return.

She looked out of the door at the long, insolent shape of her roadster, brutally reflecting sunlight pouring down on glittering hood and fenders. Then her eyes went back to Don. A torment of heat came over her and she opened and shut her purse nervously.

She experienced not the least compunction at trying to separate a man from the woman he loved, and who, she suspected, loved, or could love him. The mode of her life

had made her utterly selfish. She felt competent to intro-
duce Don to the magic mysteries of love as Gay never could;
but fear, which she hated and resented, stole over her, for she
knew that Don and Gay had an attraction for each other
which was greater, which went beyond the mere magnetism
of the flesh. That damnable enchantment she could not
fight, for she had no experience with the things of the soul.

Moll never deluded herself, even to spare herself, and she
was no longer playing; she was deeply and terribly in love
and the chances were that she would lose Don to Gay if the
flimsy barrier that she had erected between them should col-
lapse. She felt as though she were being devoured by a
cancer of jealousy and hate because Gay possessed some
elusive and intangible quality that she and her kind lacked.
It was there and had to be reckoned with. She and the girls
she had run with aroused men's passions, but Gay's appeal,
beyond that of the flesh, jumped at men's hearts, at Don's
heart anyway. She looked venomously at him standing so
still, thinking of what?

Was he picturing what life with Gay might have been
when he took her back to the ranch, had she not spoken,
killing all his hopes of ever possessing her love? Moll looked
at him from under her lashes and a slow flood of scarlet rushed
to the roots of his hair, then ebbed away, leaving his face
ghastly. He moved, perhaps trying to free himself of the
guilt of his own hasty act.

Moll stared at the toe of her shoe, thinking intensely.
Outside, sunlight poured healingly on the earth, but the
room, instead of being a place of peace, had become a place of
tumult, the silent tumult which has its home in human souls.

CHAPTER XV

GAY slipped her bathrobe over her pajamas and tied it tightly about her. Wind fingered the corners of the house speculatively, then went away into the darkness. Bending down, she picked Vixen up off the rug and going over to a couch sat down among the pillows piling it. A little shiver ran through her. Her eyes, luminous and wistful, too large for her thin face, wandered thoughtfully over the room. She still felt strange and a little lonely in it, despite the fact that her own pictures hung on the walls and her own books lined the cases under the windows.

Something must be done and it looked as if she were going to have to be the one to do it. Perhaps it was the worry of Glenn's illness that made Don strange and abstracted, or had Moll told the truth when she declared that Don had stated that he had no intention of ever getting married? Remembering the days and nights after she had been hurt she could not believe it. He had been tenderness, love personified, but since coming to the ranch a barrier had risen between them. She hugged the dog closer for comfort and it dug its head against her arm.

Her years of grinding work, pressed to the very soil itself, had compelled her to look life in the face. If Don had been swept away by an impulse of pity, and people were swept away, if he regretted having married her, it was her duty to free him. Emptiness filled her at the supposition. She loved

258

him. Who could help loving him? But loving him she was responsible for his happiness and if he would be happier with her out of his life she must go.

She sat like a tall thoughtful child, one arm cuddling the dog, the other propped on one knee, cupping her chin. Her great gray eyes mechanically followed the lines of a chair, but her heart ached in a dull way. She felt as she had felt after her father died, abandoned by life. She had fancied when she found Don, or when Don had found her, that they had turned into the straight and would go to the finish together, like horses racing gloriously, neck and neck. A breath of wind, like a ghostly benediction, came in the open windows, but she felt encompassed on all sides by the old house. Its roof spread patiently, protectingly, over Glenn and his nurse, over Ernesto, over Morse's and Sue's empty, waiting rooms, over Don sitting alone in his wing, reading, thinking, wishing perhaps. . . .

Her eyes grew deep and thoughtful and she pushed back her hair. It was cowardly postponing things; she had never been guilty of cowardice before, but she shrank from making the move which might bring the slender, recently found happiness she had briefly known, tumbling about her. Sportsmanship, fair play, demanded that she go to Don, not as a woman, but as a fellow human, and ask him outright if he regretted marrying her. She pressed her cold hands against the dog's little body for warmth.

There were so many factors which might account for Don's attitude of distant aloofness—her recent accident, Glenn's condition, the feeling of suspense and unrest which pervaded the house. Don had an immense consideration for others

259

and would be likely to subordinate or put his own feelings aside rather than . . .

She threw up her chin. She was cheating, to spare herself! If people loved each other trouble swept them together rather than apart. She slid the little dog gently into the cushions and, rising, tightened her bathrobe a second time determinedly about her, then walking to the window stared at the stars. Vixen hopped off the couch and followed her, holding her injured back leg up daintily. Gay swooped down and gathered the bitch into her arms.

"Life never lets some people off anything," she whispered, pressing her cheek against the dog's head. "I might as well go and get it over. I can stand knowing—it's not knowledge that kills." She stared with dry, tearless eyes at the great dark, kissed the dog and put it down. Thrusting her fingers through her hair she walked to the dresser, and picked up an enlarged, framed snapshot of Don which she had filched from one of the guest rooms, Don astride of a splendid horse, making a spectacular run down the polo field toward a goal. His lean hard body bent eagerly forward, and his body and the horse's were one, charged with force, joy and rhythm. Her throat ached. Don was another person whom life never let off anything! The realization made her feel close to him and she thought to herself: "It isn't I that matters; it's love; not my suffering which must be eased, but love which must be served."

Replacing the photograph on the bureau, she straightened up, jerked open a drawer and commenced searching for a brooch to pin her robe across her breast. With chilly fingers she went through a small box filled with simple odds and ends of jewelry, then her body tensed, seeing the little gold spur. Picking it up she looked at it, then her fingers closed over it so tightly that it wounded her palm. Thrusting it into the pocket of her bathrobe, she started for the door.

When she got to Don's room she hesitated for the ghost of an instant, then rapped smartly.

"Come in," Don's voice called.

Grasping the cold knob, she turned it resolutely, but hesitated on the threshold like a shy boy. She lifted her face slightly and the expression upon it was strange, searching, half frightened. Don looked astounded when he saw her. Reaching for his canes he rose.

Gay noticed a whisky bottle and a glass on the table beside the chair in which he had been sitting and a pang pierced her. He was unhappy, he was trying to get away from something. Compassion filled her. He looked very tall in his kimono, very much the thoroughbred as he waited courteously for her to be seated, but his eyes had a strained expression as if he had difficulty focusing them.

"Don. . . ." She swallowed to ease the constriction in her throat. "May I come in for a few minutes? I want to talk to you." Her gaze met his resolutely, then her eyes brimmed with tears.

"Take a seat, Gay." He indicated a chair and waited, looking straight at her, and there was something dominating in his expression, as though he were resentful or defiant of what she might be thinking or feeling at finding him drinking alone. For an instant the combative part of her nature was roused by his challenging glance, then she realized he was ashamed of what he had been doing and her spirit rushed to his, to protect it from pain.

"Don—"

"Yes, Gay?"

"Could I have a drink before I begin talking? What I have to say is hard."

The expression of his face softened and he gave her a quick, grateful look.

"You're a brick, Gay. I know you don't want a drink; you're just saying so to make me feel better."

The light on the reading table fell on her face and form, emphasizing its soft outline, fair coloring, slender delicacy and the brooding of the wide gray eyes.

"Please sit down, Don," she said. "I want to sit on the floor near you. It'll be easier for me to talk." Taking a cushion from a nearby chair Gay dropped it on the rug. Don reseated himself and pushed the bottle away. Of a sudden Gay felt very young, helpless and frightened. She looked out of the window.

"Surely, Gay," Don said gently, "you must realize that you can say anything you want to me."

Thrusting her hand into her pocket, she gripped the spur. Silence waited in the room and she and Don seemed to cower beneath a hand lifted and ready to strike them. Multitudinous soft noises came from the dark garden: a sudden gust of wind streaming through old driven trees, leaves falling, birds stirring as they took firmer hold of swaying boughs. Two limbs of a eucalyptus, bent by *kona* gales, creaked and groaned faintly as bole wore upon bole, wounding each other every time they moved. The night seemed filled with ar-

cades and avenues, leading nowhere. Gay moved closer to
Don and he took hold of her hand and they sat, two incarna-
tions of the troubled earth, sentient for an instant.

"Like a smoke?" Don asked.

She nodded abstractedly and accepted the cigarette he
handed her. Bending over, he struck a match and the tiny
flame illuminated his face lighted by a curious, still smile that
brought sudden tears to her eyes. The smile was the lone-
liest, most hopeless thing she had ever seen in her life, that of
a man who smiles because there is nothing else left to do.
She tilted back her head, trying to tip the tears back into her
eyes, but one escaped, rolled off her cheek and made a splash
on the floor. Doubling up her small fist she struck the mark
angrily.

"That's the old fight," Don said, admiringly, but his voice
shook slightly, uttering the words she had spoken to him the
morning he had gone out to ride. When she failed to command her vocal chords sufficiently to use them, he pressed
her hand. "I think I know what you are trying to tell me,
Gay, and it's all right. If——"

"Wait," she commanded, kneading her shin nervously
with her free hand. Her face was stern, her eyes serious.
It seemed impossible for one so young to be so resolute. She
sat like a straight boy, erect on the cushion, making no gesture of womanhood. To her way of thinking that would not
have been fair. She must meet men on their own ground
and keep herself on that ground without showing the effort
she made. To trade on her youth, sex, or appeal in a matter
so vital would be contemptible.

"Gay, if it hurts you too much to have to tell me, you

don't need to, but," he indicated the bottle with a slight, contemptuous gesture, "I know you are generous enough to make allowances for my doing this. You see, Moll told me before I ever asked you to marry me, but when you were hurt I forgot everything except———"

"What did Moll tell you?" Gay asked, her eyes leaping to his.

"Why," Don hesitated, "that there was a young fellow you loved and who loved you, as I do. The other day when she came to your place she reminded me of it and said———"

"There isn't any one I love, except you," Gay interrupted, scrambling to her knees and grasping him by the arms. "There was a boy from Honolulu last summer whom I took up the mountain in one of my parties and he fell in love with me and begged me to marry him. He was nice, but I didn't love him that way, so I couldn't." Her voice caught.

Don made a helpless gesture and she caught his hand and held it tightly.

"Because of Moll," he said, "I've been in Hell thinking that you———"

"Me, too," Gay cried. "You see, she told me———"

"What in God's name did she tell you?" Don asked indignantly.

"That you—that you told her," Gay's eyes closed, "that you never intended, never wanted to marry and I thought———" She could not go on.

"What did you think, Gay?" Don asked, drawing her closer.

"I thought that you married me because you were sorry for me and not because you loved me. I couldn't," she kept

264

HAWAIIAN HARVEST

her face averted, "I don't want love which isn't given with both hands."

"But how could you imagine, for an instant, how couldn't you know that I love you as I've never loved any one or anything in my life?" Don asked, drawing her between his knees.

Gay bit her lip, then looked into his eyes.

"Moll said that when she talked to you she thought that you loved me instead of her——"

"Which was correct," Don interrupted.

"And then, when she accused you of it, to prove you didn't care for me you threw——"

Don grasped her fiercely by the shoulders. Glancing up, she was shocked by the expression on his face. It was livid, distorted with indignation and anger.

"Don't look like that," she whispered, frantically.

"I can't help it, Gay," Don said, his voice imperceptibly shaking. "I'm thinking that if you hadn't been game enough to come to me, like the little straight shooter you are, I'd have lost you; we would have lost each other simply because Moll——" He thrust his hand into the breast pocket of his pajamas and brought out a tiny lump of gold. "That's all that's left of it after she threw it into the fire, but I've been hanging onto it hard because——"

With a laugh verging on tears Gay dug her hand into the pocket of her bathrobe.

"I had to hang onto mine too," she said, showing it, her cameo face aglow. "I wanted to go to sleep, but I couldn't. I've been wanting to talk to you for days." She looked up,

then remarked, as an afterthought, "You can't blame Moll
for wanting to fight for you."

"I'm not much to fight for, Gay," Don said, gazing down
at her. Then seeing the expression in her eyes, fixed on his,
a wild red tide of color ran up to the roots of his hair. "Gay!"

"Yes?"

"Are your eyes telling me the truth? Do I mean all that
to you?"

She nodded.

"Then, Gay, let's realize, feel it all to the full." He
caught her to him with fierce tenderness, gathering her
against his shoulder. "Don't let's miss anything, now or
ever."

There was a deep breathing under his voice and he held
her closer, looking into her eyes as if trying to send all of
himself into her through them.

"I don't want to," Gay said; "I want it all!"

"Gay," a fleeting smile lighted Don's face briefly, "I'm
afraid you're a desperate character."

She lifted her face, delicate, eager, alive.

"I told you that first morning we talked that I had a devil
—too," she laughed, elfishly.

"Gay, you're gorgeous!" Don said. "But I wonder if it's
possible for you to realize what you are to me." There was
a throb in his voice which rose from the depths of him,
shaking him. "From the instant I met you I gave you all
that I had. You are everything beautiful, everything fine
———"

"And for me, you are everything that's brave and splen-

266

HAWAIIAN HARVEST

did," Gay whispered, laying her forehead against his heart with a sort of proud humility.

The purity in her voice and in her simple action dazzled Don like a flame shining suddenly out of all-enveloping darkness.

"I feel," Gay spoke on a held breath, "as if we were the only two people in the world, as if the earth and stars had been given to us. It frightens me. I feel as if we had no place big enough to put such a gift."

Don's body shook with the vehemence of the spirit confined within it; then with an effort he controlled his shaking, as though afraid that if he moved he might shatter the universe and all it contained. Her words made him understand, as few men do, how in a good woman the two streams of human love, that which implies the intense desire of the flesh and the mystical love which is absolutely purged of that desire, can flow the one into the other and mingle.

"Gay," he took her face between his hands and lifted it from his heart, "you make everything I have and am seem small and yet great. What does it mean?"

"Listen," she whispered, gently taking his hands from her face. He yielded to her at once, but she retained hold of him. "Listen—the garden, the island, the earth, talking to us." She tipped her head against his arm, her eyes fixed on the pulsing darkness outside.

Infinitesimal rustlings and whisperings of grass, shrubs and trees, the remote thrilling echo of the sea, the silence of the soil, which is a deep solemn murmur—too fine for human ears to hear—the murmur of growth, of preoccupation with

267

life and the future, mingled in a vast diapason, spreading over the earth.

"What do they say?" Don asked, after a long silence.

"They say," Gay looked up and the light on the table behind her spun quivering gold through her hair, "that you are great and I am great, because we love. They are telling us that no one is small who loves, no one bad, no one wrong— who really loves."

Moll got out of her roadster and after studying her reflection in the mirror of her vanity started along the path leading to the house. She was blind to the beauty of afternoon shadows lying among shrubs and trees. Passing the kitchen, she saw Ah Sam busying himself with tea things and, stopping, spoke to him through the window.

"Mr. Don and Miss Gay go ride on mountain, but Mrs. Morse stop s'pose you like speak."

Moll went into the house and waited in the living-room. A quarter of an hour passed and her smooth forehead was marred by a frown. Well, she would go and talk to Sue to kill time until Don and Gay returned. Going upstairs, she stopped at Sue's door.

"Sue."

"Come in, Moll."

Sue was lying on her chaise-longue, a copy of a moving picture magazine open on her lap.

"Oh, my deah," she cried, "isn't this picture of Billie Dove too sweet! I think she's just precious."

Moll glanced at the picture indifferently.

"Well," Sue asked, raising herself slightly on her pillows, "what are you up to?"

Moll seated herself in a chair and crossed her legs.

"Me? Oh, just snooping around. Ah Sam informed me that the young lovahs are out riding."

"They go out almost every day now."

"What do you mean, now?" Moll asked.

"Well, I mean since Gay's stronger we hardly see them except at dinner. They take lunch with them and usually breakfast upstairs."

"Alone or together?"

"I'm not sure; I'm usually asleep at that time. I think they have it with Ernesto in the end room that used to be their father's. Really, Moll," Sue said, plaintively, "the atmosphere of purity in this house is depressing. Ernesto works or goes off with Don and Gay, Glenn is jumpy as a cat and blew up yesterday when I suggested a party might revive things, said it was rottenly inconsiderate of me to even think of such a thing when Gay wasn't up to———"

"She's strong enough to go riding," Moll interrupted.

Sue nodded.

Moll leaned her head against the back of the chair and studied her image in the mirror across the room. She smiled, satisfied that her beauty put her in a class apart. She did not realize that, aside from differences in personality and coloring, she was cast in much the same mold as her mates, slim, smart girls who all danced with equal grace, read the same books, when they read any, discussed them in the same patter, girls who prefaced, ended and interjected almost every remark with "My deah" to express sympathy, ridicule, horror or amazement. They made a fetish of frankness and in an age of shrieking headlines were obliged to red ink remarks to get them noticed at all. Words, relegated by good taste to the Bible and dictionary, fell nonchalantly from their pretty lips. Their conversation was uninhibited, free, on occasion fanciful and often bald, but they were conversant in the arts of femininity which put them in another category than the previous generation of women who had produced them. When their hands met men's, they were not hands but electric currents; when they stood beside a man, they would somehow, without appearing to do so, fit their curves into his so that he was aware of the feel of a soft, slim side against his hard one.

Snapping open her case, Moll selected a cigarette and lighted it, and reaching out Sue helped herself to a smoke from the stand by her chair.

"You know," she said, languidly studying the blue wraiths drifting toward the window, "I have the most perfectly original idea. I must tell you about it. When Ran and I move back to our place I'm going to have one part of my garden Hawaiian, with nothing but bananas, gingers, ti, bamboo and taro planted in it. Won't it be perfectly sweet, deah?"

"Gal," Moll said scornfully, "all island gardens have those things growing in them. Your idea isn't original at all. I suppose you'll don a big hat and wander round in it feeling Marie-Antoinettish, or like one of those make-believe rustic ladies. I didn't come to discuss plants and gardens with you, but to get the latest dope on Don and Gay." Then a thought occurred to her. "Are you and Ran planning to move out?"

"There's nothing to stay for, is there, with Glenn off parties and the purity squad in command. I'm all for getting our place finished as fast as possible, but Ran isn't so hot about it, because he's scared that when he goes Glenn will switch over to——"

"Inside, Glenn switched over to Don the day he came home," Moll announced. "Can't fool me. He's yearning to wash his sins away in the River Jordan and walk in purity again with the rest of the aunts." She laughed mirthlessly. "Wonder what makes me so mad about Don when he's never really batted an eye in my direction. I may land him yet," her eyes rested meditatively on the ceiling, "if things continue as you report they have been up to date!"

Sue yawned.

"My deah, why go over all that? I simply can't figure what you see in him. Being married to him would be like having a corpse for a husband."

"Don't fool yourself. I size men up better than you do."

"If I were his wife he'd drive me to seducing a new man every night," Sue announced.

"You're haywire, Sue," Moll retorted, her foot swaying restlessly up and down. "If he were your husband you'd have nothing left to seduce any one with."

Sue looked unbelieving. Moll sat up as though she had been slapped.

"I tell you I'm right," she insisted. "I'd swap all the men I've ever known for Don, and I bet I wouldn't be the loser. Damn guns and Gays, anyway! I snuck in one day when Don was out and had a little visit with her; thought I might as well get in more dirty work and plant some T.N.T.

bombs around, but she only sat hugging her dog and looking at the garden."

"Gay's not so dumb."

"You're right she's not dumb; she's mum as a man about everything. You never know what she's thinking or feeling. I've never succeeded in busting through to the real her. After her father died, I used to ask her about her work— Mother said I must be nice—but she always turned me off and talked about something else."

Jumping up, Moll walked to the window.

"About time they were coming back for—tea!" she said.

"Oh, sit down!" Sue snapped. "Rushing around won't hurry them. You'll hear them when they come along the walk."

Moll flung herself into a new chair and for a while they discussed matters of common interest. Moll tried to calm herself, remembering Sue's repeated assertions, when questioned, that Don and Gay were established in separate rooms; but a fever of uneasiness filled her. Instinct convinced her that despite Gay's aloofness and elusiveness she was a flame, vital as those buried in the earth that she loved. At times, in pure self-disgust, she attempted to disparage Don to herself, but, above all things, Moll had the courage of honesty and knew that when she did so she was lying, thereby only cheating herself. Don was, and would continue to be, more man than any one of her vast acquaintance and, because he was the only thing that life had ever withheld, triply desirable.

She picked nervously at an infinitesimal piece of skin at the edge of a fingernail and, when she did not succeed in detaching it, bit it off.

"My deah, you make me laugh, getting all stewed up over Don! If you saw him as I do every night it would slay you. He's as formal as an ambassador with Gay."

"That's probably a bluff; their kind never give anything away. If I could see them together, when they didn't know any one was around, I'd know," Moll announced.

"And if you found out that you're out of the picture, what would you do?"

"I'm not sure." She spoke slowly, an odd expression in her eyes.

"Well, it's after five," Sue said, glancing at the diamond watch on her pale, slim wrist. "They should be along any minute."

Moll got up.

"I'll go down and be a committee of welcome."

Descending the stairs slowly, she walked into the living-room and stopped to help herself to a cigarette from a box on the table, when voices talking quietly in the *lanai* arrested her hand before it had completed the action. She froze as an animal freezes when it feels the bead of a rifle drawn upon it, and her eyes went up slowly and carefully.

Don and Gay were having tea together. They had come in, not by the walk, but through the garden. Replacing the cigarette, she listened, making sure that Ernesto was not with them. No, they were alone; she could hear their voices, but not what they were saying. This was the opportunity she had wanted, but now the moment was upon her she was afraid to take it. Self-disgust swept her.

She started across the room, quietly selecting an advantageous position in advance from which to see them, in order

to size them up as she approached. Through the open doorway their faces were clear in the leveling rays of the sinking
sun, but they were too engrossed to notice nearing footsteps.
Gay set down the teapot, after refilling Don's cup, and reaching into the sugar-bowl took a cube between her fingers,
dropping it into the liquid with a faint plop. Don's eyes met
hers and they both smiled.

Watching their faces, a choking sensation hit Moll somewhere in the region of the diaphragm. It had happened!
Driving her teeth into her lower lip, marking it, she came to
a stop. They both looked as if they had been washed in
light, and Moll knew that only people who possessed each
other entirely could be so quiet. She had not realized how
wholly Don had dominated her imagination during the past
weeks until she saw that any possibility of ever getting him
was ended. Having Gay, no man would ever want another
woman, for in Gay were many women, all different, all vital.
For an instant she meditated violently, then walked into the
lanai. Hearing her, the seated pair turned their heads.

"Hello," Moll said, strolling over and jerking out a chair.

"Like a drink, Molly?" Don asked.

"I'll take tea and be in style," she replied, mockingly.

Gay filled a cup and handed it to her.

"Sugar or cream?" Gay questioned.

"Sugar."

Moll watched. Gay picked up the tongs and placed a
lump in the cup carefully, not impishly, as she had the
other. Moll studied the pair from beneath lowered lashes,
her face filled with deadly venom that charged the immediate atmosphere, then it changed suddenly.

"The air of nobility enveloping the ranch stifles me," she said. "The snake will remove itself from Eden and wind away." Her voice mocked them and she rose. "This is an honest snake, it can be trusted, it promises that it will never come again to drive you out of Paradise. This Paradise is too dull with purity, despite the fact," her eyes swept Don's and Gay's faces, "that the garden is lighted with pash!" Swinging her vanity by the chain, she strolled away. "Can't fool me, can't fool me," she sang the words as she went down the steps. At the bottom she turned. "Me for biggah and bettah pastures. Long live crime! S'long, aunts!"

When Moll got home she headed directly for her room. On the stairs she passed her mother coming down. The woman spoke, but Moll went by as if she did not exist. Taki was turning down the lace-covered bed, her plump, brown hands moving lovingly as they smoothed down covers and puffed pillows. Moll closed the door and went to the bureau.

"Go out tonight, Molly-san?" the woman asked.

The girl did not answer.

"Somekind no good, Molly-san?"

"Get me a drink," Moll ordered.

"You speak that kind all finish," Taki reminded.

"Well, I want one, a big one, Pie-face."

"What for you like?"

Moll wheeled.

"I went to the ranch. Don and Gay were drinking tea and kissing each other with their eyes," her voice rose hysterically. "I can never get Don now, Taki; he's sealed to

275

Gay!" It was the wail of a child robbed unexpectedly of a coveted toy.

"I no onderstand. Three weeks Mr. Don marry now. You been think you can steal after he marry with nother girl? What for you——"

"Shut up and bring me a drink!" Moll was gulping for breath while she fought tears. Seeing the stark misery in Moll's face, Taki shuffled off. When she returned with the highball Moll seated herself on the neatly turned bed and drank thoughtfully.

"Well, that's that, Taki," she announced.

"I no onderstan, Molly-san," the woman said gently, her large, kind face concerned. "Only I knowing you solly somekind so I solly too. Sure, I try berry good help you catch Mr. Don, before first time when you tell you like too much."

"How?" Moll demanded.

"I make prayer Japan and Hawaii love gods, but no use. Too late. S'pose you making like I tell long time before, sure you catch. I too solly. I like very much you have every-kind good," she heaved a windy sigh. "When you more old you onderstan. This kind thing, life, very hard tell, just all same flower. Some kind people, like you and the fellas you have for friend, broke petals so can get more quick to the heart. Silly, petal make flower pretty, but when all broke off only ugly stick left."

Moll gave her a deep look and walked to the dresser.

"Well," she taunted, addressing her reflection, "you thought you could trump every trick, didn't you? And you got fooled!"

276

Taki watched her.

"No use feel too bad, Molly-san," she consoled. "Plenty more good mans. You smart girl. After bime-by you learn."

"I don't want to be good," the girl cried, wheeling around. "I'm naturally bad and I'm going to be badder and badder. I'm going to be the baddest person on earth!"

"Silly, no can make all bad. No people all bad," Taki said, weighing Moll's words, her face worried and tender. "Even *hana-maki* mans who killing other peoples got little good inside too. Good, bad, all mix up."

Moll stood like a bewildered colt at bay, and Taki seated herself in a vast rocker and held out her arms. "Come, sit on top Taki lap all same baby-san time."

Moll stood like a ramrod for an instant, then collapsed into the woman's vast lap.

"Oh, Taki, Taki!"

"No cry, Molly-san, no cry," the woman crooned, rocking her backwards and forwards.

"Taki, I'd give every experience I've wrung out of life to be in Gay's shoes. She's got, and has always had, more than the lot of us together. I hate her, hate her!"

"No speaking this kind, Molly-san, no good. Bime-by *akuas* [gods] hear and very mad. Bime-by sure you catching nodder good mans."

"I don't want one. I only want Don, and I can never get him now. Never, Taki, never! Oh, I want to tear these damn unhappy feelings out of me! I hate them; they scare me. I've been angry and mad, but never unhappy before. It's a horrible feeling. I'm going to," she freed herself of Taki's arms and rose, "go out and get hellishly binged and give the whole rotten show the slip."

"Better no drink, Molly-san," the woman advised, her eyes fastened on the tormented oval of Moll's face. "Tomorrow torr much sick."

"What do I care about tomorrow?" Moll cried. "Tomorrow isn't here, yesterday's dead. There's only today."

She stood, like a person challenging gods, picked up her hat and started for the door.

"Molly-san!" the woman entreated, trying to detain her, "Molly-san! Molly-san, please no make this kind!"

Shaking her off, Moll went down the stairs.

CHAPTER XVI

"YOU know, Gay," Don said, propping his elbow in the warm grass and tilting his flower-wreathed hat over his eyes to shade them from the sun, "I feel as I used to as a kid, contented just to be."

Gay smiled and touched a fat black beetle, crawling along a spear of grass, with her forefinger. Her head was poised so that sunlight framed her face, still rounded from youth, but almost waxen pale and hollowed slightly under the eyes. Don lay in the sunshine, drugged with joy, watching her.

A short distance away, in the shade of acacia and eucalyptus trees, old Hu sat with the horses, smiling benevolently at the pair seated in the grass. Dogs nosed through thickets of fern or leaped at little white butterflies sailing airily overhead, occasionally touching each other as they passed. Bees, weighting blossoming boughs, made a continuous buzzing that sent pleasant vibrations through the air.

Each morning as soon as breakfast was finished Don and Gay went off for the day. Their happiness was too great for any house to hold and must be taken outside. For a man of Don's nature, to be out of doors with the woman he loved was of all lives the most complete. He was stirred by the tremendous light pouring down on the island, by the delicious air, by the green solitudes about them. Miles below, their car was parked at the halfway house; miles below, tractors tossed dust into the air, trucks lumbered to and fro, men toiled unceasingly and unbeautifully for gold. Up here stock dozed and grazed, breezes loitered in hollows, stirred grass on hilltops and lifted Gay's hair. Don looked at her lips, dainty and loving, and at her gray eyes, big and dreamily alive.

"When I'm dying, after I'm dead, I shall remember her," he thought.

Because of her his body knew again the exquisite sting of the fresh morning sea, the fragrance of forest pools, the pleasant weariness after days spent on the hot white sand of secret beaches and in the cool peace of silent glades. His face was still thin, but he was tanned and his muscles harder. The natural ache of his back, resulting from unaccustomed exertions, was more than compensated for by the knowledge that, despite being so hampered, he was managing to enjoy again things which he had fancied had been banished forever from his life.

He had to ride slowly, float rather than swim, pick his way cautiously with canes when they walked, but with Gay beside him the hidden man, imprisoned in a maimed body, rushed forward joyously and fearlessly. With the beautiful obliviousness of a child, Gay seemed entirely to disregard his broken back when, in reality, he knew she never forgot it. Without appearing to do so, she was delicately and determinedly making him resume his place in an old world, which was forever new, which was sound and safeguarded and stabilized people from the bewilderment of lesser things. With imperious gentleness she led him forward as though saying: "This is ours, this is where we belong, out of doors.

The earth is man's heritage given to him to use, see and enjoy."

Ah Sam packed impossibly large lunches and with pompous importance stowed them into the car, hovering about it grinning until Don and Gay drove away. Occasionally Ernesto accompanied them, and when they were riding, old Hu. They lived a life apart from that going on in the old house, divided against itself, with Don, Gay and Ernesto ranged against Glenn, Morse and Sue.

With a wisdom hardly in accord with her years, but which resulted directly from the forcing house which had been her life, Gay persuaded Don to keep out of Glenn's affairs. She insisted that Glenn wanted to return to real things and would come back to them when he most wanted to. During the weeks since Gay had come to the ranch, Glenn had recovered from his illness, but he moved about like a vague, bewildered ghost, fighting to keep from drinking, relapsing, then struggling forward again.

While outwardly continuing to be part of the household, Don and Gay kept aloof. Love had drawn its magic circle about them, excluding the rest of the world.

John Garrison's bedroom was transformed into a private sitting-room and Gay's piano moved from her house into it. In the evenings Don, Gay and Ernesto read, chatted, and smoked or the two men listened while Gay played and sang to them. On several occasions, when Moll came with friends, she had attempted, unsuccessfully, to see Don alone. . . .

Don watched the fox terriers vanish over a rise, eagerly following some exciting scent. He leaned on his elbow, studying a patch of tiny white flowers bobbing in the wind.

Each polleny spike had its family of buds, close folded on worlds of silent lovely activity. A tawny hen pheasant led her brood of chicks cautiously out of a thicket of fern, then, when one of the horses tossed its head suddenly, vanished as if she had never been, bewildered chicks running frantically for shelter, uttering wee peeps. A skylark shot out of the grass, singing as it winged its way upward. The heart-lifting ascents, the gushes and trills, the wistful falls of melody, the perfect repetitions of notes, sent pleasure which was almost a stab of pain, through Don. He removed his hat, as if in a sacred presence. He wanted to speak to Gay, contrasting their life with that of others who had strayed from the enjoyment of simple, natural things, but could not speak. Reaching out, he took hold of her hand. She smiled, returning the pressure of his fingers, and the very silence that held them made vivid their complete union.

Don folded Gay's hand against the earth while little breezes, like cool fingers, ran through his hair and sunlight poured down on them like a vast benediction. Vixen came running toward them, panting, and flung herself down in the grass beside Gay's booted leg. The little bitch had a marked personality, dignity never failed her. She could be loving, hilarious, clamorous for attention, without losing a jot of it. Gay gently crumpled the animal's ear in her free hand, and, looking up, the dog licked her arm worshipfully. After a long silence Gay fixed her great eyes upon Don.

"I feel," her lips shaped the words with strange daintiness, investing them with beauty, "that something tremendous is about to happen to us."

282

"The most tremendous thing on earth has happened to us, Gay," Don said, smiling.

She studied young trees, lithe and gay, dancing to a sudden breeze passing through them, while older ones moved solemnly, then were still.

"I know, Don," she said, "but I have a feeling that things, outside of us, are coming toward us." He did not reply and she worked her fingers deeper into his hand. "Don't you ever get feelings like that?" she asked.

"I used to, Gay, as a kid."

"I still do," she announced gravely.

"Well, you're only a kid still, Gay—my kid."

Her eyes brimmed with happy tears.

"I wish," she spoke thoughtfully, "that every one in the world was as happy as we are. These past weeks I've felt as if we were the richest people in the world, and when I see others who aren't rich in the way we are, I ache inside. When I see Glenn and Moll and so many others I feel sick. They tear around, because inside they are always running away from themselves. Sometimes," she paused, her eyes fixed on the clouds, "I wish, meanly, that we lived far away in some place where everything was beautiful."

Don grasped her hand more tightly.

"I've been thinking about that, Gay."

She looked at him, startled.

"What do you mean?" she asked, quietly.

"Well, I've been wondering these past days if it wouldn't be best for us, for every one concerned, if Glenn and I divided the ranch. I talked to him about it yesterday afternoon and suggested that we make a division of property. I'd

283

like to take over the upper portions, which aren't suitable for pineapple growing, and let him have the lower. To adjust the difference in value, for the lower sections are the most valuable, it would necessitate a cash settlement as well. If it's agreeable to you, we could have your little house moved somewhere up here. . . ." He looked at the peaceful hills. "There's sufficient land to keep us. We wouldn't be rich, but we'd have enough. The land will carry about eighteen hundred head of cattle. We could keep Paniolo and three or four thoroughbred mares, raise a few army remounts and polo ponies and sell enough beef from the increase of the herd to keep things pleasantly together and leave a bit over for an occasional trip."

Gay drew a deep breath and sat up.

"That would be heavenly," she said, and stopped.

"What is it?" Don asked.

"I was wondering if we could take our people with us— if there'd be enough for them, too?"

"Who would you like to take, Gay?" Don asked, smiling.

"Old Ah Sam and Taka, Ernesto, Kama-san, Sera and a few of the older cowboys, and all the dogs and my little animals."

Don smiled, loving her because there was room in her heart for so many things.

"We could manage that, Gay."

She sat very still.

"What is it?" Don asked again.

"I'm thinking."

He waited.

"The old house will be sorry to have us go away," Gay

remarked after a silence. "But it will always know that we love it and it would be perfect to live where everything is happy. I can help, Don. I can sell paintings; I know lots about horses and cattle. Because I'm so happy my mind is full of new things which must go into pictures. We've been taking a holiday——"

"Which we both needed badly, Gay," Don broke in.

"Yes, I've been tired for years, ever since Daddy died, and you've been tired ever since you went to the war, but we are both rested now and must go on."

"I want to go on, I'm eager to start working again," Don said. "I don't cut a fancy figure on a horse, but I can get around. It will be jolly to get up early, mess about with horses and cattle again, come home tired—to you."

Gay caught his hand between both of hers.

"I'll go out with you on Saturdays, but the rest of the week I must work. It seems impossible and wonderful to think we are sitting here, together, planning the rest of our lives. Sometimes I'm so happy I'm scared; sometimes when I wake up at night and feel you beside me it seems impossible that one person can be given so much joy."

"Two persons," Don corrected.

They sat as silent as the day, hushed by the heat of noon, wrapped in passionate serenity. The shared silence was like a song of thanksgiving in which all the green things of the earth joined. Don looked down the slope of the mountain; behind a long dark line of trees stretching across it, pastures were being steadily transformed into fields of drab earth. He thought of the horses and cattle which had been sold off during the past two weeks, of quail and pheasants and larks, still

285

nesting, and of more minute terrified wild life whose homes were being destroyed. As though divining hidden dangers, Morse, since returning from Honolulu, was speeding up the work of transforming the ranch into a pineapple plantation. Waking at night Don saw from his bedroom windows, through gaps in the trees surrounding the house, searchlights playing endlessly over the fields as shifts of tractors worked on and on, shattering the peace of the night with their roarings. Had Gay not been beside him . . .

Picking up her hand, he kissed it, and she smiled at him.

"I realize, Gay, that our holiday is over," Don said, "and it's time we got into the traces. After we've had lunch," he beckoned to Hu, "I'll run over and go through the cannery, estimate what the machinery, plant and equipment is worth, and tomorrow I'll see Glenn and make definite arrangements for dividing things up between us."

Gay shivered.

"I had to turn down a page when Dad died," she said, "and it hurt, too, but there are always new pages."

"I know," Don replied, looking into her wide eyes.

Hu came forward carrying the saddle-bags. Laying them in the grass beside the seated pair, he said, "Wait," and going to a fern bank with his peculiar half-shuffling gait, he picked an armful of green fronds and spread them on the grass like a cloth.

"*Luau* [native feast]," he said, observing his handiwork with pride; then removing his hat he selected a gardenia from the wreath about it and placed it carefully among the green leaves beside Gay. "For you," he said, stepping back.

The girl smiled, picked up the flower and looked at it, a

286

dreamy, expectant expression on her face, but her eyes were all spirit and light. Then she thrust the flower behind her ear.

"You pretty face, just like gardenia," Hu remarked, weighing her; then added waggishly, "After bime-by I think maybe sure nice little fella more pretty still."

Don looked at Gay with a deep and wholly unself-conscious inquiry, but the girl's eyes were fixed on the green sweep of the mountain above them. Picking up her hand, he covered it with both of his. Feeling old Hu's wise eyes upon him, he looked up, and looking up remembered that the first dim memories of his life had centered about this brown man. Old Hu had ridden carrying him on a pillow in front of his saddle while his legs had still been too short to cling about a horse. Hu had taught him to swim, to husk coconuts, to dance hulas, play a guitar. Hu had told him legends, had spoken solemnly of curses put upon island families, which had the deathless qualities of Greek tragedies, laid in semitropical latitudes, tales which seemed part of the earth, sea and the sky. Hu had braided the first tiny rawhide lasso that his fingers had ever held, had fashioned minute leggings and woven tiny wreaths to put on his hat. Beautiful, if some day a child of theirs, Gay's and his, should live on after they had gone, enjoying the green ways of the earth.

"Sit down and eat with us, Hu," Don said.

The old man obeyed, chatting, laughing, commenting on this and that while they enjoyed the sumptuous lunch Ah Sam had prepared. Sitting in the sunlight, Don felt kin to all animate things, to trees standing motionless, and spellbound by the sun, to the grass and to creatures too small for human eyes to see, moving about in tiny crannies under the earth.

Lunch finished, Gay fed the ample leavings to the dogs, then, for a while, she, Don and Hu stretched out in the sun. The blue day seemed to lean over the world, stilling it to peace, shadows in the mountain took on strange significance, clouds waited. Paniolo, tied a short distance from the other horses, neighed, aggressively male, and from somewhere hidden in the hills came the voice of a cowboy singing as he rode about his work, singing not in worship, not for the sake of memory, melody or love, but in the urgent need of expanding superabundant vitality and the zest of being alive.

Sitting up, Don laid his crossed arms on his knees and after an instant Gay raised herself and slid one of hers through his, linking him to her. The voice grew fainter and finally faded away. A bird darted out of the trees and flew toward the summit. A dog rose and stretched itself delicately. Don glanced at the watch on his wrist. They should go. He wondered if it was possible for people to experience more complete happiness than was theirs under the wide sky, watched over by trees, with only a brown man and animals for company. As though guessing his thought, Gay laid her cheek against his arm and whispered:

"Happy!"

Bending down, Don kissed her forehead.

"Yes," he said, "so happy that even after I'm dead I will still be happy because we are in everything and everything is in us."

Gay tightened her arm over his, then rising stretched herself as if trying to make room in her body for the joy which was hers. Hu walked over to the horses and began tightening girths and Gay assisted Don to his feet. He watched the old man lead out the red stallion which bore Gay's small, high saddle on his back. The animal moved its head eagerly, stretching out its sinuous neck, snorted at one of the dogs, leaped aside from a shadow, easing its overflowing vitality. Purple and golden lights ran through its coat and played among the fine hairs of its mane and tail.

"I'll hold him, Don, until you are mounted," the girl said, taking hold of the stallion's bridle, jerking the bit gently to soothe and distract the animal.

"Get up and take him for a run, Gay," Don said. "He's been standing for a long time."

Placing her foot in the stirrup, she swung up lightly, gathered the horse together and turned him around. He leaped once or twice, assuring himself that his rider was firm in the saddle, then tore away joyously. Don watched Gay take him up a slight slope, a restless, beautiful red shape streaming over green grass. Gay turned him, heading him for a bank, and he sprang at it like a wildcat. There was a noise of falling stones, a shower of scattered earth clods dropping, and he was up. Wheeling him, Gay leaped him down again and he raced back and came to a quivering standstill when Gay checked him lightly with the rein. He fidgeted, lifting his delicate feet restlessly, glancing sideways with dark brilliant eyes alive with nervous intelligence. Leaning over, Gay stroked his shoulder.

"Isn't he beautiful? Isn't he grand?" the girl cried, and the animal reached around with its graceful head and touched her leg inquiringly with its nose.

"Watching you, Gay, I ride again as I used to," Don said, smiling.

Taking hold of his canes, he started toward the horse Hu was leading up. With the help of a specially arranged strap, Hu's invention, and the old man's assistance, Don hauled himself into the saddle. Hu mounted and they rode off, slowly, following the downward slope of the mountain, the old man keeping a short distance behind.

Don and Gay rode in intimate silence, isolated from the world and content in each other's company. Don's body, steeped with hot sunshine, felt radiant and yet half lazy. The dark green line of trees stretching across the flank of the mountain drew nearer; slight irregularities showed in it. The air danced with light which near the ground pulsated and quivered as if invisible beings moved ceaselessly in it. Don's blood felt full of sunbeams and danced with delicious recklessness. Dogs leaped through the long grass. Nothing mattered on the mountain. Sad things had no meaning, grave things no place. Then he realized that, miraculously, he was feeling again as he had felt as a boy when he rode in the splendid isolation of Haleakala. As they neared the tall trees above the halfway house he looked back at the immaculate hills, reluctant at having to return to the world below.

When they reached the shelter Gay slid off the stallion and tied him securely to a post. Hu assisted Don to dismount and he and Gay sat on the grassy bank and smoked while Hu tied up stirrups and got everything ready to lead the horses home. A car smoked along a road just below them with furious recklessness as though fleeing from horrors. Gay took hold of Don's arm.

"Glenn," she said, pityingly, watching the vanishing streak.

Don nodded, his eyes clouded for an instant.

Removing his hat, he inspected the wreath of flowers about it, then replaced it on his head.

"We ought to be moving," Gay said, glancing at the sun. "You want to go over the cannery."

Don nodded, but did not rise, and Gay whistled for her dogs, which raced up and leaped over her, delirious with excitement and joy. She played with them for a few minutes, throwing them off, hugging them to her, then ordered them to be still, and they lay panting and smiling at her, lolling out tongues, pink as fresh ham.

When Don and Gay drove in to the ranch they saw Morse's and Glenn's cars parked in the quadrangle.

"They're in early," Don said. "I wonder if anything is up?"

"I wonder," Gay answered as they started for the house.

As they passed the kitchen windows Ah Sam signed for them to come in.

"More better dlink tea," he said, grinning; "I think maybe no enough lunch."

Gay laughed.

"Too much, Sam," she said; "always you give us too much."

"Maybe yes, maybe no," the old man said with assumed indifference.

Gay looked at Don. "I'd like a cup of tea," she laughed; "I'm hungry again." And pulling out a chair she seated herself.

The old cook bustled contentedly about the stove, pouring the steaming contents of the kettle into a pot already filled with tea leaves. Don seated himself opposite Gay and laid his arms on the table. Ah Sam hovered nearby chatting while they drank, his yellow face wrinkled with mischief as he recalled and enlarged youthful escapades of Don's for Gay's benefit. The girl listened, eyes filled with ecstasy, utterly self-forgetful, enchanted with glimpses of Don as a child and a boy. Outside, trees bent attentive heads and aisles of the garden dreamed in the sun.

An enormous, invisible curtain of blended sound halted Don as he went up the steps and entered the cannery: leather belts and wheels making endless revolutions, tins rolling down guideways and dropping into boxes, the swish of mechanical knives slicing fruit, juices streaming into containers, the endless rustle and whisper of machinery hurrying forward.

It was a large, lofty establishment, orderly, uncrowded, well lighted, displaying the deadly efficiency of the modern factory. Machinery and men alike moved with mechanical precision and without wasted effort. Neither felt his presence. He would have to shout if he wanted attention. Small wheels moved viciously and resentfully, propelling larger wheels; belts and shuddering counters shot fruit, cans and boxes down slopes to men and women who received them and, with a single gesture, furthered the process of packing. Wheels uttered monotonous, sibilant noises; belts purred; a smell of grease, fruit juices, boiling sugar and sweating humanity tainted the air.

Don walked over to a long counter where fruit was being

prepared for the cans. He watched tense hands moving feverishly, lines of intent dark faces, watching objects coming toward them, grasping them, passing them on. Wide guillotine-like knives, mechanically operated, rose, flashed, dropped, rose again, flashed, dropped, and rough, melon-shaped fruit approaching from one direction was miraculously and almost instantly transformed into semi-transparent, honey-colored cylinders which again were transformed when they passed under other knives into circular slices like exaggerated gold-pieces, endlessly sliding down a long incline. Don watched them, thinking that they could easily hypnotize people who confused wealth with money.

Passing on, he watched sliced fruit being immersed in simmering syrup, packed in tins, soldered, labeled, stacked in boxes, handed to men who hammered down ready-cut and fitted boards, then heaved aside to more men who piled them onto small cars which were wheeled to waiting trucks, backed up against the wide doors, trucks which quivered and shook with life the instant the last box was slapped in. And back and forth from fields being harvested of fruit, other trucks went and came like clumsy insects, trailing one another.

Don wandered about the vast plant, observing the sinister beauty of perfectly operating machinery. It seemed as if nothing could ever stop wheels and belts revolving, knives rising, falling, flashing, counters shuddering and shaking fruit and tins forward. They created the impression that trees, animals, pastures, the very island, was being sucked in through the doors and fed to spinning wheels and whirling belts. The high, unceilinged roofs of corrugated iron, crossed by great unfinished beams, threw back monstrous vibrations endlessly rising to them, which on their return met new vibrations ascending, until the whole atmosphere jarred destructively.

Don scanned the faces of men and women assiduously working; they were unconscious of him, of each other, of the blue day spread over the island, of everything but the machinery which directed their every movement and demanded their every thought. He contrasted them with the field workers. Bending over, hoeing pineapples, they could pause, straighten up for an instant, see earth and sky, while these others, with their standardized movements, created the impression that they were afraid, if they stopped working for a second, that the machinery would engulf them into its maelstrom of wheels, belts and knives and send them out cut into pieces and imprisoned in cans.

Spying a white man, whom he concluded must be an overseer or superintendent, he walked up to him and introduced himself. The young fellow, with a Middle West accent, seemed mildly amazed to meet him, but conducted him about, explaining various parts of the machinery, giving him approximate estimate of the daily pack. Once or twice Don was aware that the young fellow was taking silent stock of him, as though he had heard him discussed, and he wondered if Morse had prepared him for a possible visit.

When the tour of the interior of the cannery was finished, Don went outside and walked slowly around the building, avoiding departing and returning trucks, stepping over ruts and holes, giving piles of pineapple tops, swarmed over by millions of small flies, a wide berth. Beyond ploughed fields the sun was dropping rapidly toward the horizon and clouds were beginning to assume their lovely evening shapes. A peaceful quality was invading the ending day and the continued hum from within the cannery seemed a violation of something sacred.

He decided that it would be pleasant to wait until work stopped and watch rest come to the spot. Seating himself on a box, he watched Filipinos, Portuguese, Japanese and Chinese bustling and hurrying about. In the fields men were collecting in groups, hoes on their shoulders, waiting for new relays of trucks to transport them to various camps.

A thin whistle blew shrilly and peevishly for a few minutes, then people began pouring out of the doors—men, women, boys and girls in their teens, all metamorphosed into living beings the instant the machinery stopped. A babel of languages, the overlapping of languages, and the by-products of languages, filled the air. Out they came, chattering, bodies and faces relaxed, calling out to one another, exchanging badinage, jostling and pushing good-naturedly for advantageous positions in the trucks, shaking and roaring to be gone.

Don studied them thoughtfully. Most of the older folk and certainly all their parents had come to Hawaii in the noisy bowels of ships. From the rice fields of Japan and China, from far-off Portugal and Porto Rico, from the jungles of the Philippines, they had been imported by white men, who, with a magnificent disregard for posterity, indifferent and without sense of responsibility for the future, continued to contract for labor races diametrically opposed in origin, characteristics and caliber, to till sugar plantations, pick coffee and work in pineapple fields and canneries. And over this motley mass the veneer of a hurried civilization had been thinly spread. Unready minds had been fed with new ideas, new standards, forced into new channels of thought, almost overnight.

He noted the delicate, slender features of a young Chinese of the student type, the blunt dogged face of a Japanese peasant, the shifty eyes of a swarthy Porto Rican, the coarse loose mouth of an unwashed Portuguese, and everywhere Filipinos, jabbering, chattering ape-like creatures, alternately impudent and resentful, cunning and bold. They wore gaudy shirts of cheap silk, belted into impossibly small waists, exaggerated breeches and absurd hats. They leered at girls, ignored men of other nationalities, and walked in an imaginary spotlight which they focused upon themselves.

Watching them, Don meditated upon the results which would come when their shallow minds had been sufficiently fed with cheap movies in which bootleggers and gangsters were made heroes, then miraculously reformed in the last reel, and by newspapers whose front pages featured rape, robbery, and murder and in which criminals' portraits, last words and gestures were made more important than world events. They had none of the stability and honesty of the Chinese, none of the sturdy, hard-working qualities of the Japanese whose long residence in Hawaii had resulted in favorable crossing with the original Hawaiian. Their loud trappings would attract women, their assurance give them importance, they would breed and cross-breed and the resulting hybrids would be the responsibility of white men who had imported and continued to import them, and who lauded and would continue to laud the accumulation of money above all other virtues.

He looked at bright clouds gathering above the mountain aloof, withdrawn, and thought with relief that before long he and Gay would be living upon it, secure in a world where material things would not be of super-importance. Perhaps it was cowardly to flee, but it was the only possible refuge from misdirected group-thoughts which were binding tighter and tighter about humanity.

He sat on until the last truck had driven away, then drew out a cigarette and smoked it. A night watchman was walking about the cannery, looking at this and that, and he thought it would be restful to go in and look at the machinery in repose. Rising, he crossed the torn ground, scarred by great wheels, and slowly mounted the steps.

"I want to go inside," he said to the watchman, a stout Portuguese.

The man opened the door and Don entered and wandered down the aisles, studying the machinery, inspecting contrivances, noting the spots already being worn in the floor by passing and repassing feet. Reaching the end of a long passageway, he came to a locked door.

"Open this; I want to see what is inside," he said, turning to the man who had been making the rounds of the structure.

The fellow jerked up his head and looked at Don from under his eyebrows.

"No can; no got key," he said.

Something about the man's manner annoyed Don, and made him suddenly suspicious.

"Then get something and break the lock," he ordered.

"I'm Mr. Glenn's brother, and have a right to go anywhere. The ranch and everything is as much mine as his."

The man looked sullen and stubborn and Don's heart began beating hurriedly. Ah Sam's veiled warnings, Ernesto's assertions that he was convinced that Glenn and Morse were in something foul, leaped to life in his mind.

The man began to edge off, and dropping a cane Don seized him by the shoulder and shook him.

"Do as I tell you!" Don said.

At once the Portuguese became servile and cringing. Maintaining his hold on the man and using his other cane for support, Don went to the door with him and waited until he extracted a key from his pocket and unlocked it.

"Give that key to me and fetch my cane."

The man obeyed, with venomous, resentful looks as he slunk to obey. Don slid the key into his pocket and took his cane, then slowly descended a long stairway which turned into a vast room. Propping his cane against the wall, he felt for a switch and flashed on the light. For an instant he was dazzled; then, horrified, he realized that he was being confronted by the paraphernalia of a vast still.

For an instant he was paralyzed. Then he walked forward and coldly inspected barrels, kegs, machinery and stacked cans, the same shape and size of those used for packing pineapples. Leaning against the wall, he picked one up and shook it, heard liquid splashing inside. It was all very well thought out; very ingenious.

By day Morse's and Glenn's cannery packed pineapples, at night it was a still. After dark, new shifts of workers would come. Looking about, he calculated: it probably took

only a dozen men to operate this department. Undoubtedly, for their silence they were paid an extra bonus as well as a higher salary than their fellows who were engaged in legitimate labor.

For a brief moment Don hated Glenn, hated him with every atom of his being, Glenn who had destroyed beauty, Glenn who had permitted the produce of the land their father had loved, to be prostituted to the making of unlawful liquor, solely to obtain . . . He dared not finish his thought. Remounting the steps, he locked the door and slipped the key into his pocket.

CHAPTER XVII

GLENN walked toward Morse's room with heavy un-
steadiness, his approach suggestive of a ship ploughing
into head seas which threatened to overwhelm it. When he
got to the door he hesitated, then pounded his fist on the
wood.

"Come in," Morse called, irritably.

Glenn wrenched on the handle and lurched through. Seeing Sue seated at the dresser, his face got blank.

"Ran, I want to talk to you. Come to my room," he
muttered thickly, wiping his moist face.

"What's eating you?" Sue asked, turning to look at him.

"Everything," Glenn said.

"You're drunk again," Morse announced coldly.

"You're damn right, I'm drunk," Glenn replied. "Got
that way on purpose so I'd have grit enough to talk to you
the way I've been wanting to talk ever since Don got home."

Morse reached for a cigarette and lighted it deliberately.

"I'd advise you to sober up a bit before attempting———"

"I damn well won't!" Glenn shouted. "I'm going to
talk to you now. Come along!"

Morse looked contemptuously at Glenn, then rose and
followed him down the hall to his room. When the door
was closed behind them Glenn faced Morse, his savagely unhappy and festering soul crouched behind the dilated pupils
of his coffee-brown eyes.

"I'm through, Ran," he announced, "through with the whole stinking mess! I'm going to see Don as soon as I've talked to you and make a clean breast of everything."

"You've taken leave of your senses," Morse said angrily, getting livid.

"I've come to my senses," Glenn retorted, swaying slightly, but he radiated resolution and a lean sort of mirth.

"But, good God!" Morse ejaculated. "Do you realize what it means when you say you're going to make a clean breast of everything?" His tones mocked Glenn. "It means that the pair of us will be sent to jail!"

"I'd feel a damn sight cleaner there than living in Dad's house, as I am, polluting it," Glenn cried. "Christ! When I think——" He broke off and began pacing the floor.

"Look here," Morse broke in, "you've got to——"

"I've jolly well got to do nothing!" Glenn shouted. "I tell you, I'm through!"

"Tough on me," Morse said, sarcastically. "You were all for this thing at the start."

"I know I was. For years I've been rotten and all for rotten things, but having old Don back and seeing him and Gay and Ernesto together has waked me up. They are happy and safe because they've stayed with real things."

Morse stared at Glenn scornfully, but he was so occupied with his own thoughts that he did not see.

"I'm sick of muck and of messing about," Glenn went on. "This noon coming home I passed Don and Gay. They had been riding; the old fellow was white and I knew from the expression in his eyes that his back was giving him hell, but he was happy, happy because he's decent and square with

himself, happy because he's clean. I tell you, Ran, when I saw the pair of them sitting together with the dogs I felt as though I were buried in dung. God! It's years since I've laid in the grass or basked in the sun, years since I've played with a jolly bunch of dogs, years since I've enjoyed simple happy things."

Glenn broke off, wiped his face, still gaunt from illness, then looked out of the window at tree-tops bending against an immaculate blue sky.

"All the lot of us do is rush, Ran; rush to work, rush to and from parties, rush our drinks and our so-called fun. We have no time to live, no time to really enjoy. I tell you, since I saw Don and Gay I've been doing some hard thinking. There they were lying in the grass wearing carnation *leis* which old Hu makes for them every day, chatting with the old fellow, who was sitting in the shade with the horses, laughing at the dogs' antics, while I rushed along the road in a beastly car. They came in a while ago and Ah Sam collared them in order to have them lunch in the kitchen. I heard them laughing, laughing because they are happy and sound. I felt—I can't tell you how it makes me feel." He stopped and passed a hand over his mouth as though to steady it.

"Going to have a weeping jag?" Morse jeered.

Glenn said, "What?" in an abstracted way, and went on talking. "I'm through cheating, I tell you, Ran; through deluding myself. All the truck and paraphernalia of civilization, all this desperate scrambling to make money anyhow, solely to have the things that money buys, gets you nowhere. I grant you that in this age a certain amount is necessary in order to live, but why keep accumulating it?" Glenn looked about wildly. "You don't see, well, squirrels, for instance, storing away more nuts than they can use in a lifetime, wearing themselves out spending their entire lives accumulating, accumulating! I've been a bloody ass and a drunkard, but I'm not an absolute fool."

He placed his thin hands on the back of a chair and gripped it.

"As a kid I lived sanely and appreciated real things. I've drunk because I've been unhappy and I've been unhappy because I've been out of step. Old Don's absolutely right. That time we had the showdown in the office and I told him about the pineapples, he asked me how much money the ranch was netting a year. When I told him he said: 'Seems as though that ought to be enough to keep us decently.' "

A smile hovered for an instant about his thin, quivering lips.

"It isn't decent for people to have too much money, too much anything. Money! Money doesn't give peace or happiness, Ran! Look at the Hawaiians before white men came—they didn't even have the word in their vocabulary, but they were happy, they lived as men were meant to live, close to the earth. You can say what you like, I know damn well that old Don, despite the fact that his back is broken, was happier than any millionaire, sitting in the sun with the girl he loves, surrounded by horses and dogs."

His voice broke, he scowled, blinked, like a man lost in an obsession and trying to find a way out.

"Don's got the right idea; all he wants is sufficient land to run a few hundred head of stock and enough work to keep him busy. He came to me yesterday and told me he was willing to divide the ranch, giving the lower, the best portions, to me and take over the upper. It started me thinking. He loves this house, but rather than continue to live in it and be compelled to have a part in the things we all do, he said he would have Gay's little place moved up to Pupahu. All, all this truck—great houses, radios, cars—have got between people and real things. I want to get back; I must get back or I'll smash up as civilization is smashing up all around us."

Morse snorted.

"Since when have you taken to philosophizing?"

Glenn laughed mirthlessly.

"I suppose people born on far-away, lonely islands are always more or less philosophers; we have time and space enough to think—at any rate, we had when we were kids. It's natural that we should have a different sense of values from those of people born in cities, where material possessions are the false measure of happiness and success. The war started things spinning too quickly." He looked about darkly, helplessly. "We all got away too fast, like racehorses that spurt under the wire, then outrun themselves and start floundering. The lot of us, our entire generation, got off with too much momentum, got let in for things, and now we have jolly well to get out of them or the whole blasted race will be lost. Difficult, what?"

"Rot!" Morse said, disdainfully.

"It isn't rot, it's the damned truth," Glenn insisted, snatching up a cigarette and lighting it with shaking fingers. The tiny flame flickered in his eyes, filled with stained and strained memories.

"Well, all this bosh and stuff you're talking has nothing whatever to do with the fact that you intend to make a clean breast of everything to Don." Morse spoke bitingly. "Suppose we get down to facts."

"That's what I'm doing, getting down to facts, giving you reasons why I intend to get out of what I'm in and why I'm prepared, if necessary, to go to jail in order to get out of it. What the hell do I want with more cars, more clothes, more booze and a bigger house to booze in? I'm going back to sound things——"

"And because you, as you express it," Morse interrupted, "want to get back to sound things, you're willing—you intend to drag me, my name, through the mud."

"But you're in the mud, now, Ran!" Glenn protested.

"Well, suppose I like being in mud?"

"Then, God damn you, stay there! But I won't stay with you. Confound it, when I go out and look at hills and trees and sunshine, I feel like a maggot! Oh, I say, I've got it!" Glenn straightened up.

"Got what?" Morse demanded.

"An idea."

"I can hardly believe it."

Glenn grinned like a helpless boy.

"But, by Jove, I have, I tell you. The very idea. Look here, Ran, I guess to your way of thinking, what we've been doing is okay. Means justify ends and all that. You want to get enormously rich quickly, because being enormously rich is your idea of being happy. Then, that's right for you. Wealth doesn't mean happiness to me. I was a damn sight happier as a kid than I've ever been since. Dad had enough, but was never what you'd call wealthy. We lived in this jolly old house, fooled about with horses and cattle, worked out of doors, and life was fine and rich. My body and mind were sound, I was happy; and, damn it, I'm going to be happy again!"

He stared at the cigarette between his fingers.

"Now, my idea is this, Ran. I'll see Don and tell him about the bootlegging, but insist that you didn't have anything to do with the pineapple brandy end of it, say that it was my idea entirely. That you've just found out and raised Cain because of the stockholders in the company and your reputation and all that. That'll absolve you."

"He won't believe it. He hates me. He's always resented having me living here and he'll be glad of any excuse which will get me out." Morse flung about the room. "You idiot, you talk this fine talk, but you don't think! Imagine being in a lousy cell, wearing stripes, eating rotten food, sleeping on rotten beds, working on roads, breaking rocks!"

Glenn laughed immoderately.

"Well, I'd a damn sight rather break rocks than continue living as I am now. I go to bed drunk and get up still drunk. I rush all day doing filthy things that I loathe, sneak, cheat, hurry. At night, to forget, I dash here and there and drink more. I haven't waked up really sober, except while I was sick, for years. I'd like to know what it feels like again."

"Inferring, I suppose, that the rest of us are all like you?" Morse asked.

"I know every one isn't like me, but I got this way because——"

"For God's sake, shut up!"

"Right-o," Glenn said quietly.

Walking to the window he contemplated the garden. A fox terrier scented along the edge of a flower-bed with quivering nostrils. Sunlight slanted on the rough, furry green of geraniums, the black green of eucalyptus, the hot, sultry green of bamboos, the cool, jade green of young banana leaves uncurling slowly.

Gold light flickered everywhere, weaving patterns of enchantment, gliding along glossy gingers, trembling in the feathery foliage of bamboo, resting languidly on glazed, spreading elephant-ears, soaking into the crude magenta of bougainvilleas heaped on an old fallen tree, spilling off orange *huapala* vines swathing one wing of the house like a velvet mantle besieged by somnolent bees. The garden was a choir of colors singing to the sun, but above the mountains and over the sea, leaden clouds, hinting at pending rain, were heaped high.

Becoming accustomed to the silence pervading the garden, Glenn began hearing forgotten sounds coming from plants and trees. Airs were astir, helping Nature, loosening a leaf from its stem, striking a flower from its companions, giving it courage to leave its comrades and resign itself to the loss of a place that it could no longer fill with beauty.

Squaring his shoulders, he turned and faced Morse.

"Ran, I've been a cad and a rotter, but I have some decency left. Just because I've determined to get out of this mess, there's no reason to sacrifice you and your future. I'll talk to Don and, one way or another, fix it up so that you can get out without being exposed and publicly disgraced. I can't think, now, what arguments I'll use, or how I'll handle

Don, but the old chap thinks a lot of me and I'll manage him somehow."

Morse cursed.

"That's well enough, but how about the money the stockholders invested in the company when you agreed to lease your land? That's got to be taken care of."

Glenn looked away from Morse, fixing his blood-shot eyes determinedly on the garden.

"If the worst come to the worst, Don and I'll mortgage the entire ranch and pay the stockholders back everything they've put in it."

Morse looked completely confounded, then burst out:

"Seems to me that you think only of yourself. You don't take into consideration how it'll make Don feel knowing that his brother——"

"Don'll be a damn sight happier to have me admit that I've been a skunk and take my medicine like a man than have me continue living this way."

Knowing the truth of Glenn's words, Morse was silenced. His eyes roved angrily about the room until they chanced to rest on a picture of Glenn's father.

"It'll be fine publishing to the world that John Garrison, who was highly thought of in the island, has a son who is a bootlegger."

Glenn's face got so bloodless that Morse's looked red and swollen in comparison. Morse fixed Glenn with clever, darting eyes, knowing he had stabbed him in his most vital spot. For an instant Glenn looked like a man bidding an eternal farewell to all he holds most dear, then he burst out:

"You can't bully and browbeat me by trying that slant!

308

Nothing you can say will stop me from doing the only really decent thing I've ever done in my life! I don't give a hang what people think. I know old Dad would rather have me publicly disgraced than have me try and save my so-called honor dishonorably. Dad never funked anything." Glenn broke off, his voice a faint, husky whisper. His throat was dry, his eyes as dark as a crypt. Walking to the table, he picked up his father's picture and looked at it. When he set it down he turned to Morse.

"God damn it, Ran, old Dad always insisted that water would find its way back to its own level, and he's right. I got away from the things and people that I belong to and I've been working around, ever since, trying to get back, though I haven't realized it until recently. And I'm going to get back! Confound it, Ran, there are better dreams than the ones we cheat ourselves with!"

"You Garrisons are all alike," Morse interrupted contemptuously, "a pack of idiotic, idealistic, impractical fools!"

Glenn grinned. Morse stared at him for a moment, then flung out of the door.

When Don got back from the pineapple cannery he went straight to his room. Gay was curled in a deep chair reading when he opened the door. She glanced up, smiling, then seeing the grief of his face, ran to him.

"What is it, Don?" she cried, seizing his arm.

"Sit beside me and I'll tell you," he said, going to his chair.

Gay seated herself on the floor, pressing against his knee.

He took hold of her hand and told her, without passion, what he had discovered.

"If I hadn't had you, Gay, I'd have lost my head and acted like a theatrical fool, but having you, I hope I'll be able to behave as Dad would have me do under these circumstances. I shall see Glenn. Morse has to go. I won't permit him to remain under this roof another night. Of course, he's not entirely to blame, but——"

A step sounded, coming down the hall with a sort of passionate reluctance, as though some strong force were trying to hold it back and a force even stronger was driving it forward. It hesitated, halted, came on, paused outside the door. There was a rap.

"Come in," Don called.

The door opened and Glenn stood on the threshold. He looked bowed and guilty and old, fiercely unhappy. His thin cheeks had fallen in like those of a man devoured by a wasting illness, and a tinge of sunburn gave them a pallor more ghastly than that of a corpse. In his eyes was a fixed expression of ferocious grief mingled with even more ferocious anger, as if he were suffering, and cursed himself for it, as a man curses himself for some act which he elects to do and need not. He glanced at Don with a sort of terror, and his clenched hands, thrust deep in his pockets, shook slightly.

Gay's fingers tightened on Don's.

"What is it, old man?" Don asked, consumed with pity.

He felt as if he were facing his brother's spirit, tortured, perjured, and longing passionately to get back to beauty again. Looking at Glenn, Don realized that never, in the blackest hours of his life, had he known such depths of deso-

lation as Glenn was experiencing, as he hesitated on the
threshold, like a man expecting a blow.

"Come on in and sit down, Glenn," Don urged.

Glenn blinked, looked at his brother quickly and suspiciously, as though feeling a change in him, then entered
the room.

"Don, I want to talk to you."

"I'll go," said Gay, rising.

"Don't go, Gay," Glenn said, signing to her to resume her
place beside Don. "What I have to say to Don, I must say
to every one."

Don's and Gay's eyes rushed together.

"Have a smoke," Don suggested, "before you start."

Glenn accepted a cigarette from the package Don held out
and lighted it unsteadily; then he seemed to come up against
a blank wall. He looked tired, beaten and distracted.

"Get hold of yourself," Don said. "After all, we are
brothers and you should feel free to speak freely to me."

"You don't know the half of it, old boy, not the half."
Glenn laughed on a high, unsteady note. "When you do
you'll want to shoot me and it would be a jolly good thing
if you did."

Don and Gay dared not look at each other.

Glenn began pacing the room.

"Confound it, Don, I wish you could have come home
when I did; then, maybe, I wouldn't have got off on the
wrong foot, and Christ, how I'm off!" He supported himself with a hand pressed on the reading-table, radiating self-
contempt. "When I begin thinking I want to blow out my
brains." Don started to speak, but Glenn signed to him to be

silent. "Don't interrupt me or I'll lose my nerve and never finish." He looked around like a man whose reason is tottering. "Ye gods, Don," he said under his breath, "I wonder if you can imagine the bloody degradation of being alive!"

He seemed to see no one, then pulled himself together. Gaunt, haggard he stood, reminding Don of a blooded horse hitched to a manure wagon. Even knowing what he did, Don could only feel profound compassion for his brother.

"Ever since you got home, I've been feeling all sorts of a stinker, but I simply hadn't the stuff in me to tell you that _____"

"Listen, old man," Don interrupted; "I went through the cannery this afternoon." Glenn threw up his head. "I hung around, God knows why, guess I wanted to see peace come to that mess of machinery, and after the packers cleared out I went in again for another look around." Thrusting his hand into his pocket he drew out the key.

Glenn looked at it.

"So you know I'm a filthy bootlegger, a manufacturer of illegal liquor," he said, "and all the ghastly pretenses are done—thank God!"

He sank into a chair.

"It's impossible," he announced, from behind the security of closed eyelids, "but I feel better than I have for months, years. Confoundedly selfish of me when I'm simply shoving the responsibility of this mess off on you."

Don reached to put the key on the table, but it slipped from his fingers and clinked on the floor. Glenn made a sudden gesture of despair and opened his eyes. Sitting erect, he grasped the arms of his chair.

"I feel a filthy blighter, Don, dragging you into the slime, getting your name and Dad's messed up in a thing of this sort."

"That's neither here nor there," Don broke in, kneading Gay's hand. "The thing that pleases me, makes me happy, is that you were man enough to come and tell me. My finding out this afternoon was just chance."

Glenn blinked, and, seeing moisture on his lashes, Don was moved to the depths.

"What do you figure on doing, Glenn? What do you suggest?" he asked.

Glenn tore himself out of his chair.

"I? You'll laugh your head off when I tell you. I'd like to go to jail. I know it sounds fantastic and absurd, but when you've done something rotten and been punished for it, then you feel clean again, free of it. Like after Dad spanked us when we were kids. I feel just by telling you that I've burst a cocoon in which I was imprisoned. I guess life is just a trail of shed cocoons. You get out of one and begin building another around yourself, which, in time, you have to struggle out of again." He wiped his face. "The confounded part is, to get out of the rest of my present cocoon means I have to hurt you."

"That's okay, old man," Don said. "I don't in the least mind the so-called disgrace of your going to jail, if you feel you must. I'd rather have you want to take your punishment like a man than have you try to save so-called honor dishonorably."

"Stop!" Glenn cried, and his cry was a shout of triumph. "Those are the very words, the very argument I used when I told Ran about the bootlegging end of our business. Bucks me up, realizing that despite the fact that I'm such a rank rotter, we are, fundamentally, chips off the same block."

"Bet we are, Glenn," Don said, "but you are the finer performer."

"What'd you mean, finer performer?" Glenn demanded.

"It seems to me, old man," Don replied, looking at his brother, "that a fellow deserves more credit when he's let down the flag and then, by his own efforts, hoists it again, than a chap whose fingers never slipped."

Glenn looked as though he were about to cry.

"Rot," he said, walking to the window.

He stood with his back to Don and Gay for several minutes, then faced about slowly.

"Ran tried to block me from coming to you. He insisted that there was no reason for your ever knowing about the filthy side-show I'd hitched to the cannery. He was in all sorts of a rage when I told him about it——"

"You're lying, Glenn," Don interrupted. "Morse was in on this, too."

"Give you my word he knew absolutely nothing about it," Glenn muttered, looking at the floor.

"Will you give me your word—as a Garrison?"
Glenn blinked.

"You don't need to, Glenn; you were always a rotten liar and your face is answer enough."

"Suppose we try to line things up a bit?" Glenn suggested after a minute. "There are so many angles to this business. Wish to God I were the only one involved!"

314

"Aside from me, whom do you mean?" Don asked, watching Glenn.

"Hate like hell dragging old Dad's name in the mud with yours; and there's Ran. He thinks differently from us about such things." Don nodded. "To his way of figuring, the main object of life is to make a pile of money quickly. When he's made it——"

"He'll want to pile up more and keep on piling," Don broke in.

Knowing the truth of the assertion, Glenn did not go on. "What do you figure will be best to do?" he inquired finally.

"I'll be damned if I know," Don replied.

"Hell, Don, I wish I could convince you that Ran knew nothing about the pineapple brandy end of it——"

"You can't."

"But if people think he had anything to do with it, it'll ruin his future, kill him in Hawaii!"

"Damn good job if he's killed here; he deserves to be."

"There's Sue and the stockholders to be considered——"

"I'll see Morse," Don announced, reaching for his canes.

CHAPTER XVIII

BEFORE Don was halfway across the room a knock
sounded on the door. He glanced back significantly at
Glenn and Gay, then walked to within a yard of the
threshold and halted.

"Come in!" he said curtly.

The door opened and, in the act of entering, Morse
stopped and the two confronted each other.

"Want to see me?" Don asked, and despite the fact that
their eyes were almost on a level Don appeared to be looking
down at Morse and he flushed a deep, angry red.

"You're God damn right I want to see you," he answered
in loud, excited tones.

"Remember a lady is present," Don reminded him, his
lips tightening into a straight, white line.

Morse glared at him.

"I suppose Glenn has been trying to convince you that I
was in on this pineapple brandy business," he said with fiery
contempt.

"On the contrary, he's been trying unsuccessfully to make
me believe that you knew nothing about it."

Morse glared at Don, an expression of hatred distorting his
features.

Outside the windows, slowly dimming with twilight, the
spaced rattle of raindrops commencing to fall on large-leafed

316

plants sounded. Morse frowned as if the noise distracted him.

"Well, what have you and Glenn framed up?" he asked after a moment.

"We're not in the habit of framing people," Don replied in iced tones. "Come in and shut the door. I'd sooner the servants didn't overhear what we've got to say to each other."

Morse closed it viciously.

"Look here," he said, "I'll not stand for you assuming that high and mighty air with me."

"Nothing will be gained by losing your temper, Morse. We are supposed to be civilized beings; let's try to behave like them if possible."

"I'll do any damn thing I please!"

"Gay," Don said, turning to her, "you'd better go."

She looked frightened, hesitated, then walked slowly to the door. For an instant she paused, then grasped the handle and turned it. Her eyes met Don's and held them, then she walked out.

"Now, say what you want to, Morse, and when you're done I'll talk."

"What in God's name do you intend to do?" Morse demanded, angrily wrestling to maintain outward composure.

"As yet, I haven't had time to decide," Don replied.

There was a lull in the rain for an instant, as if it were giving its full attention to what was transpiring in the room, then it began with redoubled violence, hurrying and scampering over the roofs. A spasm of rage convulsed Morse's face.

"Damn you! You enjoy keeping me in suspense because

that's the only way you can revenge yourself—being a cripple!"

Glenn made a startled movement, but Don appeared not to see. His eyes were fastened on the open windows. The patter of the rain was deepening to a steady downpour. Against the last faint gleam of sunset, trees were silhouetted dark, gaunt, draggled, huddled somberly together, like old indignant birds resentful of wet plumage. Don watched the silver falling wires of water as if fascinated by them, but his eyes revealed increasing repulsion, increasing antipathy for Morse.

"I'd advise you not to say that again," he warned finally, looking around and fixing Morse with his eyes.

Life invisible, charged with the future, crouched in the room.

Morse walked up and down, his features reflecting the hidden mind, dark with doubt and torn with apprehension.

"Well, suppose we get down to business," he said, savagely wiping his face.

"That's what I propose doing," Don replied.

"I say, Don," Glenn broke in, picking a burned match out of an ash-tray and studying it, "I'd like to say a few things."

"Fire away, old chap; you've as much right to talk as any of us."

"For God's sake, Don, let me assume the blame for this business. I've been a damned disgrace to the family ever since I got home. I've been a drunkard, a blackguard and a cad. People can't think less of me than they do, and after the first flurry of excitement dies down they'll realize that it's no disgrace to you if your brother is in prison."

Don studied Glenn's twisted face and nodded.

"Do you mean to say you intend to stand by and let Glenn go to jail, when you can easily save him by hushing this matter up?" Morse cried excitedly.

"I shall do whatever I feel called upon to do," Don answered, speaking like a man who was dragging his mind back from a great distance.

"You're a fine sort of brother!"

"Don's the damnedest fine brother in the world!" Glenn exclaimed. "You aren't constituted to be able to appreciate the sort he is. Ye gods! a while back, before you came along, he tried to tell me that I'm the greater performer, because I've slipped and am trying to stage a comeback. They don't make them any finer than that, and if you go out of your way to insult him again I'll punch your confounded head."

"It's evident you know on which side your bread is buttered," Morse observed sarcastically.

"Damn you!" Glenn cried, clenching his fist and drawing back his arm.

"Easy," Don cautioned, and Glenn's arm reluctantly dropped.

The room echoed with the sound of magnificently falling rain. Its exultant voice filled the world. It raced along gutters, strangling them, spilled out, shattering itself on paved walks, changing flower-beds to pools and standing in dim sheets in every depression in the lawn. Gloom filled the room and mechanically Glenn switched on the reading-

lamp standing on the table. Its green shade cast a wide
circle of light on the floor, leaving the three men's pale,
strained faces in the half-light above.

"A few minutes ago you assured me," Morse addressed
the pair, but his eyes were fixed upon Don, "that you weren't
in the habit of framing people, but this brotherly love stunt
looks like a frame-up to me. We're told that blood is thicker
than water, and common sense should have told me that in
the end Glenn would go back on me—for you!" Morse
spoke venomously and contemptuously. "I was fool enough
to believe in his assertions that he would stick by me——"

"Don't be a sickening ass, Ran," Glenn cut in. "You
know damn well I've always thought the world of Don and
have been in hell ever since we went into this thing, because
I was double-crossing him. You know when you first approached me about the pineapples I insisted that I must
write and at least inform him what I contemplated doing.
You finally talked me out of it, insisting that he'd be the
gainer in the end, because it meant more money! Christ!
how I hate that word! I'm not blaming you. I was at
fault. I'm weak as hell. I allowed myself to listen to your
talk, which was louder than my conscience that told me I
was going into things that are considered rotten and, being
as I am, could never really be at peace doing them. I don't
deceive myself about myself; I don't try to cheat by thinking that I'm in this jam only because I've been haywire ever
since the war; I know I'm weak fundamentally." He looked
about like a person lost in immeasurable wastes. "In the
beginning somewhere I read, or was told, that life's best gift
was the ability to dream of a better life. As a kid, I did

dream of being decent, constructive. But it's difficult for a man constituted as I am to avoid his destiny. I'm weak because I desire so strongly. I want to be straight and, at the same time, rotten things have an unholy attraction for me, and between the two I've got lost. I listen to voices whispering dreams and while I'm listening I do queer weak things. Look where it's landed me! Nowhere! I've damn well worshiped Don all my life and yet I've betrayed him about as thoroughly as a man could. Here I am at thirty-one, a nothing, wrapped in a putrifying mess of my own making!" Glenn swallowed, grimaced and jammed his hands into his pockets.

Don glanced at him compassionately, but before he could speak Glenn recommenced.

"After all, of the pair of us, Ran, you're the one who should be respected. You aren't, according to standards, a good man, but you're strong. You sin, but aren't sorry afterwards. That's what I despise in myself; I want to eat my cake and have it too."

"Bosh!" Morse ejaculated. "You talk like a fool, think like a fool; your brain, if you ever had one, is rotted with alcohol! We aren't here to dissect your inner workings, but to figure some way out of the jam we're in."

Glenn flushed like a embarrassed schoolboy, unconscious that it was the finest, most honest moment of his life. Morse stared at Don.

"I suppose I must endure more high-flown Garrison sentiments before we get down to business." His manner was insolent, that of a man who feels that he has nothing further to lose.

Don did not answer. His eyes were fixed upon a point beyond Morse's head, as if he did not hear or see him.

"Don't be an ass, Ran," Glenn muttered. "Your only chance of getting off without exposure rests with Don and you jeopardize the possibility of it by talking tripe."

Morse flushed angrily. A line deepened between his brows and he stared at Glenn as if he would have enjoyed eating him. After an instant he turned to Don.

"I'm inclined to fancy you're the sort who shrinks from washing dirty linen in public. Seems to me the simplest way out of this is to keep our mouths shut. No one need ever be told about this business. The stockholders will never be any wiser——"

"Or poorer," Don cut in.

"Or poorer," Morse acceded. "You'll gain nothing by exposing Glenn——"

"And you," Don added, a grate in his voice.

"Or me," Morse retorted. "Of course, the night shift will have to be kept on, as packers, and we'll have to continue paying them what they've been getting to make them hold their tongues——"

"We?" Don asked, an increasing edge to his voice.

Morse looked stunned, then glared at Don.

"From that, I get it you intend to shunt me regardless of the fact that you have me to thank for a lot of extra money, which enables you——"

"For Christ's sake, Ran, shut up!" Glenn cried nervously, watching a look growing in Don's eyes.

"Well, some one's got to talk! That's what we're here for, isn't it, to talk?" Morse demanded, showing increasing tension. He suggested a violin string wound to snapping-point. His eyes darted over objects in the room, his skin was moist and, in the light coming up through the shade of the reading-lamp, had a greenish tinge. His manner, which, until the moment, had been arrogant and assured, changed, as if it were slowly dawning upon him that there was a possibility, a probability, that Don and Glenn were capable of exposing everything, despite the fact that by doing so their family would be open to disgrace.

There was a growing roar in the rain savagely assaulting the island. It filled the night with an immense muffled tearing, which seemed to spread across the world. The scent of drowned soil rose and mingled with the fragrance of clean water falling recklessly from the sky. There was something stirring, elemental and lawless in the sound and smell of the colossal downpour, a hint of forces steadily assembling, of pulses pounding and feet hurrying to a converging point. It worked potent magic, filling the dark with restless, incessant movement which charged the night with mystery force and violence. Don stood, his eyes narrowed, in an attitude of profound concentration, as though his very mind were listening for some message on its way to him across the earth. Then he lifted his head with an old unconquerable gesture of his boyhood.

"You say we're here to talk," he said, his eyes challenging Morse. "Well, I'll do the talking."

Rain roared triumphantly on the roofs. Glenn gripped the back of a chair, and Morse looked like a man lost in a maze and trying desperately to find a way out.

"Glenn," Don said, addressing his brother, but keeping

his eyes fixed upon Morse, "where have you been banking the money you made on this brandy?"

"At the First National, in Honolulu."

"Under your name or Morse's?"

"Under mine."

Don stood thinking.

"I see. In case of exposure or discovery you'd stand the gaff. Can you give me an approximate estimate of the amount that's been deposited to date?"

"Somewhere in the neighborhood of fifty thousand dollars," Glenn replied, looking hot and miserable.

"How long since the first shipment and sale of brandy, Glenn?"

"Three months."

Don meditated.

"A rather profitable business, bottlegging on a grand scale! At this rate by the end of a year you should clean up somewhere in the neighborhood of two hundred thousand dollars. Difficult to account for in income tax statements."

"That's arranged for," Morse broke in. "It's planned to be fool-proof."

"I don't doubt it. Glenn?"

"Yes?"

"Suppose we take that fifty thousand and start buying out stockholders, giving them, of course, much more than they paid originally. That's due them, for their good names have been used as a screen for the filthy trade that's been going on underneath. At the end of a year we ought to be able to raise enough from the ranch and canning to finish buying them out and go back to cattle raising."

"You forget that there's a heavy tax on grazing land which is suitable for pineapple growing," Morse reminded; "which will cut your profits by half."

"Glenn spoke of that the day we talked in the office," Don replied.

His eyes passed Morse and found Glenn.

"I'm all for the idea," Glenn said thickly. "Why couldn't we mortgage the ranch and finish up the blasted business at once? But," he hesitated, "what possible excuse could we make for discontinuing the growing and canning of pines?"

"I'll say that on further thought and investigation that I object to the conditions of the lease and question your authority starting this thing without having consulted or informed me about it. In a pinch, of course, we could put all the damned cards upon the table."

Glenn flushed a dark red.

"This means that you intend, if possible, to settle this affair so I won't go to jail?"

Don nodded.

"It's going to be pretty difficult for you to break that lease after having signed it," Morse said.

"But not impossible with a good lawyer," Don replied. "And of course, in case of difficulties, I have evidence which would justify my move."

Morse cursed.

"I imagine," Don spoke slowly, weighing his words, "that it won't be necessary for me to expose either you or Glenn, providing you work with me. I know Glenn will. You don't want your reputation and future ruined. People can construe your break with me to personal antipathy."

Morse flung across the room.

"You have me cornered, damn you! And you know that in order to save myself I'll have to work with you."

There was a deepened roar in the rain, coming down faster and faster. With increasing and incredible speed it rushed out of darkness, passed through the light thrown out of the windows by the table-lamp, and vanished into darkness again. On all sides there was a sensation of movement, incessant, threatening and continuous. Don turned his head, amazed at its violence.

"By Jove, it's coming down!" Don remarked, the tense expression in his eyes easing, as if the unleashed fury of the rain relieved emotions which had unnaturally to be controlled.

Morse snorted.

"Well," he asked, "what method of procedure do you suggest?"

"I haven't figured out as yet. There is only one thing I'm certain of at this moment. You clear out tonight."

"What'd you mean, clear out?" Morse cried, furiously.

"I mean that I won't have you in this house another night."

"But look here, you can't do that. It will look—what will people think?"

"I don't give a hang what any one thinks. Tell them," Don laughed in an overstrung, immoderate way, "that I chucked you out—bodily."

Morse recoiled as if he had been struck. His face went white, then red. Rain banged and thudded down, rending the dark, slamming against the earth, ferocious, arbitrary, savage, filling the night with uproar, like some frightful message of warning and rebuke.

"Tell people that you threw me out bodily?" Morse cried. "A damn cripple like you!"

Heaving his weight onto one cane, Don dropped the other and bringing back his arm swung. The blow, timed and calculated to perfection, that of a man who knows he has time and opportunity to strike only once, met Morse on the point of the chin. He went down, Don crashed on top of him. For an instant Don did not move, then sat up slowly. Morse lay prone.

"I guessed I could get in—one," Don said, grinning up at Glenn. "Gosh, it was a beauty!"

At that minute he resembled a pleased boy, miraculously young and refreshed. Rain raged outside, slaughtering the garden, plundering it of beauty; and wind, created by volumes of water spilling through the atmosphere, lashed and shook the orange vines swathing one end of the house, stripping them from the walls. Don's eyes went up to Glenn's inquiringly.

"Shall I give him another as he comes to? I can manage it, though it's not ethics to hit a man when he's down. I feel bully. Never thought I'd have an opportunity to hit him and I've ached to get my hands on him ever since I met him."

Glenn looked alarmed. Colossal masses of liquid slashed down in living, silver avalanches, making a shambles of the night, which seemed to stagger and recoil as new masses of water, with increasing force and impetus, tore downward, annihilating one another. Don sat on the floor, watching Morse.

"Give me a hand up," he said. "Enough is as good as a feast. I have Morse at an unfair disadvantage, worse luck, because I'm a crock, and it's hardly sporting to sit here waiting to hit him again."

Glenn hoisted Don to his feet. Morse did not stir, and suddenly Don, too, looked alarmed. His eyes leaped to Glenn's and he saw fear lurking in their depths.

"Great God! You don't suppose——"

Glenn bent and raised Morse, looked at the back of his head and felt his neck.

"He's okay," he said in low hurried tones. "Guess——"

Morse opened red eyes, looked about vaguely, saw Don and struggled to his feet.

He shouted in a loud, unnatural voice, wresting to tear himself free of Glenn and get at Don.

"For God's sake, Ran," Glenn panted, "you can't hit Don! It would brand you a skunk."

"I don't give a hoot in hell! Let me go!"

"I'll have to take you on," Glenn gasped, "if you don't——"

Silently, ferociously, Morse struggled to free himself of Glenn's arms locked under his. They lurched and slid about the room, colliding with furniture, knocking over the table and the lamp. The room was plunged in noisy darkness which became part of the raging rain, roaring downward, hissing with passionate fury against the earth.

"Get back!" Glenn cried warningly to Don.

With silent, deadly intent, the two men clenched and

fought in the dark, rolling over each other, bumping against chairs, colliding with the bed. The dull impact of furiously given blows, the gasp of quickly taken breath, the grunt of wind suddenly expelled by clenched fists, filled the immediate night. An avalanche of books slid with a crash from a jarred bookcase. Moments of silence, when the two adversaries were locked in terrific grips, were followed by the heavy thump of bodies flung against the floor. Stertorous breathing, scuffling, stifled grunts, sounded in quick succession.

Don edged cautiously toward the electric switch beside the door, halting to avoid overturned furniture, dodging thrashing arms and legs. There was an appalling quality to the hidden struggle, like a vast and hideous striving of spirits, felt instead of seen. Sweat damped Don's body. Blows, oaths, grunts, gasps, surrounded him. Through the house running steps sounded, voices calling out in Hawaiian, Chinese and Japanese.

Seeing a gleam of light coming through the crack under the door, Don reached out and sliding down found the key and turned it in the lock, then groping for the switch pushed it. The room was flooded, shockingly and suddenly, with garish and indecent light. In a frenzy Glenn and Morse pommeled each other, as if they were the two last persons on the earth, fighting for undisputed sovereignty and possession of it.

Fists pounded on the locked door, voices called:

"Mr. Don! Mr. Glenn!"

Don shouted in Hawaiian for silence; feet shifted about and worried voices conversed in lowered tones, and still Morse and Glenn fought. Glenn's cheek was blackened, blood was running from the corner of Morse's mouth. Wild eyes, rumpled hair, striving limbs, multiplied by incessant movement, seemed to cover the entire floor. In the steadily growing roar of rain was a note of menace and destruction, foster parent to the human tempest loosed in the room. First one and then the other uppermost, Glenn and Morse fought across the floor, half struggling to their feet, being pulled down, rolling over. Don watched, the muscle in his cheek fluttering like a thing gone mad.

"If that isn't hell's own racket!" Ernesto's voice remarked; then imperious knocking sounded against the wood. "I say, Don!"

"I think, Ernesto, we'd better let them alone," Gay said.

"It's nearly finished," Don called out, listening to Morse's breathing.

There was a wild gleam of terrific excitement in Glenn's bloodshot and blackened eyes, as if he were fighting Morse for possession of his own soul. Sweat streamed down his neck and cheeks and his thin hand looked almost insane. A fleck of foam on the corner of his mouth slid down his chin. Then a woman's thin scream came down the hall.

"Oh, what is it? Who's fighting? This is awful! Make them stop!"

"The door's locked, Sue," Gay's slightly unsteady voice said.

"O, dear, O dear, stop them!" Sue's voice, high, hysterical, quavered upward. "Ran, Ran! Glenn! Oh!"

"He's out, Glenn," Don said, commanding his voice after an instant. "Our old training in boxing and wrestling comes in handy now and then."

Glenn got slowly and heavily to his feet.

"Feel sick," he muttered, "sick as hell."

He stared at savage rain slashing downward, roaring like a triumphant clarion, as though watching a pale pageant of mirages passing mysteriously by, leaving no trace behind.

CHAPTER XIX

"GAY," Don said, as they stared out of the window at the blurred garden, "everything's finished; it's just a matter of time until things get straightened out. I ought to feel at peace, but instead my head is bursting. Sometimes life is too much for all of us."

"Perhaps it's this deluge," Gay suggested. "I feel as if I couldn't get a full breath."

Throughout the previous night and during the following day the old house, with its many spreading wings, endured the rain pouring on it with passionate severity. Choked gutters sputtered and protested at the loads of water incessantly scurrying along them; windows, grayed by sheets of liquid slashing downward, looked like dull, reproving eyes.

The garden, sullen and resentful, waited, stunned by relentless unceasing showers racing one another to the earth. Banks of flattened gingers leaned mournfully against one another, and bananas drooped disconsolate tattered leaves. Roads swirled yellow muddy water and gulches thundered their loads of it, roaring mutinously as they hurried madly for the sea. Over the whole island was the vast, strange stir of movement generating a sensation of alteration and pending change.

Don dropped a cane against the window-sill and put his arm about Gay's neck and she looked up. His face was pale and his eyes still held a deep, inward hurt.

332

"Don't mind, Don," she said softly. "I can guess a little how you feel. Horrid to have ugly things happen in this house which to you is sacred, but the feeling will pass."

Don's circling arm tightened.

"You know, Gay, no one has the right to judge another. God knows strange and dreadful things push people from inside, forcing them into deeds that are ugly viewed from without, but if the motive behind the action was okay, the deed must be, too."

Gay nodded and her eyes filled.

"I can guess all the things you're thinking and feeling, Don. It's like when you see a person drinking: often they are only trying to escape from something still more unbeautiful. Where's Glenn?"

"Sleeping. It's going to take ages for him to pull out of all this. I wonder—" Don paused.

"What, dear?"

"If perhaps it wouldn't be best for him to take a long trip, to go to new places, see new faces which will help him to find himself."

"That would be the easiest way."

Don glanced at her sharply.

"What do you mean, Gay?" he asked, looking into her wide thoughtful eyes.

"Maybe Glenn would prefer to stay and win his battle on the ground where he was defeated."

Don kissed her.

"You're a brick, Gay! I was going to suggest a trip, but we'll leave that to him. Then later, when things are straightened out, he can take his holiday. We've had ours."

Gay nodded and laid her head against his shoulder.

"Let's go out of this room for a bit," she suggested after a few minutes; "the vibrations left over from last night are still in it."

Don picked up his cane and they went to the living-room and sat down in front of the fire. Ernesto strolled in and seated himself in his deep chair. His dry old face was tired, but a sly twinkle lurked in the corner of his left eye.

"Why the atmosphere of intense depression?" he asked mockingly. "The bird of ill omen has flown away; the family, though battered, is still in the ring; honor, slightly damaged, is reestablished. Let's have a drink."

Don laughed, called out for Adaji and gave the order. The fire roaring up the chimney partially dispelled the gloom of the steadily falling rain, drawing the objects of the room comfortably together. Racing trophies, tables, books, chairs, half-glimpsed pictures, conspired together, brewing a potent magic. Dark-beamed ceilings seemed to reach down to share the firelight.

"I wish to God this blasted rain would stop," Don said. "I can't get the sound of it out of my ears, out of my head; it's beating my mind numb. When it lets up I'm going out to see the damage."

"It'll wash out a few pineapples," Travers remarked maliciously, smiling as he watched Don's face. "In a story, of course, the land would be completely ridded of the blight, the cannery washed out to sea, but in life things jog along a different way. You have the jolly prospect ahead——"

"Shut up, you old buzzard," Don laughed, reaching out to possess himself of Gay's hand.

334

Adaji arrived with the highballs and the three drank them slowly.

"This is one of those days that you could do without," Gay commented after a silence, and Don's fingers tightened sympathetically over hers.

Travers chuckled, then became serious.

"Such days are more than compensated for by those you couldn't do without," he announced with the wisdom gathered from a long life. "*Tout passe.* Tomorrow the sun comes out." He raised his glass. "To tomorrow and all the other tomorrows given us to shape as we will."

Draining his glass, he set it aside, lighted a cigar and strolling to the door went onto the *lanai.*

"Come on out," Travers called without turning. "It's letting up."

"I think the world of that old blighter," Don said, looking fondly at the old man's back. "He scoffs at practically everything, but underneath appreciates life's deep signifiance. It's probably raining harder than ever, but let's go out."

He listened: there was a lessening note in the downpour. Its steady voice halted, hesitated, increased, wandered tentatively among the trees and sodden hills.

Gay rose and they walked out and joined Travers. He stood, his cigar gripped between his teeth at a jaunty angle. For a while they listened to the melody of rain playing on the earth, stopping, recommencing, scampering here and there, running into little arpeggios and trills as trees freed themselves of water weighting their limbs. Through lifting gray veils, the beaten island stretched exhaustedly in the sea, smirched with the brown of washed earth along the shore. After a while the three on the *lanai* went in and by common assent adjourned to John Garrison's room, with its commanding view of Haleakala.

Travers and Gay threw up the wide windows, and the rich smell of drenched soil and clean-washed vegetation flooded the house. The mountain stretched a vivid ink-blue across the eastern sky, filling it. Above it spectacular clouds held mighty consultations. Soaked pastures and red fields of gutted earth below them wore the peaceful aspect of land after flood. Irregularities and gaps showed in the mechanically planted pineapples, stock began to venture forth from their shelters to go out and graze. Ah Sam stood in the kitchen doorway, hands clasped beneath his apron, his wrinkled face screwed into a grin. Back and forth along the turn of the road, visible from the window, men were trooping out to inspect the damage of the rain: Hawaiians on horseback jogging easily up the mountain, silent Japanese with hoes over their shoulders, Filipinos chattering, jabbering and gesticulating—races and the crisscrossings of races out in force to repair injuries done to the island which gave them sustenance and was gradually welding them into a whole.

"The harvest of Hawaii," Travers said, drawing on his cigar and indicating the stream of humanity pouring along the road. "Wonder what the final mowing will be?"

Gay clasped Don's arm and he looked down at her. High and splendid, crowning hilltops, like regiments drawn up in review, the plantations of trees waited for the sun to break through dispersing clouds, standing out distinct and solid from the mountain, but an integral part of it.

336

Glenn rode by.

"Where're you off to, old man?" Don shouted.

Glenn checked his eager horse.

"Thought I'd ride up there for a bit," he called, brandishing a long arm at the trees.

A mud-spattered roadster shot into sight and halted by Glenn. Moll conferred with Glenn for an instant. He shook his head and wheeled his horse for the hills. Moll rammed in the gears venomously and tore away.

Gay's eyes met Don's and bending down he kissed her.

Across the summit of the mountain marched a lingering rainstorm, like a great gray god with folded arms and aloof head in the sky.